Praise for
The Heiress

"*Pride and Prejudice* retellings abound, but none are quite like Molly Greeley's."

—Oprah Daily

"Greeley is faithful to the original story, while creating an imaginative and vivid inner life for the beleaguered Anne. This inventive novel will delight *Pride and Prejudice* fans, and win over readers who are skeptical of Austen reimaginings."

—*Booklist* (starred review)

"A perfectly joyful read."

—*BookPage*

"Greeley's expert imaginings of the life of Anne de Bourgh reveal the hidden depths of her character and highlight the societal restrictions of nineteenth-century women as Anne seeks to overcome her mother's domineering persona and find happiness. Historical fiction fans will be drawn to Anne's plight."

—*Publishers Weekly*

"With stunningly lyrical writing, Greeley elevates Austen-inspired fiction—and psychological fiction in general—to a whole new plane."

—Natalie Jenner, author of *The Jane Austen Society*

"Greeley's storytelling is intricate, masterly, and delightfully imaginative. Highly recommended."

—*Library Journal* (starred review)

"Haunting. . . . Greeley shines a light on the darkness cloaking Anne de Bourgh. . . . The result is a novel with all the hallmarks of a nineteenth-century Gothic. . . . Highly recommended."

—Finola Austin, author of *Brontë's Mistress*

THE
HEIRESS

ALSO BY MOLLY GREELEY

The Clergyman's Wife

THE
HEIRESS

The Revelations of Anne de Bourgh

MOLLY GREELEY

𝒘𝓂
WILLIAM MORROW
An Imprint of HarperCollins*Publishers*

P.S.™ is a trademark of HarperCollins Publishers.

HarperCollins books may be purchased for educational, business, or sales promotional use. For information, please email the Special Markets Department at SPsales@harpercollins.com.

A hardcover edition of this book was published in 2021 by William Morrow, an imprint of HarperCollins Publishers.

FIRST WILLIAM MORROW PAPERBACK EDITION PUBLISHED 2022.

Library of Congress Cataloging-in-Publication Data has been applied for.

ISBN 978-0-06-303201-9

22 23 24 25 26   LSC   10 9 8 7 6 5 4 3 2 1

To Jane, Ciaran, and Alasdair,
whose names contain whole worlds.

And to Ashley, for twenty-nine (and counting) years
of being my favorite person with whom to
laugh until we cry.

THE
HEIRESS

Part One

Rosings Park, Kent

CHAPTER ONE

I was not always small and sickly.

When she was in a remembering mood, my nurse sometimes liked to tell me my own story. It began with the moment she beheld me for the first time, still wet from my mother's womb.

The infant was robust at birth, she said, as if my origin was just another fairy story. *Fat and dimpled as could be, with hair sticking up from her head like soft dark feathers. Her mother, pleased her work was done, did not even mind, as so many other women must, that it had all been to bring a girl into the world, for Lady Catherine was wise enough to wed Sir Lewis de Bourgh, whose estate could pass as easily to a daughter as to a son. She praised her new daughter's nose, the unlikely slope of which already gave her the look of Lady Catherine's own noble relations, and declared that she should be named Anne, after her own elder sister. Baby Anne's father and his steward drank a toast of finest brandy to her health.*

I could imagine them together, firelight making the brandy glow in Papa's crystal glasses. I could even imagine Nurse, looking down at my infant face with her own broad face full of curiosity and good humor. Mamma was harder to picture; she so rarely lay abed that it was difficult to think of her tucked up among the cushions after the exertion of birth.

But soon enough, Nurse went on, *Anne's health declined. She turned peevish and miserable, and nothing, neither her mother's arms nor her nurse's milky breasts, could calm her. The parish doctor was called for; he said the babe suffered from an excess of wind, and prescribed a bittersweet tincture of laudanum to help her sleep.*

And sleep I did. I slept so long and deeply, Nurse said, that when she woke in the early hours of the morning, it was to find her own shift wet with leaked milk. She put me, still sleeping, to her hard, swollen breasts, gratitude for the rest the medicine afforded us both warring with worry when I suckled only a little, and so lethargically that the excess milk had to be expressed by hand into the washbasin.

When I woke at last, I turned fractious again almost at once, wailing loudly enough to be heard far beyond the nursery. *The entire household went tense and afraid, the babe's cries powerful and unstoppable as sea waves in a storm. Her poor parents were frantic, and helpless as any parents whose child is clearly in pain. But the good doctor was called back, and he brought with him more drops, which worked their magic again directly.*

Though Nurse tried to wean me from my medicine once or twice, I always wailed again so loudly—*Like a pig brought to slaughter*—and turned consumptive, hot and chilled by turns, my chest rattling. She learned to dose me—my magic drops, she called them, smiling—at intervals, which alleviated my discomfort and kept me sweetly sleeping much of the time. And though the soft rolls at my ankles and wrists melted away like snow in spring, Dr. Grant, with a shake of his graying head, said it seemed I would likely always be delicate, and Mamma gave thanks, loudly and often, for the wonder of modern medicine.

MEMORIES OF MY EARLY life begin slow and dreamy as any of my nurse's stories. They meander like dust motes in the shafts of sunlight that came in through the nursery window. I was not supposed to dance, myself, but I could pretend, in the hours I spent watching those flecks twirl and collide, that I was one of them, a member of the set.

Some of my memories are surprisingly clear—I could describe the exact pattern of fruits and leaves in the intricate molding on our drawing room ceiling, or beat out with my fingertips the cascading rhythm of the garden fountain. Scents come back to me with overwhelming clarity—my musty nursery, of course, but also the headiness of the garden in full summer bloom, and the bright scent of Cook's pea soup, one of the few dishes to regularly tempt my appetite. It tasted of spring even when she served it in winter from boiled dried peas, accented with the faint tang of onion and the salty musk of anchovies.

People had their own peculiar smells; or rather, their fingers did, fingers that were forever testing the heat of my cheeks and brow. Mamma's, laden with rings, smelled of lily of the valley, a delicate scent at odds with the robustness of her form and character. My father's fingers, when he patted my shoulder in his usual distracted manner, smelled thickly of snuff. Over the years, as I needed her less and less, Nurse's gown and apron began to smell of smoke and grease from the kitchen, but her fingers forever smelled of the medicine she dispensed to me twice daily, bitterness just masked by cloying treacle.

For my own good, the boundaries of my world lay at the far-flung edges of my father's vast estate, but Nurse widened them, just slightly, with the fantastical tales she told as I drowsed in the grips of my drops. Stories of men the length of my thumbnail; of sleeps that lasted centuries. My medicine turned me stone-heavy, a breathing statue, eyelids drawing down despite all my best efforts and thoughts drifting like milkweed fluff. In this way, I was like one of the people in the stories, for what could be more fantastical than a girl made of stone?

When the weather was fine, and the sun not too strong, Nurse sometimes took me out to the garden, where, if it was too early for my first dose, I practiced reading from the Book of Common Prayer, my tongue stumbling over sentences no more comprehensible than the whispering of the wind through the trees, and far less interesting.

If it was later, I remained so still and recumbent that all manner of creatures came to me: bees roaming from the garden hives, who perhaps mistook my gowns with their block-printed patterns of leaves and flowers for an extension of the garden beds; beetles who scuttled up my wrist on feet so light I could not feel them; grasshoppers, some striped brown as winter leaves, others so bright a green that they blended completely into the summer grasses. These startled me a little from my stupor when they bounded from ground, to bench-back, to my knee, and down again. They were so energetic that, loose-jawed and loose-limbed, I could only marvel at them. The voices of all the grown persons in my life buzzed inside my head like the whirring of insect wings, reminding me gently that I was not meant for such darting quickness.

I am happy to say that those voices were slowly replaced by others—friends, phantoms, and, eventually, even myself—who, not-so-gently, disagreed.

CHAPTER TWO

I lay on my belly under the table in the nursery, head cradled on my arms, sleepiness drawing over me from toes to chin like a heavy coverlet. At seven years old, I was just long enough that I had to draw up my knees to keep my feet from poking out from beneath the tabletop. My eyes were almost closed, but from under the quivering cover of my lashes I could just see Nurse's square feet in their striped knit stockings. Nurse's sturdy boots had been set aside, and her toes spread now and again, glad to be released from their pinching confines.

Nurse was sewing. I could tell, though her hands and their work were hidden from view by the spreading top of the dark wood table. My twice-daily dose of medicine made my ears sensitive to the tiniest sounds, and I could hear now, like a whisper directly in my ear, each tug of thread through fabric.

As she sewed, Nurse told me a story. She often told stories at this time of day, her voice was low and restful as I grew drowsy after taking my drops. Today's, about the ugly prince whose intelligence earned him the love of a princess—whose beauty, in turn, endeared her to him despite her complete lack of wit—was one she had told many times before, and it was one that soothed me, for reasons I did not fully understand. I let my lids flutter closed, blotting out the sight of Nurse's feet and making room for my mind's illustrations.

"The prince was so ugly, his mother cried out at the sight of him," Nurse said. "But a fairy told the queen not to worry, for her son was amiable and good, and what's more, he was gifted with great wit, which he could, in turn, gift to the person he loved most in the world."

I saw the little princeling inside my head, wrapped in his swaddling clothes. He had a tuft of golden hair at the very top of his misshapen head, and eyes like currants sunk deep in a poorly baked bun. He was deeply hideous; I smiled a little as he waved one lumpy fist.

"A neighboring kingdom was the home of a princess who was very beautiful, but who was so stupid her poor mother despaired of her. But that same good fairy promised the queen that her daughter would, at least, have the power to make her beloved as handsome a man as she could wish."

I saw the princess as clearly as I did the prince. She had waving pale hair, and her cheeks had pink circles painted upon them, like the cheeks of my favorite doll. I saw the palace where the princess lived, larger even than our house here at Rosings Park, and surrounded by woods that were deeper but less frightening, dappled with improbable patches of sunlight. There were gardens, too, a maze of hedges that spiraled deliciously; I watched as the princess and her sister raced through it, just the hems of their skirts visible as they whipped laughing around corners, and imagined that I raced along just behind them.

My breathing grew slow and deep, and I missed the rest of the story entirely.

It was some time later when I was drawn out of my sleep by voices. One, I knew instantly—my mother bellowed even when whispering.

"What is Anne doing under there?" Mamma said. "Why is she not in her bed?"

"The young miss likes to curl up in the oddest places," my nurse said. "I did not see the harm in it, Your Ladyship."

"Nonsense. You did not feel like moving her, more likely. I will not tolerate laziness, you know."

"No, Your Ladyship. Of course not."

I opened my eyes in time to see Nurse's feet under the table stuffing themselves back into their boots with quick furtive movements.

Then a face appeared, tipped upside down, big solemn eyes and curly brown hair. I stared at it.

"She's awake," the face announced, and then it was joined by another, a woman who crouched down and smiled at the sight of me blinking up at her.

"Anne," the woman said. "My dear, it is so good to see you again." She reached out a hand to draw me forward, and I took it, crawling gracelessly out from under the table on my two knees and free hand. I kept my head ducked until I was out and standing. The room moved in and out around me, as if I stood inside the bellows of a giant's chest as he breathed. I swayed a little where I stood, and Nurse put out a hand to steady me.

"Greet your aunt, child," Mamma said, and I blinked and dipped an unsteady curtsy.

"Hello, Aunt Darcy," I said, for of course that was who the woman was. Mamma had been looking forward to the visit for days, both her brother and sister and all their children coming to see us at Rosings Park, but I, keeping quiet in the nursery, had all but forgotten about it. I looked to the side, where my cousin Fitzwilliam had straightened and was watching me with frank curiosity. He was not quite a year my senior, but was much taller than he had been the last time I saw him, and his hair was longer, curling over the tops of his ears. He saw me looking and bowed very correctly.

"Cousin Anne," he said.

"Cousin Fitzwilliam." I felt shy of him, but safe inside the giant's chest, padded a little from his curious stare. We both knew, having been told so all our short lives, that we were going to be married when we grew up.

"Come, Miss," Nurse said. She took me by the hand and led me to the window seat, tucking me in among the cushions. Aunt Darcy nodded at Fitzwilliam and he trailed after us, looking reluctant.

He perched on the edge of the seat, looking out the window at the garden below. "I thought Edward and John would already be here," he said. "They should have been. Their journey was much shorter than ours."

My other cousins, sons of Mamma's brother, the earl, could be at Rosings Park within a day of setting out. "Perhaps their horses are not as swift as yours," I said.

Fitzwilliam looked at me. "Perhaps not," he said, thoughtful.

My face cracked with the force of a sudden yawn, and my cousin frowned. "I am still tired," I said, and let my cheek rest on the cool of the windowpane. I did not quite sleep—I was aware of the movement when Fitzwilliam stood, and heard his footsteps as he crossed the room—but I could not keep my eyes from closing.

THE EARL AND HIS family arrived before dinner. They had a very fine, large carriage, and their horses were more than equal to the task of pulling it briskly. I was still resting in the window seat when their carriage was spotted but was summoned downstairs soon enough, where my entire family, including my aunt and uncle Darcy and my cousin Fitzwilliam, had arrayed themselves on the front steps to greet the new arrivals. Our butler, Peters; Mrs. Barrister, the housekeeper; and the most senior among the footmen, stood a little behind. Wedged between my father's comfortable stomach in its silver waistcoat and my mother's broad skirts, I stood a little on my toes, neck lengthening in my eagerness—for it was a rare treat when other children came to Rosings Park—to watch as the carriage rolled to a stop.

The Earl of Brightmoor emerged first, and he turned to hand out his wife. My uncle looked a great deal like my mother—they had the same nose, dipping down, as my own did, like a hunting bird's beak; and the same way of positioning their tall, strong forms, feet so firm upon the ground that they seemed rooted wherever they happened to be—much more so than Aunt Darcy, who was shorter and rounder, more robin than hawk. My cousins, Edward and John, came next. Mamma had come to the nursery several days in a row this past week to instruct me in all the family's proper titles, and I mouthed them to myself now as the boys emerged. Edward, the eldest at eleven, tall and pinch-faced, was properly Viscount Eden; John, just a year younger, was shorter, stocky, with a sweep of unruly hair over his brow, and was the Honorable John Fitzwilliam. It seemed unfair that my cousins were so distinguished—hadn't Mamma told me countless times that I was special, niece and granddaughter to earls, heiress to one of the finest estates in southern England, betrothed to the heir of one of the finest estates in the Peak District? Though my father was only a knight, the de Bourghs—like the Darcys—had been well monied for centuries. I knew better than to complain to my mother, who had no patience for impertinence, but I did tell Papa that I wished to be known as the Honorable Earless of Hunsford in company. My father looked at me, astonished, then laughed the great wheezing laugh I heard so infrequently.

"That you will be," he said, chuckling as he walked away.

Now my uncle kissed my mother's hand, then Aunt Darcy's; there was a great deal of chatter, a lot of quick movements as my cousins rushed to greet one another, Fitzwilliam jostling me in his hurry. I stepped back, out of the fray, watching as Papa ushered the men and women inside and the boys raced off across the lawn, already shouting in some game that had mysteriously sprung up instantly among them. I turned in a slow circle to watch them run—their legs and arms leaped and swung; their hair flew away from their faces in a wind created by their own quickness. Not one of them glanced in my direction.

Inside my own body, something stirred, making my arms tingle and my feet move restlessly against the gravel drive. I was not allowed to run; too much physical effort made it hard for me to breathe. And yet I had taken five or six steps forward—quick steps!—without even meaning to before I was stopped by Nurse's hand on my arm.

EDWARD AND FITZWILLIAM PLAYED at battledore and shuttlecock while I watched from my garden bench. They hit the feather-trimmed shuttlecock back and forth, lunging and grunting, faces going red with exertion. Both had taken off their coats to allow their arms more freedom of movement. I was the Keeper of the Coats; I held the folded garments on my lap, absently stroking the soft wool.

The day was warm, but because the sun was mostly covered by clouds Nurse had allowed me to come outside. Still, she took precautions; my hat shaded my face and neck, and I had been firmly instructed to keep to the bench and not run. This would have been an easier command to obey had I already had my drops, but it was too early, and a child's body craves movement. Even knowing the way I would end up gasping for air if I were to take a turn at my cousins' game, I found myself unable to keep still; I wriggled on the bench until Nurse lay a hand upon my shoulder, a quiet reprimand. I turned a furious look upon her, but Nurse just kept sewing.

Earlier, Dr. Grant had come to Rosings Park for his monthly visit, which always put me a little out of humor. Dr. Grant's fingers were cold when they probed the sides of my neck, and he looked at me as if I were a curiosity in a jar, like the butterflies in Papa's book room. He peered into my eyes, checked the color of my tongue, felt the pulse beating through my wrist, and grunted to himself after each evaluation, as if he had discovered something very important. He seemed a very old man to me, the top of his head bald and shiny and the ruffle of hair around his ears blackish-gray, but his skin was unlined and his voice steady when he said, "Miss de Bourgh is very well," to the room at large.

Usually, the audience to these examinations consisted only of Mamma and Nurse, but today my aunts watched as well, their faces, until the doctor's pronouncement, politely interested, at which point they both smiled, as if he said something enormously clever. I felt my cheeks flush as if from fever from the force of all their gazing eyes and glowered down at my blue-sprigged lap. Dr. Grant said the same thing every time he came, unless I was actually in the midst of a bout of illness, and it annoyed me every time. If I were truly very well, I would be able to play with my cousins, or to go to London—that thrilling, fabled city—with my father.

Dr. Grant stood and took a glass bottle of my medicine from his satchel and set it on a little side table. "I see no reason to change her dosage," he said, bowing to Mamma.

Sitting on the garden bench with Nurse, I fancied, for all the warmth of the day, that I could still feel the chill of Dr. Grant's finger pads.

John had vanished at some point, but now he returned, the pockets of his coat bulging. He stopped before my seat, looking down at me and blocking my view of the game.

"See what I found," he said, and reached into one pocket to take out a handful of stones. He dropped them into my lap, where they lay upon the others' piled coats like an offering. I picked them up one by one. Most were uninteresting at first glance, rough and irregular in varying shades of dun and gray; but when I brought them closer to my eyes I could see why John chose each one. This stone was shot through with silvery flecks that made it sparkle when the weak sun caught it; that one had a vein of pink running through its dull gray body. I looked up at him, my mouth pulling up at the corners.

"And see here?" My cousin put his hand into the other pocket, which looked flat and empty compared to the first, and took out something hidden by the curl of his fingers. He picked up my hand and dropped the something into it—a fat, furry caterpillar, soft as anything but a little squashed and syrupy about the middle, and clearly quite dead.

I screamed, flinging it away from me, and Nurse turned a fierce glare upon John, who had taken a startled step backward.

"What in the *world* . . . ?" Nurse said. "Bringing a filthy dead thing to your poor cousin—"

"It was alive when I found it!" John said. He looked down at his hands, which seemed outsized dangling at the ends of his narrow wrists, as if they had betrayed him.

I had shrunk against the back of the bench, away from my nurse's vehemence and the lurking possibility of other nasty creatures falling into my lap. But I made myself stir when John, frowning, shoved his hands into his now-empty pockets and began to walk away.

"Thank you for the stones," I said; and then, when he did not look around, I raised my voice and repeated myself.

John stopped, looked back at me over his shoulder, and raised one side of his mouth in a half-smile. Then Edward called to him and he went running off before I could think of anything else to say.

I SAW LITTLE OF my cousins over the next few days. They spent most of their time outside, their play rough enough that they were banished from the house from breakfast until dinner; I was kept mostly in the nursery except when Mamma called for me to be brought into the drawing room, where I sat and listened as the ladies gossiped and sewed. Their talk was very dull, though, all about what schools my cousins would attend and which women of their acquaintance were expected to soon be brought to bed, and so I did not even struggle when, after Nurse came with my medicine, the usual tiredness came over me. I half-woke a few times, taking in words of their conversation—"Edward's master says his Latin is improving, but John's is still atrocious"—before slipping away again.

"Poor lamb," Aunt Darcy said one afternoon, her voice dropping.

I always knew I was being discussed when my aunts' and even my mother's voices dropped. They spoke of me in whispers, as if I were a secret.

"I do hate to see her like this," Aunt Darcy continued. "Children should not be so still, so silent; it's unnatural."

Moments before, Nurse had given me my second dose of medicine, tucking a shawl around me and murmuring that I should sleep a little now. And so my eyes were already closed; and though my aunt's words made some stubborn part of me ache to rise up and move, I stayed perfectly still so that I could hear what would be said next.

"Dr. Grant assures us it's for the best," Mamma said. "She requires absolute quiet. *You* did not have to contend with the screaming when she was an infant, Sister. Nothing soothed her, but her illness is quite well managed with a little medicine every day. It is a wonder, is it not, Nurse?"

"It is indeed, ma'am," my nurse said. "Keeps the young mistress happy as can be."

"She could be rather pretty, couldn't she? If only she were plumper." They had leaned closer, I could tell; and I knew, too, when Aunt Darcy raised a hand, as if to touch my cheek, though she stopped before actually making contact. The shadow of her hand had the weight of folded cloth.

"Her appetite is always quite depressed," Mamma said. "Dr. Grant says it is very normal in cases like this, with delicate young ladies."

"She is just so—small. And so quiet." Aunt Darcy lowered her voice still further. "She seems to have no spirit at all. Fitzwilliam is very serious; he will need a lively wife to remind him to—to find *enjoyment* in life."

My eyes squeezed more tightly closed. Mamma always spoke of my smallness as if it made me special, but there was something about the doubtful way my aunt spoke now, each syllable like a slap, that made my body feel brittle, like ice in spring. I thought of Nurse's story about the ugly prince and stupid princess, and wondered, fleetingly, whether when we married, Fitzwilliam might be able to gift me some of his own strength. But what did I have to gift to him in return? I was very aware of all my bones; of the blue veins showing so clearly under my skin. My face, not round and rosy as a child's should be, but sharply delineated. Only my hair looked healthy: dark as both Mamma's and Aunt Darcy's own, it was my mother's pride manifested as thick, waving strands, caught up with silk ribbons to match my gowns.

"It is a good thing my nephew is such a strapping boy," Mamma said, and *her* voice was defiant, cutting off any possibility of argument. "He and Anne will make well-proportioned children together."

Aunt Darcy's silence was very loud.

I would have stoppered my ears if I had to, against that silence. Happily, in this instance, my little glass of medicine made it easy to disappear into my own head. There, I raced along forest paths with the hoop and stick I longed to have in my waking life, my feet fleet upon the earth, nimbly avoiding tree roots and rolling acorns and hazelnuts. My lungs never wanting for air, my hair flying out behind me.

CHAPTER THREE

The blunt little church in Hunsford village, with its dark beams spanning the width of the ceiling and its heavy block floor, worn to a shallow trench along the length of the aisle from decades upon decades of worshipers' feet, did little to inspire feelings of awe or reverence. Nor did our rector's manner of speaking; Mr. Applewhite was white-haired and thin-voiced, and I spent more time on Sunday mornings staring with fascination at his bristling side whiskers than taking in the content of his sermons. My mind rambled; my eyes roved over the myriad little nicks and grooves marring the high wooden sides of our pew. I wafted along on the singing of the Psalms as if I had already taken my morning dose of laudanum.

I was grateful to our pew's tall sides, which shielded us from view during the service. But after, there was nothing to keep the other congregants—many of whom were my father's tenants—from looking at me. Papa stopped sometimes as we left the church, though the crowd tended to part for us like water before the prow of a boat; he greeted his tenants and many of the villagers by name, while Mamma merely nodded this way and that, the plume on her bonnet nodding half a beat behind, as if in echo of her condescension.

Outside, she spoke for a few minutes with other ladies of the parish as we waited for Papa to join us. I stood a little behind her and tried to conceal myself in the shadow of the ancient black poplar that grew beside the church. With its modest spire and gray stone walls blunted by centuries of wind and rain, the church seemed dwarfed by the tree, which shaded the side of the building where the churchyard lay, its headstones cluttered tipsily together. The oldest were as weathered as the church itself, and I watched as the village children, released from the enforced stillness and solemnity of the service, chased one another among the stones, dashing between pockets of shadow and tall grasses speckled with sunlight.

Snakes of ivy had begun a slow, strangling climb up the base of the poplar. They looped around the bulbous trunk and crept on tough hairy feet along the twisting branches. They moved, of course, far too slowly for human eyes to observe the actual motion, and yet I was able to track their progress over months and years of Sundays. My breast filled with affection for the ivy: its rustling three-pronged leaves, its apparent stillness and inexorable creep. And at the same time, I was sometimes punched by sympathy for the tree, for, just as inexorably, it was being smothered.

"We go to Town next week for my niece's debut," said Mrs. Clifton, our nearest neighbor, one Sunday. The Clifton estate, while rich, was only two-thirds the size of Rosings Park; I knew this because Mamma liked to pepper her conversation with such tidbits. "She's a retiring sort of girl; I worry that she will faint when her turn comes to be presented."

"She'll need to grow a proper spine if she wants to find a husband," Mamma said. "She hasn't much of a dowry, has she?"

"No, poor girl. Not like my Lucy. But of course we've a good dozen years before we need to worry about *her* debut; even your dear Anne will be presented sooner than Lucy."

"Don't be silly," my mother said; and her voice was indulgent as cake. "Anne is far too frail to risk exposing her to London's foul air. And her future with my nephew is quite settled; she will not suffer for lack of a proper introduction at court."

Mrs. Clifton's eyes flicked toward me, and then away. "Oh, yes. Of course."

I looked up at the tree in its ivy gown, and at the birds that perched there. I watched a snail, almost as achingly slow as the ivy, make its way down the church's stone wall. I listened to the thumping of the other children's feet, and tried to ignore the way the village women's quick, curious glances burned my cheeks and throat.

If I had a shell like the snail, I thought, I would tuck myself back inside of it, away from their branding pity. Inside my shell, I would not be able to hear the village children's laughter, or their mothers' whispers. I felt at once all-too-visible in my fine gowns and gaudy bonnets, and ill-defined as the edges of a ghost.

Mr. Applewhite, in his stiff white stock and flowing black cassock, said once with great authority that only humans have souls. But I watched the ivy tiptoe, and knew its clandestine desires; I felt the nervousness in the wings of moths; heard my mother's voice in the sharp reprimands of crows. I recognized violet flowers' concurrent reticence—hovering as they did in their shadowed crannies—and eagerness for notice, their petals purple splashes among so much green. I could not help feeling the personhood in all these things; and I was sure our vicar must be wrong.

MUCH OF MY FATHER'S time was spent in London, a place that sounded as exotic and faraway to me as anything in Nurse's stories. I had little idea what he did there, or why he was so often away; when I asked him, my father said, tapping the tip of my nose, that London was the place for gentlemen to conduct business.

But it was also the place where girls went to become women and find husbands. It was a place where both of my uncles kept homes, where they and my aunts and cousins enjoyed longer visits than those they took faithfully each year to us at Rosings. It was a place that was quite forbidden to me, and so of course I felt its pull all the more strongly.

Even when he was home at Rosings Park, Papa was generally out on the estate or tucked away in his book room with our steward. I caught glimpses of him from the nursery window sometimes as he rode out on his black hunter; my father was a large man, with broad shoulders and a broad belly, but he sat his horse as if he and the animal were one creature. Mamma was almost always home, and came to sit with me for a little while each day in the nursery, or instructed Nurse to bring me downstairs to sit with her. Dr. Grant was insistent that my education must not be too taxing, but I learned my letters and the rudiments of stitching, as well as how to count—a useful skill when I was bored, for Rosings Park was filled with things to count. There were twenty gold stripes in the fabric of the drawing room settee, for instance, alternating with nineteen stripes of dark blue. The nursery windows, with their sliding sashes and glass wiped clean of my fingerprints by the housemaids, had thirty-two panes in all. In the rose garden, the number of blossoms on the bushes was ever changing, and endlessly amusing.

Papa brought a doll back from London for me when I was eight years old. Her gown was a marvel of intricate embroidery; her hair was real, as dark as my own. She smelled, I fancied, like London must, itself: densely sooty, as if my father had carried her in the crook of his arm through the streets until the city's own perfume seeped thoroughly into the strands of her hair and the fabric of her gown. He lay her in the crook of my own arm when he returned from that trip, so gently that he did not wake me, and I woke to her wooden weight and her heady scent, alone.

The Sunday of Mrs. Clifton's and my mother's talk of London debuts, I returned with my parents to Rosings Park. Nurse was waiting; at Mamma's order, she led me to the drawing room and made me comfortable on a chaise there. She handed me my doll, with a smile, and then drew the bottle of my medicine from her apron pocket. My body instantly leaned forward a little in anticipation of my drops; I watched as she drew up a dropperful and squeezed the reddish-brown liquid into a waiting glass.

"There now," she said as I raised it to my lips and drank it down. Molasses and spices just masked the bitter tang. "That's it."

I handed the glass back to her, my tongue darting out to catch a bead of liquid before it fell, then leaned back, pressing my pale cheek to my doll's rosy one, and let the prickling sensation of being watched by all the parish recede.

But Mamma, sitting nearby, began telling Papa about Mrs. Clifton's niece, and I squeezed my eyes closed. Lucky, lucky girl; even if she did faint, she would first get to see a grand city. *London*, I thought, my eyebrows drawing together. *London, London, London*. The words thumped inside my head, slower and slower, in time to my decelerating heartbeat.

I turned my head, very deliberately, and inhaled of my doll's soot-scented hair.

EVERY YEAR WHEN THEY came to Rosings Park, it always seemed to me that my cousins had been stretched and altered by some invisible force between one visit and the next. Limbs lengthened, shoulders broadened. Edward, the eldest, always seemed to change the most dramatically; I could not help staring the year that he arrived with wispy dark hairs, like the tacked-on legs of insects, above the sharp bow of his upper lip.

I changed as well, of course, though less substantially over the years. I remained short of stature and narrow of frame, though Mamma did her best, with the help of the dressmaker in Hunsford village, to ensure I looked as well as possible when my cousins—Fitzwilliam, in particular—arrived. I do not think that Fitzwilliam, still a child himself, was much moved by her efforts. He and I stole looks at each other, curious and uncertain as forest creatures, but almost never spoke.

It is a strange thing, knowing from infancy the person with whom you are meant to spend your life. Usually the knowledge felt secure as a lap rug tightly tucked; but sometimes I had the sensation that all my slow and ponderous life until my inevitable wedding day held little meaning. I was forever waiting, without knowing quite what it was I was waiting for.

CHAPTER FOUR

The express came late one afternoon early in my eleventh year. I lay in the drawing room, my head on the arm of the settee, as Papa read aloud from the newspaper and Mamma improved upon each story with either a noise of assent or a scornful remark.

Peters brought the letter on a silver tray. "From Pemberley, Your Ladyship," he said, and Mamma snatched the letter from him before he could complete his bow.

"Has Lady Anne been brought to bed, then?" Papa said, once the seal had been broken. "It is another boy?"

Aunt Darcy was supposed to be delivered of a baby very soon; Mamma had spoken of little else recently as the days ticked by and no word arrived from Derbyshire. I felt a vague stirring of interest at the thought that I must have a new cousin; I turned my head so I could see my mother, who held the letter up to the light from the windows, her eyes moving rapidly over the few lines written there. She stopped when she reached the end, but did not say anything; Papa shifted restlessly in his chair, glancing back at the newspaper he held, as if he wished to return to it. Mamma shook her head and shoulders, as if to throw off some terrible, grasping thing, and read the letter again; and then, as I watched, my mother's hand began to tremble hard enough that the letter rattled in her grip; and then that grip loosened, the letter fluttering to the floor, and Mamma put her hands over her face.

Papa was on his feet in an instant, calling for a maid, but I only stared. I had never seen my mother weep before, and it was several moments before the dreadful gulping sounds coming from Mamma's throat and the tremors that wracked her body so violently made sense to me. The maid came in, and Papa, who had taken up the letter, said, "Lady Catherine has had a shock—fetch wine, quickly." He stood by, the letter dangling from his fingertips, and watched his wife, who sat in her chair folded in half by her grief.

I watched as Mamma drank the wine in three great swallows; as Papa spoke quietly to Mrs. Barrister, who came to the doorway to find out what the commotion was; as Mamma, always so solid, so immovable, stood too quickly and stumbled, nearly falling, and said, "I must leave for Pemberley immediately—Mr. Darcy will have need of my help." They all left the drawing room, Mamma now calling instructions about what her maid should pack, even as her face fell into unfamiliar keening lines, Papa hurrying to his study to write a letter to my uncle Darcy.

I realized that I had been quite forgotten. I put my head back down, looked up at the ceiling, and wished I could climb the walls like a spider so I could bask in the patches of sunlight that stretched at steep angles from the dark wood wainscoting up toward the chandelier.

It was Nurse who came for me at last, who gathered me, crooning, as if I should be feeling very sad about something. I pulled away from her, impatient, and said, "Do I have a girl cousin? Or a boy? What is all the fuss about?"

"Oh, Miss," Nurse said. "You've a little girl cousin, who is well and strong, thanks be to God. But your aunt—your aunt is dead."

I just looked at her. "But," I said; but could think of nothing more to add. My medicine cushioned me from what properly should have been a blow. I thought of Aunt Darcy, so round and smiling whenever she came to Rosings; and I thought of how my aunt had, without meaning to, made me feel so very small, in the worst possible way. *She has no spirit at all.* I frowned down at my hands, tracing the pointer finger of one over the sharp white knuckles of the other, and could not feel as sorry as I was sure I should.

"THE BABE WAS STUCK, that's what I heard," Nurse said in the murmur of someone speaking words they knew they oughtn't. I pretended to still be sleeping, though I opened my eyes just a little, peering through the slits. Nurse's head was bent conspiratorially toward one of the housemaids, who balanced a tray of tea things and shook her head, tutting.

"And where'd you hear that?"

Nurse shrugged. "I've got my ways. And after poor Lady Anne lost all those other little ones in between

Master Fitzwilliam and this new babe . . . Ah, it's a sad day."

The maid gave a shudder. "It's a bloody business, isn't it? Lady Anne seemed nice enough—gave us all little gifts when she visited at Christmas that time."

"She was a good one." Nurse blew out a breath. "Different from her sister as rain and shine."

"Shush!" The maid swiveled her head to look at me; from years of eavesdropping on servants' conversations, I knew better than to snap my eyes shut, as I instinctively wanted to do. Instead, I left them slitted, let my mouth hang a little loose and open. "Even *she* has ears."

"You don't need to worry about that one. She can't hear a thing once she's had her drops, bless her."

The maid thrust the tray at Nurse. "Well, *I* won't be the one losing my place for speaking ill of my mistress, thank you very much." She turned in a graceful arc and left the nursery.

Nurse chuckled a little as she set the tray on a table. She took a biscuit and bit into it, munching with great smacks of her lips.

I let my eyes close again. *A bloody business*, I thought. Perhaps that explained why Mamma was adamant that I would be her only child; I would not want to repeat any experience that could be described so, either. And of course, she was fond of saying to anyone who would listen that Rosings Park could be inherited by a girl, so she had no need, as other ladies did, to worry about the sex of her offspring.

I knew that a husband was required in order for a

woman to become with child, and thought of my own someday-husband, his curly hair and serious face. Rosings Park might be inheritable by a girl, but Pemberley, which Fitzwilliam would inherit, was not. But, I thought hopefully, perhaps after what happened to his mother, my cousin would not make me bear any children at all.

MAMMA RETURNED FROM DERBYSHIRE still in her mourning black, wearing a lock of Aunt Darcy's hair set in a handsome brooch. My father had accompanied her, directing the coachman to set the horses to the quickest pace they could manage, but he returned to Kent only two weeks later. Mamma had remained at Pemberley estate for three months, leaving only when she was satisfied that her nephew and new baby niece were well provided for.

"Mr. Darcy, of course, was perfectly useless; but men always are in the face of grief," Mamma said over tea the afternoon of her return. "He was speechless with gratitude when I told him I intended to stay as long as necessary. Luckily for him, I know all the best people. The nurse he engaged was not the right sort of person at all; she ate far too much meat. I found a good girl to nurse my niece, and I spoke with each of my nephew's masters to make sure they knew their business; I cannot expect Mr. Darcy to take much interest in such things just now, but there is nothing better for sorrow than hard work, and Fitzwilliam was very cast down indeed. His masters all seemed competent enough—he will be a credit to both Pemberley and Rosings Park someday." She paused here to smile at me before continuing. "Little Georgiana favors the Darcy side, I think, though of course there is time for some Fitzwilliam features to come out. I will have to be diligent about her education; I fear Mr. Darcy will be too lenient with her. He already dotes on her more than is good for the child. And my sister was very musical; I have no doubt her daughter will have inherited her talent. Did you notice her fingers, Sir Lewis, when you were at Pemberley? They were just formed for playing."

Papa made a sound of agreement, or perhaps indigestion, and Mamma smiled again at me.

"You have your aunt's fingers, too, my dear. If only your health were stronger, I've no doubt your musical abilities would even surpass hers."

THAT NIGHT, NURSE BRUSHED my hair with her usual efficiency. But as she divided it into three strands for plaiting, she paused, fingering the ends of one strand.

"Your hair is rather marvelous," she said. "So much healthier than the rest of you! It's almost a shame you'll have to pin it up when you're older."

I did not much like to look at my own reflection—it always scowled back at me, all pinched and bony—but I did like the softness of my hair. But just now, my hair made me think of Mamma's mourning brooch with its narrow little plait, and *that* made me feel a little sad, and then sorry that my sadness was not more terrible.

Mamma allowed me to touch the brooch this evening; I traced around and around the edges of it, again and again, as if I could actually feel the bumps of the plaited hair through the glass under my fingertips. Then Mamma finally said, "That's quite enough," and moved away. I later heard her telling Nurse to give me a little more medicine than usual before bed, because "clearly, Anne is overwrought."

"My hair looks like Aunt Darcy's," I said now as Nurse tied off the ends with a ribbon.

Nurse set her hands on my shoulders and made a mournful face. "So it does," she said, then gave my shoulders a little pat and turned to pick up the bottle of medicine she had set down earlier. She poured my dose, then guided me into bed and blew out the candles, leaving the room in near-darkness. I mumbled something in response as Nurse wished me a happy sleep, waiting for my drops' soporific effect.

While I waited, I raised my hand, describing an oval in the air, fancying I could feel Aunt Darcy's plait under my fingertips. Had Fitzwilliam been given a lock of his mother's hair, as well? Had Uncle Darcy thought to keep some for the new baby?

Poor motherless thing. She would never see her mother's pretty hair as it had looked when it was attached to her head.

I let my hand drop. Perhaps my new cousin squalled the way Nurse said I used to, as if someone were trying to commit murder and it was up to me to sound the alarm. I smiled a little at the thought.

But then a little noise, like the burbling of a dove, stopped the smile before it could fully form. I turned my head very, very slowly until my eyes met the too-wide eyes of the infant lying on the bed beside me.

It took a moment, but I finally realized it was my cousin. *Georgiana*. Perhaps I myself had summoned her here, through my very thoughts. I reached out, but did not touch the babe, who was sticky with drying blood— *It's a bloody business.* After a moment's thought, I took up my own plait and trailed the tip of it across my cousin's cheek, letting her feel the texture. Georgiana did not cry or even try to bat the hair away, and I felt a sudden, surprising annoyance. My cousin was not like me at all. She was quiet, well behaved, contented. Easy, as I had not been.

I withdrew my plait quickly enough that the babe tossed her head a little, as if in protestation; but still she made no sound beyond a quiet squeak, and I turned over onto my side so my back was to my cousin, waiting, waiting.

At last my limbs grew heavy. The room undulated gently around me, and I forgot my tiny cousin entirely as I fell asleep, rocked like a babe myself in its cradle.

CHAPTER FIVE

In January of my twelfth year, I first saw the sea. The journey from Kent to Brighton took several days, most of which I spent dozing against my nurse's arm in the carriage, or curled under heaped coverlets on lumpy inn beds. Mamma was thin-lipped with anger for the entirety of the trip; it was Papa who said, Dr. Grant's advice notwithstanding, they would be fools if they did not at least try to help me by any means possible. My sickliness had not seemed to worry him overmuch at first—he was, for most of my life until now, entirely satisfied with little glimpses of me throughout the day, and reports from my nurse that I was well. But my health had, it seemed, now begun to weigh upon him. Mamma might be fully committed to following Dr. Grant's advice, but Dr. Grant was, in the end, nothing but a country physician, and the London doctors that Papa recently consulted were all eloquent in their praise of the restorative powers of sea bathing.

The sky was low and heavy as the underside of a mountain, and the sea, at first glimpse, seemed all whitecaps. The thought of going into the water was terrible; I was certain I would be swept under, or snatched away by great tentacled creatures. The wind coming off the water was cold enough to freeze the tears on my cheeks. I threw myself backward, tried to scramble back up the steps of the bathing machine to get away from the churning waves, but the ladies who were paid to help holiday-goers safely into the water were undaunted by my cries and thrashing. I found myself down the steps and in the water without quite knowing how it happened; my bathing costume inflated around me, swallowing me up like one of the sea monsters I dreaded meeting. I could hardly breathe, the cold was so profound, the pain of it not really so much *pain* as a terrible wrongness. With what little breath I had, I screamed, high and shrill like a fox's cry, until one of the dippers clamped a hand over my nose and mouth, cutting off sound and breath entirely.

"Hush, child," the woman said. "You'll put everyone off their cures." Her fingers pressed into the bones of my jaw; she only released her hold when I began to flail for air. The waves crashed against our backs, one after another, rhythmic and surging, and now I clung to the woman with her rough calloused fingers and sturdy arms who had nearly smothered me only moments before, raising my chin to keep it above the water, seeking my mother's form on the beach. Finally I found her, wrapped in her warm cloak against the wind, one hand shading her eyes as she looked out over the water.

When at last the dipper concluded that I had been in the sea long enough for my healing to commence, she bundled me up the steps of the bathing machine and dried me briskly with a cloth. Nurse was inside, ready with my clothes; she exclaimed over the iciness of my fingers and toes, frowning when I shivered so violently that it was difficult to do up the fastenings of my gown. Then she helped me out of the bathing machine and out onto the stretch of wide, damp sand, where we found Mamma waiting.

"There is some color in her cheeks, at least," Mamma said, looking down at my huddled form. "I suppose that will please Sir Lewis." Then she took off her own cloak, sweeping it over my shoulders, warm and thick against the sea wind. Nurse scrambled to pick up the hem so it would not drag through the sand.

When we returned to the house we had taken for our stay in Brighton, I was put to bed, kept warm under layers of shawls and blankets, the fire in my room built up until I became too hot, throwing off my covers. Before leaving earlier in the day to meet some acquaintances in town, Papa told Nurse not to give me my usual doses. If I had any improvement, they must be able to tell whether the sea was truly the reason.

And so, once I warmed up, I was bored. Waiting for sleep, I listened to the house settle and creak, and to the wind outside; but without my drops, I was fidgety. I went to the window, the panes frosted along their edges, but my room overlooked the small back garden, which was winter-gray and dead. From somewhere down the row of terraced houses, I could just hear the voices of other children at play.

When Nurse came in to check on me, I was in the thick of a very exciting game about pirates. Though stories of high adventure were usually deemed too stimulating for me, I had watched many times as Edward, John, and Fitzwilliam played at pirates, so I knew how the game was meant to go. My bed was my ship—its tall, curtained canopy made for excellent sails—and I was a navy captain. It was night, the ship surrounded by a pirate fleet, but my crew was fighting bravely. I crouched in the center of the bed, dress and petticoat rucked up around my knees to give my legs room to splay. Amidst the chaos of battle, I could hear someone approaching—a pirate was sneaking up on me, cutlass raised. I stayed very still so he would not realize I heard him coming, and then, just as the creak of the deck under his boots gave him away, I sprang.

There was a cry and a great clatter. I was jolted from the high seas and back into my bedchamber; flat on my back at the edge of the bed, I looked up and saw not billowing sails but a stiff yellow canopy. Then Nurse slipped an arm under my shoulders, helping me to sit.

"Miss!" Nurse said. "What were you *doing*?"

Nurse sounded angry. I frowned up at her, at the deep line between Nurse's pale eyebrows and the turned-down corners of her wide lips, and jerked myself away from Nurse's hands.

"I do not need help," I said, and tried to smooth my dress down over my legs. "I was only playing."

Nurse looked at me quite blankly for a moment, then turned her attention to something easier to comprehend, tutting under her breath. "Look at this mess," she said, sweeping one hand out in a gesture that encompassed the dropped tray, biscuits tumbled everywhere, teapot smashed and leaking. She stooped to pick up the shattered bits of china, blotting with the edge of her apron at the carpet, where a pale brown stain had begun to spread. Then she looked up at me again. "You're feeling well, then, Miss?"

I swung my legs, heels thunking against the side of the bed. "Wonderfully well."

Nurse piled the last of the soggy biscuits and broken crockery on the tray then sat back on her haunches, staring at me with her mouth a little open. "Playing," she said at last and, gathering up the tray, left the room.

My game had rather been ruined by the interruption, so I returned to the window, pressing my ear to one icy pane to try to hear what the children down the row were shouting about. When the door opened again a few minutes later, it was Mamma who entered first, Nurse scuttling behind her.

"It's marvelous, Your Ladyship," Nurse was saying. "Just see—"

I turned my head so I was looking over my shoulder at them. Mamma had very dark brows, and she raised one now at the sight of me leaning against the window. "I see nothing to make a fuss about," she said.

Nurse bunched the fabric of her apron in her two fists. "She was at play, Your Ladyship, she was just there"— pointing to the bed—"acting boisterous as any normal child."

"Boisterous? I hope not. I abhor children who cannot sit still. It portends a lifetime of poor self-control." Mamma's gown went *swoosh-swoosh* against the floor as she walked farther into the room. "How are you feeling, Anne?"

I stepped away from the window entirely, folding my hands in front of me. I wished Nurse had not mentioned my game; Mamma thought games of imagination undignified. "I am feeling very well, Mamma."

My mother frowned down at me, looking into my eyes, as if for some sign of a great change.

"She is *not* a normal child," Mamma said, with a suddenness that made both Nurse and me jump a little where we stood. "She is Anne de Bourgh. You oughtn't allow such sudden excess, Nurse, for all that Anne seems to be so much better than usual. Let us see over time whether the sea truly has cured her."

I ATE HEARTILY THAT night, to Nurse's delight, soup and chicken and potatoes and two kinds of salad. After, my father came to visit me upstairs before I went to bed. He peered into my face just as Mamma had, searching for some secret that I was not sure actually existed there, then kissed my forehead with his dry lips and said, "You shall enjoy the sea again tomorrow, dear girl, and every day until we return home."

I began to cry, thinking of the bitter waves and the dipper's unforgiving hands, and Papa looked alarmed and stepped away from me. "Tell her, Nurse," he said as he sidled out the door, and waved a hand in my direction. "Tell her it is for the best."

I went sea bathing again the following morning after

breakfast. I slept oddly without my drops, waking sometimes in the night rather than sleeping like a dead thing all the way through, but I was hungry for breakfast. My parents watched as I ate three pieces of toast slathered in preserves, then began to lick my fingers. Mamma rapped me smartly on the wrist with her knuckles.

The sea was as cold this morning as it was yesterday. This time, only Nurse accompanied me down to the beach; Mamma had calls to pay, and Papa could not have come even had he wished to, for the bathers were segregated by sex to preserve the ladies' modesty. I struggled again against the dippers' strong arms, but I did not scream, and only cried a little after I was taken out of the water.

In the afternoon, though, I did not feel like playing as I had the day before. Something had settled at the small of my back, a pressing feeling like a fist that would not go away. My legs felt strange, almost as if they were not there at all, and yet there was sometimes a horrible sensation, too, like ants crawling up and down my calves under my stockings. I wriggled and squirmed, trying to get the feeling to go away, but during the moments it was gone there was only a terrible numbness, and I had to lift my skirt, to Nurse's exclamation of dismay, to make sure my legs had not fallen off.

By evening, I was shivering. It was cold in my chamber, so cold that my skin was covered all over in little bumps and my nose was running. I whinged and snapped, twisting away when Nurse tried to smooth back my hair, annoyed by the very presence of the maid who came to build up the fire. When Mamma and Papa came in to see me before their dinner, their faces grew flushed from the fire's heat, but I still shook under the covers. Papa's distress at finding me so unwell was visible, but my mother looked almost pleased.

"This is what comes," she said, "of ignoring a trusted doctor's advice."

Papa, however, was determined that the cure be thoroughly tested. Only see, he said, how well I had done the day before! I had a little cold, now, that was all—it was only a minor setback, and in a few days I would be well again and could again be dipped in the sea. The bracing saltwater could only strengthen anything, or anyone, with which it came into contact.

But the following morning, my condition had worsened. Nurse, drawn and exhausted-looking, told Mamma that the young mistress was awake most of the night, writhing about in bed and complaining that there were insects all over her, and they would not leave her alone.

I was crying out when they came upstairs, my hair stuck to my face, which was wet with both tears and perspiration. I hurt deep within my limbs, pain at the very core of me, squeezing; but I could not find the words to express what I was feeling beyond moaning, "It *hurts,* make it *stop,*" over and over.

"She says she is freezing," Nurse said, "but just look at the state of her."

"'Just a cold,' indeed," said Mamma.

THOUGH I HAD EATEN almost nothing for more than a day, it seemed my body still had plenty of reserves to reject. Nurse was not quite quick enough when I began to vomit, and the bed linens, already sweat-damp, needed to be changed immediately. Usually so placid, today I lashed out at the maids as they tried to urge me off the mattress. I crawled back onto the newly made-up bed like a half-drowned man onto shore, and then proceeded to vomit again. This time, at least, my nurse was ready with a bowl.

She was not ready, however, when my body began to purge itself from the other end, and at last she summoned a maid to bring my parents. They found me curled in a miserable ball around my cramping belly, eyes tightly closed against the light of the fat tallow candles.

A doctor was summoned with alacrity. Mamma narrowed her eyes at the unfashionable cut of his coat and the mud on his boots but kept silent at a sharp look from my father. They watched as the doctor gently straightened my body so that he could probe my belly and feel my neck; it took some persuading, but at last he managed to get me to open my eyes, to find himself faced with pupils blown monstrously wide. My lips were cracked but my skin was pale and clammy; I would, he declared, be dangerously dehydrated soon. When he listened to my chest, my heart thundered in his ear with worrisome rapidity.

Laudanum, he said, producing a bottle of the sweetened brown liquid with which we were all so familiar, was the only thing for me. It would stopper the looseness of my bowels and allow me to drink water and tea. Mamma's expression softened with relief when, only a short time after a dose had been administered, I began to relax toward sleep. Papa was wise enough not to suggest a repeat of the sea bathing experiment, and we passed our remaining days in Brighton much as we would have had we been at home in Kent.

CHAPTER SIX

When we returned from Brighton, Rosings Park seemed to stretch itself up on its toes to greet us over the bare-branched tops of the trees lining the lane. I rolled my eyes up so I could see every pinnacle as our carriage rolled closer to the drive. There was a little snow on the roof and grounds, light as sugar dusted over a cake, and when we went inside the house, Peters and Mrs. Barrister greeted us and led us to the drawing room, where a fire waited and everything was warm and familiar.

But within a day or two, the hooded eyes of all the de Bourgh family portraits lining the walls made me twitch; the fabric of the window seat cushion seemed to chafe even through my clothes. I looked out at the garden and was irritated by the sculpted perfection of the hedges and topiaries, their rustling leaves the only splash of green in the winter landscape. I thought of the sea, which seemed far less terrible now that I was no longer caught up in its watery grasp; of my booted feet making deep imprints on the damp sand. Dread clutched at my heart, making it quiver, making me gasp. Only my drops calmed the terrible vibration inside my chest, and I drank them down as if I were dying of thirst and they were the only sips of water to be found.

I looked up at the ceiling, so high and heavy, and could think only, *More, more, more, more*.

MY MOTHER SEEMED LARGER back in our home than she had in Brighton. As usual, I spent a great deal of time watching her—giving orders to the servants, holding court in the drawing room when company came to call, dispensing advice to cottagers the way Nurse dispensed my drops—and she seemed to me like a wild creature, swelling and safe in its own territory.

Papa, though, seemed restless after we returned. He came into the nursery more often than usual; I sometimes woke from my stupor to find him peering down at me, Nurse hovering by his elbow. His face seemed to be composed entirely of tight lines, as if it had been sketched in short, angry strokes. He did not go off to London but remained in Kent for weeks and weeks, as the sun slowly gained a little strength and snowdrops bloomed in one sudden effort, carpeting the woods at the edge of the garden with their nodding white blossoms.

When Dr. Grant made his usual visit, Papa, for once, attended. Once the examination was over and a new bottle of laudanum safely in Nurse's possession, Papa said, "I have been considering the matter of Anne's education." He held his hands clasped behind his back and looked only at the doctor, his eyes carefully keeping away from Mamma, whose brows dipped suddenly, dangerously, toward one another. "I believe it is beyond time that she have a governess."

Dr. Grant raised his eyebrows. "A governess? Hmm." He blew air out between his lips, and I wrinkled my nose behind his back. "I have no objections, provided the woman understands Miss de Bourgh's . . . considerable limitations."

MY NEW GOVERNESS, AT first glance, appeared average in every way, with features that were neither homely nor pretty, hair that was neither quite gold nor quite brown, a figure settled comfortably between slim and stout. She was dressed modestly in a gown that was neither too ornate for her station, nor so plain that she looked out of place in Rosings's drawing room. She came to Rosings Park fresh from Miss Briggs's Seminary— "Where you would have gone, Anne, had your health allowed," Mamma said.

We sat looking at one another, and though the silence only lasted for a few seconds—I knew, for I counted them off in the ticking of the clock—my entire body began to burn under the cool appraisal in Miss Hall's eyes. She took in my bones and my pallor, all dressed up in a gown so richly covered in whitework embroidery that it was almost stiff, despite the cotton's softness; she took in the way I listed a little against the arm of my chair. Then she looked down at her lap, shuttering her expression.

"I understand your father is insolvent," Mamma said then. "I wonder that he was able to afford your education."

Miss Hall's lips parted, but she swallowed whatever

words might have come out, her throat working as though around a bite of meat that she had not properly chewed. It took but a moment for her to gain mastery of herself, and then she said, "I was fortunate, Your Ladyship, in that Miss Briggs agreed to keep me on if I helped with the younger girls' instruction."

"Yes, she said you had some experience, and that you've all the usual accomplishments. You taught drawing, I believe? And needlework?"

"Yes, ma'am."

"French? Music? Dancing?"

"Yes, Your Ladyship. And Italian."

Mamma flicked her painted fan, as if to dismiss the word *Italian* from her drawing room. "Anne, of course, cannot be expected to do much. Her health does not permit strenuous study."

Miss Hall's eyes darted from Mamma to me and back again, as if trying to make sense of them both; then she nodded. "Yes, ma'am."

"She is at her best in the mornings; in the afternoons, she requires rest and quiet."

"Of course, Your Ladyship." A pause, and another look at me, quick as a cat's paw. "I am certain that I shall understand Miss de Bourgh's constitution soon enough, but in the meantime I would wish to do neither too much nor too little. May I ask what subjects you think might be too tiring? Music, for instance—you've such a fine instrument here. I assume you wish Miss de Bourgh to learn to use it?"

"Oh, *music*," Mamma said. "There is nothing better

in this world than music. My sister, Lady Anne Darcy, was a *most* accomplished musician. But *she* was strong enough to withstand the hours necessary to practice."

"It could be that Miss de Bourgh takes after her aunt," Miss Hall said. "I am sure that I could manage a course of musical education that would not be unduly taxing. After all, Your Ladyship," she said, "where would we ladies be without our accomplishments?"

Mamma raised her brows. "Where would *you* be, you mean. For myself, I have never held with any of that nonsense. My sister learned all the things young ladies are supposed to learn, and her performances and drawings were pleasant enough to hear and see. But she'd have done well enough without them; she had a fine dowry and our connections to ensure she would never want for suitors. I never bothered to learn, and I married quite well; and before *that* I oversaw my family's estate after my father passed, while my brother was still at Cambridge. Ladies only *need* accomplishments when they are not secure in their prospects. Anne has her inheritance, and she has a husband waiting, just as soon as they are both grown up."

She sat back in her chair, surveying Miss Hall, her lips puckered, as if she had taken too much vinegar. "Securing a governess was entirely Sir Lewis's idea," she said. "I am not at all convinced it is wise, given Anne's indisposition. But I can at least ensure that she is not overburdened by the experience." A pause, and a narrowing of her eyes. "I hope you are not prone to having opinions, Miss Hall."

Miss Hall looked down once more. "No indeed, Lady Catherine."

"YOU ARE HOW OLD?" Miss Hall said on her third day at Rosings.

I was sitting across from her in the nursery-turned-school-room, bent over a square of fabric. I was meant to be making an even hem along one edge, but my stitches stood out like bad teeth, some big, some small, none of them straight. I thought of Nurse's easy indulgent smile with its missing eyetooth, now banished to the kitchen except when I needed my medicine, and refused to raise my head to meet my governess's eyes; my cheeks were tight and hot, my eyes prickling.

"Twelve," I said to the work in my hands.

"Speak up." Miss Hall's voice was sharp. "Ladies do not mumble."

I ground my back teeth together.

"Ladies," Miss Hall said, leaning forward and tapping me on the side of my jaw, "do not do *that*, either."

I looked up at her, and Miss Hall sighed. "Stop scowling and tell me again—without mumbling—how old you are, Miss de Bourgh."

"I am twelve years old, Miss Hall," I said after a moment, and my governess nodded.

"Twelve years old, and yet you cannot sew."

"I can sew!"

Miss Hall raised one eyebrow, looking pointedly down at the disaster in my hands. "Miss de Bourgh, I do not know what to call this, but it is *not* sewing." She leaned forward. "By the age of twelve, I would have expected you to be, at the least, well on your way toward accomplishment at embroidery. But it seems you have never so much as held a needle."

Mutinous, I said nothing.

"Ladies," Miss Hall said after a pause, "are sometimes seen as idle creatures, are we not? But women *do* work, and our work is important—vital, even. It just happens to be quieter than the work done by men. A woman who can sew a straight hem will never be without something to do, for every household, however big or small, needs shirts and petticoats made and mended. Fancywork, for a young woman of your station, will serve to beautify your home and your garments, and those of your family. Not to mention all the good work you can do for the poor in the parish, all those women with more children than they know what to do with and no time to keep them properly clothed."

"Mamma never sews," I said.

Miss Hall sucked in a little breath, then let it out slowly. When she spoke, it seemed she was choosing her words with great care. "Lady Catherine," she said, "is not my pupil. And I am certain she occupies her time in other ways."

MY MOTHER HAD NO patience for poetry, and made it clear that no daughter of hers was to waste time on history; so Miss Hall made me read aloud for an hour every morning from the Book of Common Prayer. I at first protested that I knew how to read, at least—my mother had taught me from this very same book from a very young age!—but after my first stumbling attempt, Miss Hall shook her head in something like despair and said I must practice if I were ever to be proficient.

"You might have been taught," she said, "but no one expected you to keep up with it. The mind is like . . . like an arm, or a leg; it must be subjected to vigorous exercise, or risk going soft."

"I'm not supposed to do anything vigorous," I said. "And reading hurts my eyes."

"Even so," Miss Hall said, and opened the book, pointing to a particular passage. "Begin here."

"This is—oh, this is too stupid. I am too *stupid*—"

Miss Hall let out a breath; released the clenching of her fist so that her long fingers lay flat against the tabletop.

"You are not stupid," she said. "Though you do *sound* stupid when you speak so. Apply yourself, Miss de Bourgh—any young lady who will someday be mistress of an estate must have at least this most rudimentary education."

But I turned my face away.

"I am tired," I said, though the morning was only half gone and I was not due to take my medicine for some time yet.

There was a long pause, and then Miss Hall began clearing away our books and papers. "I will leave you to your rest, then," she said, her voice quite expressionless.

But I glanced up when the door to the school room opened, and caught my governess's quick, contemptuous look before Miss Hall stepped into the corridor and closed the door behind her.

IT WAS ONLY WHEN Miss Hall put columns of numbers in front of me to decipher that, at last, something came easily.

The numbers, in fact—a list of accounts, like those, Miss Hall said, that our steward, Mr. Colt, must keep for Papa, of debts owed and tradesmen paid; money in and money out in surprising and unsettling plentitude in both directions—came together quite naturally. Even as Miss Hall explained what she wanted, my eyes were moving down the column, my head making sense of what I saw there. It was rather, I thought, like slotting the pieces of my geography puzzle together; only far easier.

When I turned the long column into a tidy sum, Miss Hall stepped forward to examine my work. I watched my governess's eyebrows climb, then drop together in a V over her nose. And then climb again.

At last she turned to me and said, "Has Sir Lewis been working with you, Miss de Bourgh? I was under the impression that you had not had much instruction in mathematics."

"No," I said. "Papa has never—no." What an idea. My eyes dropped to the page, to my careful addition and subtraction. "Did I work it wrong?"

Miss Hall shook her head slowly. "No, indeed," she said. "You did it exactly right. And far more quickly than I expected." A small smile. "You did very well, Miss de Bourgh."

CHAPTER SEVEN

My father strode into the entrance hall one morning, greatcoat flapping and mud on his boots, to find me studying the painting of the old manor house that hung at the foot of the staircase. He halted his own forward momentum, head turning so suddenly that I thought he must have spotted something unexpected or startling—I looked around, half-thinking I would find that a horse or a fox wandered into the house and was standing somewhere behind me. But there was nothing there; I was the unexpected thing.

Papa hesitated a moment, and then came forward, nodding at the painting. "It was a poky old place," he said. "Drafty. Your grandmother had a sentimental attachment to it, but I could not wait to pull it down and start fresh."

We stood side by side, looking up at the old house, rendered immortal in oil paints. Its stone walls were weathered, its windows very narrow. Large trees grew up all around it, trees that, now, no longer existed.

"The roof leaked here; my father was forever having it patched," Papa said, pointing. "And there was so little light that we used candles even on the brightest days." His hand hovered above my shoulder but did not touch down. "I wanted a more comfortable home for myself and my family, but I also wanted to create something befitting the de Bourgh name. When Rosings Park is yours, I am sure you will make your own improvements."

He let his hand drop then, resting it heavily on my narrow shoulder for a moment. Beside my father, I felt even smaller than usual; at twelve years old, the top of my head reached just past his shoulder. He could have fit more than two of me inside himself.

When Rosings Park is yours. Contradictions clicked against my teeth. Rosings Park *was* mine; it was the only place, save our brief journey to the seaside, that I had ever known. But the thought that it would be *mine*— my responsibility—caused a quiver of anxiety inside my chest. And, too, was Mamma's constant refrain, that my cousin Fitzwilliam and I would marry—in which case, as the law dictated, our two estates would belong to him.

Do you think I can? I wanted to say—meaning, could I do all the things my father did to keep Rosings Park whirring like a child's top, profitable for us and for the people who worked its land? My cheeks pinked.

But before I could begin to figure out how to voice these thoughts, Papa released me and looked around the hall, as if searching for something. "Why are you on your own?" he said, as if only just noticing. "Where is that pretty little governess of yours?"

"She went to her chamber to fetch a warmer wrap," I said. "We are going to take a turn in the garden." I frowned. "Miss Hall is not pretty. Mamma said so."

My father looked amused. "Did she, now?"

"Yes. She said . . . it is the first duty of any governess, to not be too handsome."

Papa shook his head, smiling a little; and then his face grew serious. "And how do *you* like your not-too-pretty governess?"

He never asked my opinion of anything; I felt certain that I must give the correct answer now. "Very much," I said, but the words were muttered, and my eyes dropped so Papa would not see the lie in them.

But he put his fingers under my chin, tapping there so my head came up. My nostrils filled with the smell of his glove—leather and oil and horse—before he took his hand away. It was the second time he had touched me in only a few minutes; I could not remember when last he had touched me, could only remember brief dry buffs of lips to brow, the occasional, merry tugging of me onto his lap. But that was when I was small; I was becoming a young lady now, or would soon, at least. And Papa was so rarely home now. I thought of his large form galloping away across the fields; even when he was at Rosings, he was never within my reach.

Papa looked at me for a moment. Then he sighed in a way that told me he was ready to move on with his day. His gaze drifted down the hall toward his book room, and I took an instinctive step closer to him, trying to draw his eye back to me. The book room was where Papa and Mr. Colt conducted business; it was not a place for ladies or children.

"Whether you like your governess is immaterial," he said, looking back at me with clear reluctance. "You have the privilege of a good education. And you will need it. Your husband will have the running of a grand estate, and you will have the running of the household. These stones"—with a motion that took in the house that he had built—"those fields out there, that rich timber— all of it will be yours. You need a sharp mind if you are to help your husband secure the future of this estate for your children, and their children. And on and on."

Ah, I thought. *My husband*. My jaw tightened.

And then my father stepped back, closing off from me as surely as if he had already withdrawn to his book room and shut the door behind him.

"WE MUST IMPROVE YOUR penmanship," Miss Hall said.

It was an overcast day and I had been squinting at my embroidery, trying to understand at what point my thread became so dreadfully tangled. I looked up to find Miss Hall grimacing at some lines of scripture that I had copied out for her the day before; she held the paper between her thumb and forefinger as if it were a soiled petticoat.

My body pulsed with indignation—could I do *nothing* right? Other than mathematics—Miss Hall had taken to giving me increasingly complicated problems to solve, involving bushels of this or that, and all manner of questions about crop yields and the cost of lengths of fabric—our lessons were still mostly exercises in frustration, for both teacher and pupil. Nothing came as easily to me as figuring, and while Miss Hall praised my quickness with numbers—"You've a mathematical mind!" she exclaimed just yesterday, making me blush and shake my head, wondering what on earth Mamma would say to hear such a pronouncement—she was quick to remind me that hard work could, if only I let it, make up for a deficiency in natural ability in my other subjects.

"Put aside your"—Miss Hall looked down at my work, lifting one eloquent eyebrow—"embroidery for now. We are going to write letters."

"Why?" I said, not troubling to moderate my tone.

Miss Hall gave me the same look she gave the embroidery. "Because you need to practice if you are to improve. Lady Catherine"—and here she rose from her chair, moving about the room with confusing swiftness, gathering pens, ink, and paper, setting them out on the table so that she and I would be squared off, facing each other like street fighters—"may have decided that you are above learning to draw or play, but even she must agree that a lady who cannot pen a legible line is a useless creature."

She pulled out a chair for me, hard enough that the front legs thumped against the floor. I lowered myself into it warily, watching as Miss Hall sat across from me, dipped her pen, and began writing the date at the top of her page in a slow and elegant hand. After a minute she looked up, sighing when she saw that I had yet to write a word.

"What is the problem, Miss de Bourgh?"

My jaw hurt where my back teeth pressed too hard

together; I unclenched them with an effort. "I . . . I have no one to whom I can write."

Something—something—flickered in Miss Hall's eyes, there and gone too quickly for me to read it. But when she spoke, her voice was gentler than usual.

"Surely you must. You have cousins, do you not? Aunts?"

"One aunt living," I said. "And . . ." I paused, counting in my head. "Four cousins. But we do not correspond." Though it was amusing to wonder, if only for a moment, what my family would think if they received a letter from me. I could see the puzzlement on Aunt Fitzwilliam's handsome face; the baffled panic in my cousins'.

Another sigh, louder than the first. "Very well. You may write to *me*, if you must—but your hand must be steady, and you must think of something to say. No recitations; your own words, Miss de Bourgh."

For some reason, the suggestion was startling. My shoulders hunched; Miss Hall must be mocking me.

"Will you write back?" I said. My voice was strange; I had never heard myself sound so hard, or so daring.

Miss Hall considered me for a moment. "Yes," she said. "I will write back."

I nodded slowly. Miss Hall nodded in return, then bent her head over the letter she had already begun. Watching her, I wondered to whom she was writing; and then I glanced down at my own blank page. I could, I supposed, *ask*.

I smiled a little, and dipped my pen.

CHAPTER EIGHT

I slipped my latest letter into the school room letter box before hurrying out to meet Miss Hall in the rose garden for the morning's lesson. On fine days, Miss Hall thought fresh air could only do me good, and so we spent as much time in the garden as possible, always with hats and shawls at the ready. There had been many such little changes in the years since Miss Hall arrived; small enough that Mamma either did not notice them, or did not think them important enough to rail against, but large enough that my world felt wider, just a bit. I even had ponies and a phaeton of my own, which I was allowed to drive into Hunsford village in the mornings before my first dose of medicine. They were a gift from Papa on my seventeenth birthday, even-tempered beasts, which would—he said with a pointed look at Mamma, who raised immediate objections to the scheme—be easy even for a delicate young lady to handle. I thought, rather hopefully, that Papa would teach me to drive the ponies himself, but one of the grooms was given the honor instead.

Today I left the letter box—a fanciful thing we created from an old hatbox when our correspondence first started—and hurried out into the garden where

Miss Hall waited, as promised. She was bent over a book; I sat on the bench beside her, but Miss Hall did not look up until she reached the end of the page, and though I leaned over a little, Miss Hall's sleeve and fingers hid most of the page from my view. So instead of reading, I found myself studying those fingers—long, much longer than my own, tipped by round nails, neatly trimmed, and affixed at the roots to hands that were soft and dimpled at the knuckles. The sleeve was muslin, ending at an elbow as dimpled as the hand, leaving Miss Hall's forearm bare to the wrist, pinkish skin above and blue veins below. Her hair was smoothed back into a modest arrangement, and from this angle I could see the curve of her cheek and the tip of her long, straight nose. I exhaled, fidgeting, and finally, finally Miss Hall turned to look at me with an exasperated expression.

"You," she said, closing the book with a thump, "are late."

I smiled. "Not very." Feeling rather daring, I reached across and turned the book over so I could see its title. "*The Seasons*," I murmured, and glanced up at my governess. "What is it about?"

"It's poetry." Miss Hall set the book aside, signaling quite clearly that the discussion, such as it was, was over; and though this in no way answered my question, I subsided, only frowning a little.

"Are you ready to begin your French lesson?" Miss Hall said.

I sighed, suddenly weary, leaning my head back so that I could see the whispering movement of the leaves and petals above her head. The gardens in general my father allowed to be Mamma's domain, and under her direction they were very beautiful in a precise sort of way. But occasionally, Papa got notions into his head; over the years, he had instructed our head gardener to add bits of whimsy to the otherwise straight and geometric lines of the beds. A hermitage, round-walled and half-overtaken by quick-growing vines, stood in a little hollow near the woods. The rose garden where we currently sat was adorned by classical sculptures Papa ordered, sculptures with long, curving lines, round-limbed women whose state of general undress displeased my mother. The one nearest us now had one shoulder hitched invitingly; I liked to imagine she looked back at me with a fascination equal to my own as I studied her.

I disliked French; was embarrassed by the clunky way my English-rooted voice spat out syllables that, from Miss Hall, fell quite naturally—like jewels and flowers from the mouth of the girl in one of Nurse's old stories. I was more like the sister cursed to gag up vipers and toads with every word she spoke; my French landed with moist splats. But:

"*Oui*," I said.

WHEN NURSE APPEARED WITH my medicine, Miss Hall, who had been laughing in exaggerated exasperation at my pronunciation only moments before, went suddenly quite still, her mouth tightening at the corners. I kept one eye on my governess and one on my nurse, who was making her way along the garden path very slowly, grumbling to herself, the ruffles on her cap and apron bobbing as she moved. Her gouty leg must be paining her.

"Here you are, Miss," Nurse said, and handed over the glass of laudanum. She fanned her face with one hand and fixed Miss Hall with a sharp look. "What a long walk that was! Too far for this old body. Does her ladyship know you are out here? It isn't good for the young mistress to be outside during the heat of the day."

Miss Hall had picked up her book again and was leafing through its pages with every appearance of indifference. "We are in the shade," she said. "Miss de Bourgh is quite safe from overheating, I think." She looked up at Nurse with a mild expression. "And you needn't have made the walk yourself; surely a maid could have been sent?"

A scandalized intake of breath. "Trust a maid with Miss Anne's medicine? Absolutely not." Nurse nodded to me. "Drink up, Miss."

I leaned my head back, swallowed the liquid, and put the empty glass back into Nurse's waiting hands. Nurse nodded once and set off, grumbling again, all affronted dignity and tipping a little from one side to the other as she favored one leg above the other. Whether it was my mother or my father who had made the decision to let Nurse stay on beyond the point that I actually needed her, I had no idea, but Nurse still clung fiercely to her duty as the only person who knew exactly how to dispense my doses.

Miss Hall was frowning at her book. This part of the garden was shaded by climbing roses, leaves and blossoms forming a dense thicket overhead, and I reclined back against the bench, looking up at them. But my governess's silence felt close and heavy, and I could not enjoy the sight and scent as I usually did.

The first time Nurse arrived in the school room with a little glass of medicine, Miss Hall had stared openly; now, after five years together, she only shut up our books as soon as we heard the older woman's heavy tread outside the school room door, looking away, as if from something obscene, when I cupped my hands around the glass and drank down the red-brown liquid inside. I had ignored my governess's responses for years now; but sitting here, as Miss Hall pretended to read her book while simmering with *something*—something I could not place, but that still pricked me with a shame I did not entirely understand—I felt reckless enough to speak.

"What bothers you so?" I said, staring up at the roses.

Beside me, Miss Hall went still as a hare feeling itself caught in a hunting bird's sight. "Bothers me?"

I shifted so that I was facing Miss Hall. "You always look so—disapproving. Whenever Nurse brings my medicine."

Miss Hall ran her fingers along the spine of her book as if she were stroking a cat. "I have never asked this before," she said, "because I did not feel it was my place. But . . . why do you take it?"

"Why do I—" I blinked. "Because I need it. I am too ill to do without it."

"But you seem perfectly well in the mornings, before you take your first dose. I have . . . long wondered why Lady Catherine and Sir Lewis do not use these hours when you are fully awake and aware to allow me to teach you some of the—" But here she stopped, fingertips pressing her lips closed.

Yet I could guess what she might have said, for Miss Hall had hinted at it before, if never quite coming to the point of speaking out of turn. In the afternoons, while I rested, Miss Hall practiced the pianoforte— Mamma allowed that an older instrument, long out of use, should be brought to the school room for my governess's use. More than once, Miss Hall tried, despite my mother's injunctions against anything too vigorous, to encourage me to learn to play as well; but I found my stumbling fingers too stupid, the notes twisted and jarring and not coming easily enough to satisfy.

"That is why you must *practice*," Miss Hall said, irritation tucked just behind her teeth. But my mother had spent years mourning the fact that Aunt Darcy's vaunted musical ability could never be given full expression in her niece, for I was too unwell to withstand the many hours required to master an instrument. When presented with the confusion of notes Miss Hall copied so carefully, it was far easier to let Mamma's voice, always so assured of the rightness of its own words, drown out Miss Hall's.

But Miss Hall surprised me now. "You are to inherit—all of this," she said, sweeping one arm out in a gesture that encompassed the house and extensive

grounds, and the acres and acres of woods and farmland beyond. "You should be—learning about your inheritance, learning how to manage a great estate. If you
were not *stupefied* . . ."

I shook my head. "I am to marry Fitzwilliam," I said.
"He shall have the management of Rosings."

"Ah, yes. Young Mr. Darcy."

There was a snideness to Miss Hall's tone that I did
not like. She had, of course, met my cousin on each of
his five yearly visits to Rosings Park since her arrival; he
had done nothing to merit such derision. "We have been
betrothed since I was an infant—"

But Miss Hall waved my words away like pipe smoke.
"I apologize. It is only . . ." She clutched her book in both
hands so that the binding must press painfully into her
palms. I had the sudden, disconcerting urge to loosen my
governess's fingers and smooth away the red marks left
by the book's edges. To lean against Miss Hall's shoulder as my drops began to work, to enjoy the warmth of
her, the soft give of flesh. Miss Hall looked at me, and I
flushed.

"It is only—I truly wonder, sometimes, what you
might be without your medicine, Miss de Bourgh." If
anything, Miss Hall held her book more tightly, leaning
forward a little, her words quick and quiet and unfa-
miliarly urgent. "I have some . . . experience with such
things. I have not wanted to say anything—again, it is
not my place, I know this—but you are given too little
credit, I think, and it is hard to see, to sit daily beside you
and see you and your family squandering all that you

have." She shook her head. "I think—Miss de Bourgh, forgive me this impertinence, but I truly think that it is your medicine, and not your constitution, that sickens you. My brother—he was badly injured many years ago in an accident with a cart. He was given laudanum for the pain, and he became . . . quite a slave to it."

I shifted away from her. *You have no idea what I endure,* I thought, but forced myself to say instead, "I feel most . . . clearheaded when I have not yet taken my first dose. But I become very ill if I go too long without it." Proof, I was certain, that my drops were vital to my wellbeing.

"Pain?" Miss Hall said in a conversational tone, and despite myself, I warily nodded. "Violent chills? Sweats?"

I blushed fiercely, but nodded again.

"My brother was the same," Miss Hall said, voice gentle.

"But surely," I said, and then stopped. Surely, if Miss Hall was right, Mamma—or Dr. Grant or my father, or any of the many relatives who showed their concern in hushed voices—should have known, should have realized—

Miss Hall—who never fidgeted—shifted a little on her seat. "I am not a doctor," she said at last. "I do not know . . . That is, if you have some illness that is truly something only laudanum can control, then of course you must take it. I only know that *those* sensations are exactly what Richard experienced as the medicine left his body."

My exhalation was a long and wavering thing. "How long . . . how long did they last?"

Miss Hall squinted. "I . . . am not precisely certain. Several days? Perhaps more? He was terribly miserable. But after, he was clearheaded as ever. And free from pain, except for the ache of his wounds."

"He is better now," I said. I sounded very stupid, and felt even more stupid than I sounded. Panic fluttered—I had been told I was ill all my life. I *was* ill. The wooden busk at the front of my stays was the only thing holding me upright on the bench.

"Yes, for the most part. He's had a hard go of it, though. He stopped taking laudanum. But it was terribly difficult, and he has . . . returned to it more than once."

"Please stop," I said. The world had begun to feel hazy, which was just as well, for I did not like what Miss Hall was saying. There was no logic to it at all. Miss Hall subsided into unhappy silence, opening her book once more, though she glanced at me from time to time as I slipped sideways against the bench until I was curled with my head on its back.

The wind was a warm breath on my cheek, and I could hear the swish of tree branches from the woods down the hill. I had been frightened of those woods all my life; they seemed a fearsome place, shadowed and gloomy. I could never understand the impulse that drew people to seek out such untamed places, my mind skipping back to those old stories from my nurse, to wolves and bears and unnamed beasts with teeth and claws that pierced maidens' delicate flesh. It was always the maidens being pierced, in the stories.

If I tilted my head just so, I could see the trees above the border of rosebushes, sturdy trunks and snarled branches, and how did they know which way to go, to *grow*, sending up bits of themselves in all directions, reaching over and around each other toward the sky? I held my breath, straining to hear the secrets whispered between the leaves.

Some of the trees' branches were bare and brittle as bones, and I felt suddenly, unaccountably, like weeping, because *oh*, they were dying; slowly, perhaps, by human standards, but they were at the beginning of their end, little desperate shoots growing up from the bases of their trunks as if to make up for the skeletons at their crowns.

"Do you think they understand?" I said.

Miss Hall paused in her reading. "Do I think who understands what?"

"The trees." I reached out a languid hand. "Do they know they're dying?"

Miss Hall followed the trajectory of my pointing finger, and I watched her gaze flutter mothlike over the waving branches. "I think," Miss Hall said in a careful voice, "that trees are not people."

"Oh, but they are so *beautiful*," I said.

"God created many things of beauty," Miss Hall said. "That does not mean they think or feel as we do."

I knew Miss Hall was wrong—could she not hear the sadness in the trees' rustling talk?—but I also knew the uselessness of arguing, particularly when *God* had been invoked. I pushed my hat—its brim generous enough to cover my face and shoulders—back a little to let the breeze stir the hair at my temples, and closed my eyes, just for a minute.

"I HAVE BEEN THINKING about what you said the other day." Miss Hall turned her teacup in her hands; though it was empty, she made no move to fill it.

"What did I say?" I watched the cup go slowly 'round and 'round, watching the shifting tendons at the backs of my governess's hands, watching the cup's shadow shifting, too, against Miss Hall's pale muslin lap.

"About the trees. About their—feelings."

I did remember what I had said, but I could hear the trees now, their branches moving subtly, their distress quiet but clear. "Oh?"

"Yes. And I think—I think you ought to read this." Miss Hall set her cup down and picked up a book, holding it out. I reached for it, my arm dropping a little under its weight. I recognized it at once as the book of poetry Miss Hall had been reading some days before, and looked at my governess inquiringly.

"Mr. Thomson writes of nature in a way I think you might appreciate. But his is a godly appreciation that you would do well to emulate. It is nature as religion; it is nature as God's great work and glory."

I grimaced reflexively, and then tried to smooth out my expression. I had read books of sermons, and the Book of Common Prayer itself, so often that I must have seemed a pious girl to anyone who cared to look. But church services were something I endured; religion was just another part of life, its rituals as necessary and inescapable as washing one's neck or combing one's hair. The Book of Common Prayer made me itch.

Miss Hall, though, was pious in truth and not merely by rote. I had spent half a decade, after all, sitting beside her in church, watching her when I ought to have been listening to the sermon. But she listened hard enough for both of us, listened with her whole body leaning a little forward, as if to ensure the cups of her ears caught every trickling.

"Mamma does not approve of poetry," I said, and tried to hand the book back.

"These poems are well known, and all written in praise of God's work. I am"—here Miss Hall stopped for a moment, considering—"willing to risk Lady Catherine's displeasure in this. There is no frivolity to be found here, no silliness."

I looked at her, and at the book in my hands; I suspected Miss Hall was wrong about what Mamma would say, if she knew. But I ran my fingers over the book's spine, remembering how Miss Hall's own fingers stroked it, and said, "Yes, Miss Hall."

THAT NIGHT, AFTER I took my medicine and Nurse left me to my rest, I took the book of poetry from its hiding place in my dressing table and opened it to "Spring." I leaned close to the light of my bedside candle, pushing my plaited hair impatiently out of the way of the flame, tracing the short lines of text with my fingertip. I had never read poetry before—had only the faintest idea of how a poem ought to sound, of poetry's purpose—and my lips moved silently, mouthing the words, chewing them like unfamiliar fruit, letting their meanings burst sweet and surprising against my tongue.

Lend me your Song, ye Nightingales!

Shadows from the flickering candle shivered across the page; I blinked, reading the third stanza, my heartbeat faster than it should be with my drops beginning their work. I read it again, whispered the words aloud to myself, my finger underlining each line, my eyes racing from one to the next—

'Tis Love creates their Melody, and all
This Waste of Music is the Voice of Love;
That even to Birds, and Beasts, the tender Arts
Of pleasing teaches. Hence the glossy kind
Try every winning way inventive Love
Can dictate, and in Courtship to their Mates
Pour forth their little Souls.

I felt the slow beginnings of drowsiness; saw sweet souls, bright-colored as their possessors' feathers, pouring across the page like watercolors. The poem went on for a few lines in a similar vein, making my face heat with some feeling to which I could not quite put words—the only words I had for it were there, on the page—*The cunning, conscious, half-averted Glance . . . Their Colors burnish . . . They brisk advance . . .*

And shiver every Feather with Desire.

I fell asleep before "Spring" was quite finished; when I woke in the morning, I returned to the poem, but its tenor felt different, less fevered than it had the night before, the birds and animals retreating to the—far less interesting—realms of nests and burrows, of feeding young and watching them grow.

CHAPTER NINE

An express came from London at breakfast. I was looking down at my buttered toast, trying to muster some enthusiasm for it when my belly still felt too knotted and heavy from last night's dinner, and Mamma was talking, with the peculiar talent she had for believing every word she had to say must be of interest to her audience, about our relations' upcoming visit to Rosings Park.

"You, of course, must have new gowns. It wouldn't do for Fitzwilliam to see you in the same gowns you wore last year." Mamma took a bite of cake, chewed, then added, "I fear he does not want to formalize the engagement until you have both reached your majority, but it still cannot hurt for him to see you—and Rosings itself—at your very best. To remind him"—with a smile—"of what his future holds."

My cousin was widely considered handsome, I knew, and I supposed he was; but as he reached manhood I could not seem to stop my eyes lingering, with a sort of unwholesome fascination, on his side whiskers and the hair on the backs of his hands. I had petted only a few dogs in my life, but I wondered, still, whether the hair on Fitzwilliam's hands and face, so much thicker and more coarse than the hair on my own body, would feel similar to a dog's, if petted. It was an odd and not altogether pleasant thought.

But I could not say any of this to Mamma.

I was saved the trouble of forming any sort of response by a pounding at the front doors. Mamma stopped talking midsentence, a forkful of cake held aloft, and both she and I listened as Peters spoke to whomever had arrived. Our butler's heavy footsteps came toward us down the corridor.

"Ma'am," Peters said, bowing low before my mother and holding a letter out to her. Mamma set her fork down with a strange deliberateness—as if she, too, felt the same illogical disquiet that I suddenly did—and read the letter quickly. It was, I could see, but a few brief lines. And then Mamma said, "Dear Lord," in an odd voice that was utterly devoid of inflection. "Fetch Mrs. Barrister," she said to Peters. "And have my writing things fetched here. I must write to my brother."

Peters bowed, his eyes moving minutely toward the paper she still held, though he knew his place well enough that he asked nothing. Mamma set the letter down on the edge of the table when he had gone, too far away for me to read it. I took a bite of toast, but it filled my mouth, tasteless and dry, and I had to work hard to swallow it down. Mamma returned her fork to her hand but had yet to take a bite of cake, the fork poised over her plate and her eyes staring, brows gathered together over her nose, at the opposite wall.

"What is it, Mamma?" I said when I could no longer bear the silence.

Mamma gave her head a little shake and put her fork very carefully back down. "Your father has been killed," she said, still in that strange, calm voice.

It was because of this calmness—because I watched my mother lose her composure when Aunt Darcy died, heard the terrible keening sounds she was capable of making—that I did not immediately understand Mamma's words. I whispered them over to myself like lines of poetry, puzzling out their meaning. It took several goings-over before I made sense of them; and then something crashed over me—I was back in Brighton, the waves bursting against my back, Mamma remote and distant on the beach. And it was Papa who put me there among the waves, Papa's choice, Papa's fault. But Papa was gone, gone off to his friends and his pleasure, leaving me with only Mamma, who was safe on the sand, while I sputtered and gasped in the cold, cold water.

DR. GRANT CAME TO SEE me as usual after Papa's death. In mourning black, I was paler even than usual, and my appetite, never strong, was gone entirely. The doctor expressed alarm at the change in me—"Though it is natural, of course," he assured Mamma. "A shock of this sort can fell even the sturdiest of characters. And Miss de Bourgh has never been sturdy." He prescribed a few extra drops of medicine to calm my nerves and help me sleep; I drank them down without complaint, welcoming the added protection against the world.

Mamma read out letters from Aunt Fitzwilliam and

Uncle Darcy, their condolences and promises that they would visit in a few weeks as they had already planned. Miss Hall sometimes read from books of prayers. Occasionally we had callers—Mr. and Mrs. Applewhite, who came from just down the lane at the parsonage; our neighbors, the Cliftons; Mamma's friend Lady Mary, who broke her journey at Rosings on her way to visit her son in London. None of them troubled me; I was sometimes aware of their pitying glances, their murmured questions about the future of the estate, put forth timidly lest their impertinence seem too marked. Mamma always answered in the same way, confident and strong-voiced, assuring our visitors that *she* had taken on the responsibilities of managing Rosings Park until I came of age and married her nephew Mr. Darcy.

My twentieth birthday came and went unremarked.

I HAD VISITORS OF my own, beginning soon after Dr. Grant increased my dose, but Mamma and Miss Hall knew nothing about them. They were a secret I guarded closely. At night, they appeared inside my room—I never saw how they crept in, and though I asked sometimes whether they used the door or climbed the walls like soldiers with grappling hooks to reach my window, they never answered, only smiled at me gently. Their smiles made my skin prickle, and not pleasantly. I held myself tight as a harp string until tension crept up from my shoulder blades, spread across my shoulders, and set my neck to aching. It was a feat to hold myself so, for my drops urged my muscles to slacken, dragged at my eyelids, tried to tip me over to lie upon my pillow. But I forced myself to stay tense and still until my drops' pull became too strong to resist.

But this reaction, this instinctive fear, shamed me, for my visitors clearly wanted to spend time in my company. Sometimes they petted my hair, their long, clawlike nails tangling in the strands and pulling locks free of their plait; other times they crouched like gargoyles on the end of my bed, imitating my stillness, just watching me in a manner that felt at once predatory and protective.

One, in particular, came more often than the others, a very fat woman in a white gown who liked to urge me to rest against her comfortable bosom. I always longed to do so—the woman seemed very kind, and it would be so novel to be cuddled—but then sometimes when she smiled the woman's teeth looked very sharp and pointed, like the tines of a fork; and so I remained wary of her.

My father came once as well, wearing his nightshirt and a lady's elegant turban. His plumpness gone, he looked ill, as delicate as I did, myself, as if some mysterious fever burned away everything but his bones. He did not stay long, and I could only be glad that he did not come to me wearing the true cause of his death, smashed and bloody after falling from his horse onto the unforgiving London cobblestones.

WHEN ROSINGS PARK ITSELF began to communicate with me, I was not sure I could trust the evidence of my own senses. No one else appeared to notice the whispers in the walls or feel the caress in the way the floor rose up, just a little, to press against the soles of the feet treading upon it. The whispers were just low enough that I had to strain to hear them, a constant murmur like that of a brook, from which I could at first only occasionally decipher a distinct word. *Crumble. Fallow. Find.* And, more than once, *Anne.*

At night, the house breathed, and it was this that made me realize I had been hearing and feeling Rosings Park for most of my life. I remembered, when I was a child, imagining that the walls of the house were moving in and out around me, just as my own rib cage expanded and subsided with each of my breaths. It had, I knew now, been breathing the whole time; I simply had not recognized its respiration for what it was.

Night was the only time now that Rosings Park was quiet. During the day, it never stopped talking, never ceased worrying over its every stone, both those that made up the building itself—there was damp running down some of the inner walls, apparently, and slick green things taking advantage, clinging to the stones' rough texture—and those that lay in the fields outside, silent, chuckling to themselves, just waiting to make the plough horses stumble. I wondered sometimes whether it used to nudge Papa as it nudged me, now I had inherited its cares and worries. I thought of it sometimes like a cat that twined about its mistress's legs, butted its small head against its mistress's hand, intent on getting the attention it needed.

At night, though, I could relax back into the mattress, breathing in time with the house. Only sometimes was my rest disturbed, when the house muttered something or cried out weakly, like a kitten. Rosings Park, it seemed, sometimes had bad dreams, too.

THE DAY THE DARCYS and Fitzwilliams were expected to arrive, Mamma ordered the drawing room curtains closed and told Miss Hall to keep me company while I rested. Dr. Grant had warned, on his most recent visit, that too much excitement in the wake of such great tragedy could prove permanently detrimental to my fragile health.

In the dimly lit room, I lay bored upon the settee. Miss Hall dragged her chair near the window and, despite Mamma's injunction, twitched one of the curtains just a little aside, bending over her sewing in the resulting thin light. I watched her, her stitches so quick, so fine, Miss Hall's concentration so complete, brows nearly touching over her nose.

The drawing room doors were firmly shut, muffling the sounds, but I concentrated very hard, as hard as Miss Hall was concentrating on her work, and *there*, there were footsteps, rushing; and there a door banging open. One maid called to another. All of it conducted at a much more frantic pace than usual. I tried to imagine what was going on, but could not; I had watched the servants at their work all my life, had lain quietly as they dusted and polished, arranged furniture and lit fires, working around me as if I were a stick of furniture, my-self. But I had little concept of what they might be doing now to cause this unaccustomed bustle.

"Why are the servants so harried, do you think?" I said.

Miss Hall gave me an odd look. "They have visitors to prepare for."

"Yes, but." I looked up at the ceiling, and lost the rest of my thought to the shadows in the corners.

Miss Hall sighed and made another few stitches. But she said, "Belowstairs, they will have been preparing tonight's dinner for the last several days. *Acres* of food, I believe. They will all want to show off the house to its best advantage, and Lady Catherine, and the future mistress of Rosings."

The future mistress of Rosings. I watched as the words appeared before me in Miss Hall's soft, sloping hand, trailing off in curls.

"Mrs. Barrister has been in a froth over the flow-ers; I think the gardeners are quite frightened of her." Miss Hall smiled a little at her work. She was not wearing black, as I and Mamma were, but a subdued gray, with a black armband. She had taken recently to wearing the ruffled caps of matrons or spinsters, which hid most of her hair and made her look older than her six-and-twenty years. I found, strangely, that I missed the sight of her hair, the wings of it curving over either side of her high brow—like the wings of a ladybird poised to fly. I had the urge to remove her cap, to feel for myself whether those wings were as smooth as they appeared, to follow their trajectory around her skull and upward to the heavy plaited knot of hair just a little back from the crown of her head. And then down again; my finger-tips, with their whorled lines like a tree's secret patterns buried under the bark, tingled as I imagined running them over the round of her cheek, the flexible shell of her ear. I wondered what her earlobe would feel like, that soft curving bit of flesh, if I were to hold it between my thumb and forefinger, and something tightened in the very lowest part of my belly, like a most delicious cramp.

"And of course," Miss Hall continued, "the guest rooms needed airing. And everything needs polishing. There's the china and silver to be cleaned. The candles to be trimmed and lighted." She sewed in silence for a while as my wandering eyes moved across her familiar features, dropping naturally to her throat, her sloping shoulders, the shelf of her bosom within her stays. And farther still, over the spread of her hips and lap, remind-ing me of Papa's garden sculptures, under her skirt. Then she said, "You really ought to know these things. You should have been training with Lady Catherine and Mrs. Barrister already for years."

The criticism might have made me glare and blush, were I not feeling so wonderfully indifferent. "Dr. Grant has said too much responsibility is bad for me. As you know."

"Dr. Grant . . ." But Miss Hall stopped speaking, her lips pressed together like a sealed letter, and I without the strength of will to break the wax. We had not spoken of my drops since that one time in the rose garden. I watched the flash of my governess's needle in the dimness.

"What are you making?"

A little of the ill humor left Miss Hall's face. "A baby's gown. My sister is expecting her first child very soon."

More quiet. My thoughts drifted from Miss Hall's clever hands to her unflattering cap; distantly, I wondered whether my governess had entirely given up on the idea of marriage and children of her own. Even after so many years, I still knew only scraps of information about her life, much of it gleaned by peppering my letters to her with questions—some of which she answered, some of which, particularly the more bold and deep-delving, she pointedly ignored.

From Mamma, I knew that Miss Hall's father had, like so many other gentlemen, lost his money at the gaming tables; but Miss Hall herself never spoke of this, and even I knew better than to probe that particular wound. She had one sister, two years her junior, who also went to work as a governess right out of school, but who wed a London merchant with a thriving business a year or so ago. Miss Hall, however, was always with me here in Kent where the pool of eligible men could more honestly be called a puddle; at our annual harvest ball, while I, forbidden by Dr. Grant's injunction to dance, sat with my parents watching our neighbors and tenants form set after set, Miss Hall was asked to dance often—twice, one year, by the draper's son. She looked happy then, *merry*, smiling widely, a gleam of perspiration on her collarbones. But none of the men who asked her to dance had, as far as I knew, asked for her hand in any more serious way.

I said, "I will marry you."

It was a stray remark, as idle as "I wish the rain would stop," or "I might go into the village this morning"; it felt as natural as either of those remarks would, too. But all at once, the silence in the room was so complete that I realized I had been hearing the soft drawing of thread through fabric; the subtle whisper of cotton as Miss Hall turned it as she worked.

Even my own and Miss Hall's breaths had now ceased, as completely as if we both died quite abruptly, and for a moment I felt panic rush up past the dampening blanket of my drops; I drew in a gulp of air with theatrical loudness, felt my ribs expand as far as they could within the cage of my stays to accommodate my breath, and expelled it again on a sigh.

Miss Hall stared down at the needle in her one hand, at the white of the fabric in the other. I could not understand her expression; I saw no arrow, was certain I heard no gunfire. So why did Miss Hall look so exactly as I always imagined someone might look after being shot: perfectly still, stunned by the improbability of the blooming bloodstain?

"That was a wicked thing to say," Miss Hall said, very quietly. "Even in jest, as I assume you meant it." She gathered up her work with exceptional haste and said, "I shall leave you to rest." She was gone from the room between one eye-blink and the next, and I was left with a sensation of endless falling.

THE VISIT WAS ALL hushed whispers and gently pressed palms. Uncles Fitzwilliam and Darcy insisted on closeting themselves with Rosings's steward, Mr. Colt, to satisfy themselves that Mamma and the estate were in capable hands. My mother sniffed when they admitted that it seemed she knew what she was about, and said to Uncle Fitzwilliam, "And who was it, Robert, who kept Father's estate running after his death? *I* was not away at Cambridge; nor was I yet married, as Anne was. It all fell to me, as it has fallen to me now. But I have risen to the challenge; I always do."

Every evening, when we went in to dinner, Mr. Darcy led Mamma through, and though the honor of taking me in ought really to have gone to Edward, somehow it was always Fitzwilliam on whose arm I found myself; Fitzwilliam who was seated beside me at the table. Mamma smiled out over us all, the jet bugles on her gown glinting in the light from the silver candlesticks, and led the conversation—*was* the conversation, rarely needing the participation of anyone else. But her expression changed, little by little, over the course of each evening; even as she spoke without ceasing, her eyes lingered on me and Fitzwilliam, and I could feel her waiting, *waiting* for some sign of true attachment between her daughter and her beloved sister's son. And, too, I felt her disappointment—a puckered, peevish thing—and, increasingly, her worry, which was pale and papery as a pressed flower, as delicate as I was, myself.

ONE AFTERNOON, MAMMA TURNED to poor Georgiana, at nine years old my youngest cousin by far, whose birth caused Aunt Darcy's death. Georgiana was a tall, silent wisp of a girl, who positively wilted when my mother turned the full force of her attention upon her.

"Play for us, Niece," Mamma said. "Your father has nothing but good to report of your talents, but I should like to hear for myself what your music master has accomplished."

I thought Georgiana might cry, but she whispered, "Yes, Aunt de Bourgh," and sat at the pianoforte.

Miss Hall, who had been spending most of her time embroidering the baby's gown, stood immediately and offered to turn the pages of the music, smiling with more warmth than she had shown me in days. I watched, something terrible swelling in my belly like bread dough.

I did not notice at first when my cousin John took the seat beside me. But he smiled at me, and asked after my health, and his manner was so easy, so amiable, that I found myself thinking wistfully that if I must marry any man, I would rather it be John than Fitzwilliam, for all that John was by far the plainer of the two and had no fortune of his own. He sat beside me as Georgiana played, and I did my best to answer him when he spoke, trying not to feel, as I always used to with

Papa, that I had nothing to say that could possibly interest him. I pressed my slippered toes against the carpet, hard enough to hurt, a strangling frustration creeping over me like the vines of ivy whose progress over the churchyard poplar I still marked each Sunday. John and Edward and Fitzwilliam moved in the world with an easiness I would never be allowed, even if I were not ill—Edward and Fitzwilliam busy with their estates and education, John with his recent promotion in the army. They lived lives I could not entirely imagine. And because I *was* ill, nothing ever changed in my life from year to year, and so I had nothing to talk about.

None of this should matter at all, really, or so I told myself; my dullness was not my fault, and it was silly to become overwrought about it. It would be nice, though, to have something worth talking about.

Yet despite my dullness, John stayed with me for an hour or so, even when Edward and Fitzwilliam, using the excuse of looking out over the estate, escaped the dreariness of the drawing room for the outdoors.

"ANNE IS YOUR COUSIN. *Talk* to her. She deserves civility from you, at least."

My eyes opened. I must have dozed off at some point, for long enough that my cousins returned from their excursion; Edward stood across the room with his father, both nursing glasses of port that glowed like twin sunsets, and beside the fireplace, a few feet from the settee upon which I lay, were John and Fitzwilliam.

Both glanced at me, and I let my lids drop a little. When he spoke, Fitzwilliam's voice was quieter even than John's, but still I understood him clearly.

"I do not mean to be rude," he said. "But how exactly does one converse with a doll?"

CHAPTER TEN

"You never read to Anne anymore, Miss Hall; this must be remedied," Mamma said one afternoon, a day or two after our relatives departed. She had been querulous from the moment the Darcy carriage disappeared down the drive. "Anne is too weak to read much, herself, but Dr. Grant says *listening* cannot be too taxing for her, provided the material is not something that will overexcite her."

Miss Hall looked at me and I stared back, unblinking. I was drifting, too limp to become even moderately excited, let alone overly so. It was a delicious feeling. I was breathing, but so languorously that I fancied, if I closed my eyes, I could pass for dead. It had happened before—I was awoken by my maid's screams, and the entire household's rushing feet in the corridor outside my chamber. There was nothing humorous about it at the time—through my mind flitted the memory of Nurse wailing, of Mamma with her hand pressed to my breast—but for some reason, the recollection made me smile now.

Miss Hall selected a book from the small pile on the table beside her chair and removed the bit of ribbon with which, months ago it must have been, she last marked her place.

"Let me see," she said, then trailed a finger down the page, slowly, so slowly. I looked away. "Ah . . . Yes. 'Suppose a young lady educated by a mother, who to the best sense and truest breeding joined the utmost reverence for religion, and the tenderest concern for the soul of her child . . .'"

I wanted to yawn—my jaw ached with the tension of trying not to do so.

"'Let this accomplished parent bestow upon her daughter a culture worthy of herself; instructing her in every thing that can become the female and the Christian character; among the rest, recommending a lovely modesty, and graceful simplicity of apparel . . .'"

"Quite right," Mamma said, and nodded her approval of Miss Hall's restrained gown of printed cotton. By contrast, Mamma's striped silk gown, though dyed black for mourning, was rich with lace, her fingers heavy with jewels and her earlobes with large gray pearls.

Miss Hall coughed lightly into her hand, tucking her lips together, just briefly, as if to contain a smile. "'To what has been said in favor of modest apparel under this head, I must not forget to add, that it is a powerful attractive to honorable love. The male heart is a study—'" Here Miss Hall looked up at me, an odd, prodding glance; I pushed my knuckles against my mouth.

"'To gain men's affection, women in general are naturally desirous. They need not deny, they cannot conceal it. The sexes were made for each other. We wish for a place in your hearts: why should you not wish for one in ours?'"

A sound tumbled from my lips—I could see it as

much as hear it; it had the frothy quality of the water in the garden fountain. It was an inappropriate sound, not quite the laugh that I was trying to contain but somehow darker, rising from the inky spaces inside myself where I rarely ventured. I watched it leave my mouth and tried to snatch it back, but it was too late. My sound was out in the world, and so I let my hand drop back down. "'They need not deny, they cannot conceal it,'" I said, and then I let the sound out again.

"Anne!"

I looked up to find that Miss Hall had stopped reading and was staring at me, wide-eyed, over the top of the book. Mamma's mouth was pursed like a flower bud.

My nurse only used a switch on me once, for some infraction I could not even remember; Papa was furious when he discovered the marks on my palm, shouting that I was ill, and what was Nurse thinking? Miss Hall's mouth, just now, looked to me like the sting from that switch: a worried red weal.

"She's overwrought," Mamma said.

Miss Hall closed the book. "I apologize, Your Ladyship, I thought Fordyce's *Sermons* would be soothing."

"As they should be," Mamma said, and now her voice sounded like the switch, that sharp smack as it landed its blows. "Anne, stop it. You are hysterical."

My face twitched as I strove to control its expression. "I am well," I said, and patted my chest. "There was something caught, but it has come loose now." And my smile did feel loose, my lower jaw like a door half off its hinges.

Mamma eyed me. "That is quite enough excitement for one afternoon. Miss Hall, help Anne to her room to recover. And fetch Nurse—perhaps another draught is in order?"

I SAT WITH MISS HALL in the garden temple. When my maid opened the curtains that morning, the bright view through the windowpanes filled me with a sudden desire for *release*, and I all but begged Miss Hall to come outside with me after breakfast. Nurse came to us there, gouty and grumbling, as we sat sewing together and not speaking; and so when Miss Hall finally *did* speak, my usual lassitude had returned, and I had slipped down a little on the bench.

One of my arms was flung across the bench's back, my head resting upon my sleeve. A fly lit upon the back of my hand, and from this angle I had a good view of it; the shifting of its transparent wings drew my eye, and now were caught fast, fascinated. The fly was so small that it should be nearly impossible to see in any detail, but I could make out the legs, like the finest of silken threads, and the veins in the leaflike wings. I pursed my lips, blew softly—or so I thought—but the gust to the fly was like a gale, sending it tumbling over, and a little clutch of fear and sorriness for killing it breached the gentle fog of my mind. But no—the fly righted itself—flexed its wings— continued its careful exploration of my hand, creeping over the long bones that extended from fingers to wrist, climbing the hillocks of my knuckles. I didn't dare move, lest I disturb its progress again. But of course, I was accustomed to stillness.

If I were to raise my eyes just a little, I would see the house looming over us. At this time of day, the sun sat at such an angle that the house's pinnacles cast shadows across the lawn. I could not help fancying that they reached for me, long narrow fingers that would grasp me if they could, pulling me back inside the house's open, whispering mouth. It was a strange truth that it was only since Rosings began to speak to me that I felt I truly loved it, loved it the way it ought to be loved by the person in whose care it rested. Except, of course, that it did not rest with me, not truly. I was guardian of its secret cares, but I did none of the hard labor of fixing its problems, myself.

I thought, sometimes, about Miss Hall's brother; but then I felt the trembling overwhelm me at the thought of actually having to take charge of Rosings Park. A healthy woman, I was sure, would not feel faint at the mere thought of controlling her own inheritance. I often wanted to clap my hands over my ears to block out the sound of all those *things* in the drawing room, and all that vast land outside the window. All of it wanting something from me. And then I was sorry for trying to block them out, for I was the only one who listened to them; they needed me.

Out here, at least, though the roses murmured and the woods wept, their voices were easier to ignore than the voice of the house itself, dispersed as they were throughout the broad sweeping sky; and so I kept my eyes cast down, away from the house's reaching fingers.

"Miss de Bourgh."

Miss Hall had to repeat herself, twice, before I was able to pull my eyes away from my hand. I turned my head carefully, determined not to accidentally dislodge my small companion. Miss Hall's work was crumpled in her hands, and I stared; the fabric would be terribly creased when she released it.

"Miss de Bourgh," Miss Hall said again, and I raised my eyes from those hands, that fabric, to Miss Hall's face, which was also crumpling, folding in upon itself beneath the weight of whatever it was she was about to say.

My entire body hardened to stone.

"I . . . need to tell you something." And now Miss Hall's voice wrinkled, too, little shudders of sound that made no sense at all. "I am leaving. I will give my notice to Lady Catherine today, but I—I wanted to tell you first."

Miss Hall paused, watched me, waiting, apparently, for some reaction, but I said nothing—*could* say nothing. Stone cannot speak.

Another moment, and then Miss Hall said, "I'm going to my sister in London. She is overwhelmed with the new baby; I hope to help her. I will—I *will* miss you, Miss de Bourgh."

Still, I stared, stared until my eyes watered. Miss Hall had been with me for eight years; what she was saying now was impossible. But even as I thought this, Miss Hall's fingers tightened impossibly further around her work, an unlikely, *angry* noise coming from her chest. I blinked, and a little of the wetness rolled down the slope of my cheek.

Miss Hall stood so quickly that I could not possibly track the movement, gathering the rest of her things in bursts of action like the explosion of grouse taking flight. She made as if to leave but stopped, just briefly, turning to look at me over her shoulder.

"You could be—you are *more* than this," she said. She still sounded angry. "I have *seen* it. But no one else will tell you so; no one is going to help you become the woman you might be, if you did not stun yourself so thoroughly with your medicine." She paused, then said in a rush, "Rosings Park is *yours*, Miss de Bourgh. You are an heiress no longer; you are now the owner of a grand estate. Have you no understanding of what that *means?*" Miss Hall covered her eyes with one hand, just briefly, then looked at me through her fingers. "You have so much," she whispered. "And you are letting it go."

"My—"

"Do *not* speak to me of Mr. Darcy." Miss Hall shook her head. "Do not. Even if you marry him, you should still feel some responsibility to Rosings. And to *yourself.*"

"I was going to say," I said, slowly and carefully, "that *my mother* has the estate well in hand."

"Even Lady Catherine," Miss Hall said after a moment, "cannot live forever. Please—think on it." She looked down at me for a long, hard moment. "Goodbye, Miss de Bourgh."

I had to speak—had to say something to hold Miss Hall there a little longer. I opened my mouth, imagined my jaw creaking like a door in need of grease, and said the first words to present themselves.

"Fitzwilliam thinks me a doll."

I had not been able to get his words out of my head ever since I heard them; I felt the hot-cold horror of them engulf me during quiet moments. John's protestations, at the time, of our cousin's unfairness, did little to dampen my humiliation; nor did John's coming to me later, while I was still reclined beside the fire. *Anne,* I heard him say; and in his voice was a pity so cloying I might have vomited. *Anne, you know that you have many people who would be happy to have you visit, do you not? We all of us care about you—*

I could not answer him—his words were too pretty to be real.

Useless, I whispered inside my head, little mortified arrows that pierced my softest inner places. *Useless, stupid, useless.*

But in the days since, when Fitzwilliam's words came back to me, a little anger slunk into my mind along with them. Was I a doll to him, I thought, only because of my illness? Or did he suspect the amount of time and attention that was given to my gowns and hair when he came to visit? In which case, I thought—and here, the slinking anger rose like a cornered beast onto its hind legs—how was I different from any other young woman adorned for gentlemen's pleasure? True, I did not play or sing; but what were accomplishments except another form of ornamentation to attract men? If I was a doll then Georgiana, with her carefully curled hair and beautiful gowns, was a doll in miniature; the only real difference between us was our state of health.

Now, though, Miss Hall was the one staring. "Fitz . . . you mean young Mr. Darcy?"

I blinked, and hoped my governess could recognize the nod in it.

"You are no doll," Miss Hall said after a moment. She smiled just a little, without showing her teeth; but she was not one to speak or smile falsely, and pleasure rushed through me, from the top of my head to my aching core, so swift and strange and unexpected in the wake of so much lethargy that for a moment I could only stare at her, my mouth a little open.

"That is why I wanted to marry you instead," I said at last, though that was not the whole truth of it. But it hardly mattered that I could not seem to articulate my thoughts, for Miss Hall stood looking at me for a long moment, her smile falling away, leaving intolerable sadness in its place; and then she walked away.

My head dropped back upon my arm. I looked at my hand, where the fly still stood, twitching its wings as if in preparation for flight. I could not feel its weight at all, or the tickle of those wee legs against my skin.

My eyes closed.

When I opened them again, the light had changed. Rosings Park looked innocuous—not a fearful, clutching thing, but a house, just a house. I raised my head, and my arm was assaulted by dozens of pinpricks.

Miss Hall was still gone, and I was not certain whether she had ever been there at all, sitting silent on the bench beside me. Perhaps, I thought, I dreamed the entire encounter. There was a hissing sound of negation from the garden beds; the shadows slunk toward me, suffocation in their eyeless faces. I stood, throwing them off; but the feeling of breathlessness remained.

Very suddenly I recalled my little fly friend and raised my hand, searching. But though I flexed my fingers as if the fly might be hiding somewhere between them, it had disappeared entirely.

CHAPTER ELEVEN

The next few years blur messily together in my mind. They are The Years After Papa and Miss Hall Left. It is a shameful truth that the latter leaving hurt most; but not, I suppose, a surprising one.

Uncle Darcy died quite suddenly only a few months after he and his children returned to Derbyshire from Kent, and Mamma, who always had to be useful, left me in the care of a new companion while she rushed to her nephew and niece's aid. She wrote me from Pemberley estate—*Georgiana and Fitzwilliam are too stricken by grief to properly express their gratitude for my attentions, but I know they feel it just the same. They set their table far too richly; it is no wonder my niece is so retiring. I have already informed their cook that there are to be good English dinners from now on rather than the French fare to which they have become accustomed.*

I would have felt quite sorry for my cousins, had I room, just then, in my own head for others' suffering.

Mrs. Jenkinson, my new companion, was plain as unadorned cotton and a consummate nodder-and-smiler—the very opposite of Miss Hall, which pleased Mamma tremendously, for Miss Hall's defection was, to Mamma's mind, a sign of the grossest ingratitude. Mrs. Jenkinson seemed entirely composed of gratitude and awe, and within ten minutes of her arrival, she had agreed with Mamma twice as many times without ever having uttered an opinion of her own.

A childless widow whose husband's estate had passed to his brother after his death, Mrs. Jenkinson had been recommended to Mamma by Aunt Fitzwilliam, who knew her before her prospects took their sudden downward turn. She seemed to me the sort of person who had been five-and-forty forever—despite being, in reality, nearly a decade younger—and who would be five-and-forty until the day she died. There was nothing else worth knowing about her; she was boring as the toast she liked to urge me to eat in greater quantities every morning at breakfast time. When she wrote her weekly letters to her one living sister and four nieces, I wondered what she could possibly have to tell them, for she spoke little of her life before coming to Rosings Park—had lived so little, it seemed, that she had nothing interesting to say. I felt cross just looking at her.

In addition to keeping me constant company, Mrs. Jenkinson took over from Nurse, whose weak chest and bad leg afforded her a necessary rest from toil, in the dispensation of my drops. When Mrs. Jenkinson remarked on Mamma's generosity on letting Nurse stay on past her usefulness, Mamma smiled and said, "She has the strongest affection for Anne—and for myself, of course. Rosings Park has been her home for twenty years; after such long, devoted service, I see no reason not to give her a little corner of the attic to live out her last days. She knows better than to be a bother."

WHEN THE HUNSFORD RECTOR died, Mamma found a replacement in the form of a young man named Mr. Collins, whose awkwardness rivaled my own. He was lavish in his compliments to the point of absurdity, once going so far as to commend my mother on her robust health in nearly the same breath that he praised my delicacy as being a clear indication of my noble birth. Mamma, being Mamma, was perfectly capable of holding two such incompatible truths in her mind at once, and merely smiled.

IT WAS RAINING, MANY months later, when the letter arrived, a raging storm with thunder that I noticed only dimly, though water poured down the great windows as if men were standing on the roof tipping buckets over the side of the house.

I was preoccupied by my left hand, by the way the long bones that ran down to my wrist shifted under my skin as I moved each finger. *Miraculous*.

Then Mamma came into the drawing room, bringing another storm with her.

"Mrs. Marchbank," she said, rattling a paper, "has written with the most outrageous story."

I moved another finger. I could not remember who Mrs. Marchbank was; nor did I particularly care to.

Mrs. Jenkinson, though, seated across from me, turned in her chair to give Mamma her full attention. "What is it, Your Ladyship?"

"Only this—that my nephew—*my nephew Mr. Darcy!*—is engaged to be married to none other than Miss Elizabeth Bennet!"

My companion gasped, and my hand dropped to my side. I looked down at it, uncertain how it got there. Inside my body, something else dropped as well, some organ swooping down, down, but, sickeningly, never landing.

"Mrs. Marchbank had it from her sister, who heard the news from someone intimate with the Bennets. There can be no truth to it, but . . ." Mamma stopped, the letter crumpled in her fist.

"Surely Mr. Darcy would refute the claim if you wrote him?" Mrs. Jenkinson said.

That my mother did not immediately take up a pen told me everything I needed to know: however strongly Mamma might rail against the story as a falsehood, the larger part of her must believe it true. I remembered Miss Bennet well; she visited Mr. Collins's new wife when John and Fitzwilliam made their yearly trip to Kent, and she called with Mr. and Mrs. Collins at Rosings Park several times, and instantly distinguished herself by not only having opinions of her own when Mamma spoke to her but actually voicing them, though they ran contrary to Mamma's own. Rarely did anyone contradict my mother—even Papa, when he was alive, avoided confrontation with her unless it was truly necessary. In that moment, I thought Miss Bennet the most marvelous person I had ever met.

She did not seem to find me so marvelous, however. Civil enough when we were introduced, her notice of me devolved, over the course of her visits to Rosings, into arched eyebrows and a vaguely turned-up set to her mouth. It was obvious that something about me amused her greatly, and between her clear scorn of my frailty and Fitzwilliam's utter disregard for my existence over the course of his visit, I felt as though I were sinking into a swamp of mortification, sludgy waters closing over my head and cutting off all air.

But still—one morning, when I and Mrs. Jenkinson were driving out to the village, we came upon Miss Bennet on one of her frequent walks through Rosings's woods. Her hem was a little dirty, her curls a little windblown. The wind had whipped pink into her cheeks; I could not seem to look away from her.

Later that day, I studied myself in the glass—something I rarely did, for my features were familiar enough, my clothing and hair the purview of my mother and my maid. I ran my hands over my body above the white fabric of my shift, fingers bump-bump-bumping down my rib cage, over the dip of my waist, the knobs of my hip bones. My shift fell to just below my knees; my calves, beneath it, were narrow and very pale. My maid, Spinner, would be in soon to dress me for the day, swathing my form in a morning gown, disguising the horizontal ridges on my chest, just above the slight swell of my bosom, with a pretty fichu.

How would it be, I wondered, *to move through the world like Miss Bennet, with such energy and sureness?* There was strength in Miss Bennet's form, and health in the brightness of her cheeks. Her muslin gown showed the full outline of her legs as she moved, and they looked so very sturdy. I imagined running my palms down their length, feeling the soft brush of fine hair and the solidity of muscle. Cupping the backs of her calves. They would feel, I thought, very different to my own.

Now Mamma's anger hummed like the air just before a lightning strike. She called for her maid. The bit of me that had been falling settled then, with gentle care, into the cradle of my pelvis, and as Mamma made furious plans to set out for Hertfordshire, I observed my altered prospects with detached curiosity.

OVER THE COURSE OF the following week, Mamma returned from an unsatisfactory meeting with Miss Bennet, and Darcy wrote to formally announce his engagement. My mother was like a cornered beast in her fury, and I found myself teetering between a blank sort of fear, the unfilled years stretching like great sheets of empty paper before me, on which I had no idea what to write; and a curious giddiness for which nothing logical could account. Everything changed with my cousin's letter; all certainty was gone from my life, save the one that surrounded and contained me at all times. Rosings Park, I had always known, would someday be mine; but always, there was the understanding that Fitzwilliam would be the one to ensure the smooth running of both our estates. No one—no one except Miss Hall—ever expected that the burden of Rosings Park might fall to me, or that I would be able to shoulder it, if it did. The house's walls seemed to press in on me from all sides, moving themselves, their stones grinding against one another, inch by inch. I lay, terrified and perfectly still, waiting to be crushed between them.

And yet, even as I felt the house closing around me, I had the strangest sensation of freedom, of having escaped from something, so narrowly that the something nearly rent the skirt of my gown with its claws as I raced away from it.

My drops were such solace then, letting me float until at last the passage of time dampened my mother's disappointment. I awakened to find everything exactly as it had been before, except for the tattered and singed remains of my own future.

IT WAS A TIME of change for everyone else, it seemed, though our life at Rosings Park continued quite the same as ever.

When Mrs. Darcy produced a son, Mamma released the very last of her anger. I could *see* it when the announcement of little Thomas's birth came; her fingers unclenched, and scraps like ashes fluttered out of her open palms, disappearing at last, ghostlike, into the air. A few months later, my cousin and his wife were ensconced unhappily in our drawing room, the baby, drooling in his cap and gown, on Mrs. Darcy's lap, and Mamma's eyes bright and curious as a robin's when she held out a papery hand to greet her sister's first grandchild.

Darcy cast me one or two glances, but for the most part ignored me, though there was a slanted set to his mouth. Mrs. Darcy, for once, did not laugh at me, as if conscious that I might have feelings.

But my feelings were not what they assumed. I sat in my chair, looking at the infant that might have been mine, if only my body and spirit bloomed riotously. Like Mrs. Darcy's. Envy spread along my limbs, black as mold; but I could not be sure *what* exactly I envied. Not the child; not marriage to my cousin. Something else, something less solid than either of those things. There was a hint of it in the way I felt, watching the easy line of Mrs. Darcy's shoulders and hearing the quick way she answered questions, as if she had never had reason to doubt her own opinions. Mrs. Jenkinson fussed, as usual, telling the footmen to reposition the fire screen and urging me to try a slice of seedcake. A slow bloom of irritation started at the back of my skull, and I knew that, if I hadn't laudanum to temper my reactions, all the dark inky things that huddled in the hollow of my chest would come screaming from the hole of my mouth.

CLOUDS SCUDDED ACROSS THE sky like dust chased by a broom. I watched them through the drawing room window as my cousin John introduced his intended bride to my mother.

"Her manners are pretty enough," Mamma said to John, as if Miss Watters were not sitting beside him, hands folded and a smile, taut as fabric inside an embroidery hoop, on her small pink mouth. I turned my head from the window to look at her. She wore a fortune on her body, everything, from the slim feathered bandeau on her head to the slippers, stiff with embroidery, on her feet, chosen to display her wealth to the world. That her wealth came from manufacturing mattered less than it would have if it were Edward, heir to the earldom, who courted her, and not John, a mere second son.

I could not like her, for all that their marriage would enable my favorite cousin to live a more comfortable life than that of an army colonel; Miss Watters, when she acknowledged me at all, made me feel intolerably stupid, speaking to me as one might speak to a child, if one were not accustomed to being in the presence of children, or to a dog, if one did not particularly like dogs.

Miss Watters's brother traveled with her and John; he leaned now against the mantel, reminding me of a cat in the long, affectedly unconcerned line of his body. His feet were crossed at the ankle, his chin lifted above his cravat's intricate knots. He bowed to me when we were introduced; and then he dismissed me. Between one blink of his pale eyes and the next, I knew he had quite forgotten my existence.

John, however, did not. He glanced at me a few times as my mother interrogated him and Miss Watters; once, when Mamma's head was turned away, he gave me a comical, exaggerated grimace. I smiled a little, though there was something vaguely sad, like the last dull days of winter, in the careful way he and Miss Watters spoke to one another, a lack of intimacy that I might not have noticed had I not recently seen Fitzwilliam and his wife together.

He came over to me when Mamma ordered Mrs. Jenkinson to the pianoforte to entertain us all. A complicated melody drifted over the room, and John bent his head to me.

"How are you, Anne?" he said.

"Oh, she's very well," said Mamma before I could respond. She nodded at Mrs. Jenkinson, whose back was a little humped as she leaned over the keys. "She is always at her best when there is music to be heard; it is one of the reasons I allowed Mrs. Jenkinson an older instrument in her room, that she could practice daily for Anne's enjoyment. Music is truly Anne's greatest joy."

John glanced at me, as if to assess my joyfulness, and my lips turned up passively.

"How fortunate that she gets to hear it regularly, then," he said. "But if she truly loves music, she really must come to London sometime and experience a true concert with a full orchestra."

"And die from the poor air? Certainly not," Mamma said, less reprimanding than dismissive. "And those concert halls are always so hot. And the noise!" She gave John a narrow-eyed look. "If you and your wife intend to take a house in Town, I hope you will avoid crowds."

John inhaled a little, just sharply enough that I heard

it over Mrs. Jenkinson's playing, then said, "Too right, Aunt."

A moment later, after Mamma turned to say something to Miss Watters, John leaned close to me.

"We do intend to take a London house, in addition to a country estate," he said. "You are welcome at either, Cousin, whenever you like."

CHAPTER TWELVE

I t was the letter that truly changed everything.
   I woke early one morning, for no reason I could discern, early enough that the sky was only turning dusky at the horizon and the birds were just testing their morning calls. I lay for a time looking up at the canopy, which seemed heavy and precarious, something that might sink down upon me at any moment.

When I got out of bed, it was with the succulent feeling of doing something illicit. The carpet rasped against my stockinged feet, and my fingers reached for the doorknob as if they were detached from the rest of my body. But then that body went on through the doorway, glancing in either direction for early-waking servants.

I passed the door to Mrs. Jenkinson's chamber—which would always, in my mind, be Miss Hall's—then on, down the long, darkened corridor and up another set of stairs until at last I reached the school room. Which was, of course, of *course*, my destination all along.

There was a sense of waiting inside the room, of breath held and held until the very walls were blue and desperate for release. Unlike the rest of the house, this room was entirely awake; I felt it rouse further upon my entrance, like a servant whose mistress has entered the room unexpectedly, spine lengthening, chest thrust out.

I stood in the middle of the room, taking in its familiar contents—the chairs and table, the shelves for books. The bench below the big window, where I had spent so many afternoons of my life. The writing desk.

Miss Hall had been gone longer, now, than she had been with me. Nine years passed almost without my noticing; and I had not entered this room once since she left.

My eyes caught now on the hatbox perched atop the desk, incongruous as a plume-topped turban on the head of a washerwoman. I stilled entirely.

And then, without warning, my body moving without my brain's conscious direction, I rushed at the desk—my hands grasped the hatbox, fingertips pinching around the lid—and with a great heave, the hatbox went flying, landing halfway across the room with a dull thump.

And something else: the faint, barely-there rustle of falling paper.

I KEPT ALL OF Miss Hall's letters in a little wooden box, inlaid with silver, that my father brought back once from Town. "A happy place for girlish treasures," he said, and at first I could not think what I might have to put inside. But then I thought of the letters my governess and I had, at that time, just begun to exchange, all of which I had been keeping in an increasingly untidy drawer in my dressing table.

The letters were such innocuous things; certainly, to

objective eyes, not worth treasuring. I asked increasingly impertinent questions, which my governess rarely answered. Most often, Miss Hall used her responses to criticize my handwriting or the flow of my words. Only occasionally would she drop tantalizing bread crumbs about herself; I felt like a sparrow, hopping along behind, eager for whatever she cared to toss my way.

This letter was different.

It had been waiting quietly in the letter box for my notice of it for nine years. I held it for long moments before I unfolded it, my breaths coming fast and quivering. Almost, I did not want to read it; it felt a hot, augural thing in my hand, and the thought that it might be just another note criticizing my penmanship was horrible. But at last I opened it, though my stomach churned and my head fogged.

Dear Miss de Bourgh, Miss Hall began, and I could not help imagining her as she penned the words: the curve of her neck, the slant of her wrist. The serious, studious expression she would have worn as she wavered over her next words. The words she finally chose had clearly been written in haste, her impatience getting the better of her penmanship so that, briefly, it sprawled inelegantly across the page in a way she would never have countenanced in her pupil.

I wish you nothing but good in your life, Miss Hall wrote. *Your life should be nothing* but *good—for you are the most fortunate and unlikely of creatures, Miss de Bourgh: a woman with land and wealth enough to live exactly as she pleases. You may marry your cousin, as your mother has decreed; if this is your wish, too, if he will make a good husband and a good master to Rosings Park. Or you may marry elsewhere—or not at all, and retain complete control over your life and your estate.*

I regret many things from my time as your governess, but chief among them is this: that I did not push harder for you to learn; that I allowed my own need for security in my position to keep me from doing my best by your education, and your health. But I risk little in forcing this conversation— one-sided though it is—upon you now, and I hope you will forgive me for it.

I tried to tell you once before, about my brother. He wrote to me only last week; he is well and whole and still quite free of laudanum's curse. I—

But here there was a trail of ink, as if Miss Hall thought the better of whatever she might have said. Instead she wrote: *In so many ways, I failed you.*

But you needn't fail yourself. You have the advantage of having the most secure position possible for a woman in this life. Use it. Learn from Mr. Colt, and Mrs. Barrister, and your mother; and when you are of age, take up your responsibilities as mistress of Rosings. Seek the advice of other doctors about your health. You've a good mind, full of surprising creativity, and if only your senses were not dulled and your impulses not made so strange by laudanum, you could put that mind to useful purpose.

I can see you scowling as you read this. But really, my dear—have you no sense of all that you have?

I am sorrier than I can say that we are parting badly. But please know that I remain your most affectionate friend,

Alice Hall

OUR NEIGHBORS, THE CLIFTONS, came that day for tea. Mamma invited them often, as they were clearly sensible of the honor bestowed upon them by such frequent attentions. She greeted them warmly on this afternoon, asked Mrs. Jenkinson to pour the tea, and proceeded to launch a discussion about the merits of traveling in winter, for she intended to embark on a brief trip the next day to visit her brother, the earl, and was certain the clear weather would hold for the journey.

My mind was filled with Miss Hall's note; it was upstairs, folded in my treasure box, but I had to knot my fingers together in order to keep them from worrying at the shawl spread across my lap, pressing the edges of it like the creases of a letter and drawing Mamma's or Mrs. Jenkinson's attention. It was not until my mother's voice rose with incredulity that I pulled my thoughts back to the assembled company, with a sensation like trying to pull a great stone out of clutching mud; they came forth only with difficulty, and with a terrible sucking noise.

"Dr. Grant knows his business," Mamma said. "I wonder that you would question him on a matter as important as your grandchild's health, Mrs. Clifton! Why, a little laudanum never hurt anyone, and there is nothing better for an infant cutting teeth."

Mrs. Clifton looked into her teacup, and her husband cleared his throat. I rolled my eyes away from them, away from the twin looks of embarrassment they wore, as if my mother had just spoken of something they had been for years leaving tactfully unremarked-upon. But even turned away from them, I could see their faces inside

my head, familiar from a lifetime of calls paid and neigh-
borly dinner parties attended. Mr. Clifton's bald head
always captivated me, his scalp shining like a polished
table from the natural oils on his palms, which he often
rubbed over his pate in a distracted manner. His wife
had hair the color of winter clouds and a cluster of tiny
moles, like pink pebbles, just under her jaw, and was usually everything ladylike; but set a pack of cards before
her, and she suddenly reminded me of Papa's hounds
before a hunt. When she won a trick, I imagined her
tearing out the throat of a fox.

I knew these things about the Cliftons, and many others besides. Their son was at Cambridge; their daughter,
Lucy, a few years my junior, married around the time
Mr. Collins arrived in Kent, then produced two daughters in quick succession. They had all formed a sort of
comfortable, familiar background to my life, people
whose own lives I had been observing in a distant sort
of way for as long as I could remember. But somehow I
had not realized that they had been observing me just as
closely all that time, closely enough that when the word
laudanum was spoken aloud they felt the need to politely
avert their eyes from me.

"Of course, we do trust Dr. Grant, Lady Catherine,
and your own sound advice," Mr. Clifton said at last.
"But I wonder, sometimes, at how freely such cures are
dispensed. Too frequently, the papers have stories about
their abuse. Why, just the other day I was reading a most
tragic tale—a mother who accidentally killed her own
child by giving him too much laudanum for a bellyache."

His words tumbled over and around me like boulders

down a cliff, and I nearly raised my arms to shield my head from the force of them.

"That is why I do not subscribe to a newspaper," Mamma said. "Reading such dour news does no one any good. The mother was poor, I suppose? Did she have the advice of a good doctor?"

"Probably not," Mr. Clifton said. "If I remember rightly, she sent her elder child to an apothecary for a draught."

"There. You see? The poor may be excused for their ignorance in such matters, I suppose, but there is nothing to be done in such cases. And no need to use valuable ink and paper discussing the matter." She gestured toward me and said, "And listen to Dr. Grant. Only see what miracles he has worked with Anne! Though her health will always be delicate, she has overcome such violent afflictions under his care."

All eyes turned to me, considering the miracle. Feeling vaguely that I ought to offer something to support Mamma's faith, very purposefully, I picked up my cup from its place on the table near my elbow, and took a sip of tea.

WHEN SPINNER LEFT THE room and Mrs. Jenkinson brought my nightly dose, I could not keep the dead boy from the newspaper out of my head. I regretted taking my medicine for almost the first time I could remember, and squeezed my eyes so tightly closed that blue pricks of light appeared behind the lids; but still the thought of him remained. In my imagination, he was dark-haired and round-cheeked, his eyes open and staring. One arm hung off the edge of his cot. He was very dead.

All the voices of Rosings Park—the walls and floors, attics and cellars, gardens and streams, ploughed fields and fallow—spoke to me at once as my drops began to work. They rose and fell almost in unison, a cacophony that prevented me from understanding a single word and left me crying with my hands over my ears. On the dressing table, I could *feel* my treasure box with Miss Hall's letter, perched like a crow, and with a crow's eerie watchfulness.

Tell me what to do, I thought, or said, or screamed; but the voices only rose in agitation, until at last my medicine sent me keeling over toward sleep.

I woke sometime in the night, to the fire nearly out and the room shrouded in a blackness so thick I reached out to touch it. My hand found, instead, another hand, grasping at me through the dark, small stiff fingers and a cool, greasy palm. I pulled my hand back, thrashing under the bedclothes to push myself upright.

The dead boy from the newspaper sat by my feet, calm and quiet. His lifeless eyes did not quite meet mine, staring a little off to one side. It was difficult to see without good light, but there was something terrible about the color and texture of his skin. As I watched, my breath trapped behind my breastbone, he turned his head with an impossible motion, and gave me a sorrowful look.

Part Two

London

CHAPTER THIRTEEN

I first saw London through a ferocious rain, the view from the carriage window all but obscured by the water sluicing down the glass.

Everything was gray and brown: the hazy forms of horses and carts, of people walking, of buildings rising steeply on both sides of the street. There were so *many* people, in spite of the rain. Some carried umbrellas but many did not; their clothing must be wet through. The tip of my nose bumped the cold window as I looked out, and my breath made fog upon the glass, blurring the scene still more.

Even through the muffling carriage walls and above the sound of the rain on the roof, I heard the sounds of the city like an assault. I did not know where in London we were, only that this was the most noise I had ever experienced all at once. How was it possible that horses and coaches and calling voices could produce such a din? I could not stop my thoughts from going to Miss Hall and her description of London's sounds and smells from one of the many letters we had exchanged in our make-shift letter box during her years as my governess. *You cannot imagine the noise, a ruckus from dawn until well after dark, people talking, carriages clattering along the streets, merchants calling for custom. And the smells of all that*

humanity in one place—we are odorous creatures, to be sure!
There is nothing to compare to it in the country.

But with so many other things on which to rest my attention, the thought of her was not so poignant as usual; more dull ache than lancing pain.

Across from me my maid, Spinner, sat with wide eyes and pink cheeks as she peered through the window; she was so excited that I could actually hear it, a high, happy, tuneless humming coming from her throat. My own nerves snapped like nervous dogs, but in the forward motion of the carriage, the indistinct picture of the world outside, even the overwhelming tumult of the city, there was also something tentatively glorious.

I leaned my brow against the window, tucking my chin down toward my chest to hide the smile I could feel madly blooming.

IN THE SCRAMBLE TO get out of the rain, I did not take in much of my cousin John's town house until I was ensconced in the drawing room, a cup of steaming tea in my hands and John's wife seated across from me wearing as polite a mask as I had ever seen. She tilted her head, smiling with lips pressed closed, her eyes like shuttered windows for all the feeling they displayed. My eyes flitted birdlike around the room, keeping away from her face of their own accord, taking in lace curtains and framed landscape paintings and the graceful lines of the furnishings. The paper hangings were more pleasing than those at Rosings Park, an entire garden scene along one wall, archways and balustrades printed to look like marble with climbing plants bursting through every crevice available to them.

"If only you had time to write before coming all this way, Miss de Bourgh," Mrs. Fitzwilliam said, and I forced my reluctant eyes back to her masked face. "We expect my brother in but three days, and if he brings a friend, as he so often does without warning, I fear we haven't enough guest rooms for you all."

The implied rebuke made me feel as if I were surrounded by her on all sides. Multiple Mrs. Fitzwilliams, each more civilly disapproving than the last. There was an odd feeling, like insects crawling upon my limbs; I took a sip of tea and tried to ignore it, and nearly scalded my tongue. When I put my cup down again, it rattled against the saucer.

"I should have written," I said. "I am sorry; the decision to come to Town was an . . . impulse. John said once that I was welcome any time I wished."

Though that was years ago, now, before my cousin married. John had probably long since forgotten. Not to mention that the last impulse I obeyed sent the only person who ever truly cared to talk to me careening out of my life, and so logic would suggest that listening to my own impulses was . . . unwise. Yet Mamma left just that morning for a short visit to my uncle Fitzwilliam's estate, and not two hours later I was dressed for travel, urging Spinner to pack more quickly, and crossing frequently to the window, as if my seeking eyes might make the carriage ready sooner.

"*John* said . . . ?" Mrs. Fitzwilliam frowned into her tea. "Well. It would not be the first time he invited guests without informing me." She looked back up at me, false smile back in place. "The Season is just beginning; you've come at exactly the perfect time, if you plan to stay. Perhaps the Darcys have space for you."

A sip of her tea, a tip of her head. I flinched, reminded, with breathtaking sharpness, how much I disliked Mrs. Fitzwilliam when first we met.

"I must confess myself surprised," Mrs. Fitzwilliam said now. "I thought you never came to London, Miss de Bourgh."

"I do not. I mean, that is, I never have. Until today." I swallowed and tried to ignore the strangling way my heart beat in my throat.

"How extraordinary," she said. "I always understood you to be too unwell to travel. Is Lady Catherine not with you?"

"No," I said. "Mamma is visiting Lord Brightmoor."

"John's father? How nice for her to see her brother; and how odd that you are here, and not there with her. And you did not bring your companion, either? Mrs. . . . oh, what was her name? That quiet woman who played the pianoforte so nicely?"

"Mrs. Jenkinson." I shook my head, sniffed a little; my nose was suddenly dripping, as if I had a cold coming on. "No, I—she remained at Rosings Park."

A raised brow and a little silence as Mrs. Fitzwilliam looked at me, clearly waiting for something. But I'd no idea what she was waiting for, and so the silence built around us like walls.

She had not thrown me out. She *could* not throw me out, I realized, with an unexpected thrill. My back straightened, like a plant stretching up to meet the sun. I was the mistress of Rosings Park. *She* had married into consequence; I was born to it. Mrs. Fitzwilliam folded her lips together, and I looked back at her, trying to hold on to my own sense of importance.

"The colonel will be home for dinner," she said at last. "No doubt you will want to refresh yourself before he arrives. Your things will have been put upstairs."

There was a pause, and then I stood, slow and careful as an old woman. "Thank you," I said, and followed the footman to whom she gestured through the drawing room door, down a short hall, and up two long graceful staircases to the guest rooms near the top of the house.

When the door to my chamber closed behind me, I released my breath and slumped against the wall. Spinner was waiting for me, but she stood, quiet and attentive, allowing me time. Away from Mrs. Fitzwilliam's scrutiny, my body began to shake, the enormity—and the boorishness, the *thoughtlessness*—of what I had done cascading through me. I was grateful for the wall's solidity.

At last, I raised my eyes and took in the room. Well proportioned, with elegant furnishings and pale blue walls, it was less ornate than my chamber at Rosings Park, and somehow calming. The floor was dark wood, polished to a high shine, and softened by a carpet woven in a pattern of flowers. At the far end was a window framed by curtains that looked like they were heavy enough to keep out all light when drawn. It was here that

Spinner stood, hands clasped before her waist, looking at me.

"I have unpacked your things, ma'am," she said.

I cleared my throat. "I do not know how long we will be staying. It seems my cousin is expecting other company." I glanced at the bed, which was big and soft. "I think I will lie down for a little while."

"Very well, ma'am." She moved toward the bed, as if intending to help me into it, then stopped, swinging back to the window. "But first—come look." Her smile was a heady thing, her fingers beckoning me closer.

I crossed the room to stand beside her and looked out. We were up high enough that I had to look down, down, down toward the street below. It was much quieter than the areas through which we drove earlier; just one or two people were walking, and only a single carriage was driving past. The street curved out of sight, a long line of handsome brick town houses pressed cheek to cheek, each with an identical black door. The rain had stopped, and water puddled at low points in the road. Then my gaze rose above the roofs of the houses across the street, and oh, *oh*—there it was—London unfurling before me, a jumble of rooflines and chimneys that poured smoke out into the gray-white sky, on and on as far as I could see. My mouth opened; I leaned closer to the window.

Beside me, Spinner let out a soft laugh. She looked very young in the pale light from outside, much younger than her four-and-twenty years. "It's even bigger than I imagined it," she said. "Think of all the people in all

those buildings! You hear such stories of the city, but seeing it—"

"Yes," I said, breathless. "It is as if the whole world
is . . . right there."

"Well, not *quite* the whole world, ma'am," she said
with a sideways smile that made me suddenly very glad
that she was here with me; that I was not entirely alone
on this mad adventure. "This is not even the whole of
London, I'm sure."

"Of course," I said; but I did not entirely believe it.

CHAPTER FOURTEEN

The canopy above me, pale blue and thickly fringed, was deliciously unfamiliar.

So was the coverlet upon which I lay, and the room's furniture, and the walls, and the corridor outside. Beyond the window stretched a city I had longed to see for nearly all of my twenty-nine years. London lay only forty miles or so from Kent, but like so much of the world, it had always seemed like something out of the stories my nurse used to tell me as I fell asleep, a place I knew I would never see.

Yet here I was.

I thought of the doll Papa had brought me from London. I used to try to imagine where that doll had been to have acquired its smoggy perfume, only to be thwarted by my own lack of experience. It was galling, really, to think that my doll had seen more of life than I had, myself.

But today—just today, though it felt as if years had passed since I made my impulsive choice—I had seen more of the world, had *done* more of my own volition, my own choice, than ever before. *I* stood in the garden after Mamma's carriage rolled away. Surrounded by rustling hedgerows and the earliest February buds showing tight and green on the trees, *I* tipped the entire contents of my medicine bottle into one of the flower beds, watched the liquid soak into the soil, and felt myself pulled into two parts, like a paper roughly torn. One part of me blazed with triumph; the other had to resist the urge to kneel on the wet ground and lap like an animal at the dark drops before they disappeared into the earth.

The sickliness that defined my entire life felt entirely removed from me just now, here, on a wide bed in a house in London. I could feel my heart beating, a little too quickly, in my breast and in my fingertips. My body pulsed with life, like the city outside, whose clamor and rush was so distant from the incessant quietude of my life until today. My world had been limited in scope to the pattern in the Turkish carpet in Rosings's drawing room; the ornate plasterwork on the ceiling; the portraits on the walls. My father's portrait, staring sternly down at me, and my own, opposite his, showing a young woman with unfamiliar pink cheeks and an exaggerated fullness to her bosom, a book that I never read dangling from her painted hand. It was painted for my eighteenth birthday, and when it was hung, try as I might, I could not recognize the girl on the canvas.

My joints ached a little. I rubbed at my left wristbone with my right hand, and tried to ignore the foreboding knowledge that I knew what was coming. Instead, I concentrated on the room, which sparkled so with unfamiliarity; I breathed in and out of its foreign air. But insects were, once more, scuttling up and down my arms and legs, and beneath them my bones were beginning to ache in earnest.

When I began to shiver, I knew that I was not going to make it downstairs for dinner.

BY THE TIME SPINNER returned to my chamber some hours later to help me dress, I felt truly ill. Cold crept through my body like frost along the last clinging leaves of autumn. My breath came in shivering puffs; almost, I expected to see it whiten the air it touched. But no, the cold was not in the room, for the fire burned strongly in the grate; it existed deep within me, and I knew, with a despair that stole through me as insidiously as the cold itself, that I would never be able to get warm, no matter how many blankets I lay beneath, no matter how hot the fire.

I clutched one of the cushions as a child would a doll, squeezing it to keep my body from rattling apart. Spinner clutched her own hands. I would feel sorry for the position I put her in, but I was too full of my own misery to allow space for anyone else's.

I RECOGNIZED MY COUSIN'S voice, but it was all too much—too much pain, drawing deep within my joints, too much embarrassment that he was seeing me this way—and I could not look at him, even as he said, "Anne? *Anne?*"

Spinner spoke quickly, so quickly that her voice was

like an assault. I caught snatches of it—"She poured it out, sir, and she made me swear I would not let anyone give her more—"

But it was not until John said, "Hell and damnation— I'm sending for Dr. Carter," that I shook my head against the pillow.

"She doesn't want a doctor, Colonel—"

"She cannot come to my house in this state and *not* be seen by a doctor," John said. I could feel him standing over me. "How much laudanum does she usually take? He will need to know."

"I—do not know, sir—it was Mrs. Jenkinson who administered it."

My cousin swore again, more colorfully this time, and left the room.

MY BODY SEEMED A vengeful thing, trapping me inside of it. I tried to crawl out of my skin, to shed it like a cicada sheds its husk, but it would not let go, and when I crawled across the bed, I merely dragged my skin with me, and my aching bones, and my heavy cotton-stuffed head. My skin wept perspiration, and I wept, too.

Spinner and Dr. Carter spoke above my head, my maid's voice off-key and high as a note poorly played upon a flute, his deep and calm as a church organ.

"But sir—"

"—necessary, Miss Spinner—stay with her; her distress will not last forever—"

I had been here before. But this time was different;

this time I *chose* this. I keened like a babe, and thought I must be as mad as Mrs. Jenkinson claimed when she understood that I meant to leave Rosings Park.

I WAS ALONE WHEN I awakened. All was quiet, and very dark. Though I felt limp as a wrung handkerchief, my body was my own again; the aches were gone, and the chills. My skin was neither pebbled like gooseflesh nor damp with perspiration, though when I raised my arms to stretch, an unpleasant, sickbed smell wafted from my person. But the linens upon which I lay, and the chemise I wore, were both fresh; I had a vague recollection of Spinner helping me to the desk chair to sit while other maids changed the bed. With gentle prodding, she coaxed me to raise my arms above my head, undressing me as she would undress a child, replacing my soiled shift with a clean one. Smoothing my hair back from my brow.

I lay now for some time, waiting for my eyes to adjust to the dark room. Outside, I heard a carriage pass on the road below, but otherwise everything was nearly as quiet as night in Hunsford. I strained, trying to hear something—something—something like the voice of Rosings Park, which always whispered good night, and whose even, sleeping breaths helped lull me to sleep; but John's house was silent.

Slowly—as the hulking dark shapes around me reconciled into identifiable pieces of furniture; as a clock chimed four somewhere in the house below me—the full greatness and horror of what I had done stole over me. I imagined my mother returning from my uncle's house to find me gone; I felt her rage and worry like a gathering rainstorm, and wondered how long I had before she descended upon John's house and drenched me.

But I rocked my head against the pillow; I did not want to think about Mamma.

Nor did I want to think about the truly unthinkable— *I have left Rosings Park.* But the guilt twisted inside my belly and made *not thinking* impossible. Mr. Colt was still there as steward, and it was not as if I had ever had a hand in the actual running of the estate; but Rosings *needed* me. It said so, *Papa* even said so, just the once in the entrance hall standing before the painting of the old manor. And I knew the estate more intimately than my father ever did—my knowledge ran down into the house's very foundations; into the tree roots that ran below the wood.

And I left it.

As we drove away, I thought I could hear the turrets keening above the treetops. If I looked back, I felt sure I would see the trees themselves reaching out, branches extended like snatching hands. This despite not having taken my morning dose, my mind so accustomed to thinking of the estate as sentient that it did so now of its own accord. And so I clutched myself, arms tight across my rib cage, like a mother who does not like to leave her screaming infant, but knows she must.

I left Mrs. Jenkinson as well, left her angry and afraid, fingers flying to her mouth. *Miss de Bourgh, have you gone mad?* bursting from between them.

When I left—the bemused footmen, unused to

taking orders from me, piling my hastily packed trunk and Spinner's small bag on the back of the carriage—Mrs. Jenkinson was near tears. What would I do, she pleaded, without a companion? Would I really travel all the way to London with only my maid? When I told her again that she could not come with me—trying to be as immovable as Rosings's stone walls, or as my mother, while my heart thumped within my breast hard enough to hurt—she cried, *What am I to tell Lady Catherine?* And I could not answer her.

It was an unkindness, I supposed, to leave her so; but it was suddenly so clear, so perfectly clear, that I could never get free of my drops with her always, *always* there, incessantly fussing, drawing up a dose with the punctuality and precision of a clock. That this was not her fault—that Mamma engaged her for precisely this purpose—did not make me like her any better. It was not Rosings's fault, either, that I spent all my years there in a mist; but I knew not how to exist there outside that mist, feeling the full force of sun and wind and rain without my drops' shrouding protection.

I rose now and went to the window, leaning over the little writing desk positioned before it to shift aside the curtains. The darkness was nearly complete outside, too, but for a small pool of illumination cast by a tall lamp on the farthest corner of the street. I could see, dimly, other lights in the distance, little bright dots scattered across the blackness like stars across the sky. Somewhere out there, among those lights, down one of those myriad twisting streets, my father died. But so, too, did he live there; for all the pride he took in Rosings Park, he was in London more often than he was in Kent. This was the place, I could only assume, that he loved best in the world. I stared out at the trembling lights; the sight made something inside my chest unknot, and I sank slowly into the chair before the desk, reaching my arm forward until my fingers knocked gently against the window, as if I could touch the city beyond.

I MUST HAVE FALLEN asleep again, slumped over the desk with my head in my arms, for Spinner's cry of alarm woke me next. There was sunlight showing between the curtains, and my neck was crooked and painful.

"I am well," I said, though in truth I could not decide if this was true. I sat bemused as she ordered John's housemaids about, watching as they lugged a great copper tub into my room. One built up the fire while two others hauled bucket after bucket of scalding water up from the kitchen three floors below. When at last the tub was full, the sides lined with linens, Spinner helped me bathe. I kept mostly silent as she gathered my heavy hair and draped it over my shoulder, the better to wash my back and the nape of my neck. I was weak and wasted, as if I had weathered a grave illness; which, I supposed, was not far from the truth, for Spinner told me how I burned for two days with fever; how I vomited until nothing was left inside but bile.

I watched my hair tips splay as they touched the steaming water, and wondered what I was going to do now.

"Has Mr. Watters arrived?" I said at last, and Spinner paused in her ministrations.

"Yes, last night," she said.

I turned to look at her. "I assume he did not bring another guest, as I was not turned out of the room?"

A little smile. "No, ma'am. He did not bring anyone with him—though I do not think Colonel Fitzwilliam would have stood for your being turned out in your condition. He was that worried for you."

The thought of facing John made me dizzy; or perhaps that was merely the heat of the bathwater, which turned all the skin it touched an unlikely shade of pink. I thought, fleetingly, tantalizingly, of my drops, which provided such lovely padding from anxious thoughts, and then I shook my head, as if in doing so I could shake the memory of them from my skull entirely.

The cloth began moving again, over my right arm from shoulder to wrist, and she added, "There was another visitor. Lady Catherine was here two days ago."

I put my fingers to my lips, then spoke around them. "Dear God. What happened?"

"I was here with you, so I did not witness the . . . altercation . . . myself. But her ladyship was, ah, forceful enough that I could hear her tone through the floor, if not her actual words."

No—*no*—oh, the dizziness was, without a doubt, entirely due to the anxiety that was rising, rising within me like the flames of a well-stoked fire. My breath felt trapped inside my chest, emerging from my mouth only in little frantic puffs. I caught hold of either side of the tub for fear I might slip under the water. *I chose this*, I thought, and then, *I hate this*. The thought did not make me feel any better, and I wanted my drops with such frightening intensity that I bit my tongue until it truly hurt in order to keep myself from sending Spinner to the nearest apothecary to procure some.

"Is there laudanum in the house?" I said, voice tight, fingers flexing against the damp linen lining the tub, toes pressing, hard, against the tub's smooth bottom.

My maid dropped the cloth and took a step back from the tub. "No," she said. "Dr. Carter told Colonel Fitzwilliam there mustn't be." A pause. "Since you said you did not want it any longer."

That is good. I looked at the whiteness of my knuckles, and tried to believe myself. *Very good*. I repeated the words to myself as she helped me from the tub, and felt a deep, blooming gratitude for her gentleness as she dried me, and her steady presence when I was ill.

In the looking glass, I saw her nod, her eyes on my hair, damp and dark and snarled. My own face in the glass was pale and tight, the skin under my eyes smudged with purple. My body was shrouded in linen, my damp skin making translucent patches on the fabric, and above the linen's upper folds my collarbones spread, long and sharp as sticks.

Dr. Grant always said it was an innate frailty that kept my appetite so slender. My insides were knotted with nerves, but there was something else, an uncomfortable stirring in my belly that I could not account for. I sat very still for a moment until I realized, with some surprise, that the feeling was hunger.

CHAPTER FIFTEEN

A maid found me hovering at the bottom of the stairs, and told me when I asked, pointing down a narrow hallway, that Colonel Fitzwilliam was in the breakfast room.

To my relief, I found my cousin alone. But still I hesitated before entering the room, my fingers curling around the doorframe, my feet refusing to cross the threshold. I was as stupefied by nerves as I ever was by my drops, but without the easy detachment my drops also offered. I wanted to turn around and return to my room two floors above; to burrow under the covers like a mouse hides in the underbrush. But I came here—without warning, I came here, and promptly became violently ill, and brought nothing less than my mother's wrath down upon my cousin's household. At the very least, I owed him thanks, and explanation.

John sat with his legs stretched out before him, leaning back in his chair. A newspaper was folded beside his plate, which held the crumbs of his breakfast, and he was scribbling some correspondence, pausing to sip from a cup that steamed by his elbow. As I watched, he pushed the hand not occupied with his quill through his pale hair, and exhaled a breath that sounded of frustration.

But his head came up when I managed to force one foot forward, and then another, his rugged, plain-featured face going quite slack when he saw me so that, all at once, I burned with shame for the trouble I had caused him. He was up from his chair, pen dropped with no concern for the resulting trail of ink, and looking down at me within seconds, worry in his very whiskers.

"Anne!" he said. "Are you feeling better?" And then, with a shake of his head and a laugh, "Well, of course you are; you are out of your room. Carter assured me you would survive well enough, but . . ." He ran a hand over his face. "I shall have him fetched back to look at you—he asked me to keep him apprised of your condition."

"I am much improved," I said, and let him lead me to a chair, which he did as gently as if I were made of china.

"By God, you had me frightened." He sat as well, leaning forward with his forearms on his knees. For all that he was in the army for years, John was decidedly unmilitary in his bearing, and he looked up at me now, his smile sweet and twisted as it was when he was a boy. There was no condemnation there, only a gentle question, and I blinked and looked down at the fine whitework tablecloth, thinking of the boy he was, coming to me where I sat in forced repose on a garden bench at Rosings, his pockets bulging with pretty stones he'd collected to show to me.

Grown-up John now saw the way my mouth twitched into a smile, and offered his own puzzled smile in response. "What are you thinking?"

I shook my head. "Only that you have always been . . . very kind to me." My smile fell away. "I am sorry I did not write before arriving. I did not mean to—inconvenience you."

He was silent for so long that I was sure his next words would be a scolding. But "Nonsense," he said. And then, ducking his head so his eyes were level with my own, "Anne, what happened?"

I thought of the dead boy, his greasy palm against my own, and my fingers twitched. I could not say anything so alarming. So instead I said, "Do you remember my governess? Miss Hall?"

John frowned. "Yes," he said after a moment, drawing the word out slowly. "Young? Quiet?"

I smiled, just a little. "She was . . . only quiet in company. With me she was . . . opinionated." Almost, I thought to recite from her letter—it would be so much simpler than coming up with words of my own.

"She had a brother," I began at last, and then Miss Hall's story—and with it, my own, intertwined like snarled thread—came rushing forth.

"She recognized the same . . . trouble her brother had in me, and tried to . . . but I did not want to hear her."

He watched me with an intensity that was difficult to bear. "But you did anyway."

"Not immediately. Not for years." I swallowed again, but my throat was so dry there was nothing to bring down. "May I—may I have some tea?"

"Of course." John was on his feet, pouring the tea himself, before I could reach for the pot. "I apologize, I should have asked—what about breakfast? There's plenty—" He gestured toward the sideboard, where platters of bread and eggs mingled with glass dishes of colorful preserves and sun-yellow butter.

But my earlier hunger had disappeared. "No—thank you—just tea." I took a sip, then put the cup down again. But now I had nothing to do with my hands. "I would not—I did not want to listen."

If you were not stupefied—

"My mother would have dismissed her, had she heard some of the things Miss Hall said to me."

Of course, it never came to that; I managed to drive my governess away very well on my own.

John was silent for a moment. Then he said, "Do you recall the time Edward and I came to Rosings, and the rain kept us confined all morning to the nursery? To pass the time, you told us stories you'd invented."

I stared at him, seeing in his face suddenly all the enraptured eyes of my cousins fixed upon me. It was the only time I could remember feeling large, swollen with the power of their attention. "I . . . yes. But I did not invent those stories; my nurse used to tell them to me."

"Ah." He nodded. "Well, I remember how well *you* told them, so that even Edward, who thought he was too old and dignified for such things, was quite in your thrall. But I also remember your nurse, and the little glasses of quietness she brought you. Upon drinking them, you were transformed: animated storyteller to only half-conscious in mere minutes." He turned his cup around on its saucer. "I've often thought of that, particularly on more recent visits, when I saw you driving out with your little steeds in the mornings, and then turned so . . . lifeless by the afternoons. I often wondered at the nature of your illness. It was not until you came here, and I saw you in such misery that I realized . . . well. I've seen such things before. Since the wars—too many men have found themselves in a similar predicament. Men under my command, good men—strong—turned into slaves to laudanum after they began taking it." A grimace. "Forgive the impertinence. But—we should have paid more attention to you. The family, I mean. Myself. Edward. Darcy. My parents. We worried and wondered over your health among ourselves, but not one of us intervened, and I am more sorry for it than I can say."

"I do not know what you could have done," I said, weak-voiced, and oh, how I loathed this. My fingers clutched the seat of my chair to prevent me from flying from the room. "Papa tried—he brought me to Brighton, against Mamma's wishes, against our doctor's advice. After that . . . debacle . . . Mamma would not hear of anything else being tried. Not even Bath, though more than one person urged us to try it."

"Yes, she is . . . quite fierce in her protection of you." He pushed his fingers against his eye sockets. "But still, your governess—who has been gone from Rosings Park for years now, has she not?—succeeded where we did not even try. I am . . . deeply ashamed."

It was not Miss Hall, in the end, though without her prodding I do not know whether I would have been so affected by the story in the newspaper. But I hardly wanted to tell my cousin that a dead boy showed me I must leave my home or risk death, myself; and so I closed my eyes and said instead, "I understand that my mother was here?"

John's voice turned wry. "Very much so, I'm afraid. I do not think she could have been so formidable even when Darcy announced his engagement."

I flushed.

"I told her you were ill and could not be disturbed. She was—distraught. Angry. And worried, I'm sure, somewhere under all that noise. She is staying with her friend, a Lady Mary, I believe, near Portman Square."

The address meant nothing to me whatsoever. "And where—where is that in relation to this house?"

He smiled, just slightly. "Only a short drive. I am sure she will return here today to see how you do. That is why I am here—Harriet and her brother have gone out, and I could not leave you to face Lady Catherine alone."

"Thank you," I said in a whisper. "And thank you for—keeping her away from me when I was . . ."

John chuckled. "Anne, I was in a war—even Lady Catherine holds no terrors for me, fierce though she is."

My own laugh came cracking from my mouth, loud and startling as gunfire, and I pressed the back of my hand to my lips.

"May I assume," he said, grinning, "that your stay with us will be a lengthy one? What do you say, Cousin—assuming Dr. Carter gives his blessing, would you like to experience a London Season?"

I would—oh, how I would. And yet, too, I would not; not in the least. I'd only a faint idea what a Season in

London entailed, but I knew there were balls and parties. I was far too old to think of anything like a proper debut, even if the idea did not terrify me. People—so many people. And everything else the Season implied for an unmarried woman of fortune, even one who was nearly thirty. Men's eyes, weighing my purse as they slid over my form like water over rocks. I looked at my cousin without speaking until at last he chuckled.

"All right. What about a single evening out, to start? When you are fully recovered, Harriet and I can introduce you to some of our set."

"I . . ."

"They are none of them fearsome, I promise you, Anne. Indeed, some of Harriet's friends will no doubt be in awe of you; their connections are . . . not so elevated."

I nodded, slowly and without conviction, but it was enough; John grinned.

"My father will give me hell," he said, almost as if he looked forward to it. "And I doubt my aunt will let you go quietly. But once they see how well you are, they cannot help but be—overjoyed, I think, that you are able to take in the Season's delights."

IT WAS INEVITABLE, I suppose, that Mamma arrived at dinnertime. She always had an unerring sense of how to best inconvenience those with whom she was out of humor.

Mrs. Fitzwilliam took the news that I was to remain in London with a smile that more closely resembled a grimace, but said that of course it would be an honor to host the heiress to Rosings Park.

"She is not the heiress," John said. "Rosings Park belongs to Anne."

And his wife grimaced again, said, "Of course—how foolish of me," then swept away to dress for dinner.

We were all seated, the first course half-eaten, when there was a knock at the door, and then raised voices in the entryway. Everyone stopped eating, spoons forgotten midair, soup dripping back into bowls. I let my own spoon drop back down entirely, my eyes closing as Mamma's voice and footsteps grew, inescapably, louder and nearer.

I opened my eyes again when the footsteps stopped and I heard two chairs pushing back from the table as John and Mrs. Fitzwilliam's brother stood to greet my mother. My cousin wore an expression of resignation, Mr. Watters one of civil curiosity.

Mamma stood in the doorway, looking at our assembled company with lips pressed together and a tightness to her jaw that made me think, with faint, frightened amusement, of Miss Hall's fingers tapping my own jaw to stop me grinding my teeth during one of our first lessons. *Ladies,* I thought a little wildly, looking at my mother—her face framed by silver hair, carefully curled, and the wide brim of her bonnet; her pearl cross at her throat and the brooch with Aunt Darcy's hair on her bosom; her expression one of such profound displeasure that there was nothing of ladylike reserve there at all—*Ladies do not do that.*

"Aunt," John said. "You received my note?" And then, before Mamma could say anything else, "Please, do join us. Have you eaten yet?" He gestured to a servant for another place setting, and came himself to lead my mother to the chair beside his own, opposite mine.

But then—oh, dear God—behind her, my companion followed like a shadow, stealing in without looking at me. John paused, then said, "And you, too, of course, Mrs. Jenkinson," as servants hastened to fetch two bowls and fill them with soup, and the butler, who had been hovering ineffectively, stepped forward to take bonnets and wraps.

When Mamma was seated, I hardly knew where to rest my eyes, her fury so strong that I imagined, were I under my medicine's fantastical influence, I might actually see it emit from her skin in sparks. John and Mr. Watters resumed their seats, and we all sat in uneasy silence. No one ate, no one spoke; I glanced from face to face, stopping at last on Mamma's, full of hauteur and something else I could not define, but which made me shrink like a forest plant under the full strength of the sun.

"I do not think I need to explain the extent of my shock when I returned to Rosings Park and found you gone," she said at last. "And to learn from Peters that you decamped to *London*, of all unhealthful places—! I never in all my life imagined you could be so reckless, so insensible of what you owe to your estate and your family."

John licked his lips. "Aunt—" he said, but Mamma rounded on him.

"And *you*. Keeping me from my daughter—*my daughter*! I know it was you, Nephew, who encouraged this madness. Do not think I have forgotten how you whispered in Anne's ear when you came to us at Easter! Talking of concerts and amusements—you have upset us all and endangered your cousin's health. You ought to be ashamed." She looked down the table at John's wife, who sat watching us all with perfect expressionlessness. "I do not know how much *you* had to do with this, Mrs. Fitzwilliam; but if I find so much as a *hint* of your influence here, be assured you will feel my displeasure."

Mrs. Fitzwilliam inclined her head. "I promise you, Your Ladyship, I neither invited Miss de Bourgh to London nor condoned your being kept in ignorance of her whereabouts."

Mamma raised one eyebrow, then turned away from Mrs. Fitzwilliam with a sniff, looking back at John, who raised his hands, fingers spread wide.

"Anne was truly ill, Aunt. I did not wish for you to be distressed. I had the best doctor I've had the privilege of meeting attend to her, and he said this very afternoon that she is quite well—"

"Mrs. Jenkinson tells me you have stopped taking your medicine," Mamma said to me, cutting John off.

I glanced at my companion, who looked down at her bowl.

"It is true," I said. "But Dr. Carter said—"

"You would take *his* advice over the doctor who has labored to keep you well your entire life? Ungrateful child!"

"My dear aunt," John said, attempting to draw her ire his way, as a farmer will coax an enraged bull away from the child who has wandered into its pen. "Anne is much improved, as you can see; and she has not taken her medicine in many days—since she left Kent. Surely if some harm were to befall her as a result, we'd have seen it by now."

Mamma ignored him utterly. "Anne, you will return with me to Rosings in the morning. Lady Mary will happily have you at her home for the night; you needn't endure my nephew's meddling any further." A cutting look at John. "I do not know what you hoped to achieve, but you may be sure my brother will hear of your officiousness. You and your wife need not come at Easter this year; perhaps by next year Anne and I will have forgiven you."

I could feel John looking at me, but I could not look back, could not raise my burning eyes from the dregs of my soup, covered with a tight skin and looking thoroughly unappetizing. My whole body stung with heat, as if the flames of Mamma's anger had leaped out and given me a thousand tiny burns.

Mamma took up her spoon and tasted the soup, then made a face. "Pah," she said. "Gone quite cold." She stood, nodding to Mrs. Jenkinson and me. "Come. Your maid can bring your things once they are packed."

Belatedly, both John and Mr. Watters rose as well, and Mrs. Jenkinson was already at my mother's side. Still, I felt John's eyes, and the eyes of everyone else, fixed upon me. A look at John, and I knew that he would speak for

me, should I wish it; though what could he say that he
had not already? Shame held me as fast as fear.

I am the most fortunate of creatures, I thought—
Miss Hall's words again; Miss Hall's words, always.

"Anne." Mamma's voice brooked no dissent; she commanded with the easy assurance of a general. Yet still I sat.

"I am sorry, Mamma," I said.

"What are you talking about, Anne? Get up at once."

I held the seat of my chair; I would be up and beside
her otherwise. "I—no. I am staying, Mamma. With
John. For a time, at least."

My voice was so quiet that I wondered if anyone heard
me, but when I raised my head at last it was clear that
everyone had. John grimaced; Mrs. Fitzwilliam glared
at him. Mrs. Jenkinson seemed to be making herself as
small as possible, back humped and shoulders drawn
close to her ears, while Mr. Watters looked, if anything,
highly entertained.

And my mother—my tree-rooted mother, my cavalry
commander mother—reeled, grasping the back of her
chair in hands like a winter tree's branches.

"You most certainly are not," she said. "You will
come home immediately; you will rest and recover from
this—this fit."

"I will not," I said, and flinched back as she buckled a
little, leaning over so the chair back pressed into her abdomen. Mrs. Jenkinson, ever my mother's echo, gasped
in tandem with her.

Mamma's mouth worked for a moment without making a sound, before she straightened abruptly, a general

once more. "We can discuss this more later. Come." She nodded to my companion, still standing beside her. "And you, Mrs. Jenkinson—come."

"Mamma, I am staying here," I said, like a tree branch snapping underfoot. I stood and my feet spread themselves wide, planting me firmly as if they, too, had been watching my mother all my life, learning her tricks for commanding respect. Her head whipped to look at me, but I looked at Mrs. Jenkinson, who seemed to have stopped breathing. I felt rather as if I had, as well.

My mother's eyes were mere chinks of brightness between her upper and lower lids. "You would truly disobey me in this?" she said, a touch more astonishment than anger in her voice. But then more anger rushed to displace any other feelings. She shook one arm like a fighter, said, "You are headstrong—ridiculous! Running off to London without even a companion. You dishonor yourself—you dishonor me, and everything that I have done for you. You will keep Mrs. Jenkinson with you, at least."

I folded my arms across my rib cage, pressed my palms into the points of my elbows, a desperate self-embrace. "No," I whispered. My blood rushed through my body so quickly I felt I might faint, but I could not—would not—have Mrs. Jenkinson there, for all that a companion meant freedom, of a sort, for a woman alone. She belonged too fully to my mother.

Mamma kept her eyes upon me, and I felt everyone else's eyes as well, wide and waiting. And then my mother turned her head away, as if from the sight of something monstrous, and moved toward the doorway.

"Your uncle," she said, "will hear of this, as I said. I will return to Rosings Park in the morning and await your return to sanity."

We all watched her go, Mrs. Jenkinson following after a moment's hesitation, though my mother did not even look at her before sweeping from the room. Our faces remained turned toward the doorway as we listened to the sound of her footsteps disappearing down the corridor, to her voice cracking out an order for her hat and cape to be brought, immediately. And then the front door opening, closing; and silence.

My body sagged. I stumbled backward until my knees bumped the seat of my chair, and then I sank into it and pressed my fingers against my face. The air was suddenly thick and clogged my nose and mouth, and I thought, half-hysterically, that perhaps Mamma was right and London would kill me after all.

At last Mr. Watters, his voice sly, broke the silence.

"I think you could perhaps use a little more wine after that, Miss de Bourgh."

I raised my face to meet his laughing eyes.

"In fact"—he gestured to a footman, who had already taken up the crystal decanter—"I believe we all could."

The footman poured wine into each of our glasses—just a splash into mine, for I had only tasted it before Mamma arrived—and then Mr. Watters raised his glass and said, "That was a bit of a triumph, I should say."

I could not decide whether he mocked me. John rolled his eyes; Mrs. Fitzwilliam said, "David, really," though she smiled.

CHAPTER SIXTEEN

After my mother's spectacular arrival and departure, I found myself so ravenous that I had to consciously set my fork and knife down between bites to prevent myself from gobbling the entire contents of my plate. Pigeon pie, the crust buttery, the gravy rich; parsnips and beetroot; warm apple puffs. Mamma and Mrs. Jenkinson kept my diet free of heavy sauces and anything that might be too stimulating. Even vinegars, usually considered so healthful, might overpower me. The extraordinary bounty now on my plate and the sudden eagerness of my appetite were like those first sights and sounds as we drove into London: more clamorous than my anxious thoughts, more intoxicating than wine.

After dinner concluded, Mrs. Fitzwilliam and I removed to the drawing room. She took up some sewing, and I sat foolishly idle, my fingers tugging at one another in my lap. My eyes darted to the drawing room door, through which, at any moment, John and Mr. Watters would enter.

Mr. Watters had been out for most of the day, and when he returned to the house he did not recognize me, though we met once before, when he visited Rosings Park with his sister upon her engagement to John. That day at Rosings, he bowed to me quite properly, then spent the rest of the evening ignoring me in favor of ingratiating himself with Mamma. Not that I minded; the stripes on his waistcoat, created of gold thread that shone distractingly in the candlelight, were the most interesting thing about him.

This evening, however, rather than greeting me as he ought, he stood back, awaiting an introduction, which would have been right and proper if we had not, in fact, already known one another. As it was, my blood rushed with embarrassment when Mrs. Fitzwilliam at last reminded him of our prior acquaintance. There was a light of recognition in his eyes then, and though he came forward, bowing and saying how glad he was to see me again, I could feel his remembered contempt and dismissal of the invalid woman he had met then.

But after the confrontation with Mamma, there was a shift, as Mr. Watters discarded his disinterest like a coat. He watched me, *studied* me, taking in every particular from the careful curls Spinner constructed at my crown, to the pearls at my ears, to the striped green silk of my gown.

"When you are fully recovered," he said as his sister and I rose to withdraw, "I hope you will let me escort you to some of London's best sights."

I stumbled over my thanks, noticing Mrs. Fitzwilliam's sharp, contemplative gaze.

FALLING ASLEEP SOUNDS LIKE such an easy thing— falling, after all, being a swift endeavor, often inadvertent.

And so it had always been for me, except for the rare occasions when I forewent my laudanum.

But tonight my mind and body were both still restless. I listened to the creak of the ceiling above my head, the heave and thump of feet and bodies as the servants readied themselves for bed in their attic rooms. My thoughts darted toward and back from my mother's stricken face as she turned away from me; and in between, I saw Mr. Watters.

My father owned a pocket compass, small and silver, and on its face a precise eight-pointed star. He brought it out for me once, when I was a child and lying, muddled by my drops, in the drawing room, and spent an unaccustomed few minutes sitting with me there. His hands, so big and warm, caught one of mine like a butterfly in a net, turned it over gently so the palm faced up, and pressed the compass into the resulting hollow, as a gardener pressing a seed into the soil. With two fingers, he rotated the compass within my palm.

"See how the needle remains steadfast?" he said, and I nodded, astonished by such everyday magic. After a moment, Papa patted my shoulder and took his leave, but I lay there and kept turning the compass with my fingers, slowly at first, and then faster, watching and watching the needle, convinced that if I looked away it would turn contrary and jerk suddenly around to point in another direction.

When at last he and John had joined us in the drawing room, Mr. Watters's eyes had found me unerringly, as if they were the compass needle, and I were North.

And like the needle, they remained fixed and steady. For a breathtaking moment, I thought of my drops; they would cover me like a blanket, and I would revert to the safety of the chaise, recumbent and bland as the sauce-less meat and dry toast I was accustomed to eating. I caught my left wrist in the circle of my right hand; it was narrow enough that my fingers and thumb overlapped. The nails cut my wrist's tender underside, harder and harder until at last the pain became sharp enough that my thoughts went scattering.

I rolled over in bed now, rested my head on my arms, felt the dip of the mattress under my breasts and belly. My stomach was full, satisfied. My ears picked out noises from outside; my eyes roved around the shadowed room. My breaths, even and measured, came in cold through my nose and left warm from my mouth. I could *feel* everything; there was no gauzy medicinal padding to my thoughts or the sensations of my body.

There were also no distractions in the form of sleep rushing toward me like a sea wave, or visitors stealing into my bed. My neck prickled as I waited, but no one joined me; not the fat woman with the pointed teeth, not Papa in all his plumage. I was quite alone. Even the dead boy, whose existence I was so grateful not to have to explain to John, would be welcome just now; but he, too, kept away. I'd known that they were false visions; like the voice of Rosings Park, they appeared when my dose was increased, and any rational person would know that they were a product of too much laudanum. But in my sudden loneliness, I did not feel rational at all, but so sad that saltwater trailed from the corners of my eyes, leaving damp spots on the pillow.

I remembered Mrs. Jenkinson as I left Rosings—*Have you gone mad?*—and concentrated on the sliver of moonlight shining through a gap between the curtains and the edge of the window frame. My fingers plucked at the bedclothes. I wondered whether it was, in fact, madness that brought me here, and not, as I had thought, a long-delayed understanding.

To distract myself I softly, softly began to whisper, and my voice sounded, in the great dark hush, like Nurse's. *"Once upon a time, there lived a king and queen whose great sadness was that they had no child . . ."*

The story, of the longed-for princess who lay protected for so long in her enchanted sleep, was as familiar as my own. As my eyes closed at last, I saw the princess so very clearly—unnaturally still and silent on her narrow bed until the moment the enchantment broke. As I watched from behind my lids, the princess blinked, sloughed off the covering of cobwebs, and rose, looking astonished, from her bed.

MRS. FITZWILLIAM ASKED ME, AS she adjusted her bonnet, whether I would like to accompany her as she paid calls.

"It would be a perfect way to make some other acquaintances in Town," she said, glancing at me in the glass. "And, of course, it would signal to society that you are ready to receive invitations."

Pressure was building inside of me. I put one hand

against the back of a chair, leaning a little, and the other to my chest. My breath escaped in short bursts; I felt a vague dismay, as if my skin might tear apart to release the rest.

"No," I said. "I—not yet."

When she left, I stood at the window, looking out over the gray-skied city and all the glorious motion and humanity it contained. There was a draft; I felt it cool my cheek, and took it as a small triumph that there was no one, at least, to urge me away from it, nearer the fire.

If I could, if it were something ladies did, I would go out into the city on my own, with no purpose other than exploration. I would be entirely anonymous—not Anne de Bourgh, but just another person, one of thousands. I would test the strength of my legs along London's twisting streets, and the strength of my lungs against its air. I could be among people without being expected to know what to do with any of them. My feet stepped in place against the carpet.

And then I looked outside again, and suddenly there was death everywhere. It lurked behind a loose cobble on the pavement, waiting to catch walkers unaware. It rode, self-satisfied, under the heavy iron hooves of passing horses. A nurse and child were walking hand in hand down the street; I pressed my face to the window, opened my mouth in a silent warning cry. At any moment, the child was going to trip, stumble, slipping sideways into the horses' path. I *saw* it—her bonnet flung away, her bright yellow pelisse crumpled, her little body crumpled, too. I squeezed my eyes against the sight.

When I opened them, the horses had passed, and the child and her nurse were just rounding the corner.

At breakfast earlier, as John and Mr. Watters discussed their plans to go to John's club and Mrs. Fitzwilliam read some correspondence, I stirred my tea to cool it, and had a sudden flash—my father at his death—just a flash, but so vividly detailed that I shut my eyes, as if in doing so I could shut the vision out. Papa's mouth, open and shouting in surprise; Papa's eyes, wide. His fingers spread, as if braced to catch himself when he fell—but of course, he fell twisted all wrong, and headfirst. My body was left shaking, subtly enough that the others at the table did not see it.

Here I was, in the city to which I'd long dreamed of coming; the storied place into which my father spent my life disappearing until, at last, he never returned from it. I felt as if I had climbed a great crag, only to be too afraid to clamber down the other side. There I teetered, waiting, as if for some toothy thing to come charging at me over the crest of the hill, to battle me to the ground, to prove that I was not safe at all.

Almost, I wished I could still blame my drops for these terrible, intruding thoughts, for would it not be better to be crippled by medicine than by my own fear?

CHAPTER SEVENTEEN

While I held myself captive inside John's house, I ate through the days like a woman starved, gobbling up all the things I was never allowed before. Dr. Carter explained to me, when he called to see how I was getting on, that laudanum often curbed feelings of hunger; but if my appetite was held in check before, now it had been given its full head. I was sublimely gluttonous, tasting bits of everything and enjoying second helpings of many. Cheese, in particular, was a novelty to me; long deemed too rich and binding for my already bound-up insides, it was now available to me in all its endless varieties. The blue-veined Stilton was my favorite, and I ate it with fruit at almost every meal.

I was very aware of my tongue as it tasted and my teeth as they bit. My jaw working to chew and my throat to swallow; and then my belly sighing its contentment. In the mornings, for the first time in all my life that I could remember, my body emptied itself easily without first requiring a purgative. My life's rhythm had always been set to my body's sluggishness, many days in which my food bound itself to my insides like Flanders glue, followed by mornings wracked with the cramps that always attended the use of a purgative, while it all came out in humiliatingly spectacular fashion. These mornings brought the fancies of traveling, in which I sometimes indulged, crashing down around my aching head—for, other symptoms notwithstanding, I could not imagine enduring such miserable hours anywhere except in my own home. But now, I had traveled—I was *here*—and my body had proved that it could function as cleverly as anyone else's. The entire world was suddenly available, whenever I gathered courage enough to face it.

OUTSIDE THE HOUSE, NEW leaves flexed like fingers on long, branching arms as the trees stretched after a winter of sleep. I wanted to pluck those leaves; to smell them and feel their tenderness between the pads of my fingers. I tapped out my impatience with my cowardice on the window frame instead. From my bedchamber, below which so much of the city sprawled like a rolled-out carpet, I watched the rest of London bloom with spring. John's and his neighbors' gardens, with their plum and apple trees espaliered against tall walls, went abruptly heavy with blossoms into which bees and butterflies eagerly dipped.

I closed my eyes and imagined Rosings Park, where little delicate shoots would be pushing up in the fields. Our head gardener, Mr. Saxon, would be starting his spring work: separating overlarge clumps of plants, pruning, making reality whatever improvements he and Mamma had dreamed up over the long frozen months. The woods would be noisy with life, all the creatures from Mr. Thomson's "Spring" stepping into courtship rituals as solemn, and as ridiculous to an outsider's eye, as our own. When I left, Rosings sent me off with cries like shoving palms; I tried now to imagine what it would say to me, hovering here as I was, unwilling to step back but afraid to step forward. *Not yet,* it might say. *Wait just a little longer.*

Or so I told myself.

All my life, I had been dormant as a winter tree, waiting for a spring that never came. But now it had come—it was all around me. I spent my years in detached observation of the wheeling seasons, but there was nothing detached about me now. Green and birdsong burst forth across London, and I watched, avid. Like the world outside, I was *full*, full of so much feeling I knew not what to do with it all. Like a child, I was all curiosity, every moment a discovery.

This fullness extended to my body, which, with the benefit of all the nourishment I'd been putting away in greedy gulps, changed subtly under my curious fingertips. My body was a mere *thing* before, inert and trapping me inside it; but now it was a wonder. I liked to imagine myself like one of the fat, bursting buds on the trees outside, but in truth, the changes were slower, gentler, all my hollows filling in, my angles rounding out.

More dramatic was how my body felt—*that* my body felt—a quickening of blood through my veins, like the rush of white rootlings underground; a tingling at the pads of my fingers, like a gathering summer storm. Under my shift, my breasts ached. Every sensation seemed exaggerated as a line of poetry; and as poignantly true.

I WOKE ONE MORNING to blood.

The evening before, a pain had sprouted, so deep in my belly it seemed unreachable. It began dull but grew into a fist that pulled and clenched and released; by the time I excused myself from dinner, I thought I might vomit. Spinner put me to bed, her face creased with worry, her fingers, calloused from needle pricks, testing the temperature of my skin.

"You're cool, ma'am," she said, though her brows drew together to see my hand pressed futilely against my abdomen. "But perhaps I should send for Dr. Carter?"

"No," I said, miserable, closing my eyes. "I think— perhaps I ate too much." I curled on my side and eventually fell asleep.

When I awoke to the thin light of dawn, I could not at first understand what had happened. I was lying in something wet, and for a dreadful moment I thought I had voided my bladder or my bowels in the night. I scrambled back, shifting aside the bedclothes, to find the white sheets stained bright as a butcher's apron. The great, spreading stain was still wet, and as I shoved myself backward, away from it, I realized there was more coming, seeping from between my legs.

A bright rush of horror and then, suddenly, I understood. I'd had my first monthly bleeding when I was seventeen, and more, erratically, in the years since; but they were never predictable, not as Nurse and Miss Hall said they would be—though Dr. Grant assured my mother that such sparse and sporadic bleeding was to be expected in a delicate young woman—and never presaged by this burrowing ache. I was abruptly aware of my womb, of its existence somewhere in the deep mystery between my hip bones.

I rose up onto my knees on the bed. The insides of my thighs were streaked with blood; my chemise was ruined. I would be embarrassed, except that it felt not shameful, but joyful. This was a torrent; a glorious abundance that had been stored and waiting, and was now released. I felt borne along on it, like a leaf caught in a river.

I pressed my fingers over my eyes and, laughing, wept.

SPINNER CAME IN SOON enough, took one look at my sheets and shift and the tackily drying blood, and sent for a bath. While we waited for the tub to be brought and filled, a housemaid came to bundle away my soiled linens, returning with salt and a basin of cold water. She blotted at the pinkish smear on the mattress, then sprinkled it over with salt, all the while pretending, in the manner of well-trained servants everywhere, that I was not the source of the troublesome stain.

The hot water eased away the deep-down ache even as Spinner scrubbed the blood from my skin. I stayed in the tub until it cooled, then let her clout and clothe me. The pinching pain began to return, however, and I curled over, fists pressed to my belly.

"What is it?" Spinner said, alarmed.

I said, "I don't know—I have never suffered like this when I bled, before," and a look of comprehension came over her face.

"It's quite normal," she said, then hesitated before

adding, "I think perhaps—you did not suffer so because your drops kept you from suffering. Laudanum is . . . often prescribed for ladies during their turns. But I do not suppose you would want—"

"No," I said, blade-sharp, and she nodded, looking relieved.

CHAPTER EIGHTEEN

Spring's warm breath crept in through the open drawing room window the day the Amherst ladies came to call.

I had so far managed to avoid going out, though John, when he was not in busy correspondence with his steward in Surrey, asked me often whether I would like to venture outside with him. Mr. Watters, too, enquired each morning if I felt well enough to sample London's amusements; but each time, I demurred, Rosings Park's imagined voice murmuring in my head like the rustle of leaves: *Not yet. Not yet.*

But I was finding that, when several hours were not spent in a state of half-consciousness, there was so much time to fill each day, and so little with which to fill it. I had no responsibilities here in London, no friends. I could work more diligently on my stitching, now I'd the ability to concentrate for longer stretches of time. I could, like Mrs. Fitzwilliam at her writing desk, write to my mother, and to Mr. Colt. I could . . . But I found my imagination here went empty. I slumped a little on my sofa and listened to the knell of the hall clock as it struck the hour.

And then, with a feeling like fingers trailing upward from the base of my spine, my back straightened abruptly. The front door opened and closed—the butler spoke, and feminine voices answered. Frozen in place, I looked at Mrs. Fitzwilliam, and she, setting aside her letter, gave me a rainwater-cool look back.

"Ah, callers," she said, rising from her chair just as the butler entered.

"The Misses Amherst, ma'am," he said.

In an instant, Mrs. Fitzwilliam transformed herself into someone entirely unfamiliar. In all the days I had spent in her home, she had been stiff as a newly starched collar. Now it was as if her mask cracked open, unexpected warmth shining through the crevices.

"Eliza, Julia!" she said as two young ladies, bright as flowers incongruously blooming in winter, appeared in the doorway behind the butler. Mrs. Fitzwilliam clasped their hands. "It has been *ages*—is your father recovered from his illness, then?"

"Quite recovered," said the taller of the ladies. "He ordered us out of the house, saying he could bear our fussing no longer."

The other lady, though, had caught sight of me where I still sat perfectly motionless at one end of the sofa. She blinked and tilted her head, upon which she wore a magnificent hat, high and plumed, with a brown velvet ribbon that looked so lush I had the disconcerting urge to stroke it. My fingers wove together in my lap; my eyes dropped away from hers.

"Harriet," she said.

Mrs. Fitzwilliam looked around at her, and said easily, "Forgive me—I quite forgot myself in the excitement of seeing you both. Miss de Bourgh," and here she gave me an odd, pointed look, "may I introduce my friends from school: Miss Amherst"—gesturing at the shorter lady in the lovely hat—"and Miss Julia Amherst. Eliza, Julia, this is Miss de Bourgh, the colonel's cousin."

The ladies made their curtsies, and I nodded to them both, my mouth too dry for words, nerves tautening the line of my shoulders. Miss Amherst seated herself on the other end of the sofa, while Miss Julia and Mrs. Fitzwilliam took the chairs. After a moment's silence, Miss Julia began to speak, and soon enough they were all chattering, eager as songbirds. I sat silent and listened to them, self-consciousness flowing through my body like blood, unable to figure out how to add my own chirping to theirs.

Mrs. Fitzwilliam, having become accustomed, I suppose, to my awkward manners, paid me no mind, and Miss Julia, after a little hesitation, followed her example. It was very like what I was accustomed to, sitting quiet and forgotten while everyone else conversed, but now I'd no laudanum haze, no Rosings Park pressing up against my feet like a nudging friend. My drops made me buoyant, my attention shifting languidly from face to face, from object to object, in a happy heedless dance. Sometimes my attention would snag on something— our tea caddy's intricate filigree paperwork, for instance, whose loops and whorls I traced with my eyes, a sensation, I imagined, like sliding down a bannister. Without them, I was rigid as wood, and remembered too well why I had not yet accepted any offers to go out into society.

Miss Amherst flicked glances at me like marbles while I sat straight and knot-fingered. She and her sister were rather bewildering in their physical differences, Miss Julia tall and slim as a sapling, her nose and chin narrow and sharp, as if chiseled by an expert hand; Miss Amherst, shorter and fuller, with curving shoulders and blunt, irregular features—small eyes, round nose, soft, receding chin. Both had hair of an unfortunate shade of orange, though Miss Julia wore it better, her skin pale and smooth enough that the contrast was dramatic. Miss Amherst's skin was covered in freckles so scattered and numerous they looked like droplets of paint. She was elegance and irreverence at once, one foot, in its neat green slipper, swinging lightly as she sat. I watched it move, the better to keep my eyes from wandering over all the oddly appealing, clashing parts of her.

"How long have you been in London, Miss de Bourgh?"

I looked up from that swinging foot to find Miss Amherst watching me openly—it was she who spoke—and her sister and Mrs. Fitzwilliam paused in their conversation to look my way, as well. My cheeks burned.

"About a fortnight," I said.

"And is this your first trip to Town?"

"It is, yes."

She smiled. Her mouth was large, and her teeth, too, but still her smile made her almost handsome in a way that her mismatched features should not allow. Something dark flashed with her smile, and I blinked. "How exciting! What have you seen so far?"

I looked at Mrs. Fitzwilliam, who wore her polite not-quite-smile. "Nothing yet," I said, turning back to Miss Amherst. "I was—ah—ill when I first arrived, and have been regaining my strength."

Her sister answered, "Oh, so that is why you were still seated when we arrived. How unfortunate that you have been unwell! But at least most of the Season is still before us—there is plenty of time for you to enjoy its delights."

I was glad my gown's high neck hid the warmth that rushed downward from my face, staining my throat and chest. Mamma never expected me to exert myself to rise when callers arrived, and though Miss Hall had taught me all the usual rules of etiquette, they often seemed not to apply to me. I remembered, with sudden vividness, the way Miss Bennet—now Mrs. Darcy—looked at me with laughter at the corners of her mouth when we were introduced, one brow arched just a little in a way that I did not like, as if she found it amusing that I felt too off-balance to stand and bow. My smile now felt as false as Mrs. Fitzwilliam's, though Miss Julia seemed not to notice. Miss Amherst, though, continued to watch me for a moment, frank curiosity in her face.

When they took their leave, I made sure to stand to say farewell. Miss Amherst shook my hand, smiling into my face, and said, "I hope you will visit us in Cavendish Square. I would so like to learn more about you—I fear we three rather ran on today in our excitement to see each other again. I am sorry if you felt left out of the conversation; it cannot be very interesting to hear gossip about our schoolmates when you have never met them."

I shook my head, and then said, all in a rush, "I'm sorry—but—you have something caught between your teeth."

Miss Amherst stared at me; I felt my own mouth press closed, and longed to let my eyes close as well, blotting out the sight of her shock at my rudeness. But then she laughed, full-throated as a diving bird, the sort of laugh my mother would revile and Miss Hall would censure as being unladylike. Her teeth showed when she laughed, with that little dark speck between them, and her tongue, pink and startling. Then she covered her mouth with her hand.

"Thank you, Miss de Bourgh; Julia and Harriet were content to leave me in ignorance, it seems. Where is it exactly, if you don't mind . . . ?"

I touched my own teeth in the same spot, tentatively, and she scratched between hers, her other hand still acting as shield. Then she smiled at me again, quick and large, and said, "Is it gone?"

"Yes," I said, faint as a breeze.

WE RETURNED THE CALL a few days later. Mrs. Fitzwilliam, over breakfast, announced her intention of visiting the Amhersts, and I was seized with simultaneous urges—to flee back to my chamber, and to rush outside. The muscles of my legs bunched as if in preparation to leap up, and I knew not in which direction they would carry me. But there was a slight warning note to Mrs. Fitzwilliam's tone as she said, "Will you join me, Miss de Bourgh?", and I thought of how I did not rise to greet the Misses Amherst when they came. I could not refuse to return a call without it being seen as a snub.

"That would be lovely," I said.

Mrs. Fitzwilliam nodded. "Good," she said, her voice relaying none of her thoughts.

Mr. Watters emerged from behind his newspaper. "I'm glad to hear you are well enough to venture out at last," he said. "I hope you know I will not let you off your promise to let me show you some of the best amusements in London."

"Of course, Mr. Watters," I heard myself say. "I will be delighted."

THE BUTLER HELD OPEN the door when we left, and I followed Mrs. Fitzwilliam outside. I stepped, one foot and then the other, onto the scrubbed front steps with their pretty black and white tiles; I felt the bracing air with its breath of smoke. Raising my eyes to the rooftops with their pouring chimneys, and higher, to the cloud-white sky, I almost smiled.

Despite spring's arrival, the air was still brisk, but our capes and muffs kept us warm enough for the short carriage ride, passing through streets very much like the one we left, all high handsome houses. I thought at first that we would not speak at all, and turned my head to the window; I felt quite outside myself, watching the buildings flash by. With each clop of the horses' hooves, I heard an old familiar refrain—*London, London, London* beat inside me like a second heart.

But Mrs. Fitzwilliam startled me by speaking. "I

suppose Eliza and Julia are not quite the sort of company you usually keep."

I could not think how to respond beyond a shake of the head.

"They are very rich, for all that they come from trade," Mrs. Fitzwilliam said, a little color in her cheeks. "Their house is larger than ours, even. I hope they will make matches as good as mine. This is Eliza's third Season, though, and she has yet to receive a single proposal. Julia has a better chance, I think." She fidgeted with the string of her reticule. "They are not the sort of people about whose friendship one would boast, but we have known each other a very long time. Julia and I formed a bond in our first days at school, and Eliza—well, she is a dear, despite her tendency toward . . . loudness." A glance at me. "I hope she did not offend you; sometimes I think she is unrefined on *purpose*."

I remembered Miss Amherst's unreserved laughter. "I liked them both very well," I said, and looked away from her in confusion. It had not occurred to me that John's wife might be self-conscious of her background, or of the friends she retained from girlhood; she wore condescension almost as well as Mamma did.

"Of course," Mrs. Fitzwilliam added after a moment, "Eliza is also more accomplished than any of the rest of us. She positively outshone us all when it came to drawing, and her singing voice is unsurpassed except by the most classically trained musicians. It would be enough to make one hate her, were she not so completely indifferent to it all. I do not think she has touched a drawing pad or instrument since we left school; so really, what was it all *for?*"

I had no response.

The house at which we alighted was fronted with pale cream stucco that was tinted slightly gray, like linen in need of washing. The neighborhood was clearly genteel, pale brick and stucco houses with wrought iron fences. I turned while we waited to be admitted, looking out over the square's even pavement and the pretty circular garden at its center. Whatever the Amhersts' origins, they were clearly rising.

The butler took Mrs. Fitzwilliam's calling card and nodded at her murmured explanation of my cardless presence. "You will, of course, have some cards printed if you mean to stay long in Town," she whispered. I nodded, but my reticule hung light at my wrist, testament to its meager contents. I must write to Mr. Colt and ask how I can access my money. The very thought made my heart thud arrhythmically within my breast.

The butler returned and led us to the drawing room, where a fitted carpet muffled our footsteps. Both the Misses Amhersts and their mother stood as we entered. Mrs. Amherst and Miss Julia were blandly polite in their greetings, but Miss Amherst flashed her teeth at me.

"All clean, Miss de Bourgh?" she said, and I nearly laughed in astonishment.

"Yes," I said, and she smiled again, more naturally this time.

"I am glad you came," she said. "Please—sit."

I was led to a low sofa, and for a few minutes the

talk was of a party to which they were all invited. I, of course, had not been introduced to the hosts, and so was not included in the invitation my cousin received. I was glad of the excuse to sit quietly now and accustom myself to the company. The tea in my cup was too hot to drink; I held the cup gingerly on its saucer, breathed in the steadying aroma, and tried to think of something—anything—to add to the conversation.

Before I was ready, Mrs. Amherst turned to me, all bright inquisitiveness. "My daughters tell me you've not long been in London, Miss de Bourgh. Where do you come from?"

"Kent," I said. "My father's estate—" I paused. "Ah, that is, my estate is near the village of Hunsford."

"A beautiful county."

"It is," I said, and for a moment my mind was full of sloping farmland and murmuring forests.

"And with whom did you travel? Your mother?"

My throat managed a series of beetle-clicks, but nothing more for several seconds. Then I cleared it and said, "Ah, no one." And at her expression of surprise, "I—had a companion, but she was . . . unable to accompany me. And I was very unwell—"

"Oh, yes, we've all the best medical men here in Town. But how courageous you were, to travel all on your own, and while ill!" Mrs. Amherst looked at Mrs. Fitzwilliam, a strange eagerness in her posture. "With all your husband's connections, you will be able to introduce Miss de Bourgh to the very best of London society."

Mrs. Fitzwilliam's expression twisted a little, but she said, "Of course. She has been unwell, but now that she is feeling better I hope she will be able to accompany us to all manner of amusements. My brother, I know, is eager to shepherd Miss de Bourgh about."

Miss Amherst, I noticed, raised her eyebrows at this but did not speak.

"And of course," Mrs. Fitzwilliam added, "Miss de Bourgh is the earl's own niece. It should not be difficult to secure invitations for her."

"You have come to the right place, then, Miss de Bourgh," Mrs. Amherst said. "Mrs. Fitzwilliam met the colonel at a ball during the Season; it is now her sworn duty, as one of the lucky ones, to help other young ladies make good matches. I would guess you'll be engaged by April."

"Perhaps Miss de Bourgh already has a young man," Miss Amherst said, looking at me.

I thought of Darcy, and flushed. "Oh—no. There is no one," I said.

"There now." Mrs. Amherst nodded. "Of course, she has also promised to find husbands for my girls—you will be very busy these next few months, Mrs. Fitzwilliam!"

She launched into a discussion of the likeliest events at which to meet suitable gentlemen. After a moment, Miss Amherst scooted along the length of the sofa to sit nearer to me.

"Since you are so new to Town, I hope you will come shopping with me," she said. And then, before I could answer, "I know Mr. Watters has promised to take you about, but though I am sure he will take you to all sorts of interesting sights, a man cannot know the shops that will most interest us ladies."

I thought again of my few shillings. "I would enjoy that," I said, though in truth I was not so sure. In the past, Mamma had made all the choices about my attire for me; I merely went along to the Hunsford seamstress to be poked with pins and measured.

"Wonderful," she said, again with that unreserved smile. It made her almost . . . not handsome, for she was not finely formed enough for true handsomeness, her eyes small, made smaller by the roundness of her cheeks and the size of her nose. Her skin was much too freckled for fashion. But her mouth was wide and attractive, her every movement unselfconscious and sure. I could not fathom what she wanted with my company.

"I will need to figure out how to get money," I said, and then, quickly, "that is—I have money—plenty of it—but I have never had to access it before. My mother always gave me an allowance, but she is . . . well, she did not give me anything before I came to Town."

Miss Amherst stared, eyes shining with incredulity; then she laughed. It might have mortified me, but there was no malice in the sound, only true, wholehearted mirth. "Oh my," she said. "I admire your frankness. Though—and I hope you will not take the advice amiss—you might wish to temper your honesty when Harriet introduces you to other families. I would not want you to be eaten alive before you have had a chance to enjoy yourself."

I found this strange advice from a young woman whose entire being seemed frank, from her unbleached freckles to her extraordinary laugh. She smiled again.

"Your problem is not a difficult one," she said. "You can easily set up an account in any of the shops from which you make a purchase. Have you a man to attend to your business affairs?"

"Yes, in Kent. I mean to write to him."

"You can have the bills sent to him easily enough, I imagine."

The butler entered then with another card, and Mrs. Fitzwilliam rose.

"We will leave you to your other callers," she said. "But I look forward to seeing you all soon." She smiled again that warm, true smile, which she seemed only to bestow upon the Amherst ladies.

"And we must choose a time to visit the shops," Miss Amherst said to me.

I agreed, in a stammering sort of way, and followed Mrs. Fitzwilliam out, glancing once over my shoulder to find Miss Amherst looking after us, still smiling. I wondered if she ever frowned.

"Mrs. Amherst was quite right," Mrs. Fitzwilliam said as the carriage set off. "You will soon be overrun with invitations. You were so . . . unwell, at first. We have not put it about that you are in Town. But you will be such a curiosity, with your fortune and connections, and never having had a Season before." She looked out the window, watching the street outside, and then added, all casualness, "You are . . . not promised to any particular gentleman, then? Perhaps someone in Kent?"

I shook my head, but she was not looking at me so I was forced to speak. "No," I said, a mouse's squeak; and now she did look at me, eyes running over my form from bonnet to slippers, as if truly taking in every particular for the first time.

And then she said, "Hm." But before I could move my tongue to ask the question skipping down its length, she added, "I must say, I think David will be a little vexed if you go shopping with Eliza before you let him show you about." A smile, almost as true as those she gave her friends. "He did invite you out first, after all."

CHAPTER NINETEEN

The tiger in its too-tight cage was huge—monstrous. I'd heard it and the other big cats before we even entered the Royal Menagerie, the menace in their voices lifting the hairs on my arms. My fingers tightened on the wool sleeve of Mr. Watters's coat; I half-believed, as we approached the building, that I would find myself faced with beasts wandering free and fierce. John and Mrs. Fitzwilliam, walking a little ahead of us, looked back at me, and my cousin smiled and said, "Don't worry, Anne—they're all shut up quite tight." But still I stared up at the outside of the building, waiting for one of the monsters of my childhood imaginings to come rushing out at me. Mr. Watters steered me around a murky puddle, his silver-headed walking stick keeping up a distracting *tap-tap-tap* on the pavement.

But inside the long, high-ceilinged room, I found my fear drained down through the soles of my feet. Cages lined the walls, and inside them beasts out of storybooks, impossibly huge and oddly shaped. An elephant, massive and humped as a boulder, took up a cage that spanned the width of the wall at the far end of the room. A horned, leathery rhinoceros was housed beside a sleek leopard. A baboon peered out at us, soft, furred fingers curled around its cage's bars.

But it was the tiger that caught my eye. It was listless; not sleeping, but not awake. Hopeless, perhaps, if tigers could be said to have hope. I thought of our old rector at Hunsford, Mr. Applewhite, so certain that souls were the sole province of human beings; no doubt he would scoff at the thought that so beastly a creature as a tiger could understand something as abstract as *hope,* much less lose it. But this tiger was unfathomably huge within its cramped cage, power in its great platter-like feet and square, toothy jaws. It should not remind me of nothing so much as a skin mounted on a wooden form, its eyes expressionless as glass. The white fur at its great paws and muzzle looked dirty, gray-tinged like everything else in London.

I stood staring at the tiger, my head tipped back, tears crowding my eyes and throat.

"Astonishing, is it not?" Mr. Watters said beside me. He stood with his legs spread a little apart, both hands resting on the knob of his walking stick. "Look at those claws—those haunches. I wager it would be a good deal taller than I am standing on its hind legs."

Mr. Watters had taken me out into the throbbing heart of London several days in a row, with his sister or John as trailing chaperone. The city unveiled itself to me bit by bit, shedding some of its mystery like a bather sheds clothing; I took it all in, overwhelmed, as the staid and stately homes of the neighborhoods around John's house gave way to thronged shopping districts and humid concert halls; to Montagu House, with its marvelous curiosities, and sprawling parks where people promenaded in the thin sunlight and made me think of goods on display in shop windows. Without meaning to, I held myself tense in those crowds, half-expecting that I would meet Miss Hall by chance—a silly notion, but one I could not dispel. Yet still, I loved each of the city's revelations—of the wondrousness of human imagination and my own body's resilience, my feet firm upon the flagstone pavement, my lungs breathing easily of the air I'd been afraid of for so long.

But I could not love this.

I withdrew my hand from Mr. Watters's arm, and he looked down at me, narrow brows arched in surprise. But I could not speak sensibly, my mouth crowded with thoughts of tiger-souls and tiger-hope, and the hopelessly insensible urge to unlatch the tiger's barred cage and see all its potential unleashed on the world.

MR. WATTERS BOWED OVER MY right hand when we returned to John's house. His breath was hot even through my thin glove, and I tucked my lips together, feeling, too, Mrs. Fitzwilliam's and John's sideways glances, hers assessing, his amused. Then Mr. Watters and John left again, this time for John's club, and Mrs. Fitzwilliam disappeared to speak to the housekeeper, and I peeled my gloves off almost frantically. The back of my right hand was moist, as if I'd passed it through steam; I wiped it on the edge of my skirt, clenching my gloves tight in my other fist.

MY DAYS USED TO move at the pace of the sun, slow and tedious, measured in shadows creeping across the floor and the interminable *chocks* of the drawing room clock. My new life left me overwhelmed, feeling as if I'd been buffeted from one end of the city to the other by a brisk wind. But it was the constant hum of expectation in the air around me that left me truly exhausted. If it was not Mr. Watters, who seemed always to be near at hand, smiling his many-toothed smiles, offering constant amusements and his own steady arm, it was Mrs. Fitzwilliam's callers, who looked at me as if I were one of the menagerie's fantastic beasts, rich and landed and unwed; and in need of caging.

"WE WILL HAVE GUESTS in our box tonight," Mrs. Fitzwilliam said, turning so her maid could help her into her cape.

My cape, lined with fox fur against the chill of the spring evening, was already fastened around my shoulders; Spinner drew its wide-mouthed hood up over my hair with great care. I turned my head to look at Mrs. Fitzwilliam, the edge of the hood obstructing my vision a little, and nearly sighed.

"Oh?" I said.

She looked back at me with a slight smile. "You needn't look so despondent—is it really so terrible, making new friends? But these are friends you know already: Mrs. Amherst and her daughters."

"Oh," I said again, but with an entirely different inflection.

I had seen nothing of the Amherst ladies since we

called upon them. Though Mrs. Fitzwilliam did her best to promote them in society, a whiff of trade still followed them everywhere, and so they were not invited to many of the parties to which the Fitzwilliam name gained her admittance. Not one of the other young ladies to whom I had been introduced put me so immediately at ease as Miss Amherst, and though I knew how unlikely it was that we would meet by chance, I still found myself searching each drawing room we entered for a crown of red hair and a generous, laughing mouth.

"They will meet us at Drury Lane," Mrs. Fitzwilliam said as John and Mr. Watters emerged from John's study, bringing with them a faint aroma of brandy. I nodded, swallowed, very aware of the hedonistic softness of fur against my shoulders.

THE THEATRE ROYAL AT Drury Lane was a smart, square building, only just constructed, Mr. Watters told me on our ride through the city, five or so years ago. He handed me out onto the pavement with great courtesy, taking my elbow to move me out of the way as another carriage took the place of ours, spilling more theatergoers into the London twilight. Snowflakes fell, just a few here and there, as if someone far above was dropping them at random, one by one.

John and Mrs. Fitzwilliam joined us before the theater. He stood at his ease, his wife's hand tucked into the crook of his arm, while she looked this way and that, presumably for the Amherst carriage; but as the minutes passed he finally turned to Mr. Watters and said, "Take the ladies inside; it wouldn't do to have them take a chill. I will wait for Mrs. Amherst."

Mr. Watters offered his sister his other arm. Against my will, I was grateful for his steadying presence, for without his deft maneuvering I no doubt would have tripped or smashed into someone, so engrossed was I in taking in the grandeur of the building's interior. We passed through the rotunda, with its round red columns and handsome cupola, and I forgot to mind my feet on the unfamiliar staircases.

I heard the noise of the audience before we reached our seats. My fingers tightened on Mr. Watters's sleeve; he looked down at me with faint amusement and leaned down to murmur, "Do not faint, Miss de Bourgh; you will be quite safe with me, even if the crowd gets rowdy."

I blinked away from him and was saved the trouble of responding by the sight of the theater opening up before me. I must have looked like a rustic, standing there with my eyes big as oranges; but who could fail to be moved by such a place? There was a whole world there, gilded and so brightly lit my eyes were dazzled. At a nudge from Mr. Watters, I followed him to my chair, sitting without taking my eyes from the spectacle before me.

Boxes, like the one in which we sat, rose on both sides of the stage. They were filling with elegant ladies and gentlemen, while below a larger crowd gathered in the pit, people jostling one another in their haste to greet friends. All the voices melded together to produce a sort of overwhelming, wordless hum.

Mr. Watters leaned close again. "The gaslights were only just installed a few months ago," he said. "This is the first theater in London to be so well lit."

"It is astonishing," I said.

"All the better," he said, after a moment, "because it shows off your new healthfulness to advantage."

I turned to look at him, and whatever he saw in my face—outrage? bewilderment?—made him laugh. "I apologize, I did not intend to discomfit you. It is only . . ." He smiled with one side of his mouth, voice low and head bent toward me so I could hear him above the general clamor. "You have a bloom about you, Miss de Bourgh; I am so glad to see you so fully restored to health."

Quite of their own accord, my eyes jerked themselves away from him as my cheeks grew ember hot. There was a sudden flurry behind us, and Mr. Watters, to my relief, stood to greet the Amherst ladies as John escorted them into our box. I swallowed and extended my hand in greeting, first to Mrs. Amherst, who glittered at her ears and throat, then to Miss Amherst and Miss Julia. They all greeted us cordially, though I noticed Mrs. Amherst and her younger daughter offered a little more pointed attention to Mr. Watters. John edged past us to reach his chair beside his wife, while the other ladies arranged themselves on the chairs behind ours.

"This is Anne's first time to the theater," John said, his voice raised to be heard above the general din.

"No! Not really?" Mrs. Amherst said. "Though I suppose there is little opportunity for theatergoing in Kent. We come as often as we can, though Mr. Amherst never joins us—he cannot abide the spectacle." She gave a laugh, a more restrained variation on her eldest daughter's. I glanced at Miss Amherst, who was sitting directly behind me, to find her watching me. For some reason, this made the embers in my cheeks flare all the hotter.

"Unlike Papa, I love the spectacle," she said, leaning forward so I could hear her. "I hope you will enjoy yourself this evening, Miss de Bourgh; if the tragedy of the play itself is not to your liking, the pantomime after will lighten your spirits."

"Is the play a tragedy, then?"

Her face was open and amazed. "*Macbeth*? My dear Miss de Bourgh, I know you have not *seen* a play, but have you never *read* Shakespeare?"

Her question put me off-balance; yet, once again, I could sense no meanness in her words, only genuine surprise. "No," I said. "To be . . . frank—though I know when last we met you warned me against it—I have read little enough of anything, other than sermons. *Those* I could probably recite asleep."

She regarded me seriously. "By choice?" she said. "Or was the choice not yours to make?"

"My education was . . . narrow." I thought of Miss Hall and her clandestine offering of *The Seasons*. "Not, I think, by my governess's choice, but by my mother's orders. She does not approve of—theatricals, or novels, or poetry, or . . ."

"Now that," Miss Amherst said, "is a *true* tragedy. But look—" She touched me with the tips of her gloved fingers, just a bump to the top of my shoulder, and nodded toward the front of the theater. I turned back to look just as the heavy curtain was pulled back to reveal the stage.

The play's beginning hardly quietened the general noise of the crowd, and the constancy of the gaslights made me feel rather as if we were all of us part of some larger theatrical than the one being performed on the stage. There was a general air of merriment; down in the pit, people ate nuts and drank wine; in the boxes, people talked and watched each other, pointing with fans and quizzing glasses. I tried to keep my attention on the play itself, which was easier than it should be, given the general commotion; the actors and actresses had voices that rang out like cathedral bells, and even the painted sets were detailed and absorbing in their artistry. Mr. Watters directed a remark or two my way, and John and Mrs. Fitzwilliam chatted amiably with Miss Julia and Mrs. Amherst throughout the performance, but I sat mostly still and silent, watching.

Once, though, I felt a little gust of warm laughter against the back of my neck, and I turned my head a bit to catch Miss Amherst's eye. She grinned, nodded at the stage, and said, "I have seen this twice before, and the porter always makes me laugh."

AFTER THE PLAY WAS a rough pantomime, followed by a strongman with muscles like thick twisted vines. Miss Amherst touched me again, this time on the wrist with her fan.

"We have not had a chance to visit the shops," she

said. "I wonder if you are free tomorrow—if you are still interested, that is?"

"I am," I said, a touch too quickly, but she smiled at my eagerness.

"We must go early, if you can bear it after a late evening," she said.

"Tonight is nothing—my cousin assures me we will be home by eleven o'clock. Until I came to Town, I did not fully understand when people spoke of London hours."

"Ah, you are becoming acclimated."

"Not terribly well," I said. "I am too dull for much of London society."

Miss Amherst bent closer, whispering. "Most of London society is *very* dull," she said. "They are only also very loud—always in a tasteful way, of course—and their dullness is screened by fine furs and feathers." Her wide mouth stretched impossibly wider. "But then, my mother is forever telling me to temper my opinions if I ever want to catch a husband; you probably should not listen to me."

I found myself smiling in turn. "Someone once told me frankness was not much appreciated in Town," I said. "I find I rather enjoy yours, however."

CHAPTER TWENTY

Though the day was fine, weak sunlight even breaking through the general covering of clouds, Miss Amherst collected me in her carriage.

"I thought we would wander among all the shops; and so we might still, if there's time," she said. "But after our talk yesterday, there is a place we simply *must* visit before any other. Everything else can wait."

"What is it?" I said, but she only laughed and refused to tell me.

She seemed undaunted by the throngs in the streets as we drove; when I mentioned this, and how clanging everything still seemed to me, she said her family had lived in London for many years.

"My mother, of course, wishes my father to buy an estate in the country," she said, craning her neck to look at a woman pushing a flower cart. "But Papa says he would not know a single thing about being a country gentleman. He would probably ruin an estate and lose all our fortune. He knew his business, and now his money is safely in the funds, where he likes it. Mamma"—with a wry smile—"is not satisfied, however, and harangues him on the subject daily."

I pressed my lips together to keep myself from asking

what Mr. Amherst's business was; here, I thought, my frankness would *not* be welcome. Mrs. Fitzwilliam was always sensitive to questions about her family's links to manufacturing, and as she and the Amherst ladies were in school together, it stood to reason that their families might have been involved in similar pursuits.

But, yet again, Miss Amherst surprised me. "Papa had several cotton mills. If you need an opinion on the quality of fabric at the draper's, you've only to ask—I have an eye, immodest though I might sound for admitting it."

I thought of Mamma, who never hesitated to praise her own best qualities, and to my surprise, found myself smiling. "Modesty is sometimes valued overmuch, I think."

Her answering smile was quick as a darting bluebird, and just as bright. "That is just what I think, too."

"THEY CALL IT THE Temple of the Muses," Miss Amherst said as the footman helped us down. "A little dramatic, perhaps, but an excellent place to start a lifelong love affair with books."

The front of the shop bore the motto *The Cheapest Bookstore in the World*. I had never been inside a true bookshop, much less one with such a claim to make. Hunsford boasted a small circulating library, where I had gone a few times; but their selection was small, made smaller by Mamma's prohibitions against frivolous reading, and I never particularly enjoyed venturing inside.

But this place was nothing like the little library; it was nothing like my father's book room. It was something else altogether.

Tall windows along one wall let in light from outside, and the other walls were covered with shelves bearing what looked like hundreds of volumes. The books began at ankle height and ascended far above the heads of the patrons, so that the tops of the highest books met the ceiling. Two crescent-moon counters commanded the center of the room, the clerks behind them busy with customers; above curved a glass dome, letting in still more light from the sky. There was a wide, intriguing staircase to one side, with what appeared to be still more books at the top.

"How does one even know where to begin?" I said.

Miss Amherst let out her delightful bellow of a laugh and clapped her hands. "I *knew* you would like it. How could you fail to?" She took my arm and tucked it through hers. "It is said to be the largest bookshop in the world," she said, walking me toward the shelves. "And the cheapest."

"So I saw," I said faintly. I ran my fingers along the leather spines before me.

"Have you truly read nothing but sermons?" Miss Amherst said.

"I read *The Seasons,* once. Well, several times, really. But I had to return it to its owner."

She made a face. "We can do better than that. Poetry then, do you think? Or a novel?" She studied me, as if the answer might be written on my countenance, then said, "Wait here," and made her way to the enormous counter.

I watched her go. Her hair was so bright—not fashionable, perhaps, but it suited her well. Better than I thought, when we were first introduced. Her figure, too, was perhaps a touch stout for fashion, but there was an appealing energy in the way she moved, and her gowns were cut to flatter her fullness. I glanced down at myself and thought that my clothes did not flatter me nearly so well.

Turning back to the shelves, I collected courage enough to pluck a book from one of them at random. A history of some sort; I turned the pages carefully, scanning a few lines here and there. It should probably have interested me more than it did. I replaced it and took down another, for the pleasure of browsing with neither Mamma nor Mrs. Jenkinson—nor even Miss Hall— watching me.

A light touch on my elbow, and I looked up. Miss Amherst held a book out in front of her. *Waverley*, it read; *or, 'Tis Sixty Years Since*.

"It is a sensation," she said. "There are so very many novels I could recommend, but I do not know your tastes yet so well as I hope to. *Waverley* is enjoyed by both the ladies and gentlemen of my acquaintance. The author is a fine poet as well—though he pretends to be anonymous, it is difficult to remain so when your work is already so well loved. I can lend you some of his poetry, too, if you like."

"And you liked this novel as well?" I said.

"Of course!" She held it out, and then added two more

volumes on top of it, the second and third parts of the story. I tucked them under one arm and opened Volume One, though I was too conscious of her regard to take in a single word. It was too warm in the shop; I wished I could take off my outer garments, which hung from me, heavy and smothering.

"Are you all invited to Lady Clive's ball?" she said as I pretended to read. "Mamma managed to winkle an invitation, though heaven knows how."

"I've no idea," I said. "Mrs. Fitzwilliam knows all our engagements; she merely tells me where we are to go each day." This outing, I realized, was in fact the first since I arrived in London that I had chosen entirely for myself.

"Ah." Miss Amherst turned to the shelves, running one hand along them, her eyes roving over the titles. She wore white kid gloves embroidered with red flowers and improbable purple birds; they were as fine as everything else she wore, but their whimsy made me smile.

"Well, if you *are* going to be there," she went on, "I would be glad of it. I shan't know a soul other than Mamma and Julia—and I am sure no one will ask me to dance. Which is a pity; I am an excellent dancer." She looked at me over her shoulder, her grin disarming.

I could not fathom why words I could easily imagine coming from my mother's lips sounded so different from hers. "Mrs. Fitzwilliam has not mentioned it. I do not like to attend balls in any case; but if I ever change my mind, I shall keep you company as a wallflower. I never dance."

"What—not at all?"

"I never learned," I said, and now my face was so hot it must rival her hair for color. What must she think of me—I'd read nothing interesting, I could not dance. "I was . . . sickly. As a child. And . . . well, for most of my life, really. Dancing was considered too vigorous an activity, so I never had a dancing master."

"And are you still too—unwell—for such vigorous activity?" she said, her voice rich with curiosity.

"No—I think not. If I were, I could never have walked half so much before as I have since coming to London." I dropped my eyes to the novel I held. "I have always wanted to learn to dance."

"Then I shall teach you," she said, and my eyes leaped to her face. "Not everything," she added. "But I could teach you one or two simple dances, at least. Perhaps not enough to ensure your full enjoyment of a ball, but it would be a start."

I realized I was staring, and pulled my eyes away; they careened wildly from wall to ceiling, from ceiling higher still to the great cupola at the top, and down again. No one ever—save Mr. Watters, but his motives, I feared, were becoming clear enough—chose to spend so much time with me before, nor seemed to find so much genuine enjoyment in my company. Not even kind, dutiful John. I could not understand why Miss Amherst was being so generous with her time and attention.

"Well?" she said, after a moment. When I looked at her again, she was smiling, but uncertainly, as if the smile might slip from her lips at any moment.

"I would be—much obliged," I said. I raised the book a little. "I will buy it. It looks—very interesting."

"Oh, I'm so glad. As I said, if you like it, I have purchased some of his poetry, and I will happily share." She linked our arms again and led me toward the counter. "Mamma quite despairs of me; my inclination to spend most of my pocket money on books cannot possibly make me more attractive to eligible men. Though if she and Papa were not generous in furnishing our wardrobes, I daresay I would be torn between books and bonnets, for I have a weakness for both."

A sudden thought made me tug on Miss Amherst's arm to halt our forward momentum. "So I . . . just ask to open an account?" And then, before she could answer, "I feel so stupid; I know this must be a simple matter. But I have never—"

"This is a great season for first experiences, Miss de Bourgh," she said, quite gently. But she dropped my arm entirely a moment later, her hands covering her mouth. "Heavens," she said, a little muffled. "I did not think—I would call myself stupid, if I ever let anyone speak of me so meanly." The light reproach registered as she dropped her hands. "I am terribly sorry, but I should have taken you to another establishment. It is only—this shop is very impressive, is it not? I suppose I rather wanted to impress you."

"It is impressive, yes—"

"But the writing outside, the proclamation about their prices. It is only possible because they never take credit—only coin. The thought simply went out of my head."

"Oh." I looked down at the volumes in my hands; moments ago I could not concentrate well enough to read a coherent line, but now I found my fingers did not want to let them go. How foolish; it was only a book. There were—demonstrably, even just within this shop—hundreds, thousands more in the world.

"I will buy them," Miss Amherst said, and reached to take them from me. I shook my head, my fingers still gripping the bindings fiercely.

"I could never—"

"Please—this is my fault entirely. I told you, I always spend my pocket allowance on books."

I'd no experience with gifts, except those Papa brought back to me from Town; but I did not think I should allow so costly a gift as a book from an acquaintance—friend?—of such short standing. Miss Amherst looked quite determined, however, and I closed my mouth. Her fingers curled around Volume One at the opposite end to mine.

But before I relinquished it, I said, "You must let me buy you something in return, somewhere where I can open an account. A bonnet, perhaps? A weakness for a weakness?"

She was all surprise; we paused there, each grasping the book, looking into one another's faces. Then—of course—she laughed.

"Very well," she said, and took the book from me before I could think of further protests. Then she raised an eyebrow until I handed over the other two volumes, as well.

CHAPTER TWENTY-ONE

The butler showed Miss Amherst into the drawing room, then bowed and left us. She was smiling when she greeted me, and wearing her new bonnet. It suited her very well, with a wide brim lined in embroidered net lace, which complemented the roundness of her face, and a spray of charming blue silk flowers. She looked like Rosings's woods in bluebell season, the carpet of flowers rolling right out to the edges of the trees, where I could see it when I drove my ponies down the lane.

"I thought you might like to see how well it matches my blue dress, as I said it would," Miss Amherst said; but there was a question in her voice, and her head tipped sideways. I folded my lips and curled my fingers into my palms, caught looking too long.

"Yes," I said, my voice catching like a snagged skirt. She smiled a little hesitantly, taking the bonnet off and setting it on a little round table.

"I—told Mrs. Fitzwilliam I would join them at Lady Clive's ball," I said in a rush.

"Oh!" Miss Amherst smiled more fully. "How wonderful—and all the more reason for you to learn now." She looked around the room, as if deciding how to make space for us, but then pressed her lips together and straightened her shoulders, as if preparing for some unpleasant thing.

"Miss de Bourgh," she said slowly, turning back to me. "I . . . I am terribly afraid that I am going to offend you very badly, but I just—please, do not take my words amiss."

I looked back at her, baffled.

"It is only—I find I like you very much, Miss de Bourgh; and I would like to offer you any help it is within my power to give. I fear you'll find me very presumptuous but . . . may I take you shopping?"

My mouth opened and shut and opened again, without a single intelligible sound coming out of it.

Miss Amherst ducked her head. "I apologize. I don't mean any offense—your gowns are . . . very beautifully tailored." She stopped, biting the corner of her mouth.

I felt strangely calm, suddenly, in the face of her clear uncertainty. "But?" I said.

Her eyes darted over my form, and then to my face. She smiled, just a little. "*But* . . . this yellow—it simply . . . well, it does not flatter you as it ought. And the style—"

But here she stopped again.

Yellow was one of Mamma's favorite colors; yellow and red. Many of my gowns were one color or the other. I turned, just a little, so I was facing the large, silver-framed looking glass on the wall behind the pianoforte.

All my clothes were fine—the finest that could be bought in Hunsford, certainly—and Mamma always had the seamstresses do everything they could to disguise my smallness. I was swathed in ruffles—*buried* in them.

Instead of disguising the narrowness of my frame, they overwhelmed it. And now, suddenly, I could see what I never quite did before—they made me absurd.

"No!" Miss Amherst said when I said this; but yet again, she stopped herself. Standing behind me, she met my eyes in the glass and put her hands on my shoulders. Very slowly, as if I were a horse that might startle, she moved her hands down the length of my arms from shoulder to wrist, and I shivered; and then she took my wrists loosely in each of her hands, drawing my arms up and away from my body. In the glass, she looked over my form with a critical eye.

"You have such a neat figure," she said at last. "It seems a shame to hide it with so many frills. Something simpler, I think, would suit you well."

"Yes," I said, a little strangled, my own eyes on her gown of blue sprigged cotton. "Please—I would like that very much. Your help, I mean."

Her breath came out in a gust of relief. "Ah. Good." She grinned at me once more, then, dropping my arms, said, "All right—if we go to the draper's tomorrow, we should have time enough to choose fabric and have a gown made up for you before Lady Clive's ball. But for now . . ." A tilt of her head; a raised brow. "Shall we begin?"

"ONE-TWO-THREE, VERY QUICKLY—RIGHT FOOT to left to right," Miss Amherst said, and then, laughing, "*lightly*, Miss de Bourgh! On the toes, like so."

I could not achieve lightness, for all my smallness of

figure. We had pushed the sofa and chairs away from the center of the room; they sat at tipsy angles, like watchful wallflowers. I stepped back to watch Miss Amherst demonstrate the step again. She was not a small woman, but her body was not the encumbrance to her that mine was to me. Her back was straight, head lifted, a graceful line from crown to heel. Her feet in their thin slippers arched just so as she hopped onto her right foot, shifted her weight onto her left, and then, so quickly it looked like one light, fluid movement, onto her right once more. She hopped to her left foot and then shifted to right, and back again. Like everything else she tried to teach me, the step looked very simple when she performed it, but when she gestured to me to try again, I felt like a grasshopper trying to hop to an unnatural rhythm, all awkward angles.

"*Poise and ease,* Miss de Bourgh, *poise and ease,*" Miss Amherst said in an affected, deep voice, then laughed explosively at her own words. "That is what our dancing master always shouted at us," she said.

"I do not think I am capable of either one," I said, and tried to smile away my disappointment. "I suppose I am too old to learn properly; it was a silly whim."

"Nonsense! If nothing else, if you master a few simple steps and figures you will be able to dance at small parties, even if you do not feel equal to standing up at a public assembly. I think a small private dance among friends is more enjoyable anyway. All those prim rules at larger balls sometimes eliminate any sense of fun."

My mouth twisted, and she reached over, taking my hands. Hers were very soft and warm.

"Here—sometimes it is better to try the steps in a proper figure. Let us try this one together."

I MASTERED THE PROMENADE, at least, my hands clasped in Miss Amherst's, our arms crossed before us like woven threads. I was aware of every part of us that touched: palms, forearms, fingertips. Our hips bumped occasionally together. With the movement of her body beside mine, the unaccustomed heat of her skin where it pressed against my own, it was somehow easier to find the rhythm of the steps, to achieve the lightness that was lacking before.

All the figures we tried together seemed simpler, in fact; the steps that felt so unnatural when I performed them alone in the center of the room coming with greater ease the more we practiced them together. Though I would not call myself proficient—not in the least—I could at least manage a passable chassé, and when Miss Amherst murmured each coming step in the figure, I was able to follow her instructions without getting too muddled.

We were hot and laughing when she said, "If only we had someone to play for us—you cannot truly get the feel for the steps without music."

"Perhaps you could play, Miss Amherst," came a voice at the doorway, "and I could lead Miss de Bourgh through the figures."

I turned, dropping one of Miss Amherst's hands in my haste, to find Mr. Watters standing there, smiling. He leaned against the doorframe, ankles crossed; I had a dreadful feeling that he had been there for some time, watching us.

Miss Amherst's fingers tightened around mine, a little spasm. I glanced at her; her face was flushed from our exertions. Then she released my other hand and stepped back. "Of course, sir, if Miss de Bourgh does not object."

But I was stepping back, too, taking space only for myself, though I nearly reached out to pull Miss Amherst back with me. My palms, empty now, prickled. "Perhaps another time," I said. "I am not accustomed to so much exercise; I think I will . . . sit for a little."

Mr. Watters bowed. "But of course. Perhaps this evening? We could make a merry little party of it with Harriet and Fitzwilliam. I think we have no engagements tonight, and you can hardly expect to fully understand the figures if there is only one couple dancing."

"Yes," I said, and wished he would go away. His eyes pressed like thumbs. "Of course."

He smiled, bowed to Miss Amherst, and obliged my unspoken wish a moment later.

JOHN AND HIS WIFE were happy enough to indulge Mr. Watters when he suggested dancing after dinner, and to my consternation he was right, the figures made more sense with another couple to form a too-small set. The housekeeper, to my astonishment, played for us, and they were all very patient with my fumbling, for without Miss Amherst murmuring the steps to me I had trouble remembering them. I was stiffer, too, with Mr. Watters as my partner, my feet inflexible as stone. When our hands clasped, my fingers were quite limp.

He seemed not to mind; he said what a treat it is to see a woman like me at last able to take part in something so essential, so enjoyable as dancing. "For you were ill a long time, I understand," he said, holding one hand out to me, another to his sister. John took my other hand, and we circled in time to the song. "There is nothing better than dancing for invigoration, or to smooth the way to better acquaintance."

I caught John's eye; he looked between Mr. Watters and myself with something like amusement. Then I stumbled, having missed a cue in the music, and tucked my lips together, flushed not with pleasure and exercise, as I had been this afternoon, but with embarrassment.

JOHN TOOK ME ASIDE before I retired. "Have you written to Lady Catherine at all?" he said.

I had not. I shook my head; thoughts of my mother made me burn, sometimes with shame for my conduct, sometimes with anger for hers. "I know not what to say to her."

He ran his fingers through his hair. "That is understandable. But you know—she will not be the one to bend."

I knew that very well. Mamma's iron will had been one of the essential truths of my life. But then, so was my own illness, and that truth turned out to be so much nonsense.

"I received a letter from my father yesterday. He and Edward and my mother arrive in Town soon, and he is . . . eager for any rifts in the family to be mended. He wishes to invite my aunt to stay with them for a little while."

I closed my eyes.

"I asked him to wait until Mrs. Darcy is churched after she has her baby," John said. "Forgive me for saying so, but I know Darcy would not thank me if our aunt were to call while Elizabeth is confined."

At this, my eyes opened. "The Darcys are in London?" Then I remembered, distantly, that Mrs. Fitzwilliam mentioned this on the day of my arrival; but I was too full of other concerns to admit another just then.

"Yes—the doctors here are more knowledgeable than those in Derbyshire, or so Darcy says. I suppose this time has not been so easy."

A sudden flash of little Georgiana, mewling and bloody in my bed. Of Aunt Darcy's plaited hair, the only bit left of her. I winced.

"So Mamma does not come yet?"

"No," John said. "But things would be easier when she does come, *if* she does come, if relations are repaired between you."

I SAT THAT NIGHT in the center of my bed, very still, though my nerves jangled like discordant bells. This was not true life; it was a golden season, pinched from time's hoop and pocketed all for myself. But soon enough, I would have to step back into the turning hoop with everyone else and face my responsibilities.

Mamma's tender feelings, I told myself fiercely, were not my responsibility; but Rosings Park was. And the estate must be managed. I could do it myself, or I could trust Mr. Colt to do the job properly; but that would be a betrayal of Papa and my younger self, the wisps of us that I still recalled standing before the painting of the old house, speaking of the new house's future.

I could also marry—and here, the jangling bells rang out all the louder. I could marry, and the estate would pass to my husband, all my responsibility for it neatly abdicated with a few solemn vows and a church ledger signed. Except, of course, for the production of an heir; which would be a problem, no matter what I chose to do.

I knew almost nothing of physical affection. Only my nurse ever discussed such things with me, and in such odd terms that I hardly knew what to think. *Men plant a seed in a hole inside their wives, with a special . . . appendage God gave them for this purpose*, she said, when we received news of one of Aunt Darcy's pregnancies. *If the seed takes, it becomes a baby.*

I imagined babies like saplings inside their mothers, with leaf fingers and rooted toes, their features picked out in the patterns of their bark. But breeding women looked less, I thought, like they grew trees inside their bellies than fruit—grotesque, bulbous fruits.

I rather suspected that my mother and father no longer indulged in anything amorous after I was born, for Mamma said more than once in my hearing that she was grateful that Rosings could pass to a daughter so that, with my birth, her wifely duty was complete. She would, presumably, have enlightened me before my marriage as to what those duties entailed; but of course, the marriage never occurred.

I bent over until my brow touched the tops of my knees. Marriage made me think of Mr. Watters, and thoughts of him were utterly confounding. Mrs. Fitzwilliam made it perfectly clear that she approved of her brother's attentions to me; but *his* intentions felt less clear. Though he made it obvious, in the language of admiration that he always used, that he very much esteemed this new version of Anne de Bourgh, who stood up to her mother and learned to dance, there was something glass-like about him, as if his warmth was real enough but contained behind a window. I could see it, but I could not feel it; I slid off of him like raindrops.

And, too, his attentions felt all wrong. They chafed like rough fabric, and there was a wriggling sensation, like earthworms in my palms, when he took my hand this evening to lead me through the dance. And I could not account for it, for he was, as ever, everything solicitous and complimentary; so very different to my cousin Darcy's lifelong indifference to me.

Everything about him ought to be appealing. He had pale hair and summer-blue eyes, smooth cheeks and full lips. His manners were exquisite, his mind sharp. He pressed my hand, adjusted my chair nearer the fire. He escorted me everywhere. But I was unmoved by all these things; I could not get past his glass veneer, and was not sure whether I even wanted to. If I did, and I liked what I found there, should I encourage his courtship? For that was surely what it was, subtly and carefully though he was going about it. That was what people did, was it not? I'd been spared the pressure of standing at auction, both by my illness and by the assumption that Fitzwilliam and I would someday come together, but now . . .

Tension crept upward from my shoulder blades, crawling across my shoulders, climbing my neck to nudge, bruisingly, at the back of my skull. I had a duty to the estate, to care for it, and ensure its continued health after I was gone. But I had not even written to Mr. Colt yet, and Mamma, as far as I knew, was still taking charge of everything. Inside my head, I saw my motherless newborn cousin again, and Miss Hall whispered, *Even Lady Catherine cannot live forever.*

All these things clamored and crashed inside of me, and I lay down flat upon the mattress and clenched the pillow in both my fists. "What should I do?" I said aloud; but this time there was no answer.

CHAPTER TWENTY-TWO

"Mrs. Darcy has been safely delivered of another son," John said, coming into the breakfast room on the morning of Lady Clive's ball.

Mrs. Fitzwilliam fixed a smile in place. "How wonderful. Have they chosen a name?"

John glanced down at the missive he held. "George," he said. "After my uncle Darcy."

"I shall send them a note for today," Mrs. Fitzwilliam said after a moment. "And of course we will call as soon as Mrs. Darcy is accepting visitors."

John rested his eyes upon her with such weight it looked like a caress; and then Mrs. Fitzwilliam swallowed and looked away.

THE BOOK ROOM DOOR sat partly ajar, and I had already raised my hand to tap on it when I was checked by a strange noise coming from within; a gasping, choking noise that could be distress or smothered laughter. I did not think at all, just peered around the edge of the door; and then the sight before me was so startling that I did not remember to look away.

Mrs. Fitzwilliam stood before John, her face pressed

to his shoulder. He cupped her head as gingerly as if she were made of eggshells. The sounds I heard were her sobs, raw as weals but muffled by the blue wool of his coat front.

"Hush now," he murmured, searching with his free hand in his pocket. He drew out a handkerchief and held it up to her; she took it, drew back from him a little, and buried her face in it, scrubbing like a child.

"Forgive me," she said after a moment. "I should not begrudge them their happiness. It is only . . ."

"I know," John said.

Almost, I betrayed my presence with a sound, but I swallowed it before it emerged. I curled my fingers around the edge of the doorframe, bracing myself against understanding that did not quite come.

But now she tilted her face up to his. "We have not tried in far too long," she said, very softly. "There can be no reward without endeavor."

I could not see her expression, but I could see John's, the lines of his face blurred and softened. When he cupped her head again, it was with purpose.

I stepped away, my heartbeat so thunderous to my own ears that I feared they must hear it as well.

WHEN MY NEW GOWN was delivered from the modiste's shop the day before the ball, Spinner touched the fabric with the greatest care imaginable.

"This color suits you, ma'am! And it will be lovely with your amethysts," she said. "And perhaps the silver bandeau for your hair?" Then she took the gown away to press it, before I could say that I'd had exactly the same thought about my jewelry the moment Miss Amherst showed me the pale muslin with its print of deep purple flowers.

Now, as Spinner helped me into the gown, smoothing the skirt so it hung properly, I stared at myself in the glass—raised my hands to the gown's wide, low neckline, brushing over the miles of exposed skin.

Despite the thrumming changes I'd lately experienced, it was still my face in the glass; my face, but subtly altered, so that I actually looked a little more like my own portrait in Rosings's drawing room. I would never be tall like Mamma or robustly sturdy like Mrs. Darcy; but the shadows were gone from my cheeks, and with my cheeks' new fullness, my dipping Fitzwilliam nose no longer seemed quite so overwhelming.

"Do I look . . . changed to you?" I said to Spinner, avoiding her eyes in the glass.

She paused, pins in one hand, long locks of my hair in the other, and she did not answer for so long that I began to feel ridiculous, as if the faint alchemy I'd felt working upon my form and features were entirely imagined.

Then Spinner raised her brows and the corners of her mouth all at once. "As changed as if a fairy came to rescue you, ma'am," she said, and I smiled.

A moment later, she added, "Mr. Watters will be pleased to see you in such fine looks," and my smile dropped away.

I COULD SCARCELY LOOK at my cousin and his wife when we gathered in the entranceway to await our carriage. My embarrassment at having witnessed such unexpected intimacy between them persisted in the hours since I had spied on them in the book room. Watching from the edges of my vision as John helped Mrs. Fitzwilliam into her wrap, all I could see was two pairs of touching lips, two pairs of desperately grasping hands, two bodies bending toward one another like saplings in a high wind.

The carriage ride itself was short. Mr. Watters, seated beside me, complimented my gown, but I scarcely heard him, my heart tapping against my breastbone as frantically and arrhythmically as a woodpecker on a tree. "The Amhersts are going to be here?" I said to Mrs. Fitzwilliam, and she blinked.

"They said so," she said, and then raised one brow, as narrow and golden as her brother's. "*You* would know better than I, Miss de Bourgh, surely—you have been so much in Eliza's company of late."

I lowered my eyes, grateful when, a few moments later, the coachman guided the horses to a stop outside a handsome town house. Lady Clive was another of Mrs. Fitzwilliam's acquaintances from school, a wealthy young woman who married an even wealthier old man. Their house rose taller than John's, and extended farther back, and as we handed our wraps to a footman and followed the flow of guests toward the ballroom, I had to stop myself from fidgeting with my long gloves. At the swell of music coming through the ballroom's double doors, my stays felt suddenly uncomfortable, and the toes of my slippers seemed to pinch.

The ballroom was smaller than ours at Rosings Park, which put me a little at ease. Our host and hostess greeted us as we passed through; Lady Clive grasped Mrs. Fitzwilliam's hands in her own, and they bared their teeth at one another, and it was nothing like watching my cousin's wife with the Amherst ladies; this was more like two peacocks exhibiting their plumage before a peahen, but in this case the peacocks were socially conscious young women, the peahen all the rest of society. It was with relief that I saw John take his wife's elbow, his eyes merry, and steer her away from the receiving line.

The room was already crowded and hot, yet still more people came through the doors. I had thought a private ball would be less intimidatingly bursting with guests than a public one, but it seemed Lady Clive had many acquaintances who simply could not be excluded. I was too short to see over the heads of the taller guests, all of whom seemed to know one another already, crying out glad greetings. John and Mrs. Fitzwilliam were swallowed up by the crowd like fish down the gullet of a great seabird, and Mr. Watters was waylaid by another gentleman; though I was happy enough to be free of him for a moment, I almost wished for his arm to lean on, his laughing guidance. I stood on my toes, seeking one particular face in the throng.

But I could not find her. Disappointment made my eyes sting; I was a fool. I looked down at my fine new gown, which was entirely of Miss Amherst's design, from the fabric to the sleeves, and brushed my hands over the skirt, and upward to where my necklace—a glimmering circlet of purple stones—lay against my collarbones. My body burned; I'd wanted her to see it. To see *me*, in all my imagined splendor. To see her handiwork.

It was a simple gown, as far as evening dresses went; but, as Miss Amherst regretfully said as we made our way down a crowded pavement to the draper's, there would not be time to order anything elaborate before the ball. She was entirely at home among the bolts of cloth when we entered the shop, and was not shy about asking to see this bolt or that one. She showed me the sheen on a striped pink silk, and then held this printed muslin up to my cheek, that I might feel its softness and she might see how well it suited my complexion.

"I like the ivory against your skin," she said, "and the purple print makes your hair and eyes all the more wondrously dark. *And,*" with an earnest look, "it is fine enough as it is to do without embroidery or netting, so the seamstresses should just about be able to finish the gown in time." She raised her eyebrows in question, as if I might have some objection to her choice.

"I yield to your superior knowledge," I said, and she clapped her hands.

"Mind you, if you intend to remain in London very long, I would like to see you in a truly magnificent evening gown. I saw just the thing in Ackermann's." And she was off, choosing fabrics for not only a future evening gown but also a new morning gown, two walking gowns, and a pelisse in green that made me think of moss and cool, shaded places.

I thought of her hands, nudging me forward, encouraging me to make my own tastes known to the modiste. Her head, bent to mine, smiling in gentle amusement when my tongue stumbled. The brush of her fingers against the insides of my arms.

I shook my head, stepping back out of the way of the guests still coming into the ballroom. The dancing had already begun, couples lining up for the first set, the opening notes rushing out over the crowd. I pressed my back to the wall and caught glimpses between the people standing in front of me.

"There you are," said a voice beside me, and I looked up to find Mr. Watters standing, hand extended. "I am terribly sorry, my friend Rogers caught hold of me and I quite lost sight of you. Do you forgive me?"

"There is nothing to forgive," I said unthinkingly.

"Then will you honor me with this dance?" And when I stared at him, frozen, he wheedled, "You know these steps—it is but a simple country dance." A smile, and he leaned closer, lips almost brushing my ear. "I would do nothing to embarrass you."

My hand was in his without my quite understanding how it happened, and we were taking our place at the bottom of the set, which was long enough that the dance had not yet moved along its entire length. As if I had succumbed to the desire for oblivion and taken a dose of medicine, everything felt suddenly very removed; I heard the music only faintly over the rushing of my own blood and the rasp of my breath, and stared down the set, watching like one doomed as the dance moved inexorably nearer. The elaborate chalk arabesques that covered the dance floor were already disturbed, smudged and smeared by so many pairs of feet. Distantly, I saw John dancing with a woman to whom I was introduced at a card party some weeks ago, and a little nearer the top of the set Mrs. Fitzwilliam was partnered with a rather dashing young man. I watched the steps of the dance and heard Miss Amherst's voice in my ear, low and patient, counting them off.

Still, I was caught off guard when my turn came, and was a beat off from the music when I recalled myself and stepped forward, my feet self-conscious in their execution of the steps. But I took Mr. Watters's gloved hands firmly when he reached for me.

"THANK YOU," MR. WATTERS SAID. He took my hand again in his to lead me from the floor. "You honored me. And you acquitted yourself well! One would hardly have known it was your first time dancing in company."

I shook my head, shifting out of the way of other couples as they moved past us. "You flatter me. I still have much to learn."

"There is no better place than at a ball among friends."

These were not my friends, not even the ladies and gentlemen whom I had previously met. I felt their curious glances like thorn pricks, and the heat suffusing my body had little to do with the crowded room. I shook my head again, glancing around us. A number of young ladies eyed Mr. Watters, his calves in their white stockings, the fine cut of his coat, the curl of his hair; but Mr. Watters appeared entirely unaware that he was the object of so much female attention.

He licked his lips. "Miss de Bourgh," he began, but John interrupted him, appearing beside us flushed and grinning.

"Anne!" he said. "I never thought to see you out there." He smiled between myself and Mr. Watters, radiating good cheer. "I am . . . I hope you will forgive the implied condescension, but I am just very . . . glad for you." He bounced a little in place. "I don't suppose you would honor me with a dance?"

"Oh—no," I said. "I am sorry but—one dance was enough for me this evening."

John looked as if he might protest, but finally nodded. "Very well."

"Miss de Bourgh," Mr. Watters said again when John had gone; but this time his tone was less serious than before. "May I fetch you some refreshment?"

I did not particularly want any refreshment, but I did want a moment to myself, and so I nodded and thanked him and watched gratefully as he disappeared, then opened my fan and attempted to cool my heated face, looking around at the milling, chattering crowd. On the dance floor the next set had begun, and I watched it disinterestedly until a flash of orange hair caught my attention.

It was Miss Julia Amherst. She danced as well as her sister, smiling and carrying on a conversation with her partner with apparent effortlessness. The hand moving my fan dropped to my side, and I stretched my neck to see the rest of the dance floor, searching for another glimpse of orange. A moment later, I was rewarded: Miss Amherst stood near the top of the set, laughing with her partner. At the sight of her, something inside of me squeezed.

I was looking so intently that perhaps she felt my gaze, for her own eyes darted suddenly toward me, starling-quick; when she saw me, her mouth twitched up briefly before she returned her attention to her partner and the dance. But even as Mr. Watters returned, bearing two cups of ratafia, and remained beside me, making occasional comments and observations about the dance and the general company, my eyes strayed to Miss Amherst. The drink was sweet and fruity, coating my teeth and tongue.

"I greatly enjoyed my visit to Rosings Park when my sister and your cousin became engaged," Mr. Watters said. He stood very close to me, the better to be heard above the music and drone of other voices. I smiled vaguely and took another sip from my glass. When Mr. Watters and his sister came to Rosings, neither one paid me more than passing attention.

"I only wish I had the opportunity to see more of your lovely estate," he said. "Lady Catherine said you have more than twelve thousand acres?"

His voice rose at the end of this, as if he were asking a question; and to my relief, I knew the answer. "Yes," I said. "Just a little more."

A flash of white teeth. "How marvelous. And you've a steward to oversee it all, I think?"

"Yes," I said again. Miss Amherst and her partner, a

short, balding gentleman who was surprisingly light on his feet, performed a graceful allemande; and then she turned her head ever so slightly, meeting my eyes over her shoulder for an instant.

"But you've no house in Town?" Mr. Watters said, and when I looked at him, a little startled, he added, "I was surprised that you had no house of your own to which to come when you arrived. Not," he said hastily, with a disarming smile, "that your presence at your cousin's has been anything but a pleasure. I just assumed that your father would have kept a place here."

"He stayed at his club, I think," I said.

"How very odd."

I gave another vapid smile and took another sip from my drink, and listened to the last notes of the song as they lingered around us like perfume. Miss Amherst and her partner bowed, and he led her off the floor. She said something, nodding in our direction, and he bowed over her hand before releasing her. And then she wound her way through the crush, edging between people, stopping to greet one or two on her way.

"Miss de Bourgh, Mr. Watters," she said when she reached us.

"Miss Amherst," he said. "A pleasure."

She nodded, smiled, looked back and forth between us. "Are you enjoying yourselves?" she said at last.

"Very much indeed," Mr. Watters said. Another pause, lengthier, and I wondered whether Miss Amherst felt as awkward as I did; whether Mr. Watters was aware of how very much I wished he would go elsewhere.

"I was just asking Miss de Bourgh about her estate," he said.

"Oh?" Miss Amherst folded her hands before her, all polite interest.

"Yes. I hope to visit there again someday; it is a beautiful place."

"I am sure it is. Though I am so accustomed to the city; I must confess wilderness and farm life hold little allure. The squirrels in Hyde Park are beasts enough for me."

Her words hit me like stones.

"I had hoped," he said after another pause, "to convince your friend to stand up with me again."

"You danced?" Miss Amherst turned to me, and now she was all delight. "Oh, I wish we had not been late. Julia"—a roll of her eyes—"lost one of her gloves, and refused to borrow any of mine."

"Yes, I danced," I said. I angled my body a little more toward her, though not enough to shut Mr. Watters entirely out of the conversation. "But as I told Mr. Watters, I have exposed myself quite enough for tonight, I think."

"But we've still the whole evening ahead of us!" Miss Amherst said. The drawing of bows across strings signaled the start of the next set. "Oh," she said, and looked around. "Ah—Julia is dancing again with Mr. King. Good; anyone observing can see how he singles her out, so it will not be gossip to say I expect him to offer for her very soon."

"Mr. King?" I saw Miss Julia in the row of dancers,

opposite the same young man with whom she was part-nered in the previous set. "This is sudden! How did they meet?"

"Oh, I've so much to tell you. So it is just as well that you are not dancing and that no one has asked me for this one!" She smiled into my face, and I smiled foolishly back.

Mr. Watters coughed a little. "Far be it from me to intrude upon ladies' confidences," he said, with a self-deprecating smile that almost made me warm to him. "But Miss de Bourgh, I would be remiss if I did not re-quest the privilege of escorting you in to supper."

"Thank you," I said, and he bowed and left us.

Miss Amherst watched him go, then turned to me. "He pays you a great deal of attention," she said.

"Yes," I said, quietly; to speak more strongly felt akin to inviting that attention to become something more formal.

She watched me. "He is very handsome," she said; and she, too, was tentative as a child climbing too high a tree, testing each branch for fear it will not bear weight.

Mr. Watters's good looks were undeniable. "Yes," I said again, and then I took her arm and tugged gently; I did not want to speak of Mr. Watters just now. "But come—tell me your news!"

WE WERE TOGETHER UNTIL the supper dance, when a gentleman claimed Miss Amherst's hand for the set. She followed him to the dance floor, and I followed her

with my eyes. Her hair and her gown, which was yellow
as cowslips, were easy to keep in sight among the more
subdued brown and blond heads and paler fabrics of the
other ladies. Mrs. Fitzwilliam and Mr. Watters found
me and introduced me to several people, all of whom
were perfectly cordial and perfectly forgettable. And yet
they all seemed eager to meet *me*—mistress of Rosings
Park, in Kent, and an earl's niece. These facts about me
had not changed; but no one had ever seemed quite so
eager to make my acquaintance before, and suddenly I
was surrounded by ladies and gentlemen keen on knowing me better. The gentlemen asked me to dance, though
I stammeringly refused each invitation; the ladies introduced me to their brothers, or sons, or nephews. I looked
into their faces; smiled and nodded in what I hoped were
the proper places; and thought of the years I'd spent recumbent and dismissed. Miss Hall had said that I could
be so much more than I was then; it seemed that others
agreed with her.

When supper was announced, Mr. Watters led me
through and helped me to my chair. For the duration
of the meal he was solicitous and charming, drawing
out stories of my life before coming to London and, in
turn, amusing me with tales from his and Mrs. Fitzwilliam's childhoods. From time to time I saw John, seated
at another table, watching us; and Miss Amherst, seated
across from me and a few chairs down, smiled at me occasionally, though her dinner partner required most of
her attention. I ate a few bites of everything and reeled
between enjoying the feeling, as intoxicating as the wine

served with each course, that I was fully present and participating in this moment; and wishing I were seated beside my friend.

SHE FOUND ME LATER, when some of the guests had abandoned the ball for other amusements or succumbed to tiredness and gone home. There were still ten couples dancing in the set, however, and an air of general merriment. Mr. Watters was dancing with another lady, and I had retreated to a chair half-hidden by a large urn of hothouse flowers.

"You are hiding," Miss Amherst said. She sat on the empty chair beside mine and opened her fan.

I did not deny it. "It is all a little overwhelming for a reclusive country girl."

She did not laugh, as I intended her to, but gave me a chiding glance. "You are not so lacking in mettle as that."

"Mmm. Perhaps not. But my hosts are still dancing, and I am very tired."

She smiled lazily and tapped me on the wrist with her open fan. "Poor dear." Her eyes slid sideways, toward the dance. "You would not stand up with a friend, I suppose? No one else will have me." Though her tone was mild, I found myself sitting up straighter at the sound.

"With you?"

"It is not unheard of for ladies to stand up together," she said. "Though I suppose it is more usual when there are fewer gentlemen present."

"I cannot," I said. I felt slow and stupid, but I looked at the dancers and could think only how dancing with Miss Amherst would show an utter lack of propriety after having told not only Mr. Watters but three other gentlemen over the course of the evening that I was not dancing. Even I was conscious enough of social mores to know that a lady could not politely refuse to dance unless she meant to refuse *all* dances for the rest of the ball.

Miss Amherst seemed to follow my thoughts perfectly. "It is quite something, is it not," she said, apparently without bitterness, "how deeply concerned we are with men's tender feelings?"

My smile felt limp as the flowers in the urn before us, petals wilting in the warmth of the room.

"You look splendid," she said after a moment. She reached out and adjusted my necklace so the clasp sat properly at the nape of my neck. Then she drew back.

"Your gown is by far the more splendid," I said. Yellow, which made me so sallow, brought out the shine of her hair.

"Mmm. Thank you." Idly, she caught my hand, studying the scrolling embroidery that ran all down my gloves' length.

"You've such an eye," I said. "You should have been a modiste."

"Ah, no," she said. "I am far too idle for such a life. And modistes are too busy making other ladies' clothes to have the best gowns for themselves." Her lips compressed. "In truth," she said after a moment, "I love fashion. But—sometimes I cannot tell whether my desire to always look well is for myself, or . . . if it has always been expected of me. Of all of us, as females." She frowned down at my glove.

I cocked my head. "From the perspective of a—friend . . . it seems to give you genuine pleasure. Fabrics and bonnets and—and keeping up with fashions."

"Yes." Miss Amherst offered me a half-smile. "But it just—does it never bother you?" Her fingers clasped mine a little more tightly. "It seemed to bother you, earlier—I'm sorry if I misread things. But I saw you, surrounded by all those men, all of them wanting something." She shook her head, the curls at her neck dancing. "I suppose I am just—well, as I said before. It sometimes seems that men's tender feelings are always to be foremost in our minds. And that includes decorating ourselves for their enjoyment."

I thought of all the hours Mamma spent trying to keep me in looks for my cousin Darcy's approval, resentment, like spoiled milk, curdling in my belly. "Yes," I said.

Miss Amherst was silent a moment. Then she moved her thumb, just a fraction; yet it felt like a caress against my palm, sending a sudden rush right through the core of me. "I did not mean to distress you," she said, and turned her eyes upon my face for so long that I finally returned her look. "And I know how impractical my query was. I know that we cannot dance." A lifting of her shoulders and the corners of her mouth. "I only wished we might."

CHAPTER TWENTY-THREE

*M*y dear Mamma, I wrote. *I have danced at a ball.*

I lifted my pen, brushed it across my lips, smiled to imagine my mother's expression as she read my words. To imagine her face to see me now. During self-conscious moments, I was aware that I had not done anything particularly noteworthy. Coming to London, shopping, reading, attending a ball—these were the daily activities of countless ladies throughout the country—throughout the world. And yet, each time I stepped outside and surrounded myself in the clamorous rush of this mad city; each time I turned a page in a book and felt the words printed upon it leaving dimples upon my mind, some subtle as a sparrow's claw prints, others deep as a horse's tracks; each time *I* was addressed by a clerk in a shop, as if my opinion were of true consequence; I was swollen with wonder at the turn my life had taken. I thought of those people at the ball, all so interested in making my acquaintance, and a little of the resentment faded, leaving a touch of pride in its place.

But then, from no logical place, there sometimes came a great sucking feeling. It was not unlike the falling sensation I used to get with my drops; but whereas that was a gentle drifting into senselessness, this was a muddy mire that dragged at my limbs, at the hem of my gown, pulling me down, down, down. When it came over me, I was certain that I was the most useless and pathetic of women.

My back teeth clenched together; I felt the ghost of Miss Hall's fingers tapping at my jaw to release them. I waited a moment for the tension to ease and imagined my mother's face as she opened my letter, allowing myself a moment of happy fantasy—her lips tipped up, her face going soft as muslin when she read how well I have become. Then I put pen to paper once more.

You would be amazed, I think, and happy, too, to see how my health has improved. Unfathomable as it may seem, London agrees with me.

JOHN AND MRS. FITZWILLIAM WERE invited to a dinner party. I was included in the invitation, as was Mr. Watters, but at the last moment I told my cousin I did not wish to go.

"Are you sure?" he said, eyes pinched with concern. "Are you feeling well?"

"I am only a little tired after the ball."

"Of course," he said, relaxing. "Very well. Harriet can instruct Cook to make up a cold repast for your dinner."

I thanked him and waited, all impatience, for them to be off. Mrs. Fitzwilliam was a little cross, for their hostess would have a gap at her table, but Mr. Watters bent over my hand gallantly, brushing the back with his lips, and said he hoped I would be quite improved on the morrow. Then at last, with a final adjusting of wraps and gloves, they left. John helped his wife into the carriage, then climbed in beside her. Mr. Watters glanced back at the house to see me silhouetted at the window, and tipped his hat before climbing in as well. I wiped the back of my hand on a fold of my skirts, then turned gratefully back to the drawing room, which, for a few hours, was entirely mine.

I FINISHED ALL THREE volumes of *Waverley* more quickly than I thought possible. Never before had I read anything that entrapped my attention so completely; never before had I understood the compulsion others felt to spend their time reading. At night, unwilling to return to my own life when I could exist in the one I had found in the novel's pages, I burned precious candles for hours.

When Miss Amherst asked whether I had made progress with my reading, all I could say was, "When shall we return to the Temple?"

My skin rippled with pleasure when she laughed. "So eager!" she said. "Whenever you wish, of course, but you are more than welcome to borrow any volume from our library. My father is forever giving out his books; nothing delights him so much as sharing them." She tipped her head. "Does your cousin not have a library, as well? Or is his all dull works on . . . I don't know, animal husbandry and the like, now that he has his country estate to manage?"

I was embarrassed to say I hadn't the smallest idea what sorts of books John's shelves held. It felt odd to tap on the door and breach the masculine sanctuary of his book room, but when I asked whether there were any novels I could borrow, he gave me a mischievous smile.

"I am glad to see that you are determined to please yourself," he said, and stepped back, opening his arms in a gesture of welcome. "I'm afraid I am not a great reader, but I have a few; most of them are Harriet's, to be honest, but I know she would not mind you borrowing them. Take your pick."

I took my time looking over the shelves. I rarely paid much attention to the books in my father's collection; there was little point, when Mamma would forbid anything she thought would lead to too much vigorous mental activity. But I thought of the library at Rosings now, standing among my cousin's smaller selection, thought of the high shelves and narrow windows, the room all fine dark wood and soft chairs for sitting and reading. It seemed suddenly an absurd thing, that I had spent so little time there.

John's books were obviously not much touched, musty from having been shut up so long, a cloying sweetness emanating from some of their pages. There was little thought to organization, works of military history tucked between works of fiction and—I smiled a little to see them—a few volumes about farming. I finally selected a novel whose title seemed intriguing; John glanced at it and said, "Ah—*The Mysteries of Udolpho*. A touch sensational for my taste, but Harriet has read it at least twice. I hope you enjoy it as much."

I TUCKED MY SHAWL around myself and curled up comfortably as a cat on the settee, opening my book to the place I marked. There was an indulgent feeling in both the curling and the reading, a sense that I was, as John said, pleasing none but myself in these moments. Mrs. Radcliffe's novel, which I began yesterday, nearly as soon as I'd procured it, seized my imagination in a manacle grip and refused to release me. My eyes simply flew from word to word, from line to line across the page, almost faster than my mind could grasp each line's meaning, anxious to see what terrors awaited Emily in her uncle's cold castle.

I was nearly to the end when I closed the book; I wanted to enjoy the anticipation a little longer, and keep the end as a bit of a treat before bed. How thrilling to both long and dread to reach the end of something. Poor Mamma—her imagination so slender as to be nearly nonexistent. It was little wonder she scorned such books; she had no means to understand them.

Setting the volume aside, I reached for another. This one came to me by way of John's butler, who took my letter for Mamma and, like a magician, produced a parcel for me in turn. "From Miss Eliza Amherst, Miss de Bourgh," he said, and I took it eagerly. The seal on the accompanying note broke with a satisfyingly crisp sound.

It's rather radical, Miss Amherst wrote of the book, *and has not been in print for more than twenty years. But after our conversation last night, I find myself curious to know what you make of it.*

I opened the book now, turning the pages slowly. *A Vindication of the Rights of Woman,* by Mary Wollstonecraft. It was not a novel, but an intellectual work, and my mind did not reach toward the text as it had toward *Udolpho* but shied away from it with instinctive fear. Miss Amherst would want to discuss it once I finished, but that old, clutching sense of incapability tightened my skin. It was with the sense of batting away cobwebs that I managed to skim through the long dedication, to a gentleman of some importance whose name I had never heard, and begin on the introduction. And then my lips moved quickly, silently; I read sentences over again, felt my brows rise and my blood rush like a springtime stream, fed by snowmelt and eager to be on its way.

> My own sex, I hope, will excuse me, if I treat them
> like rational creatures, instead of flattering their
> *fascinating* graces, and viewing them as if they were
> in a state of perpetual childhood, unable to stand
> alone.

I was accustomed to reading sermons—I could still hear Miss Hall's voice, jarring over the sentences of Mr. Fordyce's *Sermons to Young Women* like a badly made carriage over a rutted road. But this—this was a sermon of a different sort.

Let woman share the rights and she will emulate the virtues of man.

The parish bell tolled four as I closed the book. I had retired to my room long ago, and at some point I heard the muffled sounds of my cousin and his party returning from their dinner, but even that was three hours ago or more. The candle at my bedside was burned down almost to a nub, my eyes smarted from squinting so long in the dwindling light, and yet there was a coiling within me, promising . . . something. Sleep was elusive.

I wanted to creep downstairs to John's book room and avail myself of all the knowledge to be found there; I wanted to rush out into the early morning, past the first rising merchants with their carts, past servants hauling water and emptying chamber pots, until I reached Miss Amherst's street. I smiled to think of throwing pebbles at her window until her face appeared, sleep-smudged and framed by her bright hair, just so I could speak to her a few hours sooner, hear her thoughts, and let my own cascade waterfall-like from my tongue. Foolish fancies; but my smile only widened when I imagined my friend leaning her head and shoulders out of the open window, the cold morning air brightening her cheeks, and giving one of her laughs at the sight of me, all refinement abandoned to the giddiness of feeling the muscle of my mind pumping at last.

Heady though the thought was, I knew it to be impossible. But though prudence dictated that I sleep, at least for a few hours, my mind was awake and alive, bursting with ideas as spring woodlands burst with life, and I simply could not rest. I remembered how Miss Hall struggled to interest me in improving my reading; had she been free to offer me a wider selection of material, I think she would have found that my head took to words as easily as it took to numbers.

There was a fresh candle on the mantelpiece; I lighted it with the last gasp of my bedside flame, and took up Mrs. Radcliffe's novel, turning it to catch the light, and indulged in its last few pages.

CHURCHGOING IN TOWN WAS, I found, almost exactly like churchgoing in Hunsford. The only real differences were that many more of the parishioners at John's church were smartly dressed, clearly there to be seen as much as for spiritual enlightenment; and that the building itself was so much more stunning in its proportions than our little village church. In John's church, all is tall graceful lines, pillars curving to meet and form arches, the ceiling soaring above the congregation if in reminder of what awaits us in heaven. Looking up at it, all that stone held aloft as if by magic, I wished I could conjure just some little fraction of the sublime feeling the architecture—and the sermon, and the choir in its high gallery—was meant to inspire.

In Hunsford, I was wedged between Mamma, who bellowed out the words of the Psalms as if she were commanding a servant, and Mrs. Jenkinson, whose voice was thin and high as air blown through a reed. When I was younger and Miss Hall sat beside me, I used to watch her slantwise; my governess listened to the sermon with her whole body, every muscle and nerve focused on the rector in his pulpit, and I sometimes had the wish—vivid and unholy enough to make my face blotch with embarrassment and my eyes wrench themselves back to the trough in the floor—that she would turn just a portion of that devotion my way.

Sometimes, after Papa's death, when Miss Hall was already more companion than governess, she tried to draw me outside myself, to reassure me that my father must be truly happy now, in union as he was with God. But I wondered how happy he could possibly be. Like myself, he was a regular attendant at church, but he never displayed anything like religious feeling outside its confines. Or, really, within its confines, either.

Today, I sat in the pew beside Mrs. Fitzwilliam and remembered Papa, how his eyelids drooped sometimes in church, the breadth of his hand not quite hiding his yawn. He never actually fell asleep, as far as I knew—even if he had, the clerk, acting in his capacity as sluggard waker, mightn't have dared rap Sir Lewis on the head with his stick as he would any other drowsing congregant. But his mind, like my own just now, always seemed to be on other things. If—and oh, that *if* is a perilous word, a whisper of blasphemy—if heaven was what the preachers claimed, mustn't Papa be very bored there?

Our pew had low sides and a little door that latched with a *snick,* as if to remind us that we must corral our thoughts and bodies both. But my thoughts—blasphemous whispers, all—darted and dashed. I thought of Mr. Fordyce's ridiculous sermons, which no one else seemed to find ridiculous at all. I thought of Miss Hall's arm brushing mine as she turned the pages of her prayer book. I wondered why the words in that prayer book spoke to her so eloquently, while for me they always remained hollow as trees about to fall.

I thought the reason might have had to do with my slowness. *Poor dear Anne. She cannot be expected to exert herself.* There was safety in being treated like a child; I was not expected to do much, or understand much, and so I did not. And yet, I could still recall, most vividly, the first time I read *The Seasons* and was left with the quivering sense that there was so much *more* to the world than I had been told. There was feeling in those stanzas; Miss Hall described the poet as being a godly man, and I could hear holiness in his descriptions of nature, in the thrill of the connection I felt to his creatures. My mind was capable, I saw for the first time, of something like real understanding.

And now—now I had felt that thrill again and again and again; but not here, not in the hallowed halls of this lovely church, but in theaters and concert halls and the pages of books. My mind was never still anymore, never quiet; it was as if it had been held in check for twenty-nine years and now, given free rein to exercise itself, could not stop its rushing movement for fear it might again find itself dulled and coddled, all independent thought quelled.

But I had no wish to quell it. I thought again of all the times that someone—Mamma or Mrs. Jenkinson; any one of my aunts or uncles; Dr. Grant and various visitors to Rosings Park, all so solicitous of my health—murmured what a shame it was that I *could not*. Inside my head, I stamped on their *could nots*; my slippered foot squashed their words, ground them into so much dust on the church's stone floor. Each time I rose to greet a caller, each time I conversed with someone in spite of the nervous vibration behind my breastbone and all the voices in my head that strove to remind me that a doll has as much of interest to say as I do, each time I opened a book and my mind hummed to the cadence of its printed words, I was doing more than I ever thought I could.

I tilted my head back so that I could look up at the ceiling without any obstruction from my bonnet's curving brim, and as the vicar spoke on I listened instead to the thumping of my own heart and saw not an impenetrable heaven made of stone, but everything that lay beyond it.

CHAPTER TWENTY-FOUR

Mrs. Fitzwilliam insisted we must purchase a present for the newest member of the Darcy family. "We can choose it together," she said. "But it must be today; I expect we will have word that Mrs. Darcy is ready to receive family before the week is out."

"Miss Amherst said she would call this afternoon," I said.

Mrs. Fitzwilliam clucked her tongue. "We can send her a note. She may join us, if she wishes. Julia, too, if she is at home. I want to hear more about her Mr. King, in any case." She did not really look at me, instead smoothing and resmoothing her fine embroidered shawl over her arms.

AND SO I FOUND myself trailing after my cousin's wife as she entered shop after shop, fingering the wares and, again and again, declaring none of them suitable. She was a woman seized by some undeniable urge, and though her face remained tucked away behind her useful courteous mask, there was something frantic about her eyes as we exited our third warehouse, still with nothing for little George.

Miss Julia seemed as interested in the hunt as

Mrs. Fitzwilliam, but Miss Amherst and I dragged a little behind. We had seen infant caps trimmed with flowers in colored silk thread; infant gowns decorated in exquisite holly point lace. We felt blankets impossibly soft and warm, and we tested the high tinkling bells inside silver rattles. I was beginning to think we were on a quest for something that did not exist.

"Harriet lured us out with a promise of sweets," Miss Amherst said in an undertone, watching as Mrs. Fitzwilliam examined a pair of miniature shoes. "But I doubt we shall have time to stop at Gunter's at this slow pace."

I stepped a little closer to her under the pretext of inspecting a blanket of wool spun so fine it felt like cobwebs. "And here," I said, "I thought it was the promise of *my* company that lured you out." But the words did not sound as playful once spoken as they did inside my head; I had the unnerving feeling that I just unwittingly made my first attempt at flirtation, and that the attempt was a poor one.

I thought of Miss Hall, and the thought stopped my heart for an instant. But Miss Amherst merely looked sideways at me and smiled, and I stumbled into a display of sweet lace caps. The excuse of righting myself and catching a cap that tumbled toward the floor gave me a moment to collect my likewise tumbling thoughts. It was entirely possible that Miss Amherst did not hear anything awkward in my words; or perhaps she was better at politely not noticing than I thought she was. I took more time than necessary setting the cap back in its place.

There was a little patch of damp on the back of my chemise after the ball. I felt it—an odd tensing of my lower belly at the circling of Miss Amherst's thumb, and then a rushing forth of *something*, secret as tree sap, but slick as water over river rocks. It was still there when Spinner undressed me, though I did not think she noticed. After she left me to sleep, I reached down and discovered that same disconcerting slickness between my legs.

In the days since, I thought about it often—how so innocuous a touch could cause so torrential a reaction from my body. And I had been so much more aware, each time Mr. Watters caught my elbow to help me to the carriage, or kissed my hand when I retired for the night, that my body had quite the opposite response that it had to Miss Amherst's handclasp. It shrunk into itself; not visibly, or so I hoped, but *I* could feel it, my muscles going tense instead of soft, my skin almost contracting, if skin can be said to do such a thing.

The vague stirrings I occasionally felt in the past had been strange things, made stranger, perhaps, by my drops. Was it normal, I wondered now, to see another person and feel pulled to touch the tender underside of her wrist? To be moved by clever fingers as they flew over ivory keys? To think of those same fingers doing other things—things my lack of experience ensured I could not entirely imagine, blurred pictures in my mind that elicited cascading physical reactions despite their formlessness.

Whenever I set foot in some public space here in Town, my eyes still swept over the throngs of people, searching for a familiar turn of head or slope of shoulder. I wished this odd impulse would pass, but it never did. But how familiar would Miss Hall even be to me now, after the passing of nearly ten years? How might her face have changed, her figure, the color of her hair? She might be married; she might have a pack of small children. That was the benefit of time and distance, I supposed; that she would always be young in my mind, all the rough edges of our time together smoothed over so that what I recalled most vividly was the quiet rush of pleasure her attention afforded me, and not the painful awkwardness of our parting.

MRS. FITZWILLIAM SETTLED AT LAST on a silver rattle, cunningly shaped like a horn with small bells attached. It was perfectly sized and contoured for tiny fingers, but she looked on with an expression of dissatisfaction as the clerk wrapped it.

But then she turned to the rest of us and said brightly enough, "Shall we take some refreshment?"

Gunter's tea shop was crowded with groups of ladies and with couples leaning toward one another across its little tables. We were fortunate to find a place to sit, and put in an order for tea and cake. Mrs. Fitzwilliam immediately set herself to the task of interrogating Miss Julia about Mr. King, and Miss Julia was only too happy to talk about how often he called on her and what they spoke of and how handsome he was.

I glanced at Miss Amherst, to find her gazing at her sister with an empty expression, as if she had already heard all this many times. Then she looked at me and life returned to her eyes.

"I am very happy for your cousin," she said. "A sweet little boy. You must tell me all about him when you meet him."

"Of course," I said, and she drew back a little, looking me over, a peculiar half-smile lifting one side of her mouth.

"Do you not care for children?" she said.

"I—"

"I don't," she said, and took a bite of orange cake. She chewed for a moment, patted her lips with exaggerated delicacy, and said, "I have shocked you."

"Well." I looked at our companions, but they were reminiscing about Mrs. Fitzwilliam's wedding cake, which was, it seems, created at this very establishment.

"I mean." Miss Amherst leaned toward me, in unselfconscious mimicry of the courting couples surrounding us. "I have nothing against children. In theory, they are darling creatures. But I have no idea what to do with them. Julia"—with a glance at her sister—"is eager to have a large family; I suppose when I am an aunt I shall have to learn to converse with her offspring."

"You do not want children of your own?"

"Have I any choice in the matter?" she said. "If I marry, it is a natural assumption that children will follow. I hope I shall understand my own better than I do other people's."

I paused. "What do you think Mary Wollstonecraft would have to say on the subject?"

She leaned forward. "You read it?"

"I did."

"And?"

"I am very ashamed."

"Oh, no," she said, and reached out, though her fingers stopped a hand's breadth from my own. "That was never my intention in lending it out! Why should you feel so?"

I looked down at the space between our hands. "I am—I have been—one of those women of whom she speaks so . . . so eloquently."

She tilted her head like an inquisitive bird. "You mean . . . devoted to appearance, above all else? Thinking of nothing but . . . pleasing men?"

"*No,*" I said, and then, less vehemently, "No. But . . . I have been made small—have *allowed* myself to be made small—for the entirety of my life."

And if my own circumstances were perhaps a little out of the ordinary, I had not seen very much to make me think that Mary Wollstonecraft was mistaken in her opinion that my sex in general had been held firmly back from the fullness of our potential through a lack of education and an insistence on focusing our energies on the most frivolous of pursuits. But though these thoughts were clear and definite inside my head, I feared they would spill from my mouth in an incoherent patter, like pebbles from the pockets of a child. To the child, each pebble was lovely and valuable as an emerald; to the grown persons to whom she showed them, they were merely rocks.

Miss Amherst said, "I believe Mary Wollstonecraft had children; though I suppose that is not proof of whatever feelings she might have had on the subject."

"I do not know whether I like children," I said. "I've little experience of them. Mr. and Mrs. Darcy brought their firstborn to visit us once in Kent, but he remained with his nurse most of the time."

She looked down at her cake, but made no move to take another bite. Then she looked back at me. "Forgive me for my impertinence," she said, lowering her voice, "but Harriet once mentioned that *you* were expected to marry Mr. Darcy."

I felt myself flush, and glanced at Mrs. Fitzwilliam. I wondered what else she had told her friends about her husband's odd, sickly cousin. "It is true," I said. "Or my mother thought it was, which made it an irrefutable truth in my mind. I do not know that Mr. Darcy ever saw it so, though, even before he met Mrs. Darcy."

"Your mother sounds formidable."

"Oh, she is," I said. "Though not formidable enough to make my cousin marry me. Which was a hard blow for her; she is unaccustomed to having less than perfect control."

"Ah." We both ate some cake, so sweet it filmed my tongue and teeth. Then Miss Amherst said, "*My* mother hopes your friendship will prove advantageous to my prospects." Her smile was wry. "She says she rather wishes I were in the company of a young man as often as I am in your company; but that a wealthy young woman who is niece to an earl must be the next best thing."

There was a strange fullness in my throat, which I had to swallow down before I could speak. "I fear I do not know many young men, eligible or no," I said. "But if my company widens your prospects, then I am . . . happy to offer it, even more often."

"I shall hold you to that," she said, and speared her last bite of cake.

SHE CALLED THE NEXT day, with the excuse that she thought we could improve my dancing.

"If you choose to attend more balls this season, you should be comfortable dancing more than a single set," she said.

I was reading when she arrived, and Miss Amherst grinned when she saw the volume of poetry in my hands, then asked whether I had been practicing my steps.

I followed Miss Amherst's nimble feet. Occasionally she paused to correct my posture or to remind me to smile. ("For no man," she intoned, mimicking her own dancing master's deep voice, "wants a partner who shows her true feelings if they are anything less than happiness.") We pretended there were other couples forming the set, laughing as we held out our hands to invisible dancers to either side of us. Miss Amherst led me down the center of the imaginary lines, holding my hand aloft in a courtly gesture.

At last, however, we stopped, breathless, and rang for tea, settling into chairs near the window.

"I quite like your new gown," she said. "The lace on

those sleeves! It's perfection. But next time, you must make some choices yourself. What happens if you need a new gown and I am not there to direct you?"

"I would not know where to begin," I said.

"Oh?" Miss Amherst smiled. "Who on earth chose your gowns before you came to London?"

"My mother," I said; and even to my own ears, my voice was stone-hard. "I had no say in the matter."

Her cheeks puffed. "Whyever not?"

I turned to the window. Without my noticing, it had begun raining at some point as we danced, and the street ran now with water. A carriage made great splashes as it passed. "I was ill," I said. "I was not . . . expected to make decisions for myself."

"But you are better now," she said.

"Yes." I thought of the sucking feeling, but it seemed far away. "I am better now."

She watched me as attentively as Mr. Watters sometimes did; but her gaze felt less like a pressing weight than a hand stroking just lightly over my brow. I returned my own eyes to the window. And I did not mean to speak, but somehow, suddenly, I was anyway, my words faltering and unsure but unstoppable as the falling rain. I described for her the haze in which I existed for all of my life until just recently; how the clear mornings gave way to the tender fog of afternoon and early evening. The terrible clutching in my lungs when I did something too strenuous, my breath disappearing.

"Only one person ever intimated that my troubles might be the result of Dr. Grant's cure rather than some natural weakness." I kept my eyes focused outside the window, my neck stiff as stays, unwilling to turn and know what Miss Amherst's expression might be.

"My father tried to help me, but he . . . I know he cared, he took me to Brighton to bathe in the sea . . . but he was overcome by Mamma's . . . by Mamma's . . ." But I could not think of the right word, something inside of me turned hot and seething—boiling. I clenched my fingers into fists tight enough that my bones ached all the way down to my wrists, and my nails cut half-moons into the flesh of my palms.

"I do not know why my mother preferred me"—I searched for the word, and remembered Miss Hall's voice, the bite to it, the anger—"*stupefied.*"

Miss Amherst was very quiet. Her eyes dropped to my hands; her own hands reached, darting like humming-birds before she aborted the movement and pulled them back. I wondered whether she meant to take my hands in hers, uncurl my fingers, knot her fingers with mine in a gesture of sympathy. The thought made me swallow.

"I cannot speak to your mother's feelings with any . . . true understanding," she said slowly. "But what you said about how unsettled you were as an infant—I can imagine that would be frightening to a new mother, to think her child was in distress and to be unable to help her. And if a doctor offered relief—well, it would seem a prayer answered, would it not? And you have spoken of her as someone who feels best when she is in control of all the particulars of her life. If she believed she could not control your illness except by means of laudanum—"

I shook my head, violently enough that she startled back. My hands came up to cover my face.

After a pause, Miss Amherst said, "I apologize. I have never met your mother. I've no idea what she might have been thinking."

I did not answer, and we sat silently for a moment. I breathed openmouthed into my palms; I could feel my breath, warm and moist, and smell it, faintly sour with fear. The only sound in the room was the rain on the windows, an infernal, endless drumming that put me in mind of Mamma's fingers on the arm of her chair when she was irritated.

My eyes opened, lashes fluttering like moth wings against my hands. Through the narrow gaps between my fingers, I could see Miss Amherst sitting still, her elbow propped on the back of her chair and her chin settled on her fist. I waited, but to my surprise she did not say anything about leaving.

"I used to see things," I said into my palms; and found that it was surprisingly easy to say with my face mostly hidden.

Miss Amherst turned her head away from the window to look at me. There was no wariness in her voice when she said, "What sorts of things?"

"People, mostly. They came to me at night, sometimes. Once or twice my father, after he died; he wore a lady's turban." She smiled a little at this, her teeth showing white. "There was a woman who sometimes stroked my hair."

She shifted closer to me, close enough that I could make out the faintly floral scent she wore on her skin. "Do you miss them?" she asked, very softly.

My response sounded like nothing so much as an exhaled breath. "Sometimes."

Very slowly, Miss Amherst raised her hand. Her fingers touched my hair, the top smooth and pinned close to my scalp. They trailed toward the back of my head, just firmly enough that I closed my eyes unintentionally in pleasure, my own hands hanging forgotten before my face. Then her fingers lifted, just for a moment, before coming to rest on the curls at my temple. She touched them with the greatest of care.

We both startled at the sound of the front door banging open. Miss Amherst jumped in her chair, her hand falling away from my hair, and my own hands dropped as I twisted in my seat to look over my shoulder at the doorway. Mrs. Fitzwilliam's voice, high and agitated, echoed eerily off the entranceway's ceiling, her every movement overly loud as a servant hurried to take her outer garments and exclaimed over the state of her umbrella.

She entered the drawing room, calling over her shoulder for tea. The hem of her gown was shockingly wet, and her hair, always so carefully arranged, straggled against the nape of her neck, as if the rain were blowing sideways under her umbrella's wide awning. Her face was very pale, and she came into the room without seeing Miss Amherst or myself, patting at her hair, her neck, her sides in a distracted manner. It was Miss Amherst who stood, and I who belatedly followed; Mrs. Fitzwilliam's entire body jerked as we moved, and she let out a yelp.

"Good gracious," she said. "Whatever are you doing here in the dark? Why are the candles not lit?"

CHAPTER TWENTY-FIVE

I had been sitting in the courtyard garden for nearly an hour, missing Rosings with a deep-down longing that felt almost animal in its intensity: the particular creaking of the tree branches in the wind, and the calling birds, and the lazy sound of the working bees. I ached to see the broad sweep of the sky overhead. Here it was all penned in by tall houses on every side; in the country it could stretch itself out to its full length, and one imagined it sighing with relief. Not even the parks here were anything like Rosings's grounds, however carefully cultivated the garden beds. There was little chance to sit and enjoy even the likeness of the outdoors; it was all forward momentum and smiling and bowing. I could not hear the plants whisper there; though, without my drops' magical assistance, perhaps I would never hear such a thing again. It was a melancholy thought.

John's garden was nothing—nothing—like the gardens at home; there was little enough space for anything beyond a rectangular pavement with bench and table. The high stone walls bore espaliered fruit trees, and the middle of the courtyard was given over to prettyish topiaries. The sky was still hampered by the neighboring roofs, and the natural clouds were still almost indistinguishable from the smoke belching from the chimneys, but I was alone except for myriad small scuttling creatures, and if I strained I could almost—almost—imagine that there were voices among the hedges. A spider, hard at work on a most marvelous web in a tucked-away corner, was probably humming to itself as it wove.

The door to the house opened; I stared for a second longer at the spider, long-legged and graceful, the threads coming together in pleasing acute angles. Then I turned my head to see who was there, and a smile broke out across my face.

Miss Amherst came forward, smiling, and for a moment of exhilarating confusion I thought she was going to embrace me. But no; she sat down beside me, hands tucked into her lap, and said, "I hope I am not disturbing you."

"Of course not," I said.

"You look—tired."

"I am tired." I smiled a little. "But only because I was awake most of the night worrying." At her raised brows, I added, "We went to the Darcys' today to meet their new son. I was . . . well. I had not seen my cousin or his wife since leaving Kent."

"Ah." She tipped her head to one side. "How is the child? In health?"

My voice caught in my throat; I was back, quite abruptly, in my nursery, hearing the creak of my nurse's chair and the low drone of her voice. "Robust," I managed, and blinked against ridiculous tears.

Mr. and Mrs. Darcy welcomed us all—myself

included—warmly. Indeed, Fitzwilliam was the most gregarious I had ever seen him, holding his new son out for our inspection almost before we crossed the threshold. Mrs. Darcy, still confined, resting, to her sitting room until she was churched, could not prevent the startlement that crossed her face when I entered, bowed, and greeted her. It was a very small triumph, but I had been savoring it ever since.

Aunt and Uncle Fitzwilliam arrived in Town earlier in the week, and joined us in welcoming the new child. My mother, however, remained in Kent, having refused her brother's invitation. There was a hollowness inside when I thought of her alone in that house—or had she kept Mrs. Jenkinson as her own?—embittered and proud.

But then the babe was passed around, and we each took our turn holding him in our arms. Though I feared I might drop him, I found that my arms closed easily around his frame. I could not quite find the beauty in his rumpled face and hairless head, but when one hand worked its way free of its wrappings I was appalled by the fragility of those little fingers, something bursting inside my chest as I touched them tentatively with one of my own. I watched his small face contort through myriad expressions, cycling in his sleep from distress to worry to toothless joy, as if he were practicing the art of being human, and I wondered whether Mamma looked at me as I was looking at him: a little awed, a little terrified, more than a little amused by my infant funniness. It was hard to imagine.

"You look quite natural with a child in your arms, Anne," my aunt said, and I was at once piercingly grate-

ful, despite my hollowness, that Mamma had not come,
for who knew what leaps her mind might take to see me
holding an infant? And, too, I could almost hear her
voice as I looked down at him, dissecting his features
into Darcy and Fitzwilliam, making no room whatsoever for Bennet; fussing over his nurse's figure and diet;
demanding to know how Mrs. Darcy expects his limbs to
grow straight without a swaddling band.

"My mother did not come after all," I said.

"I am sorry," Miss Amherst said after a moment.

I shrugged one shoulder, glanced away. "I can only
imagine that she does not want to see me. Nothing else
could keep her from greeting her new grandnephew."

"You are quite magnificent these days, you know. She
is missing a great deal."

Miss Amherst spoke lightly; but my face heated.

"Well. Ah. In any case, I have been wallowing here
in the sun to chase away the shadows," I said, trying to
smile. Miss Amherst smiled as well, her laughter thrumming warmly, kindly through the air between us at my
poor jest, for the sun was weak, the garden dim and cool.

"Do you think she has any secret sorrows?" I said,
pointing. The spider darted from spoke to spoke within
her web, weaving it together with deft mysterious movements.

Miss Amherst was resting her cheek on her fist, but
she raised her head now, glancing from the spider to me.
I spoke unthinkingly, and now felt again that blooming
panic, that my words were too strange, that she would
grow stiff and silent.

But her grin burst across her face like sparks from

a fire, and she said, "I doubt it; but then, I have never thought about it before. Do you spend a great deal of time considering the inner lives of spiders?"

Relief loosened all my joints so that I slumped back like a rag doll. "I do," I said.

Her brow puckered. "And beetles?" she said, with mock seriousness.

"I am convinced that their inner lives are as varied and colorful as their shells."

A little smile, quickly hidden, though her eyes were laughing. "But surely lowlier beings—earthworms, for instance, or . . . or oysters—haven't many worries."

I raised my brows; for in truth, I wondered. "I am no naturalist," I said.

"No," she said; and now her smile was slow and wicked, and my heart kicked like a pony against my breastbone. "You are a poet."

I laughed, incredulous. "I have scarcely ever *read* poetry; I cannot begin to imagine how one goes about writing it."

She looked down, and I realized that our hands held one another still, resting on her lap. With one thumb she described a circle in the center of my palm, the motion deliberate enough that I could not possibly think, as I did at Lady Clive's ball, that it was accidental. "You needn't write a word to be a poet," she said. "It is in the way your mind works. You see things differently."

"Strangely." The word came out on a puff of air. Every nerve in my body seemed suddenly centered within the mound of my palm.

Now she shrugged. "A little," she said, and soothed the sting of the words with a gentle smile. "But think how very tedious life would be if no one ever had a strange thought."

And still her thumb moved, languorous and distracting. I swallowed, looked at the spider, who wove on, oblivious. Or perhaps not. She might be listening to our conversation, amused to think I imagined I understand what is in her heart. A laugh frothed up from my belly, and I pressed my lips together in a vain attempt to smother it. Miss Hall once told me I had a mathematical mind, but why should I not be a poet, too? I expected my strangeness to vanish with my drops, but it seemed that—perhaps from having taken them so long—it had made its way into my blood. Or perhaps it was always there, all along, innately part of me since I lay curled inside my mother's womb.

But Miss Amherst did not mind my fancies, however unnatural they might seem to others; she did not recoil. She smoothed her thumb across my hand and called me a poet.

She looked at me, and now she was the one who seemed strange, her expression unfamiliar in its sudden potency. Her breathing, I could hear in the near-quiet, hitched and stumbled a little. I thought of my cousin and his wife in his book room, and my own breath came a little too quickly.

I wanted to lean in, to touch; the little space between our two arms was suddenly thick as custard, and vibrating softly. Did other creatures experience such a complicated brew of feelings? Did foxes both fear and long to nuzzle one another? I looked up at the flying birds and wondered if things could possibly be so simple for them as they appeared.

Then I looked back at Miss Amherst, and impulsively, I bent once more and touched my lips to the back of her gloved hand.

And there I might have remained, eternally motionless but for the thud of my pulse at my throat; but Miss Amherst drew her hands away from mine. I stayed curled over, swathed in humiliation. And then her fingers brushed my jaw, lifting my face; and then my cheeks were cupped by the supple leather of her gloves. Her face was very near, her eyes holding a question. I suppose I must have answered it to her satisfaction, though I did not form actual words, for she drew impossibly closer, and her lips brushed mine.

CHAPTER TWENTY-SIX

I congratulated Miss Julia on her engagement, and listened as she talked at length of the wedding plans. All the while, I felt Miss Amherst—Eliza—watching me, and when at last there was a pause in the flow of her sister's words, she said quickly, "Miss de Bourgh—I was hoping to show you my new gown." Her hand was hot around my wrist as she pulled me up the stairs and down a short corridor. We walked as quickly as decorum allowed, and she sent an arch look over her shoulder at me before opening her chamber door.

Inside, I had only a moment to take in the green bed curtains and soft gold carpet before she kissed me, the hard wood of the door at my back, the softness of her body pressed all along my front. The room was silent but for our working mouths. I was heavy and full as storm air; and then Eliza's thigh pushed between both of mine, dragging my shift against my skin, startling me into an entirely new knowledge of myself.

And shiver every Feather with Desire.

When she released me, Eliza stepped away, the back of her hand against her reddened lips. "I . . . did not mean to be quite so . . . forward," she said. Her cheeks were flushed enough to disguise even her vivid freckles.

I pushed myself away from the supporting door, and found to my faint surprise that I was quite able to stand on my own. "You did nothing," I said, breathless with my own daring, "that I have not longed for you to do these past days."

"In*terminable* days," she said, and reached for me once more.

"AM I MUCH DISARRANGED?" she asked a little later.

I looked up at her, woozy and disbelieving. "Beautifully," I said. A few pins were loosened; anyone who saw her now would think she had been riding hard through the country, or napping with restless dreams. I was like a dreamer myself, caught in a world that did not seem entirely real.

She laughed, touched her hair and her bodice, then pulled up her legs so they were tucked around her and smiled down at me with such affection that I could not endure it for long.

"Mrs. Fitzwilliam once told me you are very accomplished," I said, for want of anything better.

Eliza collapsed onto her back and blew out a breath. "I suppose I am," she said.

"She said"—and now, to my bemusement, my voice teased—"that you were quite the most accomplished girl at school." I rolled onto my side. Her proportions were as generous as her laughter and understanding. I reached out a hand, and though I was not quite audacious enough to touch her so intimately as I wished to, I took a coil of orange hair that had sprung loose from its pins and let it run through my fingers like strands of silk thread.

Her eyes closed as, emboldened, I let my fingers drift to explore her apple cheeks and the short, hard bridge of her nose; the indentation between nose and upper lip, furred like lamb's ear leaves; the lips themselves, wide and smooth; the small hard knob of chin, all but lost between the roundness of cheeks and the slope of her throat. "It came rather easily to me," she said. "I should not say so, but almost everything we learned bored me."

"Not so surprising, I suppose, from a devotee of Mary Wollstonecraft."

Her lips turned up under my fingers, though her eyes remained closed, reddish lashes nearly invisible. I wanted to count the freckles on her face; I longed, with an explorer's insatiable, questing desire, to know whether they existed elsewhere on her body.

"I suppose," I said, stroking the side of her throat— there were freckles here, but only a few—"that it is also unsurprising that you would choose to . . . spend time with . . . a woman who has no accomplishments at all." Her pulse fluttered under my fingertips, as frantic as my own.

It was the closest I could come to asking her why she seemed as drawn to me as I was to her.

She pulled away, eyes opening. "That," she said, "is a very roundabout way of speaking for someone so frank as you."

I bit the side of my lip; shook my head.

"Oh, Frank," she said, emphasizing the word so that

it sounded more like a name. "I like you very well as you are." She curled herself around me, wrapping me in her arms and legs, tucking her face into the nook between my shoulder and chin. "I've never quite . . . fit," she said against my skin. "I can pretend quite well—sometimes I suppose I am not pretending at all. But school was nearly all pretense for me, years of it. I was merely lucky that it was easy to pretend, for I did not have to work very hard to learn the lessons they pressed upon me." Her arms tightened around me, and she dropped a kiss on the tender spot just behind my jaw. "I fit here, though," she murmured.

I relaxed back against her. I never fit, either, of course; but I lived most of my life in such a strange state, and so secluded from the wider world, that I never quite understood what it was I was supposed to be fitting into.

But still: "This is not . . . usual," I said, though with a questioning rise at the end of the last word; for I truly was not certain. I should be certain; but there was so much of the world that I had not encountered, even then.

Eliza sat up, and she looked as guarded as I felt whenever I remembered Miss Hall's reaction to my absurd proposal. "No," she said. "I suppose it is not . . . usual. If, that is, by usual you mean—what is generally accepted. But did we not—that is to say, *un*usual is so much more interesting, is it not?" She smiled, but it was false, possibly the first false expression I had seen her wear, and by it I understood that she was as terrified of frightening me away as I was of frightening her. I rubbed my lips together without meaning to; they felt larger than usual, swollen from being pressed to hers.

"There are others," she said, a touch too quickly. "Other women who—and men, too. And we ladies are the lucky ones, for we . . . for the consequences of being, ah, found out are not so grave for us as they are for gentlemen who prefer one another's company."

I could not fathom what two men might do together. But everything, everything was so new; and if two men felt together even a small measure of what I was experiencing now, I could not wonder at their pursuing it. There was damp, again, between my legs, just as there had been on the night of Lady Clive's ball, welling as mysteriously as dew on night-grass; a great, unsolved puzzle of my own body that I was determined to decipher.

Eliza spoke to fill the silence, leaning earnestly forward.

"There are ladies who live together as husband and wife," she said, keeping her eyes on mine.

"How do you know about such things?" They were hardly within the scope of gently bred ladies' educations. I thought again of John and his club; how women could not walk down the street there, let alone enter the club itself. I only knew this because I asked, once; my cousin and Mr. Watters spent so much time there that I could not help but be curious about it. Mrs. Fitzwilliam looked aghast, and then laughed in an affected manner.

"Those places are the purview of *men*, my dear," she said, as if that were all the answer required. Which, I suppose, it was.

"There was a story in the newspaper," Eliza said. "It was one Papa would not read out to us, and so it interested me all the more. A pair of women—a wife and a husband-wife, who goes about in breeches and cravat and beaver hat. Can you imagine such a thing?"

I could not imagine *her* in such garb, with her love of a well-fitted gown; and yet, even as I thought this, all at once I suddenly *could*. The breeches and stockings would show the shape of her calves, hidden now under her layers of gown and petticoat and shift. Her hips and bosom would offer a challenge for a fitted coat; but a proper seamstress could rise to it. She flushed as if she could hear my thoughts, and I covered my face until helpless laughter enveloped us both.

I TOUCHED MY OWN body in the darkness, and thought of Eliza, slipping a hand under the thin fabric of my chemise to explore the skin of my thighs and the rough hair between them. Tentatively, my fingers sought out the shuddering, shocking place I'd discovered when Eliza's leg pressed it. I imagined that my hand was not my own; wondered what someone else would feel as she touched me. My belly was no longer a hollow to be filled; my hip bones were a little cushioned. I bled now with a regularity that was strange to me; there was a rhythm to my body that was absent when it was not properly nourished. But my breasts were still small, not quite filling my cupped palms.

I'd seen the way men's eyes dipped to a lady's bosom and then back up, taking in the sight in genteel sips, the same way they would sip at a glass of good claret. I had done the same—indeed, at the ball, I found my eyes flitting from female form to female form, quite impervious to the charms of the men. But I thought that the impulse to drink in the particulars of other women's bodies, my admiration for Mrs. Darcy's vigor or Miss Hall's long fingers, was simply another of my drops' peculiar effects. But perhaps I was simply not made to admire male figures. And Miss Amherst—*Eliza, Eliza!*—had experienced the very same impulses.

This was, I thought, how husbands and wives must enjoy one another. A natural impulse—*Nature's great Command,* as Mr. Thomson wrote. But never, ever had the sight of a man made me feel so questing an inclination.

I cringed from the thought of Miss Hall's stillness when she understood where my inclinations lay. Every muscle in my body turned stiff and miserable with the recollection. And then, like a tonic, I thought of Eliza— bright and quick, bold and yet as nervous as I, myself— and my limbs relaxed, my belly softened. The taste of her lips and teeth and tongue; the fear and desire writ clearly upon her face. Something pulled and pulled behind the bones of my pelvis, taking me back to Brighton, to the ineffable, surging waves of the sea; but these waves were not cold. They warmed me, thrummed over and through me until at last I let myself be carried along by them in a great rush.

Surely, I thought after, slack and bewildered, turning my face into my pillow; surely there could be nothing so terrible in these feelings if someone like Eliza felt them, too.

CHAPTER TWENTY-SEVEN

We could not, of course, see one another privately every day, but we could, and did, keep our servants busy running notes between John's house and Cavendish Square. And between letters, we took moments together like thieves, wherever we could be alone even for an instant. Our chamber doors muted any sounds we made, and our palms did, too; we pressed them to our mouths—to each other's mouths. We muffled laughter around our own fingers; we swallowed down one another's moans.

Even when we were in company with others, we were sometimes bold enough to steal touches. The curl of little fingers as we walked together in the park, hidden from view by the curtains of our skirts; the press of slippered feet under a table. Her arms solid around my ribs, lifting me so my toes came up off the floor—just the quickest snatch of warm touching cheeks and the tickle of her lips over the pulse at my throat before she set me down again and continued on her slow and decorous way down the corridor toward her music room, which had been our destination. Only the self-conscious roll of her hips and the smile she tossed back at me—quick as sunlight on water—betrayed that anything unusual had just occurred.

ELIZA HAD SLIM SILVER furrows running along the insides of her thighs; and the outer curves of her breasts; and her hips and belly, rounded as the sloping hills of Kent. Learning of their existence, I could not stop stroking them, fingers dragging lightly up and down and back again. "Like tree bark," I murmured; and she batted my fingers away.

"Tree bark! What—am I so rough?"

I smiled at her. "Not rough," I said. "But they make a pattern—see? Like the skin of oak trees." I traced one furrow across her breast until it ran into another; and then I circled her areolae, which were darker than my own, and wider, the skin impossibly tender. Looking at them, I thought of flower petals; when I said so, she laughed.

"Of course you would," she said.

Each of her breasts filled my hands, paler than the rest of her, the only part of her body, I had at last discovered, not peppered with freckles. Released from the confines of her stays, they gently dropped, their own weight pulling them down to hang against her ribs. My palms curved instinctively, forming cups to hold them; and the smoothness of her nipples went pebbled as a riverbed.

"You truly are peculiar," she said, catching my hands and holding them more firmly against her, so that her breasts swelled up over the top of my thumbs as if my hands were a corset. "I think you would make a perfect resident for a hermitage. I can see you now, clothed in a gown of moss, your hair snarled, odd lines of poetry falling from your lips like prayers." She kissed the plane of my chest. "Do you truly see bark and petals when you look at me?" she whispered into my skin.

I hummed a little. "Well. It isn't *all* I see."

Another kiss. "It makes me feel . . ."

My chest tightened. "Like flora?"

"Mmm." Her breath a vibration, loosening the muscle of my heart once more. "*Lush.*"

IN HER LETTERS, SHE copied out poems and asked what I thought of them; she mentioned articles in the newspaper, and requested my opinion, and I nearly laughed at the surprise on John's face when I asked if he would keep the paper for me when he was through with it.

I was reminded bittersweetly of my yearslong correspondence with Miss Hall; a similar eagerness filled me whenever John's butler brought me a folded letter in Eliza's neat hand. And yet, there the similarity ended, for unlike Miss Hall's, Eliza's letters spilled over with generous measures of herself. She was liberal with her thoughts, her feelings; and there was an urgency to her questions for me, as if she could not know me quickly enough.

She told me that she detested Mr. King, Julia's intended, for the dismissive way he spoke to her sister.

The only benefit to woman's constrained circumstances that I can see, she wrote once, *is that men often look upon us as they do children, never guessing at the thoughts and passions that run through our minds and hearts. If I must marry—and I fear I must—I pray that my husband will be very stupid.*

If only I had been born a man! I think I'd have liked to go into business, like my father. Regardless of what society thinks of manufacturing as a means of earning an income— my father loved the challenge of it. I hated school so very much. Not the other pupils, for they were mostly lovely, but the course of study . . . ! If I have girl-children, I will have to find some unlikely, progressive school, of which my husband will no doubt disapprove; or else found one, myself. Let them learn to use their minds, as men are taught to do.

MISS HALL NEVER OPENED HERSELF to me. For all the years we were together, as governess and pupil, and young lady and companion, even as the difference between our ages came to feel slimmer and slimmer and as her initial frustration with me began to fade, I had to work for every scrap of understanding I had of her. I wondered, now, whether she was always so reticent with everyone, or if she somehow sensed the attraction I felt, even if I did not fully understand it yet, myself.

Eliza was entirely open. She spoke her thoughts, and wrote them, too, trusting me with her truths, however socially unsuitable. She laughed too loudly when mirth overtook her. She spread her thighs and let me right inside her very body, where it was warm and seeping wet as the ground after a rain. I smelled her there as I always wanted to smell the earth, close and intimate, my nose in the hair between her legs. It was darker than the hair on her head, and coarser than the hair on her legs and under her arms; though I loved to smell her there, too, where the faint traces of rosewater that clung to her wrists and throat were buried under the scent of Eliza herself.

No matter how I turned the question over inside my head, I could not account for how easily I accepted the gift of her candor; nor how I allowed myself, from our earliest meeting, to be so forthcoming with my own thoughts and feelings. I felt easy with her from the first; it was the sort of easiness I had never experienced before. It took all my usual disquiet and smoothed it away like the tide over the sand. It made me willing to speak of things I'd never spoken of before—my nighttime visitors; the anger that rose in me with frightening strength when I thought about my mother.

It made me willing to try things, even when I hadn't the faintest idea what I was doing; even when my attentions tickled instead of pleased, leaving Eliza with her fist pressed to her mouth to stifle her laughter and fat, delighted tears spilling down her cheeks. Instead of turning thorn-prickly, I laughed as well; and when our laughter faded, tried again.

ELIZA'S WATERCOLORS WERE EXQUISITE, delicate. Perfect renderings of what she saw. Landscapes; dogs; vases of pinks. I looked at them all, one after another, and then, half-teasing, said, "What else can you do?"

She cast me an irritated look and then, half-defiantly, half-laughingly, she showed me the embroidered linens she had made for Julia's wedding trousseau, the stitches so perfectly even that even Miss Hall would have been impressed, the design a complicated interweaving of thistles and flowing leaves.

I kissed her. "What else?"

She murmured to me in French, sentences that would have made her schoolmistress blush. I was pleased that I could understand her, even if my own clumsy responses made her snort, more like a barnyard creature than an accomplished young lady. She played for me, three songs one after the other, and sang, too, her voice almost as resonant as the voice of the singer at a concert I attended with the Fitzwilliams and Mr. Watters. That lady's voice had made me think impiously that if only she had sung weekly at our church in Hunsford, I might have grown up with a better understanding of the Divine than I gained from a thousand tepid sermons.

But Eliza suddenly struck her palm against the pianoforte's black-and-white keys, jarring discordant notes ringing out in the air.

"None of it *matters*," she said in a mutter.

I approached her slowly. "What do you mean?"

She stared down at her fingers, curled into fists. "I do not . . . love any of this. In fact, I rather hate it all. And it—it is the same as fashion, which I love despite wondering if I have been *trained* to care about it. I cannot decide whether my feelings are true—whether I truly dislike needlework and painting and—or if perhaps I would find joy in it had it not been forced upon me, and other endeavors discouraged." She rolled her knuckles along the keys, a little looping melody.

I touched the pianoforte's shining wood top. My own

feelings were knotted as the threads of my embroidery projects, all those years ago in the school room. "Is it pointless?" I said slowly. Eliza looked up at me, and I hastened to add, "That is—is art, of any kind, *pointless*?" My thoughts were on the voice of the concert singer; how it raised me up, higher and higher, until I was floating above the crowd in their spindly chairs. It was all the joyful freedom of my drops with none of the mindlessness. It was transcendence.

She listened silently as I tried, ineloquently, to explain. "What of your beloved novels?" I said at last. "Cannot a well-played song transport a listener the same way a reader can be transported by a well-penned story?"

Eliza was a portrait of misery. "I just . . . want something else," she said.

I swallowed down my frustration, though it tried to lodge itself in my throat. "And I envy your skills. So very much."

SHE WROTE ME THE following day.

I did not mean to negate your experience by bemoaning my own, dearest Frank, she said. *It is only that, sometimes, I cannot see a way out, and I find it hard to be cheerful.*

Out of *what*, she did not say; but I supposed she did not need to. I bit the inside of my cheek, glanced up at Mrs. Fitzwilliam, who sat across from me on one of the drawing room's elegant chairs, sewing and humming a little to herself.

If only ladies did not require the presence of other ladies to move freely through the world, I wrote back later. *My cousin and Mr. Watters leave the house whenever they wish, in each other's company or entirely alone, at any time of day or evening. Their strides are long and full of purpose. And why should they not be? For men are told from boyhood that they have charge of their lives and of the world. Whereas I cannot walk down St. James's Street, where John's club is located, without being assumed to be a lady of low reputation.*

I had a friend once. She called me exceptionally fortunate and urged me to take control of my estate and my inheritance. I am beginning to think I might have the strength to do so; but I hardly know where or how to start.

Her reply was swift and clipped; I felt, rattling through it, the same choking frustration I'd felt with her.

You've relations who manage their own grand estates; surely they can provide guidance, she said. *Start with small things. Ask them.*

CHAPTER TWENTY-EIGHT

M r. Watters and Mrs. Fitzwilliam were urging me to accompany them to the park for the fashionable hour, and I was resisting.

"It would be so much more enjoyable with you on my arm, Miss de Bourgh," Mr. Watters said, and then, when I demurred, he added in a teasing voice, "Surely Miss Amherst would not call at this hour."

The mention of her name made me bite my lip, and I turned away, pretending to busy myself with my mostly untouched whitework, to prevent his keen eyes from noticing. But he leaned around and said, "What feminine secrets do you two ladies expose to one another in those notes Preston is always bringing in and taking out, hmm?"

There was something I did not like in the odd lilt to his voice; in his pale, raised brow. The fine hairs all along my body sprang to attention, and it was I who looked away first.

I WAS SOMEWHAT AFRAID to approach John's book room again, but when I knocked and he bid me enter, I found him alone at his desk, looking over some correspondence.

"Anne," he said, looking up. "I thought there was some scheme to go walking. Did you not wish to go?"

"Not today." I took a seat across from him. "I see you are not out, either."

"Hyde Park at this hour has long since lost its allure for me," he said, with an almost-smile. Then he set down his quill, running a hand over his head so that his hair stood to military attention, and sighed. "And I've rather a mess to contend with on the estate. It seems a windstorm knocked over a number of trees—my steward says the damage to some of the cottages was devastating. No lives lost, thank heaven, but a few injuries, and the rebuilding will take some time. In the meantime, there is the problem of housing those who have lost their homes. I really must leave for Surrey directly."

He pinched his brow, just above the bridge of his nose, then grinned at me. "The perils of estate management, eh? It would be much easier, I sometimes think, if I could be like so many other gentlemen, and leave everything to my steward. But—"

"But your tenants are under your protection, and thus are your responsibility," I said, and he gave me a startled look.

"Yes, exactly," he said.

Harriet Watters brought with her a substantial dowry; when she and John married, they were able to buy a modest estate of some four thousand acres in the same neighborhood where John had grown up. I, of course, had never been there, though I'd heard much of it from Mamma, who visited not long after the couple returned from their wedding trip; she saw great potential in the size of the house, though the kitchens, she said, must be improved if Colonel and Mrs. Fitzwilliam were ever to host ample dinner parties.

I realized I was picking with one hand at the skin at the base of the opposite thumbnail, and forced myself to stop. "I have been . . . thinking about that, as well," I said. "My—responsibilities, that is." I looked at the papers scattered on the desk before him and said, "I am sorry; you have more than enough to worry about just now."

"No, no." John leaned forward, hands clasped together atop one page of his steward's correspondence. "Please, go on—is it your estate that brings you here today?"

"Yes. I . . . have been avoiding questions that I should not have . . . for far too long. And I think you might be able to help me." I licked my lips. "How—how does Rosings Park do, in your estimation? Is Mr. Colt a good manager?"

"Ah." John frowned. "Yes, I think Colt does well enough by the estate. And I believe my aunt likes to keep her hand in things as well."

"Which is part of the problem. Rosings Park is profitable, but I do not know any of the details. And I do not know . . . I do not *know* my tenants at all. I've no idea of their lives, or their needs, or . . . And I do not know whether they have those needs met, at present. Or even what meeting them would mean." What I did not say— that my tenants were, for the most part, not people at all to me but shadows, anonymous bowing figures in the fields and village as I passed them—was too contempt-ible to admit aloud.

John's smile unfurled like a leaf in spring. "Anne," he said, "are you preparing to take your proper place?"

I flushed. "I am . . . not sure. Perhaps."

"Then I would suggest beginning with a letter to Mr. Colt. He could answer these questions better than I. I can only say from once-yearly observations that Rosings does appear to be well managed; but I cannot speak to your tenants' thoughts."

I released a shaky breath, and he laughed softly.

"Cousin—this is truly admirable."

"Mamma will not approve."

"No," he said, and rested his chin upon one fist, the picture of thoughtful ease. "But when does she ever?"

OUTSIDE THE CARRIAGE WINDOW, I watched the passing scenery. This part of London was less chaotic than more commercial quarters, but still the streets teemed with horses and vehicles; passing ladies and gentlemen strolling arm in arm; servant girls carrying baskets from the market; a small boy scuttling along the pavement, a message clutched in one fist. The afternoon was bright and pleasantly cool, and the whole of the city seemed golden to me, a cup filled to the brim with beautiful life. I thought at last that I was in the place I was meant to be at the time I was meant to be there, and my lips spread irrepressibly wide of their own volition.

Mrs. Fitzwilliam seemed less pleased with her current circumstances. "You were upstairs a long while," she said, as if making a simple observation; but I heard the criticism in her tone.

But even her sourness could not induce me to feel less than perfectly content. "I apologize," I said. "I did not intend to be gone so long."

"Mrs. Amherst was rather put out," she said, and I shook my head. She would never dare speak so to my mother. But I held my peace, for in truth, I knew she was right that I behaved badly, leaving her and Mrs. Amherst alone in the drawing room while Eliza took me upstairs with the flimsy excuse of showing me a new book. I touched my fingers to my lips to stop the smile that longed to grow there. My body hummed.

"As I said, I am sorry."

She looked out the window as well, but I doubted, from her expression, that she enjoyed the view as much as I did.

We had scarcely handed off our gloves, hats, and spencers to the servants when Mr. Watters poked his head out of the drawing room. He affected surprise upon seeing us, and hesitated a moment before coming forward down the hall.

"Harriet," he said, nodding to his sister, and then to me, "Miss de Bourgh. I hope you had a pleasant visit with your friend."

"Yes, very pleasant, thank you."

"I wonder," he said, looking down at his fingernails, as if they held some great fascination for him, "would you care to take a turn in the garden with me? There is something I would speak to you about."

"I . . ." I looked at Mrs. Fitzwilliam, who, to my eternal frustration, was smiling *now*. She nodded at me, all encouragement. "Very well."

The garden was not particularly conducive to exercise, and I felt a little ridiculous as we began a slow circuit around the center topiaries. Mr. Watters kept his hands clasped behind his back and his eyes on the toes of his boots as he took one measured step after another. I watched him from the periphery of my vision.

"Miss de Bourgh," he said at last when we had achieved a full circle and were standing before the table and chairs near the door. And then, reaching for my hand, "Anne." I was too startled by the contact, my hand trapped between his, to protest the intimacy. "You cannot have failed to notice my attentions these past weeks. I think—I *know*—others have marked my preference for you, as well."

My mouth opened, closed, opened again.

"And so I think the time is right to offer you my . . . hand"—with a faint smile down at our own layered hands—"in marriage." He raised his eyes to finally meet mine, adding, with an almost boyish earnestness, "I very much hope you will accept."

There were calluses on his palms, I noted from some distance, probably from riding. I tugged gently and he released me, surprise darting across his face before he returned his expression to one of patient expectation.

"I would like to sit down," I said, and half-fell into

one of the chairs. He perched on the edge of the other, but I did not look at him. My eyes sought rather wildly for the spider in her corner, but she was gone, and all that remained of her web were a few tattered strands of weaving. For some reason I felt like crying.

"Are you well?" Mr. Watters said.

I managed a small smile. "Yes. I am well. And you are right, this is not . . . entirely unexpected. But I did not . . ." I glanced at him and then away. "May I speak plainly, sir?"

"Of course."

"I rather hoped I was misjudging your intentions. I intend no offense whatsoever, but I . . ." I paused, for there was no possible way for him to take my meaning without taking offense.

"You speak not a word of affection," I said at last. "I imagined you would . . . pretend to it, at least."

When I chanced a look at him, Mr. Watters was very still, his face quite impossible to read. "Do you require affection from your husband?" he said in a strange low tone, and then added, "Do not misunderstand me, Miss de Bourgh, I hold you in high regard. You have . . . quite subverted my earlier understanding of your character, and I find I like you very well. But affection of the . . . romantic sort . . . I cannot offer."

He tapped his steepled fingers together in a way that spoke of some internal disquiet. I looked at him for a long moment, not speaking, then said, cautiously, "I think, sir, that I do not entirely understand you."

He rose abruptly, paced a few steps in one direction,

then wheeled about to face me. "*I* think, madam, that you are in possession of all the affection that you require."

I pressed back against the chair. "I do not—"

"I saw you," he said, lowering his voice until I had to strain to make out the words. "Here, in this very garden. I came into the breakfast room for a moment, and there you were. You and Miss Amherst."

"No," I said; and my voice was even weaker than his.

My fear seemed to calm him; he regained his seat and his earnest expression. "I would not curtail such . . . activities as your husband," he said quietly. "For you see, Miss de Bourgh, I am . . . sympathetic . . . to your plight. I would require little from you in the way of wifely duties after we'd an heir in the nursery."

"I . . . oh." The garden seemed to be tilting rather alarmingly around me; or was it I, myself, who was tipping over? Apparently it was the latter, for quite suddenly Mr. Watters wrapped his hand around my arm, steadying me. I pulled away from him, wishing, for the very first time, for Mrs. Jenkinson; she would probably have smelling salts somewhere about her.

"You needn't answer now," he said. "But can you not see how agreeable such an arrangement could be for both of us? My fortune can help enrich your already prosperous estate—"

I waved him silent, as irritably as ever Mamma waved off unwanted conversation. I did not need to hear the rest, for I understood him perfectly. Our union would provide him instantly with an estate of his own; for once wed, my property would no longer belong to me.

Mr. Watters, by contrast, would be elevated instantly by our marriage into the class of the landed gentry.

"Please take as long as you'd like to consider," he said after a time.

I did not look up as he returned to the house.

CHAPTER TWENTY-NINE

Eliza had a subscription at Minerva Press, one of London's many circulating libraries. She liked this one, she told me with a playful smile, because it lent out its own printed works—"The very lowest of the low novels, my father thinks; but he lets me read what I please."

Today she was in search of something "deliciously sensational," and I followed her into the building. The sudden hush when the door closed behind us, dampening the noise from Leadenhall Street, disoriented me, as if someone stuffed my ears with rags, leaving me with nothing to listen to but the clerks' and customers' humming conversations and my own thoughts, turning like a hoop and leaving me dizzy. Eliza made her selection while I waited, and took my arm as we stepped back out onto the street, her hand squeezing my sleeve lightly.

"Shall we walk a little?" she said. "It is so fine today."

I nodded, and we walked for a short while as she told me about Julia's wedding preparations. "The entire household is running quite mad," she said. "I would invite you in today, but I fear there would be little privacy; Julia is wont to burst into my room without knocking these days, frantic over the silliest details. I cannot wait for it to be over."

"Will you miss her?"

"Of course. But not *this* iteration of her. She is usually fairly sensible."

"Will you still see her often, do you think? After she marries?"

"Oh, yes, I expect so. Mr. King's house in Town is not far from Cavendish Square. And she has promised me that I will be invited to their house in the country as soon as may be, though in truth the prospect holds little enough joy for me. All those insects and cows. Give *me* a street full of carriages." She sent me a sly glance. "I know *you* are quite at home among the beetles and spiders, though, darling Frank."

I tried to smile. "I hope you will visit me at Rosings as well," I said. "I promise, our cows are quite tame."

"For you," she said, lacing our arms more closely together, "I will brave the fiercest cows in Kent." A pause. "Are you—thinking of returning soon, then?"

"I . . . am not sure." I looked up at her, but the angle of the sun was such that it was directly behind her, and I blinked, dazzled. My steps dragged. She looked sideways at me again, her brow furrowed as a farmer's field, but did not question me further.

Mr. Watters proposed. The words were there, dancing a quadrille on my tongue, but I swallowed them down. If I told her and she believed our continued . . . friendship . . . too great a risk to her reputation—well, the thought made me think of my bittersweet drops with a ferocious hunger.

BACK AT JOHN'S HOUSE, I lay flat upon my bed. The scent of lavender lingered among the linens, and the now-familiar reek of London rolled in through the open window.

As offers of marriage went, Mr. Watters's was not a bad one. Like the arrangement I assumed my own parents enjoyed, he would make no demands upon my person once Rosings Park had an heir. And he would pretend not to notice if Eliza and I crept away together for a few hours; just as, I supposed, I would ask no questions about him and any of his more intimate friends. It was truly the best possible offer I could ever hope for, and everyone, *everyone* in the family would be pleased that poor sickly Anne had caught a rich husband. He might not have a fine estate like Darcy, but he had wealth and an abundance of charm. He was a great friend of John's, which spoke well of his character, however little I felt I truly understood it myself. This was more than any of my family probably dared hope for me, at this late point. Mamma might even forgive my running off to London, if this were the result of my folly.

My fingers flexed against the coverlet. A marriage like my mother's. I thought of her and Papa in the breakfast room, him with his paper and her with her letters, and neither with very much to say to the other. Papa off to London every chance he got. And marital relations—I could not help thinking, from Mamma's apparent unwillingness to continue them after my birth, that they must be very different to what I enjoyed with Eliza. I already recoiled from Mr. Watters's touch; how much harder would far more intimate relations be to endure? To give up my body to him, when I had only recently gotten it back for myself—

And all the rest. I had completely bared myself to Eliza—she had seen all of me. Not only my body but all the strange and secret corners of my mind and heart. I had no such desire to be so naked before Mr. Watters.

I sat up on the bed, a hand pressed against my rib cage. A seed seemed to have been planted somewhere between my heart and stomach. It had grown over the last few days into a cold, stonelike ball that I could not seem to shift. It was all very well for *him*, I thought, speaking so casually about producing an heir, as if it were a small thing to demand of a wife. *I* recalled, with dreadful vividness, Nurse's gossiping words with one of the maids after Aunt Darcy's death. So many infants lost between my two cousins, and then—*a bloody business*—Aunt Darcy lost as well. Women's bodies were such strange and mysterious things, swelling and shrinking and swelling, again and again, until we were at last too old to swell any longer; or until the swelling killed us. Perhaps it should shame me, but I felt nothing strong enough, holding little George in my arms, to induce me to take such a risk for myself. I had, after all, only just begun to live.

I feared the only way to move that cold heavy thing inside of me was to give Mr. Watters my answer, and the easy thing would be to accept him.

I was accustomed to doing the easy thing.

Downstairs, two floors below, I heard the front door opening and the murmur of faraway voices. Someone had come home. My hand pressed harder against my ribs, as if to keep my insides from spilling out between them.

MR. WATTERS'S WALKING STICK, WITH its distinctive silver knob, was resting against the wall in the entranceway when I went downstairs. I stood staring at it, the seed abruptly putting out strangling vines inside of me, which wrapped around my heart, squeezing until I thought it might burst.

There was a noise from the breakfast room, a clink of china-on-china. It could be John or Mrs. Fitzwilliam and not Mr. Watters at all. But my feet, braver than the rest of me, were already moving down the hall, and when I reached the doorway I found it was, indeed, Mr. Watters inside, sitting at the table with the four pages of the newspaper spread open before him. A cup of tea steamed on its gold-rimmed saucer, and Mr. Watters appeared very casual in only his shirtsleeves and dark-patterned waistcoat. His cravat was so extravagantly knotted that I could not help wondering how long he had to stand this morning, chin raised as his valet constructed it.

My greatest fear was that he would use his knowledge of me and Eliza as a means of forcing me to marry him. Our actions might not be subject to prosecution, but we could both be utterly ruined were rumors to circulate. I cared less for myself than for Eliza, with no country home to which she could escape. I studied him for a moment—sharp profile, long legs stretched out in front of him—and thought, heaven help me, that I wanted to believe he would not be so unfeeling, though I'd little reason to think either well or badly of him. Really, I knew him hardly at all.

I was going to turn around—he was so clearly at ease, it would be a shame to disturb him just now—but he looked up, saw me, and rose. "What an unexpected pleasure," he said.

When I said nothing, my tongue suddenly as knotted as his cravat, he moved to pull out a chair for me. "Please, will you sit?"

I sat as carefully as if the chair were made of glass.

"Am I right in hoping," he said, holding each word in his mouth for a moment before releasing it lightly into the air between us, "that you are here because you have made a decision regarding my offer?"

I breathed quickly through my nose, in my lap my hands clutching each other tightly as lovers. "Yes," I said, and then, "No. That is—I mean—"

"You mean . . . your answer is no."

"Yes," I said, and then added, "I mean, yes, my answer is no." I could not even reject a proposal properly, I thought; and closed my eyes in misery.

When I opened them again, he was holding his cup in his hands, turning it around and around.

"I am sorry," I said.

His laugh was small and humorless. "Do you know," he said, "I actually believe you are." A faint smile; and this, at least, held some warmth.

My own smile was at first tight as a locked door; and then, as understanding of what I had just foresworn

flowed suddenly through me, a waterfall of relief, it
broke wide open on all the other possibilities for which
my "no" cleared the way.

ELIZA WAS AN ENTIRE world. I could spend my entire
life exploring and still there would be more to discover.
She lay spread like a quilt over my bed, her stays loosened so that I could feel the natural curves of her. Her
gown was laid carefully over the chair by the window,
with her silk stockings atop it. Mine was draped across
the clothespress. Our slippers tumbled together at the
foot of the bed.

My chamber door was locked. Except for the servants,
the house was quite empty. We had all afternoon if we
wished it, and no one to disturb us. I walked my fingers
over the bend of her shoulder from freckle to freckle.

As usual, this morning's newspaper had mentioned recent arrests and trials, sentences and reprieves. But one
in particular had caught my eye: a groom in a genteel
household, convicted of an unnatural crime and sen-
tenced to death.

I'd looked across the table to where Mr. Watters was
still sipping his coffee. Whether he had seen the story
or not I could not have said, for while my own face felt
locked in an expression of horror, his was as cool and
unreadable as that of a classical statue.

When I first ventured into London on his arm, I'd felt
as if the city was undressing before me, each new door I
entered like a piece of clothing discarded, baring more of

London's secrets to me. And now I had the same delightful feeling; I undressed Eliza the way I once imagined I undressed the city. But it was just a fancy; I had come to understand that, unlike Eliza's form, London would never be entirely revealed to me. As a woman, and a gently bred woman, at that, so many pockets of this place would always be barred and mysterious to me.

I had a vague notion that there were places for men like Mr. Watters to go and be in the company of other men like him; and, too, the vague notion that they were not safe from persecution within the walls of such establishments. Gentlemen had their clubs, free of ladies' prying eyes. Gentlemen had the entirety of the world in which to room. But we, I thought, stroking my hand down Eliza's arm, over her side and the slope of her belly, had one advantage. In the expectation that we must be retiring—that we must always be in one another's company because of the risk that men's appetites pose to a woman alone—society kept us hobbled, even as it offered us sanctuary to be our true selves.

I cupped Eliza's cheek. "I am nine-and-twenty," I said, "and I have never once felt like this before." I would once have been ashamed of my age; embarrassed by the littleness of my life until now. But at last, at last, I was not.

"Mmm." She turned her head, dragged her lips along my palm. "Are you truly so very old?" Her eyes gleamed up at me.

I tried to reclaim my hand, but she held my wrist fast. "And how old are you?"

"Twenty-one. And quite hopeless when it comes to romance."

I'd known she was younger than I, but old enough to have had three Seasons. And it was not her age that made my skin suddenly itch. "Have you so much experience with romance, then?"

A soft laugh. "No. Not so much. There was a girl at school. But she married years ago, at just seventeen; I have not seen her since." She raised her eyes to mine, and now they were very serious. "Nor," she added, raising herself up on one elbow so our faces were on a level with one another, "have I thought about her at all in a long time. Nor anyone else, since I first walked into Harriet's drawing room and saw you sitting there, all haloed in your little patch of spring sunlight. Not since you told me with such spectacular frankness that I had something in my teeth."

Her words felt impossible in their loveliness. "And what of men?"

Eliza dropped back down onto the bed and rolled onto her back. "Men," she said, and sighed. "Men and romance do not fit together in my mind at all." She stared up at the canopy for some minutes, while I stroked her wrist and forearm. "Papa said his friend Mr. Andrews has been speaking of me in . . . flattering terms."

My hand stilled. "Mr. Andrews?" I said, though the name meant nothing to me; she had never mentioned it before.

"He is almost as old as my father," Eliza said, her eyes

still fixed overhead. "When I was a child, he used to bring sweets for me and Julia. His wife died several years ago. He has no children, but he would like some."

I was silent, watching her.

"He made his fortune in shipping."

"Oh," I said.

"It is not the match my mother envisioned for me, but I think Julia's intended will make up for Mr. Andrews's lack of connections. And in a generation or two, our descendants will seem genteel enough to satisfy most people."

The room swirled a little around me. *No, no, no, no*—

"Has he—offered for you?"

She looked at me, eyes water-bright. "Not yet," she said. "But soon, I think." She reached for my hand, but I pulled it away, drew my knees up to my chest, and encircled them with both arms. This was impossible—I had only just rejected Mr. Watters.

"Could you—how could you—" I breathed in and out, then said the first thing that entered my head in a coherent manner. "How could you bear to share a bed with him?"

Eliza scrambled to her own knees and perched so, her jaw working strangely.

"My mother has always said that women have the burden of endurance," she said at last. "We endure all the things that men cannot, for the good of society. Childbed, and quietness. I suppose I could bear his attentions as well." She pushed her knuckles against her lips, then let her hand drop.

"This is probably the best chance I have," she said. "This is my third Season, Anne. I have not had a single offer. One or two young men seem amused by me, but none wish to marry me."

"Then they are fools," I said simply, for it was the truth.

"Oh, Frank," Eliza said, and now when she took my hand I did not resist. She held it again to her cheek, and it absorbed the wetness there.

CHAPTER THIRTY

I was invited to Miss Julia's wedding purely because I was a guest at the home of her intimate friend. I knew this, but still I was grateful for the opportunity, for I had not seen Eliza for nearly a fortnight. She was busy helping with wedding preparations, though she did find time to write to me nearly every day, if only a brief note.

Julia insists that only Gunter's will do for the cake, she wrote one day. *Mamma has acquiesced, though our cook makes perfectly delicious cakes for ordinary occasions, and would almost certainly do as well for extraordinary occasions.*

The letter continued in this manner for several lines. And then:

I think of you every hour.

She never mentioned Mr. Andrews at all.

THE RECTOR'S VOICE RESOUNDED throughout St. George's, amplified by the high arched ceilings. I had been to only a few weddings in my life, those of neighbors and important tenants; my cousins' nuptials took place too far away for me, in my supposed weakness, to attend them. I sat now between Mrs. Fitzwilliam and

Mr. Watters as the familiar words of the wedding service were spoken, the ring given.

I glanced at Mr. Watters, his profile smooth as pressed linen. We each knew something of the other, now; truths few others did, or ever would. A fragile trust laced us; if I were still taking my drops, I thought I might have seen it woven between us now, thin and strong as spider threads. Almost, almost I wished things could be different; that I could be happy doing the easy thing; but attraction is a mystery, and an affinity of minds even more so. I felt neither of these things with him, and so, sitting in a lovely cathedral on a summer's morning, I could not feel sorry that he and I would not be standing together before a clergyman, solemnly vowing things neither of us meant.

When Julia promised her obedience, a sweet smile upon her lips, my jaw clenched in its old, impotent way.

I thought of Miss Hall's silent fury when I spoke to her so casually of marriage, probing the memory as I might a sore tooth; but there was no tenderness at all left. In its place was Eliza and a story, as fanciful as those I loved as a child, wherein we had more than stolen hours together, but could live together as devotedly and affectionately as any husband and wife.

"Blessed are all they that fear the Lord: and walk in his ways," the rector intoned; but I scarcely heard him.

WE WERE ABLE TO snatch a few moments together during the wedding breakfast. The Amherst home gleamed with polish; the food was plentiful; the guests merry. We all admired the wedding cake, all the more so once we tasted it, heavy with dried fruit and sweet with sugar. Mr. Watters escorted me into and out of the church, and into the Amherst residence, with no sign of ill will, his teeth as determinedly gleaming as ever.

Eliza was, of course, much engaged in helping her mother ensure their guests' comfort, but she spared me many quick smiles, and at last she came over to the corner where I secluded myself, away from so much required conversational effort, and whispered, "Come." The tips of her fingers brushed the inside of my wrist.

I followed her from the room, noting that Mr. Watters watched us leave. When I looked at him, though, he merely lifted one corner of his mouth, then turned to engage the gentleman beside him in conversation.

The Amherst garden was a little larger than John's, and better tended. Eliza slipped her arm through mine, moving us briskly away from the house, where a pretty stone bench sat half-hidden by a small fountain.

"I am so glad it is over," she said.

"Your sister seems very happy."

"She is," Eliza said, but she looked about us, restless as a dragonfly and just as bright in her made-over gown.

"What is it?" I said this even as my breath grew short, suspended somewhere between my breast and my throat, from the fear that I knew what her answer would be.

Eliza leaned back on her palms, raising her face to the feeble sun. "Mr. Andrews asked to speak to me after the breakfast."

I did not ask which gentleman Mr. Andrews was.

I had marked him almost instantly, his hair gray and thinning, his coat well cut, his face amiable. He spent much of the breakfast speaking with Mrs. Amherst, who was unmistakably attentive to him. I spent much of the breakfast trying to ignore his existence, and failing utterly.

I spoke now only because I must know the answer, but the words tore at my throat. "And . . . what will you say to him?"

Her eyes squeezed. "What I must."

I seized her hand. "Come back to Kent with me," I said, and when her eyes opened and her head began to shake, I spoke frantically to forestall the inevitable. Not of marriage—I was not so naive now as I once was. But of creating our own sort of forever, our own terms. "You can be my companion—that is what we can tell people. It is perfectly respectable. You will have everything you need; we can take a house in Town so that you can see your family often."

Her eyes widened, full as twin moons. "Anne—"

"*No.*" I shook my head. "No. I—love you," I said; and the words that we had not spoken to one another before trailed between us now like candle smoke. "I would spend my life with you, if you will let me."

She stared at me for so long that I had to release my breath or die for want of air. The next breath I took was a ragged, hopeless thing. She shook her head, slowly, as if the motion pained her; and I began to weep.

"Anne, please," she whispered. She took my wet face in her hands and kissed me. "Please."

I drew back and wiped my face with the back of one

wrist. "How can you marry him? How can you bear to—to become a man's possession? *You,* of all people?"

"What would be different if I lived with you? I am not independent as you are, Anne! I have no land of my own, no income of my own. I would give anything—*anything*—to be as fortunate as you; but I am not, and I must be practical."

I was shivering, though it was not cold. "You show very little imagination," I said, "for someone who reads Mary Wollstonecraft and delights in the most extraordinary novels."

"That is unfair!" Eliza's mouth was a slash of color in her white face. "Mary Wollstonecraft was *reviled* after her death when her indiscretions became known! Hers might have been different to ours, but make no mistake, Anne; we would be reviled as well."

My voice came out like a stranger's, stark as lightning against a black country sky. "And do *you* know how Mary Wollstonecraft died? Just like so many other women, bringing a child into the world."

Eliza pressed her palms to her forehead, her fingertips in her hair threatening to unravel her maid's fine work. "As a companion," she said, "I would have no standing in society. At least as a wife I will command some respect." She dropped her hands and looked at me. "Did you mean to give me an allowance as your companion?"

I knew not what to say, for I had not thought so far. "I . . . I could, certainly," I said, and she laughed, sharp as onions.

"Would you really insult me so?"

"I do not mean—of course not. But I understand . . . does not a husband give his wife pin money?" I reached for her hands again, and she let me take them, though they lay limp in my own. "What of your talk of wives—and husband-wives? If your choices are a life of dependence . . . or a life of dependence . . . would it not be better to at least enjoy the benefits of affection?"

"Affection," she said softly. Her hands twitched a little; and then her fingers curled over mine. I nearly began weeping again, this time with relief.

And then she spoke further. "You will have my affection for the rest of my days," she said. "But can you not see that what you imagine is impossible? Lovely"—with a brush of her mouth over mine; and now her mouth tasted brackish—"but impossible."

I DID NOT SPEAK to anyone when we returned to John's house, except to complain of a headache that I did not have. Spinner came to help me out of my gown, despite the early hour, and to take the pins from my hair one by one. I lay down under the bedclothes and closed my eyes, listening as she tidied the room. When at last the door closed behind her, I let myself cry in earnest.

I WAS IN BED for four days. Once or twice every day Spinner asked whether I wanted a doctor; always I said no. Mrs. Fitzwilliam, too, came to see me, frowning when she saw I was not feverish. She asked whether she should send a servant to the apothecary to purchase some medicine for my relief. Relief from what, she did not say; indeed, perhaps she did not know, herself. But my drops were cures for every imaginable ailment, and so I supposed there was little wonder she thought of them now.

Almost, almost I said yes.

ON THE FIFTH MORNING since Mrs. King's wedding, I rose and went to the window. London was still there. For some reason, I was mildly surprised to see it.

I would not—could not—think of Eliza. Instead, I thought of Miss Hall, whose specter waited around every street corner. For all that I looked for her so many times since arriving in London, our eyes never met, giddy with surprise, over a display of fans or lace. We never encountered one another in the reading room at the Temple of the Muses, despite my having pictured such a meeting many times. I imagined slipping into the chair beside hers, smiling to myself, a thick novel in my hands, or perhaps a volume of love poems, while I waited for her to notice me. Her incredulity at finding me in such a place, well and whole and strong as she urged me to be, would be sweeter than lemon creams.

But even now, after being in Town for so long, I had not done all she wished me to do. I looked down at my hands, which were still so stupid with the needle; at the blank sheets of paper on the writing desk before which I stood, which lay unfilled. Even after my discussion with

John, I still had not summoned the courage to write to Mr. Colt.

I meant to leave my old life behind, my old *self* behind, when I came to London—she should still be sleeping softly on a window seat in Kent, her neck uncomfortably crooked, her knees drawn up so her legs form a gentle curl. She was never meant to rise from there; was too weak, in both body and spirit. I thought that I had changed entirely, that released from my drops I would be a completely different creature to the one I used to be. But I was not different at all. The last few months were a rush of newness, and I was borne along. Only here and there, in pockets of time like secrets hidden within a treasure box, did I willfully make my own choices. Otherwise—for all that my mind was clear and my lungs breathed freely even of the gray-tinged air, for all that I had seen such marvels as I only dreamed of as a child—I may as well have been at Rosings Park, following my mother's word as law, no matter how it chafed, and enduring Mrs. Jenkinson's hollow echo.

But oh dear God, how I longed suddenly to be *home* again.

I searched the corners of my room for . . . something. But they were empty. This house never spoke to me; and perhaps Rosings Park never did, either. I might return there and discover that without my drops' inspiring attendance, my home was nothing more than dumb stone blocks and trees cut and carved. The brooks might only sound like water, the wind like wind. There might be no whispers among the grasses.

Or perhaps I would put palm to tree trunk and feel the sap running under the bark like blood. Perhaps the earth would press up against me in greeting, the walls would exhale their welcome, the attics would hum with gladness.

I blew out a breath, so gradually that I was able to track the gentle descent of my chest as it emptied. Then I sat at the writing desk and dipped my pen.

Part Three

Back Again

CHAPTER THIRTY-ONE

Rosings Park came into view as we rounded the bend in the lane. At this time of year, with the trees dressed in their abundant summer finery, only the very tip of the rooftop was visible. I knew that returning home would likely be strange after being away for the first time since Brighton; but I was unprepared for this, for the sight of a rooftop to turn me at once thick as an oak trunk with longing and thin as a rootling with fear. Quite suddenly, there were two Annes approaching the house—one who would lean outside the carriage window if she could, the better to smell, and hear, and see; and another who would scramble back to the far side of the carriage, away from the place where she once lay dormant. In reality, of course, I did neither of those things, but sat still and outwardly serene, eyes on the high hedgerows and the approaching tall iron gate. Spinner showed no sign of noticing that I was being rent in two.

A FOOTMAN HELPED ME down from the carriage at the steps to Rosings's front door, and I stretched my shoulders and arched my back. The air was thick with moisture, and I looked up, up, up at the house, which returned my look with such blankness that I had the unsettling feeling I was gazing at a corpse. The house was silent with a silence that is louder than screams.

I tipped my head and closed my eyes and listened, waiting for the thrumming voices of the estate to greet me, but though the leaves of the trees that lined the drive whispered secrets to one another, I could not make them out.

What I heard, instead, was the murmuring of my own body. My breath swelled easily within my lungs; my legs stood, firm and substantial, upon the drive. I could hear the *thud-thud-thud* of my heart inside my breast, reminding me that I was stronger now, and equal to Rosings's vastness.

Spinner came to stand beside me, moving a bit stiffly after our journey. "It is good to be back, is it not?" she said, and I opened my eyes.

Mamma, conspicuously, was nowhere in sight, though I wrote both her and Mr. Colt to tell them when to expect my return. I fancied I could feel her watching me from an upstairs window.

"Yes," I said, for somehow, despite Rosings's cold silence, despite the thumping of my heart, it truly was.

THE DRAWING ROOM LOOKED exactly as I remembered it, from the gleam of dark wood to the angle of the late afternoon sunlight through the windows. I supposed it was rather silly to have expected otherwise; I was only gone a few months, after all. But it felt as if I had been away for a hundred years, and returned to find the house suspended in time, deep in an enchanted sleep.

I prepared myself as best I could for this moment, but standing before my mother while she looked at me—chin lifted, eyes narrowed, mouth thin as a thread—I had the disorienting sensation that I was a child again, small and trembling before her parent's anger; and like a child, I had lost my words, they had gone skittering away from me and were cowering in the corners of the room. I was acutely aware that I was standing in front of Mamma like a chastened servant while she sat her chair as a queen would her throne. I cleared my throat, looked down at my hands, and tried to call my words back to me.

Mrs. Jenkinson sat beside my mother, and I was, unaccountably, relieved. I had treated her poorly when I left, and had no reason to think Mamma would keep her on with me gone. I thought far less about my companion than I should have since I went away; to my shame, if not for Eliza, I might not be so relieved to see her here now. But I could not forget Eliza's words about the precariousness of a companion's situation: her dependence, her lack of respect from society. Though I had never warmed to Mrs. Jenkinson—though, in truth, I simply wanted to be away from her—I was glad she did not suffer for my thoughtlessness.

Mrs. Jenkinson said nothing, but her bland, watery gaze felt, incongruously, supportive as a corset, straightening my spine and keeping me from bending to my mother's will. I moved deliberately to the chair across from Mamma's and sat down, drawing in a breath. If only some clever person could distill the bits of my medicine that made me not *care* so very much—just for a time, just for now!—and remove the crippling lethargy. I was never so frightened in my life.

"Mamma," I said.

"I am glad you have returned," Mamma said. "Your room is aired and I've ordered a bath prepared. No doubt you will wish to rest."

"No, indeed," I said. "I am—not tired at all, Mamma."

"We are having guests tonight, for supper and cards. The Boltons and the Cliftons. I expect you have something appropriate to wear? Mr. Colt kept me apprised of the bills from modistes in Town."

I flushed. "I do not need to rest," I said again. "I am not tired."

"Not tired?" Her eyes sharpened, slicing like knives as they looked me up and down. She sat, if possible, even straighter in her chair. "Hmmph. Well. You do have a bloom about you. You are feeling well, still, I suppose?"

"Yes. As I said in my letters." I realized I was twisting my fingers together, and forced myself to stop. "I no longer take laudanum. I will not have it in the house."

Her mouth opened, and I put up a hand; to my complete surprise, her mouth closed again.

"I am the better for being without it; so much better that I—that I am prepared to take my proper place as mistress of Rosings." Again, her open mouth; again, my hand forestalled her words, and now my own words, the ones I spoke again and again inside my head during the drive from London, unspooled themselves. "You have done so much—I am forever grateful. But it is time for me to take up the duties I should have taken up long ago."

She was silent for a moment, and I could not guess her thoughts. Then, "Nonsense," she said. "Dr. Grant must evaluate your health before we even consider allowing you to do something so arduous. *If* he agrees that you are ready—"

"There is no need to call for Dr. Grant—"

"He has treated you since you were an infant, Anne, who knows your health better, except myself? In the meantime, you really must rest before this evening—in health or not, such a long journey will have tired you."

She nodded at Mrs. Jenkinson. "Take Miss de Bourgh upstairs, and instruct her maid that she must be dressed for company this evening."

I was a walker, scrambling to get out of the way of an oncoming cart. Mrs. Jenkinson seemed to feel much the same; she looked between myself and my mother, no doubt uncertain whose instructions she ought to follow. Almost, I retreated to my room to regroup; but if I were to do so now, I might forever be a quivering, fearful thing, my time in Town just a brief interlude in a life of controlled uniformity.

"No," I said, a satisfying snap to the word. "I do not want—I will not allow Dr. Grant to be called for on my behalf. *I* know my health better than anyone, Dr. Grant especially. If it were left to him, I would still be a slave to my medicine, good for *nothing*—"

"You malign the name of a good man and a good

doctor, who has always done his best by you!" she cried. "Such ingratitude—such repulsive pride, I could never have imagined! I hope you will show contrition after you have thought about your circumstances—"

Her voice was rising; but for once mine rose higher, like a wind that blows so fiercely it overwhelms all other sounds. My wind blew the words from my mother's lips and left her shocked and ruffled.

"Did you not read my letters?" I said. "I have been in London for weeks upon weeks, and the foul air has not killed me. Indeed, I walked farther and felt better while I was there than I ever have in the country—not because of the air, but because I was not suffering the effects of a medicine that was more curse than cure." I was standing—how was it that I was standing?—and I spread my arms wide. "And you—you *allowed*, you *encouraged* me to stay in a state of—of incapacitation! *Look at me now!*" I struck my breast with one hand. "I am *well*, Mamma. Well and whole and quite capable of being a proper mistress to Rosings."

My voice soared to a pitch just short of shouting, and I dropped my arms and consciously breathed in and out. I was flushed from hairline to toe-tips.

"I am appreciative of all that you have done for the estate," I said, more temperately. "And I . . . am appreciative of all that you tried to do for me."

Her throat worked and worked, as if there was something caught there. Her eyes stared.

I swallowed; and then the words I had rehearsed all the long drive from London came forth like a sprung leak. "I wish—I wish us to live peacefully, but that cannot happen if we are ever at odds. I think the best solution is separate households. Mr. Colt and I will go tomorrow to look at the dower house and decide what must be done to make it habitable again. You may take—almost—anything you would like from the great house to furnish it; or I will gladly provide funds for any furnishings you need."

She was shivering. "That house," she said, tight, furious, "is meant to be used after the heir marries. Am I to wish you joy?"

I shook my head. "No. I am not—I will never marry."

"I see." Mamma rose, too, forcing me to look up at her; but still she trembled, and somehow I did not feel the disadvantage of my height compared to hers as I used to. "You are a foolish girl," she said. "What will happen to Rosings Park if you produce no heir? Do you truly want some distant de Bourgh cousin—"

I had thought about this, but I was not willing, just yet, to share these thoughts with her. I met her eyes.

"That is my worry now, not yours," I said.

I ESCAPED TO THE stables, dashing across the drive, though in the distance thunder growled like an animal warning. Inside, a stable boy, leaning against the wall oiling a harness in a desultory manner, jumped when he saw me, stumbling over his own feet in his haste to bow. I nodded to him and assured him I needed no assistance; I was merely there to see my ponies.

The surprise on his face made my heart seize within its cage. But then he pointed to the stalls near the far end of the building, and my heart beat again, and my feet followed the direction of his pointing finger.

The stables smelled of hay and manure, warm and dusty with an underlying musk of animal. The carriage and plough horses were shut away in their stalls, and one or two flicked their ears as I passed. But, oh, my ponies knew me—I feared they would not, that, abandoned so suddenly, they would have forgotten me. But they came forward to the doors of their stalls, pressed their soft noses against my outstretched palms, huffed their warm moist breath in welcome. My temples tingled, and I rolled my eyes upward to keep the sudden tears from falling.

I TOLD SPINNER TO dress me well for supper and cards, armoring myself in silk and net lace, with heavy pearls at my ears and throat. When I descended the stairs and Mamma saw my gown, she raised one brow at the filaments of lace about the low neckline and the pale green color of the silk, so different to the reds and yellows she preferred for me; but said nothing.

Mr. and Mrs. Clifton, who had known me from infancy, expressed delight at my looks. "I never thought I'd see the day," Mrs. Clifton said. "Your return to health is a miracle, Miss de Bourgh; it truly is."

I managed to thank her without stammering. And when Peters announced that the meal was served, I drew in a breath and held it, and took my place at the top of the table.

There was utter silence, for far too long. And then the scraping of chairs as the others took their seats. Mamma's face, when I finally looked at her, was pale as paper.

ONCE THE FIRST SHOCK passed, Mamma did not consent to relinquish her grip quietly, and I found I must prise her fingers away from each aspect of life at Rosings Park, one by one by one. The key to the book room I had to demand, for she did not offer it; when she tried to instruct Mrs. Barrister about what food my stomach could best tolerate, I was overcome with a rage that rose as swift and as deadly as floodwaters, and had to clap my hand over my mouth to stop myself from screaming. Anything I left her she used to her advantage, her lined face desperate in a way that made me want to cry; yet still I took everything from her, everything except dominion over her own person and bedchamber, for I could not go back to being quiet and controlled, I could *not*. The servants, unaccustomed to answering to me, were very much caught between us like shuttlecocks batted back and forth; it was this that told me my decision that we must live apart was a sound one.

The dower house, situated near the village, had stood empty since Grandmother de Bourgh died before my birth. It was shut up, and smelled of dust; Mr. Colt and I sneezed and sneezed as we explored its rooms, laughing into our elbows as we covered our noses and mouths with our sleeves. In the end, he said that aside from the obvious need for a thorough cleaning, he thought repairing the roof, sweeping out the chimneys, and replacing a few windowsills that had succumbed to wood rot should be all that was necessary to accomplish before Mamma could take residence, and that he would set some men from Hunsford to the task immediately.

I looked around the rooms—fine rooms, well appointed, with good light—and tried not to think about how small they were compared to the rooms at Rosings; tried not to feel as if I were packing my mother away in a box. I would encourage her to choose new paint and paper hangings; and perhaps she would consent to venture into London for new carpets.

My days were spent mostly in Mr. Colt's company. He was a pleasant and patient man; and a competent one, which was a relief. I did not want, in addition to everything else, to have to find a new steward. We went over the accounts, the neat columns of numbers oddly soothing, this one thing, once more, coming quickly and naturally to me, the unexpected talent I had discovered at the age of twelve suddenly vitally useful. We discussed the home farm and the tenant farms—crop rotations, livestock, the prices of wool and grain and so many other things that my mind sloshed within my skull at the end of each day.

When we ventured out onto the estate, I found myself tucking my elbows in and bending my neck, making myself even smaller. Mr. Colt greeted the tenants naturally, and they greeted him with respect, but I feared they would find me strange, Sir Lewis's sickly daughter, who had never taken an interest in them before; and I was at once that girl again, dumb and witless, braced for laughter.

But they were deferential when they saw me; and if there was curiosity in their eyes, there was at least no ill will. It took nearly as much courage to face them as it took to face down Mamma; but with an effort like heaving boulders from my back, I straightened my shoulders and began to know them.

MOST NIGHTS I WAS too tired to do anything but sleep, and for the first time since I stopped taking my drops, I toppled each night into a state of heavy insensibility so quickly that I rarely remembered Spinner putting out the candle. Mr. Colt assured me that I needn't exert myself so much in the actual, physical going-over of the estate, but until I had a true understanding of all its particulars, I felt I must. Soon enough, however, I confess I knew I would be more than happy to hand over the bulk of the running-about to him; but just now, when I still sometimes feared that Rosings Park was going to close around me—that I might not be able to live here without the familiar dampening solace of my drops—I was glad to go manic with work.

But tonight was my first night on my own in my own house, and though my body ached with weariness, I found I could not sleep. I went with the rector's wife to visit some of the least fortunate among the cottagers that afternoon, those who were too old or infirm to maintain farms, and who existed on Rosings's charity, and was shocked by the meanness of their homes. I knew not what could be done about their sad circumstances beyond what we did already, however; I would have to bring up the matter with Mr. Colt. The thought was not a pleasant one; for all his geniality, Mr. Colt's one fault was an excessive devotion to my father's memory, which made it difficult to criticize any long-standing practices that Papa had initiated.

But this was not the reason for my sleeplessness. While I was out, Mamma and Mrs. Jenkinson—my companion no more, she had formally become Mamma's—moved with the last of their things to the dower house. Breakfast that morning was almost entirely silent, the sounds of silverware on china dramatically loud by contrast. Mrs. Jenkinson seemed glad enough, but even she was solemn, her eyes downcast, as if in consideration for Mamma's unspeaking anger.

I quit the room as soon as I could, saying, truthfully enough, that I had letters to write. But I did not write them; instead I locked myself in my book room and cried, a shawl pressed to my mouth to cloak the noise.

CHAPTER THIRTY-TWO

She appeared in the doorway to the book room—*my* book room—without any warning whatsoever. If I were less engrossed in my book—*An Exposition of English Insects,* which I discovered among Papa's collection, and which was teaching me the names of some of the beautiful flitting, scuttling creatures I had observed in ignorance for so long—I would have heard the front door being answered, and perhaps even Peters's request for Mamma to wait for him to announce her. But then again, until just the week before he was *her* butler, and he, and the other poor servants, were all having to accustom themselves to this strange new world, wherein Lady Catherine was a guest, and not the mistress, in this house. I stared at her now, losing my place as my book dropped to my lap, and wondered whether Peters hovered just out of sight in the hallway.

"Close your mouth, you are not a simpleton," she said, and swept into the room to sit across from me without invitation. My jaw obeyed her reflexively, my teeth clicking together.

"You spoke falsely when you returned to Rosings," she said with no further preamble. "I am here to fix the record."

I could think of nothing to say but, "Very well."

The muscles of her face relaxed at my words, and she looked down, just briefly, at her lap. "Men," she said, looking up at me again, "haven't the faintest notion what it means to be a mother. They do not *feel* what their children feel as mothers do. Your father was very proud of the seed he planted in me, but it was *my* body that tended it, increasing to give it space to grow. *I* brought you into the world. That is not something that can be—cut away, not even once the birth is completed. I felt you on the inside, and I thought, once you were outside my body, that I would no longer be able to feel you so intimately; but that was not so. I felt your every cry—every scream tugged at me as if the navel-string still tethered us and your cries *pulled* on it."

I flinched. She saw it, and nodded.

"Yes. You screamed without ceasing, and I felt every second of it in pulls and *scrapes*, like nails over my skin, and your father just—slept on." A flick of her fingers. "He never heard you in the night, and he was out of the house all day. He never felt your distress as I did."

"He tried to help me," I whispered. "At Brighton—"

"Do not speak to me of *Brighton*," she said, and there was a wildness to her that I could never have imagined. She turned her face from me and spoke to the bookshelves lining the wall. "Your father and I had the most spectacular argument after Brighton. You were perfectly well, *perfectly* contented, and he insisted we go to that—that place. I endured your screams as they pulled you into the sea once; I refused to do it again, not even if it turned out to be the cure Sir Lewis believed it to be.

It was all very well for *him*, away from it all; *he* did not have to stand in the bitter cold and listen to his child suffer. And then you became so violently ill, as I knew you would—!" The fingers of one hand rubbed a circle around the rounded edges of her brooch with its plait of dark hair. "Well, when he said we should try Bath next, I refused. Dr. Grant said it was a city of charlatans, and I believed him. My judgment was always sounder than your father's. A mother," she said, looking up at me, "cannot be wrong, not when she is acting for the good of her child."

I held on to the edge of the desk. My fingernails bit into the wood like teeth.

"I know not by what methods my nephew's physician tended you, nor how he managed what Dr. Grant could not. Whatever his methods, they have proved incendiary; I never thought my daughter could treat me with such disrespect as you have."

I thought of how I felt when I returned to Kent and confronted her; but now she was the walker, and I the runaway cart, forcing her from the road she knew and onto another, unfamiliar one. Like a thief, I had stolen her life from her, and for all the hurt and anger I carried inside me like a brazier, and for all that it was mine to take, my shoulders hunched now in shame.

"Mamma," I said, but she talked over me in the old familiar way.

"You shall never understand what I mean, I suppose," she said, "since you are being so bullheaded about marriage."

"I do not want Rosings Park to belong to my husband,"

I said. "Depending upon his temperament, I might have no hand in its running at all—"

Mamma squinted at me the way she always did when she thought I said something stupid. "Rosings Park," she said, "is yours now and forever. Just as my father's estate will always be mine, even if my brother is the *official* master there. Our ancestral lands are in our bodies, our blood; we are part of England in a way that lesser citizens can never understand."

She stood. "Even so," she said, "I am glad to see some stubbornness in you; it is a necessary attribute in a woman." She looked at me down the sharp curved length of her nose. "You get it from me, of course; your father melted like wax in the face of adversity."

And then she departed, and I was left with a mad desire to laugh, for it turned out Lady Catherine de Bourgh—like her daughter!—was something of a poet.

THOUGH IT WAS EVENING, I had to walk once she was gone. I went out on the grounds, where darkness crept across the lawn, the sun no more than a faint red light at the horizon. I looked out at the edge of the woods, where the trees crowded together, and was almost tempted to slip between them. The air carried the faintest nighttime chill under its warmth, and I walked faster and faster until I was running, *running*, my skirts bunched in my hands, my poor slippers thumping against the grass. My breath came sharp and fast, but it *came*, and as I passed one of the benches on the lawn, I imagined my younger self sitting there, watching me pass.

There was a peculiar buzzing in my ears, as if I had stumbled into a hive of bees, and my eyes smarted as if from bee stings. I staggered the last steps to the wood, as the stinging resolved itself into blinding tears. Catching myself on a tree—palm scraping against the rough bark—I clung to it. For just a moment, I half-expected the droning in my ears to become intelligible murmurs, my heart tight with missing. Almost, I called Rosings's name.

But then: "Mamma," I said instead, choked and helpless, sorry and glad at once for the way the word felt upon my tongue. It was so like her, that when at last she said exactly what I always needed to hear, it should be in such self-righteous terms.

When at last the torrent passed, I opened my eyes. The woods were water-blurred; I had only soft impressions of trees and undergrowth, made softer still by the gathering dark. It was, I thought, the way a newborn babe must experience the world, and almost, I smiled. I was made fresh again.

CHAPTER THIRTY-THREE

A letter from London, ma'am," Peters said, interrupting my concentration.

I murmured a distracted thank-you and nearly set it aside to return to the list of costs from Mr. Colt. But it was from Harriet, and the novelty of thinking that she chose to write to me was enough to arouse my curiosity. I broke the seal.

The first few lines were full of questions about how I was enjoying my return to country life. But then—

Eliza was wed this morning with much less fuss and fanfare than Julia, though with no fewer good wishes. She and Mr. Andrews are off to visit his relations in Scotland next week for their wedding trip, though why they would choose a place so wild and dreary I cannot fathom. She asked me to tell you about the marriage, which surprised me, as I thought the two of you were on such terms that she would have written to you herself. I do hope there has been no falling-out.

I should have expected this. But distractions were plentiful in this new, busy life, and whenever thoughts of Eliza tried to intrude, I quickly found something pressing that I must *immediately* see to, sometimes to my steward's bewilderment. And so the sight of her name—and linked so inextricably to another's—was like a boxer's blow, leaving me gasping. I shut my eyes tight as spring buds, but still I saw Eliza behind the lids—showing me her teeth and asking if they were clean; leaning over me, cheeks bright and lips parted, as I rocked, shuddering, against the heel of her hand. She had offered me a world inside books, and taught me that joy was something bodies could feel, as well as souls.

But after several moments, I set Mrs. Fitzwilliam's letter aside and returned to Mr. Colt's list. Yet even as I did, my mind began composing a response.

Give her my warmest felicitations, I would say. *And please do tell her that I would welcome correspondence from her, whenever she has time.*

MAMMA'S BUTLER SHOWED ME into her drawing room, where she and Mrs. Jenkinson were taking tea, sitting in two chairs beside the window. I glanced about the room for a moment before my mother acknowledged me; she had made the house her own, the paper hangings and furniture all similar in color and style to those she chose for the great house when she was its mistress.

Mrs. Jenkinson offered me a thin smile in greeting; Mamma made a show of taking another sip from her cup before looking at me. "Your hair is a disgrace," she said. "What in heaven's name have you been doing?"

I put a hand to my head. "Driving."

"Was there a gale I missed?"

"No," I said, and endeavored not to blush. "I was—" But I stopped, for to explain myself would be too much like offering an excuse, and I needed no excuse for enjoying a brisk drive over my own property.

"I came to tell you that I am going to Pemberley for a short while," I said instead.

"Pemberley! Did my nephew invite you?"

"Not . . . precisely. I rather invited myself."

"*I* was not informed that the family had removed to Derbyshire! They are not still in London?"

"It is August, Mamma; almost no one is still in London." I thought, fleetingly, of Eliza and her new husband, who would, I assumed, return to Town once their wedding trip was over; but my words did not apply to them, as they had no country house. And, of course, I was trying not to think about Eliza.

My mother swished her fingers. "Of course it's August." She frowned, as if this were something about which *I* should have been aware.

I hastened on before she could inquire further. "Also, I have a . . . that is, Mr. Colt and I . . . We have been considering a new, ah, project. And I wondered—I hoped—that you would help us with it."

She tapped the nail of one finger against her teeth. "Such condescension."

I swallowed my instinctive retraction of the offer, and waited; I meant it as an olive branch, after all. She rewarded my patience in a few moments by saying, "Very well, what is it?"

"A school," I said. "So many of our tenants' children— of Hunsford's children—are taught at home by their mothers, *if* their mothers have the learning and time to teach them. You have so many more connections than

I do; I feel certain you must know a woman—either within the village or outside of it—who would be a willing and able instructor."

Mamma pushed her tongue into her cheek, twisting her mouth off to the side. "Rosings, I presume, will be paying this woman's wages?"

I nodded. "I have been over the accounts scrupulously; we can easily afford the modest wages a teacher will reasonably expect." A pause. "You and Mr. Colt have kept the estate prosperous."

There was a flicker at the corners of her mouth, before she turned them down as if by force of will. "And what shall these children be taught? And to what purpose?"

That she was asking rather than telling me was rather unbelievable. "All the usual things—reading, writing. Sewing for the girls. Chores and basic deportment." Unwillingly, my mind flew to Eliza—*Let them learn to use their minds, as men are taught to do*—and with a wrenching pain, I pulled it back.

Her eyes slid away from mine. "I might know a suitable person."

"Well—wonderful." I paused, but she did not invite me to sit down, or ask if I would like some tea. She did look me over, frowning again at the state of my hair and raising one brow at the cut of my pelisse. That she had no further criticisms said as much as if she had actually condescended to offer me praise. "I will write you when I arrive in Derbyshire; I do not think I will stay more than a week or so."

"You have done something different with your hair," Mamma said. She glared at the flyaway strands.

Again, I touched my head. "Ah—yes."

"It is becoming. Though if you are truly serious about this nonsense of never marrying, you ought to start wearing a cap."

I blinked, recalling how Miss Hall's caps somehow seemed to hide not just most of her hair, but much of her spirit. "I will consider it, Mamma."

I ARRIVED IN DERBYSHIRE, travel-weary and stiff from several days in a jolting carriage and several nights in lumpy inn beds. Beyond the stiffness of my body, however, a terrible nervousness was spreading like a root system within my chest. Pemberley estate sprawled, lush and hilly; the house itself was larger even than Rosings, and very beautiful. I was grateful to Eliza, for it was her influence that prompted me to dress so well for the journey, in a pelisse of blue and a bonnet adorned with lace and curling feathers. A memory pricked me, very suddenly—sharp as a seamstress's pin, bringing tears to my eyes. It was, perhaps, the very earliest memory I had: Mamma, seated across from me in the nursery, her back very straight and her mouth smiling. She was describing Pemberley, in terms almost as loving as those she would use to describe Rosings, and she was stroking the back of my small hand.

"It is very grand, my dear. I have excellent taste in architecture, and I was happy to be able to tell my sister when she wed that her new home was every bit as attractive as she claimed. And with such extensive grounds!

When you marry your cousin, *your* union shall also unite two of the richest estates in the country." She smoothed my hair as tenderly as if it were her beloved sister's. "Your aunt and I promised you to one another when you were both still in your cradles. Nowhere could be found two more affectionate sisters than ourselves; how could our children fail to feel less for each other?"

Inside the house now waited two people whose opinions of me had never been high; what I meant to ask of them was ridiculous in the face of Mrs. Darcy's laughing dismissal and Fitzwilliam's words, so long remembered: *How exactly does one converse with a doll?*

Others, though, found me capable, people who knew me far better than my cousin or his wife ever cared to. I held this truth in my mind as I ascended Pemberley's steps, my half-boots a little too loud upon the stone.

My cousin greeted me with his usual stiff formality; his wife was cordial, though as usual she appeared to hold some private amusement just behind her eyes. She apologized for not rising when I was led into the airy family parlor, but she had good reason to remain seated, as little George was deeply asleep in the curve of her arm. I stumbled over an assurance that I was not offended, glancing at the infant with some apprehension only to discover, to my surprise, that the sight of his slack, toothless mouth made me smile. Tea was rung for, and then we all subsided into an awkward silence that probably would have stretched interminably had Darcy not had the good sense to marry a woman with far more social grace than either he or I possessed.

We passed an amiable enough hour, during which Mrs. Darcy expressed pleasure in seeing me look so well, and actually laughed—though she quickly stopped herself—when I thanked her and said I truly was well, so much so that I had taken over my proper duties at Rosings Park, much to my mother's dismay. Even my cousin's mouth quivered a little, as if he were inclined to smile.

They very politely did not ask why I was there, and I was glad enough to take a little time to acclimate to this strange new reality, in which I was no longer a doll but a person able to not only converse but also amuse with my conversation.

AT DINNER, HOWEVER, DARCY and his wife exchanged a significant look, and he sighed and put down his fork and knife and patted his mouth with the edge of the tablecloth. "Cousin," he said, "you know we are very happy to receive you, but I must admit to some curiosity. You said in your letter that you had an important matter to discuss."

The meat I was chewing turned to leather in my mouth, and it was a struggle to swallow it. I set my own cutlery down with great care and took a fortifying sip of wine.

"Yes," I said at last. "There is."

I paused, trying to decide how best to state my purpose, and Mrs. Darcy leaned forward. The candlelight gleamed in her dark hair; her round face shone with interest. "This is all very mysterious," she said, smiling.

I could not make my mouth work properly in order to smile in return. "I do have a question of great importance to ask you both," I said. "And one, I fear, that you will find . . . impertinent." I swallowed, but my mouth was too dry, and I took another sip of wine to wet it. "I told you I have taken my proper place as Rosings's mistress. What I did not say is that I . . . intend to remain single. Which makes the matter of inheritance rather . . . difficult."

Again, the couple exchanged one of those glances that speaks to a deep intimacy of minds. I blinked away the thought of Eliza, my lips tightening. "It does, yes," Darcy said. "But—Anne—there is no reason in the world that you should not marry. Particularly now that you are in such robust health. If it is a question of . . ." But here he stopped speaking, clearly at a loss as to any possible explanation for a woman to choose spinsterhood.

"The more intriguing question, I think," his wife said after a pause, "is not why Miss de Bourgh would remain single, but why she has come all the way to Derbyshire to tell us so."

"As I said," I said slowly, "the matter of who will inherit Rosings Park is made uncertain by my decision never to marry. My steward looked into the matter, and there is a distant cousin on my father's side who would stand to inherit should I die without an heir. I have never met him; apparently he has a smallish estate somewhere in Hampshire. It might be that he would be good for Rosings; but Papa was . . . well, in his way, he always did what he thought best for the people who relied upon us. Though he was never cruel enough to say so, I think it was a burden to him, believing his only child was unfit to take on the responsibilities of the estate once he was gone. Since I *am* able to do so, I feel the—the weight of ensuring that the person who inherits after me has the same care for the property and the people that I do."

I had been looking down at the table, but I now dared a glance at each of my companions; both wore the same startled look, as if a piece of furniture suddenly began addressing them in French. I looked down again.

"I am here because—it seemed too impersonal to ask something so . . . large . . . in a letter. I would like to name your son George my heir."

There was such utter silence that it felt like a physical thing, pressing against my ears.

It was Mrs. Darcy who finally spoke. "George?" she said, and in that single name was a world.

I HELD THE CHILD for the second time since his birth on the day I was to leave Derbyshire. I would write to my solicitor in London as soon as I returned to Kent; it was time I made a will.

George was heavier in my arms than he was a few months ago, and much more alert. I'd seen only glimpses of him and his elder brother, Thomas, in the few days I had been in Derbyshire, through windows or in the distance when I walked over the grounds. Most of the time they were with their nurse, but once I spied them with their parents, picnicking beside the lake. Fitzwilliam invited me to join them, of course, as civility demanded,

but I declined; to break into their happy little party felt
like an intrusion of the worst sort. I did not want to im-
ply that I was one of them, *part* of them. That their son
should take my surname was intrusion enough.

I was dressed for travel, poised to say my goodbyes.
My cousin was called out to one of the tenant farms on
some urgent business, but Mrs. Darcy waited with me
for my trunk to be loaded into the carriage. The children
were here as well, on the steps with their nurse, Thomas
squirming a little to get away from the stillness im-
posed by her patient hand upon his shoulder. Mrs. Darcy
shaded her eyes against the midmorning sun, then finally
turned to the nurse and took her youngest son into her
own arms.

And then, to my startlement, she pressed him into
mine.

My arms dropped slightly at the unexpected weight
of him, and he looked up at me with eyes that were beginning to change color. He was a person—small and
untested, but a *person*—and I had taken on much of the
responsibility for ensuring his future. The intellectual
question of who would ensure Rosings's survival was
quite suddenly answered here, in this child's mind and
muscle and eyes, which would be brown.

"George Darcy de Bourgh," his mother said, the second time she had spoken his new name; there was less
bitterness now, and a more testing quality to the words,
as if she put them into the world to hear how well they
rang out there.

"Yes," I said, staring down at him. We agreed, my

cousin and I and Mrs. Darcy, that George would come yearly to Rosings when he was old enough, that he might begin to learn the breadth and secrets of the place that would someday be his. Otherwise, he was still, and always would be, theirs.

It was Mrs. Darcy, to my great surprise, who saw the merit in my proposal before Fitzwilliam did. "He will have a home," she said, "ready and waiting for him, just as Thomas does. He will not have to scrabble his way up in a profession like Colonel Fitzwilliam; or marry for baser reasons as he did, either."

The lot of a second son can be a challenging one; indeed, John's situation served as the inspiration for my proposal. The thought that I could offer greater freedom to Darcy's child than our cousin had enjoyed, while also having some influence over the education of Rosings's heir, was a heady one, tempered only by the fear that his parents would not be so excited by the thought of my influence.

But Darcy nodded at last, slowly enough that it might have been reluctant, but with the comment, "You are, as ever my dear, in the right."

"People surprise me but rarely," Mrs. Darcy said now, taking her son back from me. She stroked a finger down his nose, wrinkling her own at him in a playful way that made him smile. Then she looked up at me with the forthright dark eyes George seemed to have inherited. "You have, and I am not ashamed to say it."

CHAPTER THIRTY-FOUR

Dearest Anne, began the letter that waited for me when I arrived back in Kent, in a hand so familiar and dear that it brought me, shamefully, to tears. The rest of the letter was nothing exceptional—anyone reading it would see only correspondence from one friend to another, a series of busy, flippant sentences about bonnets purchased and books read, with very little information offered about the sender's new married state. But then, at the very end, she wrote, *I hope you meant it, darling Frank, when you invited me to write you; for you see, I have missed our correspondence greatly, almost as much as I have missed your company.*

And so began four years of letters.

"IT'S ABSURD," MAMMA SAID. Mrs. Jenkinson held her arm, and today, for the first time, I realized that my mother, somehow without my noticing, had grown quite old. I recoiled from the understanding, my teacup halfway to my mouth, my mind, which had been only half-attending to whatever complaints Mamma was about to voice, stopping in place like a horse whose reins were tugged too hard. Even from this distance, several feet between our two chairs—Mrs. Jenkinson lowered my mother into hers, then scurried to the teapot to pour her a cup—I could see the new yellow cast to the whites of her eyes and the flaccid skin of her lower cheeks and jaw.

Mamma took her cup and glared at me, and I realized I was meant to respond to something. "I am sorry, what was that, Mamma?"

"I said, it is *absurd* for a woman of your age to have engaged a dancing master. Particularly a woman who has chosen to forgo the joys of courtship and marriage! I hope this rumor is not true."

"Oh, but it is true." I smiled. "My friend Mrs. Andrews was good enough to recommend a dancing master who is very much in demand by the best families in London. He arrived yesterday, and I am confident that with his tutelage I shall be able to open the harvest ball this year."

There was a deep, tender ache under my breastbone whenever I referred to Eliza by her married name, like prodding a bruise that is still new enough that it keeps changing shape, the purple spreading. I wondered whether enough time would ever have passed for it to start yellowing about the edges.

"You have entirely lost your senses," Mamma said; but then, delightfully surprising me, moved on to other matters.

WHEN GEORGE WAS THREE years old, Darcy brought him for the first time to Rosings Park.

I spent the days leading up to their arrival in a panic.

Everything had to be perfect, from the menu planned for their visit to my own wardrobe, which felt suddenly inadequate. I snapped at Spinner as she dressed my hair on the morning they were expected, my paper curls coming out limp and drooping in the summer's unaccustomed humidity. And then I had to bite the side of my finger to keep from crying.

When their carriage had been sighted down the lane, I stood to wait for them on Rosings's front steps, which had been swept and scrubbed so vigorously it was a wonder the maids had not worn right through the stone. My hands locked together before me; all I could think as the carriage rolled to a stop was that this was lunacy. I knew nothing of children; my cousin would regret our agreement before the first day of their visit was over.

But: "Anne!" he said as he alighted, and came all tall and stately up the steps to kiss my hand. "You look very well."

"Thank you," I said, and then, before I could think of anything else to say, he turned back to the carriage and reached inside to lift a small, sturdy little person down from it. He set George on his feet and took him by the hand.

"Bow to Cousin Anne," he murmured in the boy's ear, and George, after giving me one rather terrified look, bobbed a bow, awkward as a trained bear.

I licked my lips. Fitzwilliam had stepped back and was watching us. Stooping so my face was in line with his, I said, "It is so good to see you, George. You must—be very hungry after your journey. Cook has made her best seedcake, just for you—shall we go inside and have some?"

To my ears, my words were terribly stilted; but George's long, homely face changed. He smiled, showing impossibly small, square teeth with funny little gaps between them, and let me take his hand. I felt again that odd lurching behind my breastbone when I felt how soft and round his hand was, still; with dimples like divots at the root of each knuckle.

THEY STAYED FOR THREE weeks. There were, of course, the required calls paid at the dower house, and dinners at Rosings with Mamma and Mrs. Jenkinson in attendance. But most of our time was spent exploring. On fine days, we went marching out over the estate, George running through the fields, dragging a stick behind him, while Fitzwilliam and I trailed in his wake. When it rained, George and I explored the house, every hidden cranny of it, while my cousin wrote letters to his wife and steward. George taught me how to make a diver-call, and we stood in the shut-up ballroom letting loose those trilling, ghostly bird sounds, which echoed off the tall ceilings until Mrs. Barrister came running with two footmen to investigate.

When the rain had mostly stopped, we walked in the sopping gardens, the air still gently misting. George discovered a toad among the hedgerows, and we crouched to admire it; and then a dragonfly, with its long brown body and flickering wings of lace.

"I have a book inside," I said as the dragonfly flew away, "that teaches about all sorts of insects. Would you like to see it?"

George looked up at me doubtfully.

"There are pictures," I said, wheedling. "Lovely illustrations, almost as good as seeing the real thing. And it shall be *your* book someday, you know, just like the rest of Rosings Park."

On this point, George had seemed puzzled throughout our visit. But now he looked after the dragonfly, which disappeared behind a cluster of flowers, and then down at the toad, still fat and bumpy and happily damp on the path beside us. "This is my toad, then," he said, and seemed so pleased by the notion that I could do nothing but smile in agreement.

MY LETTERS TO ELIZA were not nearly as frequent as they were when we both resided in London. Indeed, sometimes I had the miserly thought that I should ration my attention to her, as punishment for her desertion. And yet, whenever a letter from her arrived, I found myself reaching for a pen almost instantly so that I might answer it. Inside me existed a depthless well of things to say—little daily happenings, amusing passages from books, worries I could not voice to anyone else—filling and filling to an almost unbearable level over the weeks between our letters; and then, in the action of putting pen to paper, a little of the well was drained.

I foresaw, with an odd brew of gratitude and dread, a

lifetime of such meager pleasures, scratched out in lines of ink, replacing what I had once imagined would be a lifetime of talking and touching and working and resting together. Eliza mentioned her husband only peripherally, in the sense of, *We are considering a trip to the Lake District* or *Our housekeeper has grown terribly forgetful of late.* She never spoke of him as a distinct person, never gave any hint as to whether she had any affection for him, or he for her. I was by turns thankful for her discretion, and seared by the sort of curiosity that would likely only burn me further were it satisfied. I waited miserably for the day when a letter would arrive bearing news that she carried his child inside her belly; but it did not come.

Sometimes I noticed other women—at church, in the village. But Hunsford was so very small, and I could never be sure that my body's response to a pressed hand or tilted head would be reciprocated. And my heart was entangled in lines of ink and strands of bright hair; I could not seem to free it, however I sometimes wished to.

In her letters, Eliza never spoke of love for me, though her words tumbled across the page as messily as my own, as if her thoughts came too quickly for her pen.

I NEVER THOUGHT I could find such joy in work, I wrote. *But I have—I have! There is nothing so satisfying as greeting a tenant by name, and his wife, and his children, too; in being part of something that enriches us all. I used to be so frightened of the world, and now I am a part of it.*

Mamma's school is doing well; there are eighteen chil-

dren in attendance this year. Fewer than I would like, but too many farms cannot spare any hands, even small ones, that might help in the fields. There is more emphasis on sermonizing than I would prefer, but for now I am content that the children are at least learning their letters and sums. Educational reform will wait for another day; today I am merely glad that they have any education at all.

She wrote back: *You write of your satisfaction, and I am so very happy to hear it. I have found my own, as well: Lady Godwin complimented me in the most generous terms on the cushion I embroidered for our parlor. I cannot think of anything more satisfying than having so noble a lady approve of my work.*

I read these lines over and over, and could not decide whether they were meant in earnest or in jest. The chance that it was the former, somehow, felt sadder even than the latter. I traced her signature with my finger as I once traced the curve of her cheek.

CHAPTER THIRTY-FIVE

The oak lived deep in Rosings's woods, where the shadows were thickest. I imagined it might have been there for hundreds of years, patiently edging its way up through the canopy to reach the sun, sucking like a greedy child at the light until at last it spread so tall and wide that little except moss and mushrooms could grow close around it. The tree should not have been beautiful, lumpy and misshapen as it was, its trunk a mass of tough knots, its branches stretching up and up like the muscled arms of strongmen. But when I found it, I loved it instantly. I reached out to cup my hands over one of its great whorled knots and felt a prayer beneath my palms.

I had braved Rosings's woods at last in the earliest days of my return to Kent. Before Mamma and Mrs. Jenkinson removed to the dower house, when they were united in their disapproval of my insurrection and even a house the size of Rosings felt too small to contain us all, I sometimes needed, quite desperately, a place to disappear for a time—even just an hour. A reprieve from the oppressive atmosphere of the house and, yes, from my new responsibilities, from columns of numbers and the newfound sense of visibility, which was by turns exhilarating and disconcerting. All my life I had seen other people—my cousin John, for instance, or Mrs. Collins, when she lived in the parsonage—slipping away for walks in our woods; it took desperation for me to follow their example, but oh, how glad I was that I finally did.

Today it was autumn, that quivering period when some leaves have turned to fire and others still cling to summer green. My footsteps were muffled by last year's leaves, and I wore no bonnet, my skin shielded from the sun by the forest canopy. I'd spent the morning sequestered with Mrs. Barrister, going over the details of this year's harvest ball, and I relished, now, each lungful of chill-edged air. I followed the narrow deer trails to my oak; leaned against its friendly bark and listened for a time to the chattering of squirrels and scolding of birds before turning at last, reluctantly, for home. My fingers brushed the mossy trunks and low slender branches of trees as I passed them, my mind still full of all the particulars that are so necessary for a proper party, but that invariably left my head aching.

There was still much to do today. But I paused before stepping out from the trees and onto the lane, as I always did, though with increasing brevity as the years passed. My feet pressed against the earth; my ears would have pricked like a fox's if they could, listening for something—a greeting, a cry, anything at all to show me that Rosings Park lived, still; that its sentience matched my own; that it was glad I had returned. But, as ever since I stopped taking my drops, there was no response, even as I sent my own whispered greeting into the air.

Out on the lane, I passed the dower house, where Mamma was no doubt enjoying her afternoon nap, and waved to the rector in his garden at the parsonage. There was a figure a little distant, standing before the gates to Rosings; I shaded my eyes with my hand to better make it out. A woman, wearing a blue pelisse and a spectacular bonnet, her head tilted sharply, as if she sought a face at one of the upper-story windows.

A little closer now, something tickled at the nape of my neck; there was a discordant familiarity to her, to the span of her shoulders and the way she held her hands together at her waist. I thought, *No,* even as my pace increased without my conscious intention, and my quickened footfalls on the lane reached her ear. She turned her head, and even from so far away I could read the leaping, colliding hope and terror in her expression as easily as if she were one of her own letters.

"Anne," she said as soon as I was near enough to hear her, and then she was in my arms and I was squeezing, squeezing, squeezing, as if she might disappear if I let go.

"MY TRUNKS ARE STILL in the village in the carriage. I thought there would be an inn," she said hours later, laughing into my hair. And then, sobering, "I should have written before coming—I just—I could not. I could not take the risk that you might turn me away before I even had a chance to see you again."

"I would not have turned you away."

"You might have. I did not know—"

I looked at her, so very close—our brows touching, our toes tucked together. Four years added a few freckles to her nose, a new solemnity to her eyes, though her smile, when it appeared, curled wickedly as ever.

"I would not have," I said again; and when she opened her mouth to say more, I closed it with kisses.

"WHAT HAPPENED?"

It was almost the first question I asked her, but she refused to answer then, and I allowed her to demure. If this was but a passing fancy for her—if she had not come to stay, as I immediately thought she must have when I recognized her in the lane—I did not want to know until I had to. But now it was morning, and the world insisted upon intruding; already, Spinner disturbed us, startled, when she brought my usual morning cup of chocolate, to discover that I was not alone. She said nothing, however, except to ask in a voice that sounded half-strangled whether Mrs. Andrews would also like a cup.

We meant for Eliza to return to the guest quarters, but sleep claimed us both before she could. I wondered what her maid would think when she saw the undisturbed sheets on her bed; and then I had the unwelcome thought that perhaps her maid was used to such things; perhaps, after I left London, even after her marriage, Eliza enjoyed the company of other women. The thought cut, even as I tried to dismiss it, even as I wondered about my other servants and how they might react to seeing my friend leaving my chamber so early. But I knew almost nothing about her married life, and so I rolled until I was pressed against her side and said again, "What happened?"

"You keep such ungodly hours in the country," she said; but then she saw my face and scrubbed her own with both palms, leaving it blotched with red. "Charles—Mr. Andrews—died a fortnight ago. At a card party, of all places—just—slumped over and died." She pushed herself upright and spoke to the blanket over her legs. "It was dreadful, as I suppose you can imagine."

"I—"

"Do not say you are sorry," she said, and gave an odd little smile. "Because the terrible, terrible truth is that I—am not. He was—a good enough man, in his way. He was not a *bad* man. But I . . . regretted my choice almost from the first day of our union, and now he has . . . freed me. You will think me the worst sort of person, but when he died I thought, *Thank God*. And then I prayed God would forgive me, for Charles did not hurt me, he did not—but I could not speak—I could not speak when I was in our house, I could not . . . It was the strangest thing—"

She scrubbed her face again, and then her hair, which already lay loose and tangled around her shoulders, but which stood up in a frizz under her hands' abuse. Her words came faster and faster, all the things I imagined she wanted to say in her letters, but that were stoppered inside her as if she were a bottle.

"He loved my playing—he loved to show it off to his friends—I don't think I ever hated the pianoforte more.

They talked and they talked about business and politics, and we wives *sat,* and I was the only one who knew how to play, so he trotted me out like a trick horse, and then I sat down again and exchanged pleasantries with the women and served *coffee* and . . ." She looked around at me, eyes full. "It sounds so—petty, saying it now. To hate a life like that? It's the same life most other women live—fortunate women—I was *fortunate* compared to so many women, and I wanted to—to scream." She gulped a laugh that sounded more like a sob. "And I missed you so very much, Anne—all I could think, once the funeral was over, was that now I could come to you."

She reached out for me, but let her hand drop back to the coverlet before she touched me.

"He wanted children so badly," she said; and now she took her hands and ran them over her own body, over the gentle, empty slope of her belly. "He never said he blamed me for their lack. But when he—when we—" Her fingers tightened into fists. "When he touched me, it was . . . my body *recoiled*. I cannot imagine he did not feel it."

She was wretched, hideous with tears; and I wanted nothing more than to kiss her. That other women endured lives of such smallness—that other women were less fortunate, still—did not mean that Eliza ought to have resigned herself to a similarly frustrated existence. I knew this, I *knew* it, and though I could not quite find words eloquent enough to express it fully, I hoped, when I took her hand, that at least some of what I felt transferred to her through our fingers.

TO THE REST OF the world, we must have seemed quite the pair of eccentrics.

Eliza was a widow now; respectable and rich and able to do as she liked. I was at once glad and ashamed of that gladness; hurt that it took his death to bring her to me, and grateful, with a beautiful, uncomplicated gratitude, that she came with such immediacy once she had absorbed the first shock of her husband's passing. And she came to me free now, unencumbered by dependency or fear; the jointure her husband settled upon her was more than generous.

I did not introduce her, as I once imagined I might, as my companion. Instead, I called her my friend Mrs. Andrews, a truth that even Mamma accepted easily enough, though Eliza's quick tongue and propensity toward overloud laughter and the discussion of novels proved more difficult for her to accept. But Eliza slipped into Hunsford society with an easiness that I rather envied. And so when, after several weeks, I finally mentioned to the rector's wife that my friend decided to move into Rosings Park permanently, she looked startled for a moment and then said, "How lovely! We do all need companionship, do we not? Even someone so independent as you, Miss de Bourgh."

Eliza did endear herself to my mother at least a little with her effusive compliments on the village school, for which Mamma did indeed furnish a woman from somewhere within her web of acquaintances who instructs the children of Hunsford parish from the back parlor of her house. Here, Eliza found a purpose in village life, though she was careful to be discreet in her augmentation of the school's books and supplies; I wondered how long it would take for Mamma to realize the narrow course of study she urged upon Mrs. Lynch was being expanded upon, inch by patient inch.

When we grew restless, we traveled. To London, often, to visit Eliza's family, and to Surrey to see John and Harriet and their children: a boy and a girl who grew, tangled tight together, and surprised everyone with their double birth after so many years of barrenness. And to the Continent, all the places whose exotic names— *Venice, Geneva, Paris, Lisbon*—I used to trace on my geography puzzle. But always we came gladly home again to Rosings Park.

I grew accustomed to this new life of purpose and parity, though it was impossibly far from anything I imagined could exist between husbands and wives. In the evenings, I looked at Eliza across the dining table. Sometimes we were joined by neighbors, but more often, it was only the two of us, and as she smiled at me over our mutton or fish, occasionally I felt myself falling backward, the jolting fall of a dreamer about to wake. As if I had slipped, somehow, into a dream world, and that someday, inevitably, I would wake to the real one. I licked my lips for traces of bittersweetness, but found none; and on nights when these thoughts intruded, Eliza held me close and murmured reassurances. "Does this feel real?" she whispered. "And this?" I felt the weight of her upon me, the reassuring way the mattress dipped when she moved; dug my fingers into her skin and reveled in the sourness of her evening cup of coffee on her breath.

Yet the sense that I must be dreaming, that this life was all unreal, persisted in coming back; and would, I feared, until my dying day.

Part Four

The End

CHAPTER THIRTY-SIX

I wake to the sound of weeping.

For a moment, I cannot remember why I ache so in all my bones; why it feels as if someone has set a thick book upon my chest. The weeper cries as if her throat is being torn open; as if her heart bleeds. I hover between concern for myself, my own heartbeat ponderously slow, my breaths shallow and rattling, and for her, whomever she is.

My eyelids are heavy as stones; there is a vague memory, scratching at the edges of my mind, about stones on the eyes and why I should be afraid of them. But I bat it away, actually managing to raise one shaking hand before it falls once more to the coverlet.

WHEN I WAKE AGAIN, it is to my maid's familiar arm under my neck, and her voice urging me to drink. Cool glass against my lips; bittersweet liquid on my tongue. A shock of recognition, though it has been more than forty years since I last tasted it. A feeble attempt at protestation, though I have already swallowed.

I FLOAT ALONG A placid river, my body, unnaturally heavy, undulating with the currents, my thoughts scattered like autumn leaves along the water's surface. A part of me knows that my true body lies still and alone in my high soft bed. But this body—the floating body—is so much freer than the other, which is tucked into the bedclothes like a child, and the eyes belonging to this body can open, can enjoy the way the sunlight flickers through the remaining leaves of the willow trees along the river's banks.

I pass my father, fishing; he is hatless and coatless, his sleeves rolled up so his pale forearms are exposed to the sun. I think at first that he does not recognize me, with my hair silver as shillings and my skin crinkled from years. But he turns his head at the last moment and watches as I drift past him. "Anne!" he calls, and grins when I wave.

If I had the power to stop my forward momentum, I would pause before him and stand with him awhile in the shallows, the minnows dashing about near our ankles. I would ask him whether he watched at all, these many years, as I took hold of my birthright at last and refused to let go; and, too, I would ask whether the taking hold pleased him, or if, like my mother, he could never quite believe me strong enough.

But I cannot stop, and so I watch as his figure grows smaller and smaller, until at last the current carries me around a bend and I lose sight of him altogether.

This river meanders through my favorite parts of the estate, and for all that I know no such body of water truly exists on Rosings's many acres, I am content merely to enjoy the journey. I pass the cows grazing in their pasture

on the home farm and the pasture containing Mr. Mont-
gomery's herd of heavy-wooled sheep, where I turned
my ankle once in the early days of my return to Kent.
His wife, who refused to let me return to the great house
without a good rest by the fire and an herby poultice, became the first of my tenants with whom I was on truly
friendly terms. I glide through the rose garden, which
blooms more prolifically now even than it did in my father's day, the roses twining lovingly around the arms
and throats of the sculptures he had placed there.

The river skims along the edge of the lake I ordered
dug when George was still a small boy; and here I find
Darcy, looking younger and more hale than he was when
he died by a good twenty years. He is laughing, one
hand shading his eyes as he watches someone paddling
in the shallow reedy waters near the lakeshore. It must be
George himself, though his figure is hazy, as if he does
not quite belong in this netherworld with the rest of us.
I suspect, watching as I pass, the river's current merci-
fully slow here, that I can only see him at all because this
particular part of his life is over; he will never again be a
small boy swimming in a lake.

I must make some sound, or perhaps he only feels the
pressure of my eyes, for Darcy turns. When he sees me,
his handsome face is so glad, so easy, it is hard to recall
a time when he was stiff and uncomfortable in my presence. It only took a journey to Derbyshire and an offer
of adopting George, removing all the uncertainty that is
necessarily attendant upon a second son. Darcy brought
George here often when the boy was old enough; he and

I stood together in this very spot and watched him test his swimmer's strength in the calm water of the lake. As husband and wife we could never have been happy, but in our odd arrangement as far-flung guardians of this sweet, sturdy soul, we found a peculiar form of contentment together.

George must come here soon, I think—the real here, with my bed-bound body from which I am so grateful for this brief escape. He has been in London with his brother, but my steward will have summoned him by now. He will be riding through the night to reach Kent quickly. I think of his dear face, framed on either side by ears like pitcher handles, for which he was teased mercilessly at school but which now, in his middle years, look like nothing so much as parentheses drawing attention to the gentleness of his countenance. He was not always so dear to me, of course; indeed, he remained a sort of curiosity to me for years, until he grew old enough to come to Kent for extended visits. But time and familiarity can indeed breed love, it seems.

THE RIVER CONTINUES ON its illogical, wandering way, through meadows I once trod in fair weather and foul; beside the lane where I used to drive my ponies. I think of their warm, happy greetings upon my return, their breath moistening my palms, the way they nudged their noses against my belly. They were the first residents of Rosings who seemed truly glad of my return.

Beside Hunsford's church, in a shaded, snaking curve

of riverbank, Nurse squats beside the water, dress and petticoat hitched up around her knees, bare toes wiggling in the mud. She sees me and smiles. "It's good to get my feet out of those boots," she says, and I see her boots and striped stockings where they lie abandoned a little distance away among the tough snarled willow roots that form a trailing shelf over the water.

I pass Miss Bennet—Mrs. Darcy—who pays me no notice, her attention on the blue of the sky and the satisfying briskness of her walking pace. I pass Aunt and Uncle Darcy, who walk with arms linked and look after me with mild surprise, and Uncle Fitzwilliam, who is so intent upon the novel over whose pages he is chuckling that he only waves at me absentmindedly, without any true recognition. I pass others, walking, riding, picnicking on the river's shady banks. Some I remember clearly—Mr. Collins, the previous Hunsford rector, and his wife, an infant lying on the blanket between them, fat legs kicking at its long white dress; Mr. Colt, who stands beside a stone wall, conversing with a cluster of farmers—and some are like wisps of recollection from dreams, their faces nearly familiar but still unplaceable. One, a stooped old woman whose long fingers curl around the knob of her walking stick, startles at the sight of me, squinting with eyes that are the only familiar thing about her. I thrash a little in the water, turning my head to see her more clearly, to place those eyes; and it is only when she is nearly out of sight that I think, *Oh, it is Miss Hall!* with the faint pleasure that comes of seeing an old friend.

John waits around a bend near the woods, hands behind his back and back still straight despite the whiteness of his few remaining hairs. He passed this way only a few years ago; not a month past, I received a letter from his widow, with whom I still correspond regularly. John says nothing, but he does not need to. He nods in welcome, affection in his eyes; and it is enough.

At the entrance to the woods themselves, the water flows more quickly, as if eager to speed me on my way to some unknown place. It steers me with unnerving splashes and jolts around sudden rocks, leaves and sticks rushing along before me. Then a swift, frightening turn around a gnarled tree, and a drop of several inches down a miniature waterfall and at last into a slower spot, where I swirl in the cool and struggle to catch my breath.

There are two figures on the shore ahead of me, and *they* I would know anywhere. Mrs. Jenkinson smiles in her bland and dutiful way, but Mamma, her hair magnificently white, her eyes dark with displeasure and hurt feelings, begins shouting the moment she spies me. In a fit of instinctive cowardice, I nearly block my ears, like a child being told to return to her nursery.

We lived uneasily together until her death, every day a battle still, the war never won by either of us. I do not know what winning would have looked like to her; Rosings Park back under her control, I suppose, and myself with it. But there were moments—scarce as they were, tender, and easy to overlook as early spring ferns—when she praised some choice I had made, be it a new carpet for the breakfast room or a settled dis-

pute among my tenants, and her face flashed with pride
for me. These make me uncertain of the size and form
her victory would have taken, and make me all the more
embarrassed for my display when I returned from London, like a child asserting its independence.

For myself, who veered wildly between shutting out
the noise of her and seeking her counsel like a supplicant
before a saint, I think perhaps victory would have been
the sort of sinew-deep understanding of my mother
that is impossible between humans except in those rare,
shining moments of connection that occur only once or
twice in a lifetime.

NOW THERE IS ONLY one face I seek among the
breezes and the shadows, and I know where I shall find
her. Sensitive as a well-trained horse to its mistress's bid-
ding, the river turns gently and deposits me among the
thick spreading roots of the ancient oak tree at the heart
of Rosings's woods. I am able to stand here, and shake
off the clinging gold-brown willow leaves, and clamber
onto the woodland floor, which smells of vegetable de-
cay and the secrets of birds and voles and beetles.

I can see the edge of her wide skirt around the trunk,
and I can hear the soft swish of a turning page. I round
the bend and stop, drinking in the sight of her, which
quenches me as if I had been wandering a desert land
and not floating in a river. She looks just as I remember
her, the orange of her hair dulled by time, her lips ridged
with vertical lines and her hands spotted not just with

freckles, but with age. She wears her favorite gown, gray silk with a narrow stripe of sapphire blue running through the fabric, the pale under-sleeves covered in delicate whitework. Her shoulders curve with the years, years that ought not allow her to kneel with such apparent ease among the wide lumps of the oak's roots, the layers of her crinoline, petticoats, and the skirt of her gown spread around her like a silken puddle.

Indeed, before her death, it had already been several years since we had sat here together; our knees and backs could no longer manage.

THIS WAS OUR TREE; our place. An irony, for until I returned to Kent, these woods held nothing but the nameless, formless terrors of children's stories for me; and then there was Eliza, whose distaste for the wildness of the true outdoors—rather than the carefully cultivated outdoors of parks and gardens—she had not exaggerated.

But she indulged me in my relish for untamed growing things once she came to Kent; and, too, we needed a place to escape together. For no matter how discreet the servants nor how stout the locks on our chamber doors, there was something delicious about making space for ourselves, for the shape and heft of *us,* in the greater world, even if only we, and local fauna, knew we had done so.

SHE SETS ASIDE HER book when I clear my throat, marking her place with a scrap of blue ribbon. Her face, when she looks into mine, is unsurprised, her smile broad and calmly glad. It transforms her web of wrinkles into a wreath of welcome. Patting the hump of tree root that we used to lovingly call the tree's settee, she says, "Sit awhile, love."

I arrange myself as best I can, given the width and breadth of my skirt and petticoats. I told her almost daily during our life together how I loved her softness, and she pulls me against it now. We listen to the hum of forest insects, the calling conversations of chaffinches and nuthatches, the branches of the oak rubbing against the intersecting branches of a nearby ash in creaking affection. We listen to each other's breathing, hers calm and even as it was before her illness, mine rattling in my chest like dice in a cup. Eliza does not remark on the alarming sound of it, only tightens her arm around my shoulders.

I should ask her whether the preachers in their tall pulpits are right about the nature of heaven; but I do not. Cowardice, once again. I never did manage to achieve anything like true feeling for the God of the prayer books, only ever finding something like a union with the Divine in the music and words of my fellow humans, and in the quiet lives of my other fellow creatures, both those whose roots run through the earth and those who scamper across it or wing their way through the sky. But I fear such a union is merely the product of my own imagination.

In my imagination, heaven looks like home. Eliza got there first, and so this time it is I who will make the long walk up the lane toward the great house, a little afraid, a little tired. And it is she who shall meet me there in the lane, surprised in her daily routine to find me standing there, looking up at the house's highest window; she who will run to me and enfold me in her arms; she who will murmur words of welcome and weep hot glad tears, as I once did when it was she who followed me.

THE RIVER HAS CREPT up between the tree roots, filling in the bark's deep crevices. It dampens the hem of my gown, tugging like a child's hands, insistent that I come along with it. I am slipping away before I know it is happening, my cheek falling from Eliza's shoulder. "Oh, Frank," she says, and grasps my hand until she can hold on no longer; and then she releases me.

I WAKE NOW TO two people speaking together. Their words are all but meaningless, but I know both their voices—my Welsh maid's musical, George's deep and boggy. I listen to them for a time, their whispers rising and falling.

Eliza had not been jesting about not being fond of children; nor had she been wrong about loving her own anyway. And George was as much Eliza's as mine, as Darcy's and Elizabeth's. I do not know whether George suspected the true depth of our affection for one another, but he loved us both as almost-mothers. Knowing that he is here now, as he was here when she died, I feel a small snap, as of a frayed rope mooring a boat to its dock.

Like the freed boat, I bob and drift, unhurried but still moving steadily away.

Slowly, over the whispers of their human voices, I become aware of another voice, ragged and choking. It is the same weeping voice I heard before, but it is coming, I realize now, from the walls, the windows. Saltwater eddies under the wallpaper, pools on the floor. My eyes open, blink against the firelight; but the room remains blurred, as if I am looking at it through a windowpane that runs with rain. My lips, dry as bones, crack as I smile. Rosings Park has been silent for me for forty years, though I never lost the habit of listening for it. I lift my fingertips from the bed and hope it understands the gesture as I mean it—that if I could, I would run my hands over every inch of wall and floor, in greeting and farewell.

"Quiet for decades," I say, still smiling, though my voice is dry and cracked as my lips, "and now all you can do is weep?"

ACKNOWLEDGMENTS

I need to thank several people whose advice and help were invaluable while I was writing. Natalie Jenner, thank you for your careful beta-read, and for pointing out that George deserved an extra scene. Laurel Ann Nattress, thank you for your thoughtful comments on my early draft. Thank you to Dr. Julian North for sharing your expertise on laudanum addiction. Rebecca Howe, thank you for the many (many) late-night texts encouraging me to keep going when I was stuck.

To my incredible agent, Jennifer Weltz: thank you for being the advocate you are, and for helping me prune that out-of-control first draft. Thank you to the entire team working behind the scenes at William Morrow—we authors, and our books, owe so much to your hard work. In particular, thank you to Shelly Perron, copyeditor extraordinaire; and to my editor, Rachel Kahan, for your enthusiasm for Anne's story from the very beginning.

And finally, thank you to my husband, Stuart Campbell. You wrangled our children, listened patiently to half-finished passages, and let me moan about edits. I (really, truly) could never have gotten this book written without you.

Insights,
Interviews
& More . . .

Meet Molly Greeley

Stuart Campbell

MOLLY GREELEY earned her bachelor's degree in English, with a creative writing emphasis, from Michigan State University, where she was the recipient of the Louis B. Sudler Prize in the Arts for Creative Writing. She lives with her husband and three children in Traverse City, Michigan. ◡

Behind the Book

When my oldest child was a newborn, her needs were constant and utterly overwhelming. She cried almost all the time. I sat staring, in a sleep-deprived blur, around my house, wondering how I was ever supposed to get anything done when she never, ever wanted to be put down. Wondering how women centuries ago had managed the hard work of caring for their new babies alongside the brutal labor that comprised day-to-day life—scrubbing clothes, building fires, cleaning, sowing, harvesting, hauling water, sewing, mending. They must, I thought, looking down at my daughter with a sort of dark humor, have drugged their babies in order to get other work accomplished.

It wasn't until years later when I was researching my first book that I discovered, horrifyingly, that my dark mental joke wasn't far from the truth. Names kept popping up as I researched Regency-era childrearing; clever, sinisterly calming names. *Godfrey's Cordial. Mrs. Winslow's Soothing Syrup. Daffy's Elixir. Street's Infant Quietness.* These were the names of just a few of the laudanum formulas that were peddled to parents, beginning in the eighteenth century, as cures for everything from teething to colic, and which were used widely in both poor ▶

3

Behind the Book *(continued)*

households and in the nurseries of the rich. Laudanum is a tincture of opium, and the unregulated nature of these formulas had tragic results—children died of overdoses with terrible regularity, and sometimes wasted away because they were too lethargic even to cry from hunger.

Appalled and morbidly curious, I looked into these drugs further, and when I learned of some of the symptoms of laudanum use—among them appetite suppression, lethargy, and respiratory depression—my mind leapt immediately to Anne de Bourgh, sitting limp and too thin as her companion fussed over her lack of appetite; incapable, according to her mother, of braving London or learning to play the pianoforte.

Oh, I thought; and even as I worked to finish *The Clergyman's Wife,* my debut novel, I was already starting to write *The Heiress* inside my head.

My first book, which explores the life and choices of *Pride and Prejudice*'s Charlotte Lucas after her marriage to Mr. Collins, is very preoccupied with dowries and social mobility. Women living in Jane Austen's time, Charlotte included, were in general very reliant upon men for their well-being. Few jobs were open to them, and except in exceptional circumstances, a woman's personal wealth, if she was fortunate enough to have any, went to her husband upon their marriage. And in an era when wife-selling was not unheard of and death in childbirth was a very real danger, relying on a man could be a bleak prospect.

But Anne de Bourgh is an exception. With her vast riches and the estate she inherits from her father, Anne is incredibly lucky for a Regency-era woman, and the more I thought about her, the harder it was to rid myself of a niggling irritation with her. She seemed, I thought, both entirely oblivious to her good fortune and willing to squander the opportunities—for travel, for education, for making a difference in the world—that came with it. Compared to Charlotte Lucas, and certainly compared to the thousands of even-less-fortunate women living in Austen's time, Anne had *everything*, and yet she did exactly nothing with any of it.

I've always tended toward curiosity about people's—and characters'—inner lives and motivations, however, and *Pride and Prejudice* leaves us with a lot of unanswered questions about Anne. She is something of an empty vessel in Austen's book, sitting quietly in the corner, filled only when other characters express their opinions of her. From Mr. Collins, we learn that Miss de Bourgh is "unfortunately of a sickly constitution," but "perfectly amiable," though of course his opinions are hard to trust when we know how overawed he becomes in the presence of wealth. Lady Catherine makes no apologies for her daughter's frailty, and even seems weirdly proud of it—and prouder still of Anne's imaginary talents, which would, her mother assures anyone who will listen, be prodigious had her health allowed. To her cousin Mr. Darcy, Anne might as well not exist; he spends his visit to Rosings Park, or at least that part to which Elizabeth Bennet is privy, completely ignoring her. And Elizabeth herself finds Anne alarming for her thinness and pallor, amusing for her poor manners, and, ultimately, completely insignificant.

But Anne's thoughts and feelings about herself and the people around her are left to the reader's imagination; she never speaks except offstage. Even when she and Lady Catherine both smile at the mention of Anne's someday-nuptials, Anne's smile can be interpreted as either gladness at the prospect or as a reflexive response—vaguely polite and easier than making the effort, particularly in the presence of her overbearing mother, of voicing her own opinions.

If her illness was not truly an illness at all, I thought, but a dependence on laudanum, then perhaps the perceptions of just about every character in the book were wrong. After all, the nature of her illness is never disclosed in Austen's novel; we have to take the word of Anne's mother that Anne is, indeed, ill at all. And if she wasn't truly ill, her wealth gave her an independence ▶

Behind the Book *(continued)*

that offered more freedom of choice than most women had in Regency times.

In *The Clergyman's Wife,* I wrote about a woman constrained by her circumstances. Charlotte Lucas's story will always mean a great deal to me, but it was, I have to admit, gloriously freeing to write *The Heiress*: the story of a woman whose life wasn't filled with only obstacles, but with possibilities. A woman who, with enough courage, could live, and love, however she chose. ✀

Reading Group Guide

1. At the start of the novel Anne de Bourgh tells us, "I was forever waiting, without knowing quite what it is I was waiting for." What do you think she is waiting for? When do you think she discovers what that is?

2. How does the arrival of Miss Hall affect Anne's small world? Is she a true friend, or merely a paid companion?

3. When the doctor increases Anne's dose of laudanum after her father's death, she says, "I drank them down without complaint, welcoming the added protection against the world." What kind of protection does the drug provide? Why do Anne and those around her see the drug only as protective instead of harmful?

4. Anne is cut to the quick by Fitzwilliam Darcy's comment: "How exactly does one converse with a doll?" But is that doll-like quality seen as a negative by anyone other than Fitzwilliam? Would being physically frail and quiet have been tolerated in a boy—particularly a male heir to a great estate? Or—as Anne suspects—are all women at least a little doll-like in a society that expects absolute compliance from them?

5. What do you make of Anne's relationship with her cousin John Fitzwilliam? Why does he say he was "deeply ashamed" not to have done more to intervene in her addiction?

6. When researching this novel, Molly Greeley studied a great many sources from the eighteenth and nineteenth centuries that chronicle the effects of laudanum addiction, which she drew on for stories like the ones Miss Hall and Colonel Fitzwilliam tell Anne. Firsthand accounts of ▶

laudanum-induced hallucinations also inspired her descriptions of Anne's nightmares. How do these stories compare with addiction to opioid drugs in modern times?

7. After Anne has recovered from her addiction, her maid, Spinner, describes her as "as changed as if a fairy came to rescue you." What does she mean by that? What is the greatest change in Anne?

8. Is Anne wrong to turn down Mr. Watters's proposal? Why does she reject a marriage of convenience, but Eliza does not? What would you do if you were in their shoes?

9. In trying to justify giving Anne laudanum, Lady Catherine tells Anne, "I felt you on the inside, and I thought, once you were outside my body, that I would no longer be able to feel you so intimately; but that was not so. I felt your every cry—every scream tugged at me as if the navel-string still tethered us and your cries *pulled* on it." Did you feel sympathy for Lady Catherine as she explained herself? When she says, "A mother cannot be wrong, not when she is acting for the good of her child," did that exonerate her? Was she cruel, or only misguided? Would you have been able to forgive her?

10. When Lady Catherine grudgingly tells Anne, "I am glad to see some stubbornness in you; it is a necessary attribute in a woman," do you agree? Is she right that Anne gets her stubbornness from her mother?

11. What do you make of the novel's final scenes? Were you pleased to see how Anne's life had progressed in the years after she rediscovers herself? Did she make the right choices for herself?

12. Had you read Jane Austen's *Pride and Prejudice* before you read *The Heiress*? How do Molly Greeley's versions of Austen's characters align with your own feelings about them as a reader? Were there any surprises for you in this book? ∾

An Excerpt from *The Clergyman's Wife*

Chapter One

Spring, Three Years Later

I stand at the window in my parlor looking out over the rear gardens. From here, I can see William's beehives and the flower beds just waking from their winter rest. Gravel paths meander throughout the garden; to the right, they curve toward the hedgerows, and onward toward the lane, and to the left, they bend around the side of the house toward the kitchen garden, and the pen where the pig lives, fattening, and the dusty ground where the chickens peck and squawk.

Behind me on my writing desk, a fresh piece of paper sits ready. The salutation at the top—*Dear Elizabeth*—has been dry for some time. I never feel the quiet uniformity of my life as fully as when I am trying to compose a letter to my friend. Eliza's own letters are full of amusing stories about her neighbors, both in Derbyshire and in London; her life seems full to bursting with her husband, her son, her estate, and her rounds of parties and social calls.

Society here in Hunsford is limited, even by the standards of one who spent her girlhood in modest Meryton. Besides the de Bourghs there is only one truly genteel family with whom we socialize, and though William claims to be comfortable in *all* circles, he prefers to be among people whose station in life equals, or exceeds, his own; and so we spend much of our time at home, and much of *that* is spent apart, William keeping mostly to his book room and the garden, and I to my parlor and the nursery. This does not usually bother me, for it is easy to fill my hours with things that need doing. There is always the menu to plan, the accounts to balance, the kitchen garden to tend. I embroider a great deal more than I used to, and my designs have improved, I think. But descriptions of embroidery do not an amusing letter make.

This afternoon, we are expected at Rosings Park for tea. Perhaps, I think with a touch of hopefulness, Lady Catherine will share some wisdom that Elizabeth might appreciate.

THE DRAWING ROOM at Rosings Park is silent but for the sound of the pendulum clock, which marks the passing of the seconds. I sit, teacup cradled in my hands. Beside me, William clasps his hands together tightly as if to keep himself from fidgeting, something Lady Catherine cannot abide.

The lady in question is dozing openmouthed in her chair. She has been asleep for nearly a quarter hour. I am tired as well, so tired that I yawn, the opulence that surrounds me blurring into a haze of gleaming wood and gilding. I catch William's repressive glance as I cover my mouth with the back of one hand.

Miss Anne de Bourgh and her companion murmur together beside the hearth, too far away for William and me to partake in their conversation. The fire blazes strongly, too strongly for the warm spring day, yet Miss de Bourgh wears a heavy shawl. Her companion, Mrs. Jenkinson, by contrast, appears flushed from the heat, though as ever she is uncomplaining.

I shift subtly to stretch my aching shoulders and try to hold ▶

in another yawn. *Chock, chock, chock* goes the pendulum. I sip my tea, which is now tepid; stare down at the leaves settled in the bottom of my cup; and read the tedium of the next few hours there.

A muffled snort; I look up to find Lady Catherine looking around the room in apparent befuddlement. She slipped inelegantly downward while she was asleep, and now she pushes herself upright, fingers fixed clawlike around the arms of her chair. Her eyes dart from me to William and back again; from the corner of my own eye, I can tell that he is avoiding her gaze, his head tipped back as though he is studying the large portrait of her late husband, Sir Lewis, which hangs on the wall behind her. I return my own gaze to my teacup. At times, William shows surprising wisdom.

"Play, Mrs. Jenkinson," Lady Catherine says abruptly. "It is too quiet."

Mrs. Jenkinson startles, interrupted, it seems, midsentence. Miss de Bourgh presses her lips together and looks at the fire as her companion rises to her feet and moves to the pianoforte, where she sits and fumbles through the sheets of music to find a song.

Lady Catherine makes a sound of annoyance. "I hope your daughter will outgrow her ill temper," she says, turning to me. Her voice, forceful under any circumstances, seems especially startling as it breaks the silence; Mrs. Jenkinson jumps a little on her stool. "Anne told me she could hear her wailing away when she took her drive past your home yesterday."

For a long moment, I keep myself very still. I think of Louisa crying for me as William and I left the parsonage to come to Rosings; she squirmed miserably in Martha's arms as I kissed her head and walked through the door.

Mrs. Jenkinson begins to play, and Miss de Bourgh looks up. Her eyes meet mine just briefly, and then she looks away.

"Louisa has a happy disposition much of the time, Lady

Catherine," I say at last. "But I believe she is cutting her first tooth, and it is making her a little fractious."

Lady Catherine sniffs. "Anne was never so disruptive," she says. "Dr. Grant recommended a solution that kept her very quiet; her nurse said it was a marvel. You must ask him about it."

I hold my tongue, actually hold it between my teeth, as William bobs his head, though my mind is filled with frantic thoughts. My eyes stray to Miss de Bourgh, to her hollow cheeks and the sharply delineated bones at her wrists.

"Indeed we shall, Your Ladyship," William says. "Your advice, as ever, is both timely and sensible—"

"Yes, yes," Lady Catherine says, waving a hand, and then she raises her voice slightly. "You play with so little *feeling*, Mrs. Jenkinson," she says; Mrs. Jenkinson's shoulders jerk, and I look down at my lap.

"Roses!" William says over dinner. He slurps a spoonful of soup and I glance away until he speaks again. "Such condescension on the part of her ladyship. I never expected this—did you, my dear?"

I take a sip of my wine before answering. "No, I did not."

There are, we learned today at tea, to be roses at the parsonage. The garden wants improving, Lady Catherine said, and nothing but roses will do to add the necessary elegance to the house's prospect from the lane. William, of course, was gratified by his patroness's interest and made certain to tell her so, at great length.

"And to think," he says now, around a mouthful of bread, "that she even considered the delicacy of the plants—for roses, I understand, are very temperamental. That she has not only purchased them but insists upon sending someone to plant them properly and instruct me in their care—she is munificence itself."

"Indeed. As always." ▶

An Excerpt from *The Clergyman's Wife*
(continued)

He pauses delicately, then says, "Do you recall in which spot her ladyship said the roses were to be planted?"

"Near the road, past the hedgerow path." I can only assume Lady Catherine wishes them to be visible to all who pass.

"Ah. Yes. I thought so." William blinks a little too rapidly. Then he shakes his head and dips his spoon once more into his bowl.

I watch him for a moment. "Did you have other plans for that space?"

"I . . . Well." I feel a pang of sympathy at the sight of his bemused expression. "It is of no consequence," he says at last. "I thought perhaps to put a new bed of . . . But her ladyship is very good to take such an expense upon herself, to adorn our humble abode so extravagantly. Roses!" he says again, and slurps his soup. ∽